Natasha Solomons

Natasha Solomons is the author of the internationally bestselling *Mr Rosenblum's List*, *The Novel in the Viola*, which was chosen for the Richard & Judy Book Club, and *The Gallery of Vanished Husbands*. Natasha lives in Dorset with her husband, with whom she also writes screenplays, and their two children. Her novels have been translated into seventeen languages.

D0036934

THE SONG COLLECTOR

NATASHA SOLOMONS

SCEPTRE

First published in Great Britain in 2015 by Sceptre
An imprint of Hodder & Stoughton
An Hachette UK company

First published in paperback in 2016

1

A CIP catalogue record for this title is available from the British Library

Paperback ISBN 978 1 444 73641 0
Ebook ISBN 978 1 444 73640 3

Typeset in Sabon MT by Hewer Text UK Ltd, Edinburgh

Printed and bound by Clays Ltd, St Ives plc

Hodder & Stoughton policy is to use papers that are natural, renewable
and recyclable products and made from wood grown in sustainable
forests. The logging and manufacturing processes are expected to
conform to the environmental regulations of the country of origin.

Hodder & Stoughton Ltd
Carmelite House
50 Victoria Embankment
London EC4Y 0DZ

www.sceptrebooks.com

For Luke and his grandparents

Woman much missed, how you call to me, call to me.

Thomas Hardy, 'The Voice'

Worse than thieves are ballad collectors, for when
they capture and imprison in cold type a folksong, at
the same time they kill it.

John Lomax, introduction to
American Ballads and Folksongs (1932)

March 2000

Edie sang at her own funeral. It couldn't have been any other way. Most people first knew her by her voice. New acquaintances took a few weeks or months to reconcile that voice, that thrill of sound, with the slight, grey-eyed woman holding the large handbag. She was a garden thrush with the song of a nightingale. It was one of her nicknames – 'The Little Nightingale' – and the one I felt suited her best. The nightingale isn't quite who we think she is. Contrary to what most people believe, the nightingale isn't a British bird who winters in Africa. She's an African bird who summers in England, and the sought-after music of an English summer evening is really music from the African bush, as native to Guinea-Bissau as to the moss-sprung and anemone-speckled copses of Berkshire and Dorset.

Edie once told me that the English countryside never really made sense to her. Her tiny Russian grandmother had looked after her while her parents manned their stall in Brick Lane, and she used to tell Edie stories. In winter they'd huddle under blankets beside the electric fire in their grotty flat, passing a cigarette back and forth, Edie listening, her Bubbe talking. Bubbe's stories were all of Russia and the white cold, a cold so deep it turned your bones to ice, and if the wind blew hard, you'd shatter into a billion pieces, fluttering to the ground as yet more snow.

In summer Edie and Bubbe would take apples out to the scrap of green that passed for a park and sit on a tarpaulin square (for a woman raised in Siberia, Edie's grandmother was remarkably anxious about the ill effects of dew-damp grass). On sun-filled afternoons, when grubby daisies unfurled in the warmth, young men unbuttoned their shirts to the navel and girls furtively unpeeled their stockings, Bubbe would tell stories full of snow. Edie would lie back and close her eyes against the jewel gleam of the hot sun and envision snow racing across the grass in waves, turning everything white, smothering the sunbathers who had only a moment to shiver and scream before they shattered into ice.

It was rare for Edie to confide anything about her childhood. She kept it close, self-conscious and uneasy under the barrage of my interest. 'I'm not like you. It wasn't like this,' she'd say, gesturing to the house with its lobes of wisteria or at the trembling willows by the lake. I'd feel embarrassed and overcome with a very British need to apologise for the quiet privilege of my own childhood, which, according to Edie, must have diminished any loss or sadness that dared intrude in such a place.

For all their charm, the gardens at Hartgrove never quite touched Edie. She admired the tumbles of violets, and the slender spring irises the colour of school ink, but she never troubled to learn the names of the flowers. I always had the gardener fill the pots on the terrace where we breakfasted with golden marigolds, so she insisted on calling them the marmalade flowers. It confused Clara sufficiently that, when she was about five, I caught her trying to spread the marmalade flowers on her toast.

But when it snowed, Edie longed to be outdoors. She was more excited than the children. At the first flake, she'd put on three coats at once, bandage her head in coloured scarves like a babushka and rush out, staring at the sky and willing a blizzard. Long after the girls were tired and damp from sledging in the fields, Edie lingered. Clara and Lucy would flop before the hearth in my study beside the steaming spaniels, and present to the fire rows of cold pink toes. Under the pretext of putting on a record for the girls (*The Nutcracker* or a swirling, cinnamon-sprinkled Viennese waltz – our children's taste in music was as sugar-sweet as the candy they lusted after), from the window I'd watch Edie as she'd start towards the house and then pause every few steps, turning back to gaze at the white hills and the huddle of dark woods, like a lover reluctant to say a last goodbye.

So many people think they knew her. The Little Nightingale. England's perfect rose. But Edie didn't dream of roses in summertime, she dreamed of walking through snow, the first footsteps on an icy morning.

November 1946

Hartgrove Hall is ours again. It's a strange sensation, this supposed homecoming – the prodigal sons returning all at once to Dorset on a bloody cold November morning. We are silent on the drive from the station to the house. Chivers steers the cantankerous Austin at a steady twenty miles per hour, the General parked beside him on the front seat absolutely upright as though off to inspect the troops, while Jack, George and I are jammed into the back, trying not to meet one another's eyes as we stare resolutely out of the windows.

I'm nervous about seeing her again. Hartgrove Hall is our long-lost love, the pen pal we've been mooning over in our thoughts for the last seven years, but each of us is submerged in lonely and silent anxiety at the prospect of our reunion. We know the house has had a tricky war – a parade of British regiments followed by the Americans, all of them tenants with mightier preoccupations than pruning the roses or sweeping the drawing-room chimney or halting the onslaught of death-watch beetle that has been gobbling through the rafters for ever.

As the car creeps higher and into the shadow of the hill, hoarfrost is draped across the branches like banners and where the trees meet across the narrow lane, we plunge through a tunnel of silver and white. The car turns into the long drive-way and there she is, Hartgrove Hall, bathed in early morning haze. To my relief she's still the beauty I remember. I can't see her flaws through the kindly mist, only the buttery warmth of the stone front, the thick limestone slabs on the roof drizzled with yellowing lichen. I climb out of the car and absorb the multitude of high mullioned windows and the elegant slope of the porch, and out of childish habit suddenly recalled, I count the skulk of stone foxes from the family crest that are carved on the flushwork. Ivy half conceals the smallest fox, so that he pokes his snout out from amongst the leaves as if he's shy. I'm frightfully glad to see him. I thought I'd recalled every detail of the house. I'd paced its walks and corridors each night before falling asleep and yet, already, here is something I'd quite forgotten.

The yellow sandstone façade is the same but the wisteria has been hacked away and without it the front looks naked. All of the windows are unlit and the house looks cold, unready for guests. We're not guests, I remind myself. We are the family returned. Yet it's an odd sort of homecoming: instead of Chivers or one of the maids lingering in the porch to welcome us, a major from the Guards waits on the front steps, stamping his feet to keep warm. On seeing us, he stops abruptly and salutes the General. The major thanks him for his honourable sacrifice and generosity even though we all know it's bunkum and the house was requisitioned by law. Although, I suppose, knowing the General, he would have surrendered the house in any case out of a sense of duty. The General takes great pleasure in doing his duty. The more unpleasant the sacrifice, the more he enjoys it.

The major clearly wants to be off but Father keeps him talking outside for a good fifteen minutes while it starts to sleet. We all stand there rigid with cold and boredom. I'm amazed that Jack doesn't declare, 'Bugger this, I'm off to inspect the damage done to the old girl,' and disappear, but then he and George have been demobbed for only a month or so. Beneath the civvy clothes they still possess a soldier's habits and to walk away from a senior officer wouldn't just be poor manners but a disciplinary offence.

After an age, the General allows the unfortunate major to depart and marches indoors. Jack, George and I hesitate, unwilling to follow. I want our reunion to be private and, as I glance at my brothers, it is clear that they feel the same. Jack lingers for a moment, then turns back down the steps, making for the river, while George heads in the opposite direction, crossing the lawns towards the lake. I wait for a minute, gulping cold, fresh air, feeling the bite and tang of it on my teeth, and then slip into the house. The great hall is almost as frigid as it is outside. In the vast and soot-stained inglenook there is no fire. I am almost certain that there used to be a constant fire. The requisite carved foxes gaze out from the stone-carved struts, chilly and forlorn. I suppose there is no one to light a fire now and I don't suppose there will be again. I notice that the mantelpiece is missing. I can't think how it was taken or why.

The walls are bereft of paintings. The good ones haven't hung here for years. They were flogged, one Gainsborough and Stubbs at a time, but my ancestors were sentimental chaps. Until the army requisitioned the house, copies of the originals used to hang around the hall – gloomy reminders of what was lost to Christie's to pay inheritance tax, veterinarian bills, servants' wages and to replace rotting windows. Some of the copies were rather good, others less so – peculiar, carnival-mirror distortions of the originals. For years, Jack, George and I used to play 'spot the imposter' and attempt to guess which of the bewigged and unsmiling portraits were copies. Then the General told us that none of them was real and the game was rendered pointless.

The last painting to go was a dear Constable landscape of the woodland beneath Hartgrove barrow. The painter stands at the top of the ridge, gazing down at a brown wood dabbed with autumn light. Somewhere in the painting a nightingale sings – the last of the year. The copy of the Constable is quite decent. I've always liked it, even though the colours are second rate and the lines muddy – but I can still hear the nightingale and that's what matters. George sent it to me, along with his letter explaining that the house was to be requisitioned. I'd been alone at school when the news had come, and it had left me disconsolate. Only George would have thought to send the painting with the horrid news – a kind memento of home to sustain me. Inevitably the painted view began to supplant the one in my imagination until I began to see the barrow and woods third hand – Constable's vision re-daubed by a copyist.

I return to the car, retrieve the picture from the boot and rehang it on a nail in the hall. It looks lost and small.

I'm chilled and feel queasy from the pervasive stench of damp. Disheartened, I retreat down the steps and out across the tangle of gardens before striking uphill towards the ridge of Hartgrove barrow. I set off at a lick until, breathless from exertion, I pause at the first of the grass terraces rippling the hillside to look down at the house. It's different for me than for the others. I was eleven when she was taken in '39 and I don't remember how she's supposed to be, not with the absolute clarity of Jack or George. From my vantage point I can see the burned-out south wing. An accident with an ember smouldering in an unswept chimney, according to the letter sent by the War Office, although Jack heard rumours it was a game gone awry in the Officers' Mess. They'd been bottling farts into brandy bottles – such an ignominious end for four hundred years of history: sent up in smoke by a lit fart.

I'm not surprised no one could face confessing the truth to the General. I spent much of the war evading him myself. Not that it took much effort – the General's war was spent preening in Whitehall; he was delighted to partake in another helping of battle even at a distance. Between school and holidays dawdled away at the houses of pals, I managed not to endure more than the occasional uneasy luncheon with him at the club.

From up here I can see the exposed timbers, looking like broken ribs, and the house appears unsteady and uneven, her former symmetry quite spoiled. An invalid with her shattered limb still attached. The lawns are sloshed into mud. Half the limes on the avenue are missing so that the driveway resembles a mouth with most of the teeth knocked out. The woodland under the ridge is balding in patches, where scores of the trees have been felled so that only the stumps remain, stubbling the hillside.

I sit down on an anthill and cry, relieved no one can see me. I wonder how the bloody hell we're going to put the old girl back together. There are no paintings left to flog. No forgotten Turner lurking in the attic. Canning, the aged and recalcitrant estate manager, is muttering about wanting to retire. But then I swat away my doubts and revel in the pleasure of home. I take a breath of cold, larch-spiced air. Happiness rises up through me, fierce as brandy fumes.

~

In the dreary lull after Christmas, Jack informs us with great delight that he has persuaded the General to host a New Year's Eve party. The General doesn't like parties. They distract from the important things in life: namely shooting pheasant and fishing. Oddly, however, he enjoys a good war, even though it disrupts the same things. George is perfectly thrilled – he can't quite believe Jack's managed it. I'm not surprised. The General will agree to almost anything so long as it's Jack who asks.

George and I set about readying the house. No mean feat as each day brings the discovery of yet more damage. The panelling in the great hall has been stripped away in places – whether for a lark or for kindling, we'll never know. Not only is the mantelpiece missing on the grand inglenook, but part of the chimneystack has been knocked off so that when it rains, sleets or worse, water pours down the chimney and puddles on the hearth. Someone left the front door open a few nights ago, and when I stumbled up to bed I saw two blackbirds taking a bath. They looked quite self-possessed as they dabbled, eyeing me with great condescension as I swayed past with a glass of whisky. I thought I'd dreamed it, but when I came down in the morning, not a little hung-over, I found a spotted trail of white bird shit across the hall. The General appears to have neither the cash nor the inclination to make repairs. Planning for a party is a much pleasanter task than considering the larger future of the house.

On the morning of New Year's Eve, George and I wander dismally from room to room, wondering how on God's earth the place is going to be fit for a hundred of the county's finest by the evening. At least we don't have expectations to live up to. Even in the years before the war, Hartgrove wasn't renowned for the calibre of its hospitality: there was always decent grog, but even then we couldn't afford the staff or compete with the swagger of our neighbours. The family name is as old and threadbare as the sixteenth-century carpet that George and I hang on the wall in the drawing room in a futile attempt to keep the wind from sneaking in through the cracks in the plaster.

Jack, of course, isn't with us. He imparted a variety of instructions over breakfast, informed us somewhat vaguely as to how many had accepted the invitation ('Fifty or so, I should think – almost certainly not more than sixty, a hundred tops') and then immediately left for the station – no doubt to collect his latest rosewater-scented poppet. Clearly his role was simply to persuade the General to acquiesce to the party, not to bother with the actual organisation. I'm torn between irritation at Jack and pleasure – we've been apart for so long that there is still a novelty in his irksome habits. I'm oddly reassured to discover that the army has not reformed him.

One of the new dailies flicks a rag over the floor and the other pokes half-heartedly at the fire in the dining room that at half past nine is already threatening to give up with a whine of damp wood. There has been a parade of help through the Hall in the last few weeks, each girl more belligerent than the last. None can stick it for more than a few days. It's never quite clear whether they've walked out or whether Chivers has dismissed them or, as Jack suggested, buried them under the roses. We never *do* see the girls again. In the years before the war the house was mostly staffed with Chivers' relatives. He always introduced them vaguely, saying, 'Katy, Maud, Joan, the youngest daughter of my sister in Bournemouth,' or 'My Liverpool cousin's girl', but I suppose even Chivers had to run out of relatives at some point.

George and I survey the two surly maids, neither of them acknowledging our presence. Long gone are the days when our appearance would make them withdraw with a blush (not that I can remember, but so Jack tells me and perhaps it's true).

'I say, would you two lend us a hand getting the old place ready for a bash tonight?' says George with false camaraderie and an awkward smile. George is never easy in company. I'm surprised that he's so keen on the party – I suspect he's pretending for Jack and my sakes. George is a thoroughly decent fellow, the best I know.

The girls look up. They do not smile back. They know instantly we're amateurs. I fear it's hopeless. We need Jack. Jack has all the charm; within two ticks he'd have the two girls eager to help, just to please him.

'We got a lot to get through,' says the larger of the girls.

'We're only paid through till twelve.' She's stout with deep-set brown eyes, like a pair of little wet stones.

'Oh, gosh, bother,' says George, deflating. I can hear him cursing Jack in his head for going off and leaving us like this.

I reach into my pocket, pulling out a portion of the General's Christmas cash ('Presents, unless they're guns, are for girls'). I stuff it into the large maid's stubby fingers. 'When you're finished for the morning, then.'

At twelve on the dot, they reappear in the drawing room, ready to help. They're almost smiling. I wonder how much of my Christmas money I handed over, but I don't care. I want this bash to be splendid. Jack and George have had parties in the mess, and they've travelled, seen things. Terrible things, perhaps, but at least they've been somewhere, done something. I spent the whole war at school. As we hunt out unbroken chairs from the four corners of the house, I try once again to ask George about it. I've attempted to persuade Jack and George to divulge details on various occasions with a notable lack of success.

'What was it actually like? I think it's rotten that you won't tell me.'

He shrugs. 'There's not much to tell. In the most part it was frightfully dull.'

'And in the other part?'

'Unpleasant.'

'Dull or unpleasant, that's all?' I ask, incredulous that this is all he'll give me.

'Mostly yes. Sometimes, when we were particularly unfortunate it was dull *and* unpleasant.'

I wonder if he's teasing me, but that's not like George. He doesn't like to be ribbed himself, so rarely pokes fun at anyone else. We set down a small and only slightly stained sofa in the corner of the drawing room, pausing for a minute to catch our breath.

'I can't really picture you as a soldier, George.'

He smiles. 'No, neither could I. I think that was part of the problem.'

'What was the other part?'

He chuckles but doesn't answer. 'It's jolly nice to be home. I missed the rain. Never thought that was possible but it is. Sunshine's all very well but I've discovered that what I like best is the surprise of it after rain.'

I'm not sure what to say to this. Freezing rain is smashing against the windows, sneaking in through the ill-fitting panes and making small pools on the sills. We could do with a surprise of sunshine about now.

'What were the other chaps like?'

'Oh, all sorts. Every type. You know.'

I don't know at all. I sigh and abandon my questioning.

Cambridge is pleasant enough – they're decent fellows, precisely the sort I knew at school – but I hanker for something different, less familiar. I can't study music (chaps like us don't study music. It simply isn't done, according to Father) so the entire rigmarole feels utterly pointless, a dreary extension of school. If the war were still going on, I'd be in the thick of it instead of banished to endure cosy little tutorials in fireside snugs and listen to the assorted triumphs of Henries Tudor. And if I can't have music, then I'd like a bit of war. I can't say this to anyone. Even Jack's wayward grin would falter and George, well, George would quietly walk away, head bowed. The General would approve the sentiment and that would be the worst condemnation of all.

~

The guests arrive meticulously late at a quarter to nine. In the dark the house doesn't look quite so dilapidated. Candlelight, branches of holly and carefully placed globes of mistletoe conceal the worst of it. With the help of the two girls, George and I have made a pretty decent show. There's a surprising amount of wine. When the house was requisitioned, the General didn't fuss about packing away the carpets or the furniture (all strictly third rate anyhow – more decrepit than antique) but he and Chivers did hide away the good drink. They had the gardener build a false wall in the cellar, and while the soldiers graffitied obscenities in the downstairs loo they didn't defile the pre-war burgundy, so in the General's view the place has survived unscathed in essentials.

The night is cold, several degrees below freezing, and even before midnight the ground glints, thick with frost. The yew hedges are unkempt, overgrown from years of neglect and brushed with white like a drunk's untrimmed beard. It's too icy for cars – for those that still own them anyhow – and most people choose to walk. We've staked torches along the driveway and they flare out, banners of red flame in the darkness. The gloom provides a mask of perfect restoration and from outside the house looks splendid once again. You can't see that the southern wing is burned out or that several windows along the front are boarded up or that the lawns are mown only by the sheep, at present snoozing in the shelter of the garden wall. All the party guests perceive is the yellow light spilling from the unbroken bay windows onto the terrace, ivy patterning the sandstone porch and the frost feathering the slate roof. I vow silently that if ever I'm rich, I'll return the Hall to her former beauty so that she always looks like this, even in daylight. I drink a glass of sloe gin and watch the river, a black ribbon spooling noiselessly below.

'Jack's still not back, blast him.'

George is angry. Well, as angry as it's possible for George to be. I really can't picture him as a soldier, sallying forth full of rage and fury. He glances around the crowd of party goers, tense, his forehead sweaty. We need Jack to play host. Neither of us is up to the task. George huffs and grumbles.

'Every time. Every bloody time. He swans in, gives his orders and swans off again. I'm tired of it, Fox. Next time, he can do the hard work. Where the devil's he got to anyhow?'

I say nothing. Jack's undoubtedly in a pub somewhere, nestled beside a toasty fire with his latest popsy, having lost track of time after his second or third pint. We move inside and we're immediately engulfed in fur. The county girls have cracked them out again, now the war's done and it's no longer vulgar. I'm enveloped in the camphor whiff of mothballs and armpit.

'Vivien. Caroline. How wonderful to see you.'

The girls incline their cheeks to be kissed.

'Freezing, isn't it? Where's Jack?'

I deflate. No one even comments on the constellation of candles we've dug out or the huge log we've managed to drag inside that roars and crackles in the mantel-less hearth. A gramophone that wasn't new before the war scratches out a tune, but it isn't loud enough to be heard over the voices. No one dances. Half a pig with a tennis ball in its mouth lazes on the vast hall table. Chivers presides with a knife long enough to be a sword but I notice that only the men are eating. The women veer away from the spectacle, slightly revolted. We didn't think of providing anything else. George and I assumed a pig would do it. Vegetables seemed superfluous.

One of the girls wafts over. Her dress is made of a fine, gauzy fabric and her skin is speckled with gooseflesh.

'Hello, Fox. Splendid show. It's all thoroughly charming.'

'Is it, Vivien?'

She laughs. 'No. Not really. But you've tried terribly hard and that's charming enough. But in a house of men, what could anyone expect?'

'Have some pig. If you eat, then the other girls might follow.'

She takes my arm. 'All right, but only if you tell me where your dastardly brother's got to.'

At least there's enough to drink. Everyone clusters near the fire, which is starting to smoke. I turn off the gramophone; the incessant scratching is making my ears itch. It's only half past ten. God knows how we're going to make it to midnight. Everyone appears to be waiting for something but we've planned nothing else.

The General moves through the crowd, a cigar in one hand (even during the war he never seemed to be short; I wonder what poor Chivers had to do to secure the things), and attempts small talk. If I wasn't so anxious about the failure of the party, I'd be amused. The girls listen with toothy smiles that match their tiny strings of polished pearls – they're all far too well bred to allow their boredom to show and everyone remains afraid of the General. He's an old dog but one always senses the snarl and ill-humour under the curl of his moustache.

And then, all at once, the uneasy chatter blooms into laughter. Just as the applause of the audience signals the arrival of the conductor, I know without turning to look that Jack has arrived. I can't quite make out the girl with him. She's small and half concealed by the throng that instantly forms around Jack.

'Right. Lead me to the drink,' he cries.

The crowd part to let him pass and now I see a slight, dark-haired girl, her little gloved hand tucked into his arm. Jack signals to me. I cross the room. I stop, quite still. I recognise her.

'Fox. This is Edie. Edie Rose.'

'Of course. Yes. Edie. Miss Rose. A real delight. I'm a pleasure. To meet you.'

15

To my horror, I feel colour rising to my cheeks. Edie only smiles.

Inevitably the girls I like are already Jack's girls. Each time he was on leave he'd show up to lunch with another wide-eyed, slim-legged thing who would flap a tear-soaked handkerchief as his train pulled out of the station and pen him letters that, knowing Jack, he never read. I've seen pictures of Edie of course. I even kept a postcard of her in my school trunk – she's the nation's sweetheart, as well, it seems, as being Jack's – but seeing her standing in our mildew-ridden hall, amongst the press of girls in their well-worn frocks and the usual chaps with their ruddy cheer and their muddy shoes, I nearly forget to breathe. She's smaller than I imagined from her photograph. Even in the midst of my awe, I notice how tired she looks.

Holding my elbow, Jack steers me through the crowd to a corner, with Edie still attached to his other arm.

'There's no music, Fox.'

He frowns, troubled.

'No, the gramophone's broken.'

'Dammit, Fox. That thing's quite useless anyhow. You should have hired a band.'

I sag, about to apologise and concede that that would have been a jolly good idea, when I remember Jack bloody well left us to it. I'm ready to snap back and ask him what I was supposed to hire a band with, since the General is hardly awash with cash, but Jack's already turned away and is pleading quietly with Edie.

'Go on, darling, be a doll. Just one.'

'It's never just one, Jack, you know that.'

'All right, two then.' He grins and strokes her cheek. 'It would mean the world to young Fox here.'

Jack's trying to persuade Edie to sing. I'm torn. I want to hear her sing, I really, really do, but she looks exhausted. She

16

wrinkles her forehead and chews her fingernail in a sudden, childlike gesture, then gives a little sigh.

'Yes, all right, I'll do it. But one short set and that's all. No requests. No encores.'

I've never heard a girl speak so firmly to Jack. He places a solemn kiss on her lips.

'Agreed, madam.'

'And now, you lured me here with promises of champagne. Are you all talk, Jack Fox-Talbot?'

With playful remonstration he leads her away and presents her with a glass of the General's best pre-war Veuve Clicquot. I can't help but stare after them. Edie might be the one who's famous but the same aura of glamour shines on Jack. When we were children our grandmama played several games with us but her favourite was to pluck a buttercup and hold it under our chins. If it cast a yellow glow, she'd declare, 'Yes, Little Fox likes butter very much indeed,' and we'd squeal, perfectly delighted. My brother lives permanently in that buttery glow.

As I watch Edie and Jack colluding by the fire, they seem set apart from everyone else – like figures in an old master in a gallery full of amateur works – and I feel a pulse of envy, hot and sharp. George perceives the direction of my gaze. George always does.

He chuckles. 'Forget it, Fox. Not a chance.' I look away, pretending not to understand.

I don't pay attention for the rest of the party. The minutes drift by. Edie Rose will sing us into the New Year. This soggy failure of a party is transformed into a triumph. Everyone will talk about it for years to come. The church bells boom the half-hour and I look around for Edie but I can't see her.

'Hello. Harry, isn't it?'

She's beside me.

'Yes. That's right.'

I notice that she has a dot of a mole on her left cheek. I want to reach out and brush it with my fingers. I wonder whether Jack already has.

'Jack tells me that you can sing and play the piano.'

'Yes.'

Silently I curse myself. I want to appear dashing and sophisticated and yet in her company I'm apparently unable to stutter more than monosyllables.

'Will you play for me, Harry? I'm frightfully tired. I don't want to sing alone tonight.'

'I would. But – the piano. She's not in tip-top condition. She's had rather a hard war, I'm afraid.'

Edie laughs. 'She?'

'I'm sorry. I always think of her, it . . .'

Edie reaches out and touches my arm. 'It's terribly sweet of you.'

I'm nettled. I don't want her to think I'm sweet. I'm not a child.

'The army moved the piano into the mess bar. Goodness knows what's been poured over the keys. Not to mention the general damp. When I tried to tune her – it – one of the strings just snapped.'

'Please play for me, Harry.'

'Fine. But—' I remember she said no requests.

'What is it?'

'Will you sing one of your early pieces? "The Seeds of Love" or "The Apple Tree"? Not that I don't like the wartime songs, of course.'

This isn't true. I dislike Edie Rose's wartime hits intensely. They're patriotic guff. Tunes in one shade of pillar-box red. I walked out of a café once when 'A Shropshire Thrush' came on the wireless, even though I'd already paid.

Edie gives me an odd look. 'They won't like it.'

She glances at the assembled crowd and I'm pleased that

she's no longer counting me amongst them. Jack bounds over and kisses her on the cheek, tucking a curl behind her ear with easy familiarity.

'It's time, old thing. Or do you want this first?'

With a flourish he produces from his pocket a disintegrating fish-paste sandwich. Edie shakes her head and I point mournfully at the hog squatting on the table. 'What's wrong with my pig? No one seems to want it.'

'It's splendid, Fox. Just not really Edie's thing.'

She turns to me. 'Well, Harry? Shall we?'

Edie doesn't sing my song. I sit at the rickety piano and cajole the keys into some sort of accompaniment, feeling as if I'm riding shotgun on an unsteady, half-dead nag that might either bolt or flop into the hedgerow at any moment. Edie's a true professional and doesn't let the screwball sideshow rattle her. She lulls the county set with that honeysuckle voice as she floats through the wartime hits that made her famous but which I cannot abide. I'm sweating from the effort of forcing the piano to obey and I have a headache. It's past midnight and we've slid into 1947 and I haven't even noticed. I need a drink and a clean shirt. The guests cheer and toast Edie and then me as she hauls me to my feet. They holler and even the General raises a glass.

'Shall we get out of here?' she whispers through her teeth, giving them a playful curtsey.

'Dear God, yes.'

We race outside before the crowd can smother her with well-lubricated enthusiasm. She lights me a cigarette and I take it, somehow too embarrassed to confess I don't smoke. I can't stop staring at her. She smiles at me, and it's slightly lopsided as though she's thinking of a mischievous and inappropriate joke. It's horribly attractive.

'So how come when all three of you boys are Foxes, you are the only one called "Fox"?'

I swallow smoke, trying not to cough, grateful that in the dark she can't see my eyes water.

'I was always "Little Fox" but somehow now that I'm eighteen and nearly six foot, it seems, well, silly. So now I'm just Fox.'

'I see. Fox suits you. Although I've always liked the name Harry.'

I wonder whether she's flirting with me, but I'm so unpractised that I can't tell.

'You need a new piano,' she says.

'And a new roof and a hundred other things. But I thought I played her valiantly.'

'With absolute chivalry. A lesser man would have chopped it, sorry, her, up mid-performance for kindling.'

'Are you trying to charm young Fox here?' asks Jack, appearing at my side so clearly unperturbed by the prospect that I'm thoroughly put out.

A trio of girls and their beaus step out onto the terrace in Jack's wake. Oblivious, he pulls people along as if they were the trail behind a shooting star. They say he was one of the best officers in his battalion, that his men would follow him anywhere, do anything for him. I believe it.

The low balustrades of the terrace are smashed, but spread with frost they catch in the light and glisten.

'I didn't get my song,' I complain. Drink has made me bold.

'You first,' says Edie. 'It's only fair and Jack says you can sing.'

'He can, he can. He's splendid,' says Jack. My brother has the kindness and generosity of the utterly self-assured.

'Fine. What shall I sing?'

'That one you do for me and George. I like that one. He's terribly clever, he wrote it himself.'

I wince at his enthusiasm. Jack's referring to a bawdy and frankly filthy ditty I made up to amuse him and George, but it's too late and Edie's turning to me expectantly.

'In that case I demand a Harry Fox-Talbot original. I won't accept anything less.'

I rack my brains for something neither too simple nor too rude. Others have gathered on the terrace, but I don't mind. I never mind an audience for music. According to my brothers, before Mother died I used to come downstairs and sing for dinner guests in my nightie. I hope Jack hasn't told Edie this. I can't ask him not to because then he certainly will. I clear my throat.

'All right. Here you go. This isn't strictly written by me, but I heard it once upon a time and this is a tidy variation on a theme.'

I'm not a distinguished singer, but my voice is pleasant enough and, I suppose, expressive. I can make a few instruments say what I'm thinking – pianos, church organs and my own voice. I'm not quite six foot and not quite handsome. My eyes aren't as blue as my brothers' but I've observed that when I sing girls forget I'm not as tall as they'd thought and not as handsome as they'd hoped.

I sing without accompaniment. I don't look at Edie or the other girls. The frost is thick as snow and I watch the song rise from my lips as steam. I've never seen a song fly before. The words drift over the lawn. It's one of Edie's old songs from before the war. I sing the names of the flowers and they float out into the darkness – yellow primroses and violets bright against the wintry ground. I sing a verse or two and then I stop. I can fool them for a short while, but I know if I go on too long my voice can't hold them. That takes real skill, and a real voice. A voice like Edie Rose's.

'Jolly good. Bloody marvellous,' shouts Jack and claps me on the back.

The others applaud and the girls smile and, for the first time that evening, try to catch my eye. I should make the most of this – it's a temporary reprieve from invisibility. The effect of a song is much like that of a glass of champagne and lasts only as long. I glance at Edie. She doesn't look at me and she doesn't clap with the others.

May 2000

I knew the girls were worried about me. I could always tell when a lecture was coming. Clara would telephone and inform me that they were coming round for tea, so I would check the cupboards for the good biscuits. Dinner or lunch with the assembled grandchildren and Clara's harassed, distracted husband was a social call but tea with both daughters could mean only one thing.

On this occasion, they sat down side by side on the Edwardian sofa, a little too close together, as both of them avoided the place nearest the fire, Edie's spot. No one could bear to sit there. I was tempted to because then she'd have to come in and shoo me away as she always did, but I knew that was daft. They perched there, two birds on a branch, Lucy, my little chaffinch, small and dark with fluttering, uncertain hands. I copied that movement once, when conducting Debussy and I wanted a ripple to run through the strings. I didn't tell Lucy. She wouldn't have taken it as a compliment.

Clara settled against the cushions with studied ease, ankles tidily crossed, expensive handbag on the floor beside her. Edie bought those cushions from Liberty on a spree a hundred years ago and I never liked them. A bit gaudy if you ask me. Though of course she hadn't and now I'd never part with them. Ridiculous how ugly snatches of household bits and bobs suddenly become precious and imbued with sentiment.

Both girls sat facing me with porcelain teacups perfectly balanced on their knees (I never know how they do this; it's one of the many things their mother must have taught them) and informed me that I needed a hobby. Distraction. I

needed To Make Friends. They were brimming with suggestions – I could join the bridge club, I could grow my own
vegetables. When I suggested joining the local Women's
Institute as an honorary gentleman member and trying my
hand at treacle sponge, I gained a stern look from Clara
who clearly didn't think I was taking this seriously enough.
So I listened politely to their advice (I always listen carefully
before doing precisely what I want – children, even when
over forty, don't like to be ignored).

'Are you managing to write at all?' asked Lucy, her forehead
notched with concern.

'Not at the minute. Another biscuit?' I thrust the plate at
her and took a biscuit myself, shoving it into my mouth all at
once so that I couldn't possibly answer any more questions.
She didn't take the hint.

'You're playing the piano, though, aren't you, Papa?'

I pointed to my bulging cheeks, but the girls smiled politely
and waited until I'd finished.

'No, darling, I am not playing the piano.'

I've never been good at lying to Lucy. Even as a child she'd
stare at me with those huge guileless grey eyes, believing every
word I uttered to be a fixed and unalterable truth, so that in
the end I couldn't bear to tell her the tiniest of fibs. I wanted
to be as truthful as she believed me to be.

I hadn't played the piano since the day Edie died. I'd tried.
I'd opened the lid when I arrived home after the funeral. I'd
slunk away from the visitors and their pocket recollections of
Edie that they were all too eager to share over the sandwiches
and vol au vents, so that in the car on the way home they might
console themselves that they had done their duty and given a
pleasant memory to the poor old sod. I'd disappeared into the
music room with a glass of decent Scotch and a cigar, and
closed the door, grateful for solitude, but when faced with the
keys, I hesitated – my hands suddenly unsure where to land.

I'd never had to think about playing, any more than I have to think about forming words with my mouth when I speak.

My fingers were terribly cold, and I couldn't fix on which was the appropriate piece for the occasion. Since I was playing for Edie it needed to be the perfect choice performed just so, but my joints were clumsy and stiff. When I reached into my memory for Bach he wasn't there, nor was Schubert. Even the little Chopin nocturne I'd played as a joke when she couldn't sleep was hiding somewhere in a recess of my brain. I'd ended up closing the lid of the piano and announcing to the empty room that tomorrow I'd play. I'd compose something especially for Edie and play it for her. However, when tomorrow arrived I discovered that even though my fingers were no longer cold and unwieldy, my mind remained stiff, and all melody eluded me.

Lucy took my hand in hers: warm and small – pretty yet useless for a piano player, but then neither of my daughters had ever shown the slightest inclination towards music. No, that's not true. When Clara was fifteen we had a handsome young trumpeter staying with us for the July concert series, and Clara declared that she wanted to learn the trumpet. Her passion for both boy and trumpet waned with the long summer nights.

It would have been nice if the girls had displayed even an amateur interest, a casual talent. I had offered each of them lessons upon a variety of instruments. Always more willing to please than her sister, Lucy had worked her way through the entire woodwind section with utterly astonishing ineptitude until neither I nor her teacher could stand any more. One Saturday morning when she was about twelve, instead of dropping her at the music teacher's house, I deposited her at tennis lessons at which, to everyone's profound relief, she was rather better.

It was Clara's turn to fix me with a steady look.

'Well, Papa, if you're not writing and you're not playing, then it's even more important for you to have a hobby.'

The thing is that I did have a hobby of sorts, although probably not one my daughters had in mind. I'd taken to visiting doctors. I'd seen all different kinds. I'd tried each of the partners at my own practice and I'd gone up to town to see a specialist on Harley Street at great expense (I told the girls I was going to the opera, which would have been significantly cheaper). I needed a diagnosis. There was clearly something very wrong. I was always cold even when I sat huddled in front of the fire. I couldn't eat. I could neither write nor play. If they'd only give me a pill, then maybe I'd be whole again. However, every doctor had said the same thing – I was perfectly fine, nothing was physically wrong. I should eat a little more and drink a little less, and at that I'd known each one was yet another quack. The blasted doctors knew nothing.

In the end I'd gone to see a new partner at the local practice. I tried to explain.

'A huge piece of me is missing,' I wanted to say. 'I'm more holes than man.' But it had come out all wrong. 'I'm a Jarlsberg,' I declared. The young, weary-looking doctor stared at me. Starting to sweat, I'd tried again. 'I'm full of holes like a Jarlsberg.'

The doctor smiled and sat back in his chair with a practised air of patience. 'Ah, yes, that Swiss cheese. I know. My daughter has it in her lunch box. My wife buys it in slices from Marks and Spencer.'

I'd stared at the doctor for a moment, then reached for my hat, wondering how it was that we were now talking about cheese instead of whatever cataclysmic ailment I had. Surely it was cancer. At that moment I'd been quite sure of it and had decided it wouldn't be such a terrible thing. I couldn't have fought it for long, not without Edie. It would be hard on the girls, but they were grown up and in the end it would be for the best, although I preferred not to suffer. I was definitely against suffering. I was about to start considering the most suitable pieces for my funeral – Bach, there would definitely have to be Bach – when the doctor put down his pen and removed his spectacles. He had pale blue eyes and he looked to be about the same age as Clara.

'You're not ill, Mr Fox-Talbot. You're sad.'

I'd inhaled sharply, affronted. Sad was the wrong word. Sad was watching an old weepie when it was raining outside or taking down the Christmas tree on the first day of January or listening to the last concert of the season knowing that afterwards all the musicians would depart and the house would be much too quiet. I'd wanted to rise to my feet and inform the young doctor that I took offence at his most inappropriate use of language but for some reason my legs wouldn't move, and my tongue was dry and fat, and it stuck to the roof of my mouth.

All I'd managed was, 'This wasn't the plan. Women live longer than men. Everyone knows that. This wasn't the plan at all.'

'No, of course not,' agreed the doctor.

He sat patiently for a few minutes while, to my profound dismay, I wept noisily and inelegantly. When my tears slowed, silently he passed me a tissue. I blew my nose, disgruntled and unnerved by my display; it appeared that I had no control over anything at all, not even myself.

He'd asked, 'Have you tried writing anything down about—?'

'Edie. Her name was Edie.'

'Have you tried writing down some things about her?'

I shook my head. 'I'm going to write her a symphony. Well, I've been meaning to. I'm a bit stuck.'

'How about starting with something a little less ambitious? You could jot down a memory.'

I frowned. 'That's all rather personal.'

'So what? No one else needs to read it.'

'No, thank you.'

He'd gone back to scrawling notes on his pad. 'As you like. Some people find it helps.'

He'd offered no sympathy, for which I was grateful, and I'd left shortly afterwards with a prescription for sleeping tablets – although I observed that he wouldn't give me too many in case I did something rash. As I'd walked through reception the secretary hailed me.

'Mr Fox-Talbot? Can I just update your details?'

I'd waited at the counter while she fumbled with her computer.

'We don't seem to have a recent phone number, Mr Fox-Talbot.'

'Yes, of course. It's—'

And I found I couldn't remember. I'm a half-decent mathematician – most musicians are. But I couldn't recall my own telephone number. I could remember our very first, the one we were given when we had the telephone installed in the house in 1952, but our present number had disappeared.

'It's all right, take a minute,' said the secretary.

I'd looked at her with her orange lipstick and her too many earrings as she suddenly became very busy, tapping at her keyboard, and I understood that she pitied me. I'd become that old man who'd lost both his wife and his telephone number.

A few days later, as I sat in my armchair facing my daughters, I wondered for a second whether the surgery receptionist had called them but I supposed she couldn't have done – confidentiality and all that. For a second I saw them not as they were then, but as they'd once been. Clara, stern and immaculately attired in her party frock, patent shoes shining and her long blonde hair in two perfectly gleaming plaits which she twirled as she spoke. Lucy, tiny and quiet, dressed in an identical blue frock but somehow contriving to be as untidy as her sister was neat, her dark hair sprouting from the ends of her pigtails and her small feet stuck out before her, revealing two odd socks and no shoes.

I blinked and my grown-up daughters replaced the apparitions. I pushed the biscuits at Clara, who declined, and at Lucy, who took two.

'Stop fretting. I'll be all right,' I said, not because I believed it but because they wanted it to be true.

'Will you go to this dance then? It's for OAPs. They always need men.'

'No, darling, I won't. I'm not going to foxtrot with strangers in the village hall.'

'When will you start arranging this year's music festival?' asked Lucy.

'I thought I might take this year off. I'm a little tired,' I said, not looking at them.

Immediately I knew that I'd said the wrong thing. I could feel their intake of breath. I wished I'd fibbed and said something about this year's theme being loss and hope or some such nonsense, even if I knew I'd never go through with it and would have had to pretend in a few months that all the soloists I'd invited were mysteriously busy this year. But I didn't think fast enough and as soon as the words left my mouth I knew that I was in for it and Operation 'Buck Up Papa' was moving up a gear.

I waited for a week but nothing happened, apart from the usual calls from Clara on her car phone during the school run with the children shrieking in the back about forgotten swimming kits and unfinished homework. Clara always called me when she was occupied with something else as though proving to us all just how many things she could juggle at once. I wished she'd call less often when she actually had a moment to talk.

There were messages on the answer phone from Lucy who, I'm certain, timed her calls for when she knew I'd be out or in the shower. She wished me to know that she was concerned but would prefer not to actually speak to me when the conversation was both predictable and uncomfortable.

Lucy: 'How are you today?'

Me: 'I've been better.'

Lucy: 'Did you manage to play at all?'

Me: 'No.'

I would have preferred to leave messages on my answer phone and avoid me too.

I spent the week as usual, drifting through loose and identical days, dreary except for grief. At night I couldn't sleep. I'd lie awake in the small hours, aware of every creak and click of wood and the cold space beside me. During the days I was so tired. A weariness settled in my bones, as if they'd been boiled too long and softened into marrow. Even though I'd potter quietly through the afternoon and be careful not to nap, not for a minute – come night-time, there I was, lying awake in the dark, listening to the hum and rattle of the house.

Memories drifted through my mind unsummoned and I'd be forced to watch, passive and powerless to staunch them. All I wanted was dull and dreamless sleep but instead I'd see Edie trying to pin up her hair before a concert, hands shaking so badly that I had to help. She suffered from terrible stage fright throughout her career, but no one ever knew apart from me. Sleep receded from me, and I found myself holding a trembling ghost of Edie in the wings of the Royal Albert Hall, her dress slick with sweat. A stage hand appeared and politely enquired as to whether she was all right, to which she replied, 'Absolutely fine,' and promptly vomited in the fire bucket.

I remembered how Edie used to disappear off on her snow walks in the night and, half awake, I'd try to fool myself that she'd just gone for a wander through the gardens, perhaps as far as the hill. But Edie went walkabout only on the wintriest of nights, and inevitably the next thing I'd hear was the warble of a chiff-chaff or I'd inhale the treacherous scent of jasmine through the open window, and I'd know it was summer and I wasn't even permitted the respite of pretence. I'd lapse into an exhausted doze shortly before dawn, wondering whether this was to be the rest of my existence: an endless replay of our marriage, the repeats slowing losing their clarity and colour.

Before Edie died, I'd never lived alone. Even when she took a trip without me, the housekeeper would live in while she was gone – I'm of the generation where men are considered useless, helpless creatures unable to boil an egg without assistance. I'd achieved the age of seventy-odd, having spent hardly a night in the house on my own. But when Edie died, I couldn't bear the thought of a stranger sleeping there. I feared an outsider would drive away the last pieces of her. I didn't want a stranger looking at Edie's things with an uninformed eye. Objects divorced from their stories are downgraded to mere knick-knacks.

I rejected Clara's and Lucy's suggestion that we find a permanent live-in housekeeper. They were baffled by the vehemence of my refusal. I declined to explain. The truth was that it seemed perilously close to assisted living. One day the housekeeper would no longer simply cook and clean and shop but help me dress and then wash and, before I knew what had happened, I'd have a live-in carer. Even if I lived off microwave meals and suppers at the pub, I would remain independent. I found a pleasant and efficient woman from the village, Mrs Stroud, who agreed to come three times a week to cook and clean.

It might have been the right choice-but I was unprepared for the loneliness. Some days it was worse than the grief. If grief is the thug who punches you in the gut, then loneliness is his goon who holds back your arms and renders you helpless before the onslaught. For the first time in my life, silence taunted me. I despise background music, incidental music, music to create ambience – whatever you want to call it. Music must be attended to or there must be silence. However, it had rarely been silent in my head; my mind had filled any quiet with music. Sometimes it would be my own – a piece I'd written or that I was about to write – or perhaps just a little Mozart. Not after Edie. Then the world became horribly quiet. A dismal hush crept through everything like a scourge of damp.

My thoughts echoed through the house. I heard the shuffle of my footsteps along the hall – when did I start to have the gait of an old man? To my shame, I started to watch the television for company during lunch, and found myself caught in the concocted melodramas of the soaps. I spoke aloud to myself, as otherwise, if the telephone didn't ring, on the days Mrs Stroud didn't come, by four or five o'clock I wouldn't have uttered a word all day. When the postman knocked on the door with a package that needed to be signed for, I talked at him for too long, with too much focus, and he backed down the steps to escape.

In desperation one night, I reached for the notepad I always left on the bedside table in case musical inspiration appeared in the small hours. Perhaps the GP was right. No one needed to read a blasted word if I didn't wish them to. Instead of melody, I tried transcribing stray memories and wondered whether by doing so I could store them safely, recall them by choice instead of being assaulted by them in the dark. I discovered that scribbling was better than lying awake fretting. Writing turned one's own thoughts into a companion of sorts. It helped, only a little, but it was something. I popped down anything that came to mind, bits and pieces about our early years but also details about the last days, weeks and months: my other life, life after Edie.

After a week or two, I'd nearly forgotten about the girls' visit and I'd stopped wondering what they were plotting. Even now, I can't be quite sure that what happened was a scheme. Clara – self-contained, elegant Clara, the girl who used to brush her dolls' hair before school each morning and set them homework (which she marked with a stern red pen) – was much too upset, too chaotic for me to be certain it had been planned. If it had, then my eldest daughter was a much more accomplished actress than I'd ever given her credit for.

That morning, shortly before nine o'clock I heard a car tearing along the gravel. The unhappy squeal of brakes. I hurried downstairs in my dressing gown to find Clara already in the kitchen and in tears.

'Darling, what happened? Is everyone all right?'

'Yes. No. I need a break. I have to have some time to myself or I'm going to go completely potty. Can you watch him? Just for a couple of hours?'

It was only then that I noticed Robin, my small blond grandson, in the corner of the kitchen. He'd opened one of the cupboards and was foraging unabashed.

'The nursery is full today. Staffing issues or some such nonsense.'

I hadn't seen Clara cry since the funeral. And here she was, weeping in my kitchen, clutching at the counter.

'It's all right.' I reached out ineffectually to pat her shoulder.

'It isn't. Will you take him, Papa? Just for a bit?'

I looked at Robin, who'd finished hunting through the cupboard and, having filched a box of chocolates dolefully forgotten at the back, was squatting on the floor and proceeding to unwrap them one by one, squashing them improbably into his mouth all at once. He dribbled chocolate ooze onto his T-shirt.

'He's impossible. The girls were never like this. I just don't know what to do with him. He never listens to me. Not a word,' said Clara, making no attempt to reprimand him, and then crumpled.

I looked at my usually rigid and far too stoic daughter, and wondered how long this trouble had been festering. Had I been told? I couldn't remember.

'You go,' I said. 'We'll be quite all right.'

'Really?' She managed to sound simultaneously hopeful and doubtful.

'Of course,' I declared with a confidence I did not feel.

Clara left, her eyes red from crying, and I turned back to the boy. Robin, a sturdy little chap of four, had just the same blue eyes as his great-uncle Jack. I softened.

'Well, here we go then. Shall we have a splendid day together?'

'No,' said Robin, the only word he'd uttered since entering the kitchen.

Edie was the one who was good with the children. She adored being a grandmother. The children rushed at her, brimming with joy, while they knocked on my study door with quiet obligation, eager to receive the square of chocolate kept in my desk drawer for this purpose, then scampered off, more eager still to escape back to Edie. It would have been pleasant to know them a little better, but I hadn't the time, nor, if I'm quite honest, a powerful enough inclination. I was still working then, and the music in my brain buzzed as powerfully as a headache, needing to be transcribed, and, selfish or not, I wanted to write more than I wanted to be bothered with scraped knees and the rattle of young creatures.

When Clara had her first two children – both girls – she was still living in Scotland. Edie vanished up there for each birth and the weeks that followed, while I sent encouraging messages. Allowing Edie's prolonged absences without – well, with only minimal – complaint felt like sufficient solidarity. I knew rather than felt that I liked being a grand-father. Everyone told me I must be very proud and so I supposed it must be true. It was gratifying to see the family line continue but I felt little responsibility to nurture or tend the individuals adding to it. I'm not suggesting that this shows the better side to my character, but that's how it was. When Edie became ill and Clara moved closer I was grateful. But already lost in anticipated grief, I barely noticed the tottering boy who now accompanied his older sisters on their visits. He seemed a trifle loud, a touch unruly perhaps, and, if I think about it, there were a few more breakages than there had been with the granddaughters: smashed china bells and things ending up on the fire that really shouldn't have. But when I did notice, I simply put down the spoiled teapot or the singed telephone directory to the dastardly ways of boys.

I had never been alone with Robin before. I tried to remember what to do with a small child.

'Have you eaten breakfast? Are you hungry?'

It seemed a little moot as the young fellow was standing amidst the confetti of discarded chocolate wrappers.

'No.'

'No to which, Robin? You need to be clear. No, you haven't had breakfast or no, you aren't hungry?'

He studied me for a moment before screwing up his face.

'No.'

I decided that whatever the little bugger thought, I wanted breakfast – I sensed already that I might need some suste-nance for what lay ahead. He watched me, motionless, as I ate toast and drank tea. He stuck a finger up his nose. I offered him a hankie. He declined. He grabbed a glass of orange juice and tipped it down his front. I handed him a towel. He chucked it on the floor and proceeded to remove his damp shirt, and then also his shoes, followed by his trousers. I felt a creep of unease as I contemplated the hours before me.

'Aren't you cold?' I enquired, politely.

'No.' He removed his socks. 'Where's Grandma?'

I suddenly felt terribly tired. Surely Clara had explained it to him. I rifled through the appropriate vocabulary. 'Grandma's passed away.'

'Is she in heaven?' asked Robin.

'I suppose so,' I answered, anxious to have the conversation concluded, whether or not I believed it was true.

Robin paused for a moment, considering.

'I hate heaven,' he announced. 'It's full of dead people.'

'Have some toast and marmalade,' I said.

Concerned for the fate of the kitchen cupboards, should I have left him alone while I showered and dressed, I persuaded him to come with me to the bathroom. He came along surprisingly meekly and watched with interest while I tried to pee.

'It takes you a long time to wee-wee, Grandpa.'

'Yes, but it's not polite to make a comment.'

I took off my spectacles and stepped into the shower, keeping up a veritable tirade of chit-chat. I was considering that perhaps company wasn't such a bad thing, when I stepped out of the shower and onto the contents of an entire tube of toothpaste, coiled like a white turd on the bathmat. As I put on my spectacles, I saw that a packet of eight toilet rolls had been disembowelled and shoved down the loo. Robin stood before me in his underpants, wielding the ancient and foul toilet brush like a sword.

I cleared up the mess as best I could and, failing entirely to persuade Robin back into his clothes, dressed myself sharpish. The boy followed me into the dressing room, chucked out all my shoes onto the carpet and then started to try on Edie's high heels. As yet I hadn't been able to face clearing out her things, and Robin took full advantage, yanking a sequinned gown from its hanger and careering around the dressing room with it wrapped around his neck like a spangled python. After one or two feeble attempts at objecting – the boy sensed right away that my heart wasn't really in it – I watched him. The odd thing was that he didn't seem to take any pleasure in his mischief. He wreaked havoc but, like a criminal meting out a perfunctory beating on the orders of his boss, his naughtiness had an habitual weariness to it.

He careered along the corridor towards the open door to the music room, yelping and trailing Edie's gown along with him. I followed, more curious than anxious as to what he might do, until I saw him rush straight for a photograph album. He pulled it off the chair where I'd left it and started to tear out photos. Pictures of Edie cascaded on the carpet, and I lunged to catch her, but the boy grabbed them out of my hand and with a shriek crumpled them. Desperate, I tried to stop him, but I was too slow and he dodged out of my grasp. I'd never felt such anger towards a child – I'm glad I hadn't caught him, for if I had I surely would have struck him. Rage spooled inside me. Pure glorious rage. After weeks of nothing but vacant grief I was flooded with colour. I took a moment to revel in it and then looked again at the blue-eyed boy with his fistful of photos. He looked at me and ripped one in half. I cried out. The pictures were old ones. Black and whites taken decades ago. He was stealing fragments of Edie from me. I wouldn't let him.

In the end it was Edie who saved herself. I heard her voice in my head – calm and soft, saying one of those things she always said: 'There's no point simply scolding them. Distract them.'

So I did the only thing I could. I went over to the piano, sat down and started to play. Leopold Mozart's *Toy Symphony* tumbled from my fingers. It took me a minute to realise that Robin was absolutely still. He dropped the photo album and walked over to the piano, shedding the sequinned ball gown en route, until he stood quietly beside me in nothing but his Superman underpants. I didn't have the requisite whistle to hand for the piece, so I drummed out a rhythm on the piano lid. Robin joined in the second time, tapping the seat of the piano stool, repeating the beats precisely.

'Jolly good!' I cried.

I continued to play, this time singing the part of the nightingale with my left hand. Robin shuddered, stared at my fingers and then quickly at me. At the end of the movement, I paused. Robin tugged my hands back to the keys.

'Again, Grandpa. Again.'

'All right.'

I started the nightingale section once more but, after a bar or two, Robin placed his hands over the keys, an octave above my own, and then to my absolute astonishment he began to play alongside me, shadowing the melody in absolute rhythm and time. I stopped, amazed, but the little fellow continued on alone until the end of the movement, not missing a note.

'You've played this before?' I asked.

'No.'

'But you've had piano lessons? Music lessons?'

He shook his head, impatient. 'Again, Grandpa. Again.'

'All right. But perhaps you could put your trousers on first?'

He watched me for a moment, considering the request.

'Afterwards.'

'Promise?'

'Yes.'

And so we played again. Me seated upright on the piano stool and Robin standing beside me in his underpants, only just able to reach the keys. I glanced over at his fingers and saw how the melody slipped from his fingertips, easy as water, and

I observed what beautiful hands he had – small, still a child's hands, but with the long fingers of a real pianist. He looked at me and, for the first time I could remember, he smiled, and it was a drunken smile of beatific joy.

New Year's Day, 1947

The following morning dawns colder still. The channels of condensation on the inside of the windowpanes in my bedroom have frozen fast. Even lying in bed in my clothes I shiver. Deciding to give up on sleep, I sling on a dressing gown and, grabbing a blanket off my bed for good measure, hurry downstairs in search of a cup of tea or a glass of whisky – anything to warm me up. I've always liked being the first awake in a house full of sleepers. I know that one day Hartgrove Hall, along with her third-rate furniture and mouldering pictures, her farms and rivers, will go to Jack, but in those moments before anyone else is awake, she is mine. Even when he is master of the house and married with fat children squabbling through the halls, he won't be able to inherit these moments. As a boy on my first morning home from prep school for the holidays, I'd get up before it was light and revisit every room, staying long enough to throw off the sensation of unfamiliarity, the stranger returned. I'd stray outside onto the lawn in my pyjamas and bare feet, feeling the dew between my toes, and watch dawn fire along the river.

I hurry into the kitchen and find to my regret that I'm not the earliest riser this morning. Chivers is trying to shoo George and Edie from the kitchen. Before the war none of us would have dared to venture this side of the green-baize door. We may not have had the staff nor the wealth of our pals, but we kept up the pretence as the least we could do. The upstairs might have been very nearly as shabby as the downstairs, but we maintained the illusory barrier. It was expected, after all. Now, by silent accord, Jack, George and I simply can't do it any more. There's a shortage of bedders at Cambridge, so it seems perfectly ridiculous to pretend that I can't brew a simple pot of tea. Standards have fallen, and Chivers and the General are the only ones who wish to see them reinvigorated.

'Sir, miss, I believe you'd be much more comfortable in the morning room. I'll ask one of the dailies to light a fire.'

Chivers attempts to conceal the note of pleading from his voice but he's the last man standing in Camp Civilisation and it's been overrun by us Champions of Informality, and he knows it.

George waves him off. 'They won't be in for ages yet, Chivers. It's bloody freezing in the morning room and it's toasty by the range.'

The aged butler sighs and retreats to the far side of the kitchen. It's true. The daily girls won't be in for an hour at least. Gone are the days when fires were lit before the family ventured downstairs.

'Thank you, Mr Chivers,' calls Edie. 'It's very kind of you. We don't mean to put you out.'

For the first time, I grasp that she isn't quite one of us. She doesn't realise that her polite apology, her 'Mr Chivers', will be taken by the man as an affront to his dignity.

'Tea?' asks George, hunting for the kettle, and at that poor Chivers withdraws to his pantry, unable to bear witness to standards having slipped so far that one of the young masters is brewing his own pre-breakfast cup.

'Oh, good morning, Fox,' says George, spying me at last. 'Bloody cold, isn't it. I went for a piss and the bloody bog's frozen solid.' He pauses, remembering Edie. 'Sorry.'

She waves away his concern and shudders with cold. Looking down, I see that she's wearing several pairs of Jack's old army socks and no shoes.

'Here, have this,' I say, offering her the blanket.

'I'll share it with you,' she says and comes to stand right

beside me, draping the blanket around both our shoulders. I'm acutely aware that I haven't washed since early yesterday and I smell of brandy and fags.

'Have you seen Jack?' I ask.

Edie smiles. 'He's still asleep. He can sleep through anything. Bombs. Irate landladies. Arctic bedrooms.'

I glance at George and try to appear nonchalant and sophisticated, taking in that Edie has admitted not only to sleeping with Jack – which we suspected – but to having actually shared his bedroom here at Hartgrove Hall. I'm torn between dizzying, hopeless envy of Jack and intrigue. I hope she's more guarded around the General or the morning will be very interesting indeed. It was jolly good luck that Chivers had made his exit before her confession or he'd have dashed straight upstairs and told him everything. There are no secrets between those two. They're worse gossips than the old women in the village.

The three of us lurk beside the ancient range, watching the light ripen through the high kitchen windows. I want to go outside onto the terrace, watch the morning slink across the white fields and count the sets of footprints dimpling the lawn, then choose a journey to follow into the hills – a deer, or a hare perhaps – but I don't want to break the spell. I like standing here with George and Edie, my back warm from the range fire, the gurgle and hiss of the boiler. It's a comfortable quiet, an orchestrated rest between notes, and automatically I count the beats. Edie's laugh punctures the pause.

'Are you counting time, Fox?'

'Yes.'

'Whatever for?'

'He's always done it,' says George, laughing. 'Conducts us all like we're a ruddy orchestra.'

'I don't. I'm marking time to something I hear in my head.'

42

'That's what I said.'

'No. It's not the same thing at all. I don't even mean to do it.'

Edie's staring at me and she doesn't find it funny. 'What are you hearing now, Fox?'

Suddenly self-conscious, I don't hear anything any more. The silence rings and the moment is quite broken.

'I'm going for a walk,' I say.

As I leave the kitchen I hear George making jovial remarks about the cold and the likelihood of my freezing my balls off. I wish that for once he could remember he was talking to a girl and not to Jack or me or some fellow in the mess.

Snow has fallen through the night and in the early light the gardens and hills glint a weird and unearthly white. The lake is frozen solid, its surface a flawless expanse. The slate sky stoops low, brimming with snow yet to come. The cold is fierce and I can hear the creak of ice. The trees are ringed with white, branches tinselled with hoarfrost. Her imperfections concealed by the fresh blanketing, the house and garden appear as elegant as a debutante. The white lawns are smooth and perfect, the weed-strewn beds quite hidden. The broken statues on the loggia appear to float, lost in some kind of macabre, injured dance.

I'm pierced by longing – if only the house could always be like this. When we were children, Jack and George used to tell me that before Mother died the gardens looked rather smart. Then the formal ponds had not been drained nor their stone linings smashed, but were kept stocked with squirming golden fish. The lawns were rolled and cut every other week. They teased me with stories of summer drinks parties on the loggia where Mother held court; the General had even been known to laugh and neglect to wax his moustache. It all seemed frightfully unlikely – a distant bed-time story – and I'd once made the mistake of telling them so, at which they'd closed ranks and stopped talking about that time altogether.

And yet perhaps it's out of kindness that they don't talk about her any more, not wanting to rub it in that they remember her and I don't. I know they pity me for not having any memory of our mother. I was barely three when she died – from complications arising from diabetes. The truth is that I'm sorry for them. They know what was lost. They remember the house and those days before the fall. The present can only ever be some sort of sad imitation. For me it's a relief not to be weighted with such sorrow and regret. I don't miss her. I have no memories of grief.

At the far end of the garden, the ugly corrugated Nissen huts erected by the army are buried under a foot of snow so that they're more like witches' cabins. Mist hovers like steam above the river. I'm cold from standing still and, shaking the stiffness from my arms, I stomp across the lawn. I want to be the first one to mark it. It's a childish satisfaction – like dashing red crayon across a white page. This morning a fox has beaten me to it; there are the slinking pads of his feet and here the tick-tick tracks of a bird. Then I notice footprints. Someone with small feet has been out before me this morning. I picture Edie standing in damp socks beside the range and I wonder whether it was her. I decide it must have been and choose her tracks to follow. It feels strange to trace a person's journey rather than that of a fox or a hare, a little like spying. I suspect she wouldn't like it, but somehow this doesn't stop me.

Her footsteps travel straight across the lawn towards the shrubbery and then, rather than slip-sliding down towards the river, she veers sharply upwards towards the ridge of the hill. Her prints are even and steady – she seems to know precisely where she's going and she hardly ever pauses to catch her breath or to stop and admire the view. After a mile or so, I'm surprised – she's travelled quite a distance. I stood beside her in the kitchen watching the dawn less than an hour ago so she must have been out walking through the dark.

I trace her into the woods. Half the trees were felled for fuel during the war – but the oldest part remains. Great thick-trunked Durmast oak and slim alders stand silent amidst the endless white, masts of an armada adrift on an arctic sea. I like the sensation of being alone amongst the trees but this morning I'm uneasy. The snow has muffled the world – I hear a rook call echoing through the trees but it's distorted and strange.

I nudge further into the heart of the wood. The glare of snow and the clear, leafless sky makes it weirdly bright, brighter than the boldest summer's day. There are no berries left on the branches; the birds have picked them clean. It seems that all colour has leached out of the landscape and then I glimpse the streak of a fox's brush, a smear of orange on white, as it slides between the trunks and vanishes. It's more sheltered in the wood than out on the bare back of the hill, and the trees themselves dispense a tiny sliver of living warmth. The bracken and brambles grow more thickly the deeper I go and I struggle to trace Edie's footprints. I lose her for a minute under the greenish shade of a yew, only to find her again in the well of a badger path, then she's gone again. I cast about but can see no more footprints. It's as though she's walked out into the woods and disappeared.

Irritated now with the game, I turn for home, ready for a decent breakfast and a pot of coffee. I have an unpleasant sensation of being watched, that something is waiting out of sight. I hum a Bizet ditty to drive away the feeling but my voice is thin. I don't want to look for more prints. I don't want to know what I might find. I'm well on the way to frightening myself and I'm angry at how ridiculous I'm being, brimming with schoolboy terrors.

Suddenly I hear a crashing near by and my blood is electric, stinging through my veins. I start to run, leaping over felled stumps and knotted roots, but I'm not as fast or as fit as I'd like. Yesterday's brandy bubbles up into my throat and pools there, burning. I'm forced to slow, and then stop. I bend over, wondering whether I'm going to be sick. I hear the jangle of bells. Rushing bodies smash through the undergrowth. My heart thunders in my ears. Slamming myself flat against a beech trunk, I look up to see half a dozen men weaving through the wood, great pairs of antlers strapped to their shoulders, encasing them like a cage. Others join them. At the sight of me, they halt.

'Happy New Year, young Master Fox-Talbot,' says one, reaching up to touch his cap, but on finding only antlers he chuckles.

I remain leaning against the beech, quite spent, adrenalin seeping away. 'And to you all. I'd quite forgotten you'd be coming. You gave me quite a scare, I must say.'

At that the men roar with laughter, clearly delighted.

'It's a good thing, to have yer all back in the big house, sir,' says a cheery fellow, and I wonder whether our principal role is to provide entertainment for the village.

'We're jist on our way to the Hall.'

'You go on. I'll follow in a minute. Don't start without me.'

'Right you are, young sir.'

I watch for a minute as they weave through the holly and ash, somehow managing not to tangle their antlers in the branches, the bells strapped to their ankles crying out shrilly as they run. I follow them, emerging from the wood to see them careering down the slope, half-men, half-stags, racing through the snow. I'm struck with nostalgia for things I've never known. I yearn for a world unmapped, filled with hidden places and wild things, where there are still dark places concealed deep in the woods where people dare not go. A place of long-forgotten songs.

~

We all gather in the porch to watch them. Jack is thick with sleep. He's wearing his overcoat but the blue stripes of his pyjamas are still visible underneath and the effect is natty. I expect he's about to start another trend. His arm is draped around Edie and they're sharing a cigarette. The General is washed, shaved and immaculately dressed in his uniform, although I can't imagine why. Several girls and a couple of chaps have slept here after the night's festivities and they shake with cold, bleary-eyed, in last night's party clothes and borrowed boots, wondering what on earth they've been summoned outside to witness.

I'm restless with excitement. This is the first horn dance since the war. Or the first we've been here to witness, at any rate. I'm curious as to whether the villagers carried on doing it without us. It seems rather presumptuous to assume they stopped simply because we weren't here to watch and tip them a few shillings. There are twelve men, six of them shouldering the vast pairs of antlers, and one holding an accordion. They stand on the white lawn in their hobnailed boots, half human, half animal, pawing at the snow, waiting.

At last, with a nod from the leader, the accordion player strikes up. It's an uncanny tune and one I don't recognise. The dancers pause for a moment, seeming to sniff the air before they move into the dance, slipping into serpentine patterns. The knock of boots on the iron ground is a counterpoint to the melody. The pace quickens into a clattering run, and they break apart into two lines, surging forwards and then back again, horns scoring the sky but never touching one another.

I study the leader, our gardener Benjamin Row, who sports the largest pair of antlers, which are so knobbled and ancient, so black and solid, that they look more like stone than horn, and I speculate about the beast who shed them. It seems impossible that such a creature haunted the woods in this green and pleasant county of smooth hills and dappled woods. Despite the cold, fat beads of perspiration speckle Benjamin's forehead and drop onto the snow. The dancers shout and stamp, and the wail of the accordion oozes around us and drifts out into the morning, sinking towards the river where it will be carried out to sea.

The dance is hypnotic and strange. I turn to see what Edie is making of it all and I observe that her face is flushed, her eyes bright, her expression rapt. Jack is proffering her his cigarette but she doesn't notice and, when she does, she bats away his arm. Jack stifles a yawn and I turn back to the dance suffused with irritation.

The lawn is a churned-up mass of grubby white as the horn-men alternate back and forth in their two lines, grunting and red faced from exertion. I watch them surge and fall and it seems to me that they're slipping forward and then further back in time, back and back towards the beginning of things. I picture the woods rise up and bloom across the hills, until the back of Hartgrove Hill is darkly forested. The ground cracks open to swallow up the few houses and the pins of light from their windows blink into nothingness. The music is a heartbeat that thrums inside me.

Then I see that the dancers have stopped and the accordion is no longer playing and the General is signalling for whisky, while I can still hear nothing but the music and I know I shall have no peace at all until I've written it down. I excuse myself and race upstairs to sprawl on the bed with a pad of manuscript paper as the music spews forth and my hand cramps around my pen and then I'm finished and at last the room is quiet. In relief, I close my eyes. There is only the faintest of aches behind them.

I return downstairs. The dancers mill in the great hall, swigging whisky and making conversation, and they no longer seem other-worldly. The smell of sweat mingles with woodsmoke and ever-present mildew. They laugh uproariously at some joke of Jack's but Edie isn't listening, she's watching me. I walk over to her side.

'Where did you vanish to?' she asks.

'It's an odd tune. Not one I know, so I had to write it down.'

She studies me for a moment. 'Is that something you do often? Collect songs?'

'From time to time.'

She makes it sound as if I'm a butterfly hunter and I suppose I am in a way, a hoarder of melodies. When I find one I don't know, I have to catch it, pin it into my book and fix it there. I don't need to look at it again once I have it. Writing a melody down, I transcribe it twice – once into my manuscript book and once into my memory. The horn-dancers' song will always be with me now.

'Will you show me later?'

'If you like.'

I shrug, feigning indifference, but I'm perfectly thrilled. No one's been remotely interested in my song-scribbling habit before.

After dinner I prowl beside the fire, eager to go to her, but no one may ever leave the dining room and return to the ladies before the General declares we may. Jack attempted it once but even he was rebuked. I have stashed the manuscript book in the cubbyhole in the ladies' sitting room that we still call the Chinese room even though the stencilled chinoiserie wallpaper was spoiled a decade ago and the sole Oriental item remaining is a japanned cabinet that is missing a door. We no longer use the drawing room after dinner when we are so few. It is too large and on bitter evenings frost gathers on the inside of the windowpanes, stalking along damp patches on the wall.

Jack is yawning and only George pretends attention as the General recounts a gory battle during the second Boer War that we've all heard before. I wonder how they can bear his nostalgia for *Boys' Own* adventures after all they've seen. Again I wish they'd furnish me with the details. I feel peevish and the distance of the years between us grates. I feel much as I did when I was a boy of eight, and they at the grand ages of sixteen and thirteen sloped off to the barn to get blind drunk on filched cider, leaving me as their resentful lookout.

At last, piqued by our indifference, the General slams down his brandy glass and, muttering oaths of disappointment under his breath, stalks to the door. Chivers opens it for him, and I feel the echo of his disapproval as we file out. Edie waits alone in the Chinese room; she's reading but puts her book aside as we enter. It does not occur to the General that keeping her in purdah for nearly an hour, while he regales us with stories of his youth, was rude. I spy my manuscript book in the cubbyhole beside the fireplace and I'm all eagerness to show her but it's Jack at whom Edie's smiling with simple pleasure. She lets him kiss her cheek but when the General gives a cough of displeasure Jack kisses her again, this time on the mouth. Edie squirms and gently pushes him away.

'Yes, yes, righto,' declares the General. He squats on the edge of a low chair, his back ramrod straight. I've never known anyone who makes after-dinner relaxation look quite so uncomfortable. 'I suppose you travelled about a bit during the war, Miss Rose.'

She pulls Jack down to sit beside her and neatly crosses her ankles. 'Yes, a fair bit.'

'Did you get east? Cairo? Luxor?'

'I went to Cairo twice.'

'Palestine?'

Edie nods.

'God, it's a bloody mess over there. Skulduggery, murder. Civil war.'

'I thought you enjoyed a decent war. It's your favourite spectator sport after the Badbury point-to-point. You could put a fiver on each way,' says Jack.

I glance at him in alarm, presuming he drank too much at dinner, but to my surprise he seems quite sober.

George looks worried. 'Steady on, old chap,' he mutters.

The General chooses to ignore Jack and simply carries on. He regards a second voice in a conversation as unnecessary. Company is present merely to provide him with an audience.

'It's the ingratitude of the bloody Jews that galls me. Bloody ingratitude.'

'What would you have them be grateful to us for?' asks Jack sweetly, and with that I know the conversation is becoming dangerous but I'm not quite sure why.

Edie places her hand firmly on Jack's knee. 'Would you mind ringing for a glass of water, darling? I'm terribly dry.'

While Jack gets up to ring for Chivers, Edie turns to me. 'May I take a look at the song?'

To my chagrin, I grasp that she's asking only in order to alter the course of the conversation. They all watch as I pull out the manuscript book from the cubbyhole. Edie shuffles along the sofa to make room, patting the spot between her and Jack. I squeeze in, jammed between them both, and Edie opens the book. It's a battered, leather-bound volume that was once blue but has faded to grey.

'There are heaps of songs in here,' she says.

'Nearly a hundred.'

'How long have you been collecting songs, Fox?' she asks.

51

'Ages. I have to write down a song if I haven't heard it before, otherwise it buzzes around like a mosquito in my brain. My problem isn't remembering tunes, it's trying to forget them.' I shift on the sofa, suddenly self-conscious, and wish the others weren't here. 'I always keep an eye out. Or rather an ear, I suppose. Gather up what I find.'

Edie laughs. 'You make it sound as if songs simply sprouted like berries on a hedgerow and sat there until you plucked them and popped them into your book.'

I laugh. I never really envisioned anyone else being interested in my song habit, far less a woman. Yet her enthusiasm appears sincere, and little spots of colour are daubed on each cheek. Jack fidgets and yawns, and George fiddles with the fire. I wish they'd jolly well leave us to it. Edie leafs through the pages, turning them carefully as though each one is a precious, fragile thing. She pauses, running her finger along the last.

'I've never heard this one before. It's the one from this morning?'

I nod.

'Well, I've sung hundreds of folk songs. I even recorded a few—'

'I know. I have some of your recordings.'

She smiles. 'Of course you do. Anyway, I've not come across this one until today. I don't know, but I think it's possible that no one's collected it before.'

I have a tingle in my belly; the satisfaction of discovery. Like an anthropologist rummaging through the jungle for lost tribes, I've found something ancient, as yet unrecorded and unfixed.

Edie smiles at me and returns the book. 'It's an odd tune. Tugs at one. It's always nice to have made a find, don't you think?'

'He's a clever old thing,' says Jack. 'Much brighter than the rest of us. None of us is musical in the least.'

'Mother sang,' says George.

No one speaks. I'm suddenly aware of the crackle and spit of logs on the fire. The General stiffens and blinks. Once. Twice. Jack grips Edie's hand more tightly.

The silence jangles.

'She sang to me,' says George, insistent now. 'And to Jack. And Little Fox.'

'What did she sing?' I ask and it's suddenly desperately important that I know.

George shakes his head. 'Can't remember. I don't have a head for tunes.'

~

It's splendid to be at home from Cambridge for the long summer vac. Three blissful months at Hartgrove Hall. Most of my pals are staying on in digs for an extra few days to drink and punt but I couldn't. Today is Mother's birthday picnic. We hold it every year. Apparently this is what she always chose for her birthday treat – a picnic under the willows by the River Stour. The General would strip off and go for a bracing swim amidst the ducks and the waterweeds, while the rest of us cheered him on from the bank.

I wonder whether Mother sang to us then and, if so, which songs. I don't remember any of it, but Jack and George are quite sentimental about the whole thing – as much for the man our father used to be as anything else. Chivers has winkled out an elderly cook from somewhere, and we ask her to make us up a hamper with cheese-and-pickle sandwiches, seedcake – Mother's favourite, apparently – and a bottle of hock, to which she was also partial. It's always a jolly afternoon. The General never comes. We invite him with careful politeness and there's inevitably a dreadful moment when we worry that this will be the one time he accepts but of course he doesn't.

George and I check the hamper in the kitchen. It's stuffed with all the usual goodies and a pound of early cherries, glossy and black. Jack isn't here. We're to collect him and Edie from the station at a quarter to one. It's the first time there's been anyone other than the three of us. Jack sent us a cable last night: 'WILL BE ON THE TWELVE FORTY-FIVE STOP BE A SPORT AND PICK ME UP STOP BRINGING EDIE STOP'. He never telephones or writes, he inevitably selects the most expensive form of communication much as he chooses the best wine or cut of beef on the menu. I'm pleased Edie's coming and don't mind that he didn't consult us first. A little too pleased if I'm honest. I can't tell whether George minds or not.

George pokes at a pork pie wrapped in wax paper. 'I'm hungry already.'

I nudge him away and rewrap the pie.

I study him surreptitiously. He's chosen not to find a job and instead has been attempting to fix the most desperate of the damage to the house – it's a forlorn task, akin to sticking his finger in a dyke, but I'm taken aback by his skill. There's now a hefty slab of silver oak as a mantelpiece in the great hall, and he's carved three running foxes into the wood. They're both crude and beautiful. I found him in the attic, gathering up all the old photographs of the house and estate, scrutinising them for God knows what. He has piles of ancient almanacs and farming magazines in his room – some of them dating from before the First World War. I can't think what use he can put them to. This morning I watched from my window as he hurried across the lawn, I presumed returning from an early walk, but now I wonder whether instead he'd been out all night. He never talks about pals or girls and I hope he's happy. I can't ask. It's not the sort of thing we do.

In the distance the church clock chimes the half-hour.

'Shall we?'

I nod and together we shoulder the hamper into the boot of the car. It's already hot and my shirt sticks to my back. The ancient and magnificent magnolia tree on the front driveway is still in bloom, the flowers huge and blowzy, with fleshy pink petals – like fat, tarty girls in ball gowns. I've always liked it. The General would prefer it chopped into firewood. I pick fallen and browning petals from the car's paintwork and, somehow unable to discard them, shove them into my pocket.

'Bags I drive,' I say, leaping into the driver's seat before George can object.

I drive too fast because it's a gorgeous day and I'm filled with happiness at the thought of the picnic and seeing Jack whom I haven't seen for simply ages. And Edie. I bat her name away and swerve around a pothole. George grips the door but doesn't tell me to slow down. It's a ten-minute drive to the station but we make it in eight and I feel a surge of triumph.

'Do you want to go and meet them? I'll wait with the car,' says George.

'Righto.'

I leap out of the car and am jogging onto the platform as their train pulls in, and I wish for a moment that I'd picked some of the cowslips sprouting on the lawn to present to Edie. It dawns on me how daft that is – as if she's a visiting dignitary or my girl or something – and then they're here and Jack's thumping my back and Edie's standing behind him, leaving space for the effusion of our reunion, and she's even prettier than I remember in her yellow summer dress and her crooked half-smile and I almost can't breathe.

'Hello, Fox,' she says. 'You can kiss me if you like.'

I don't. I glance at my feet and mumble, 'Hello, Edie. Jolly nice to see you.'

We return to the car and to my exasperation I see that George has nipped into the driver's seat. Sneaky so and so. Jack and Edie climb into the back and, as we hurtle along the narrow lanes and I glance back, I notice how Edie slithers into Jack as we take each bend. George catches me looking and quickly I turn away.

We park near a tumbledown mill. George and I heave the basket between us, leaving Jack and Edie to go ahead with the piles of blankets and scout a spot to sit. It's the first hot day of the year and the ground still has the soft bounce of early summer. The grass is long and thick. A cricket ticks in steady crochets. The river sloshes in easy curves, gnats misting the surface. Several cows watch us, bored, flicking flies with mucky tails. We halt in a field of dandelions. There are thousands upon thousands of them, constellations of vivid, sickly-yellow flowers. Jack flops down and instantly his shirt is tarnished with pollen.

Methodically, George unpacks the picnic onto a blanket. Edie tries to help but he waves her away. We eat in lazy silence until there is nothing left, passing the bottle of hock between us. As a concession to Edie we brought glasses but we entirely forget to use them and she doesn't complain. The hock thrums in my head and I'm still thirsty. We should have brought water to drink in this heat. Jack lies back amongst the dandelions, his hair so gold in the sunlight that the flowers look gaudy beside him.

'Lie here with me,' he says to Edie but she shakes her head, lolling in the shade of a willow. She's removed her stockings and I can't help noticing that her white skin is almost translucent. There is a fine fuzz of pale hair on her legs. Jack reaches over and tickles her foot. He gazes at her with something uncomfortably like adoration. I look away.

'How old would your mother have been today?' she asks and I'm taken aback. We come here every year on Mother's birthday but we never speak about her. We eat. We lark about and perhaps take a dip in the river and then we return home. I glance at George and register his surprise but he doesn't seem to mind.

'Fifty-two,' he says. 'She would have been fifty-two.'

I don't wish to talk about Mother as that would mean I'd need to pretend to be sad. The sun is too hot and the sky is glazed in a too-flawless blue for sadness. Jack clearly feels the same.

'And how old is your mother?' he asks Edie, propping himself up on his elbow. 'And when does she get the pleasure of meeting me?' he adds, turning it, as he does everything, into a joke.

Edie smiles and digs in her bag for cigarettes but Jack continues to stare at her. It occurs to me that, beneath the teasing, he's quite serious. He wants to meet her family, I think. He hasn't yet and he wants to.

'I'm not telling you how old my mother is, because it shows you how old I am,' she says archly, plucking a dandelion and flinging it at him.

He loves her, I decide, but he doesn't really know her at all. I thought loving someone entailed knowing every little detail about them – but then perhaps that's not love, merely familiarity. I'd like to be more familiar with Edie, I think, and then, embarrassed, I feel heat rise into my cheeks. That bloody hock. I check my watch – it's nearly five, we've been here for ages.

'I have to go soon,' I tell the others.

'Whatever for?' asks Jack.

'There's an old bloke near by who knows a good many songs, apparently. I've been invited to tea.'

Edie leans forward, hugging her knees. 'Found anything good lately?'

'A few. Mostly around Cambridge but I want to hear the

old Dorset songs again. Those are my favourites. Nothing sounds half so pleasant as the songs of home.'

She studies me for a moment and then asks, 'Can I come with you?'

'I don't see why not. Can't think why the old chap would mind. We should get going, though.'

As Edie starts to put her stockings back on, Jack sits up and grabs her ankle. 'Don't leave me. I shall be bereft without you.'

She shakes him off. 'Stop it, Jack, you're being a pest.'

He flops back in the grass, unconcerned. 'Come for a swim first.'

'Absolutely not,' I say. 'We simply don't have time.'

Dripping wet from our swim, we hurry across the fields in bare feet. I wonder how it is that Jack invariably gets his own way. It's a rare and unacknowledged gift. In the pub after several pints we sometimes debate what special power we'd like best and I always thought it would be super to fly, but really I think it would be better to always get my own way.

'Slow down, Fox,' says Edie. 'You're going awfully fast.'

'Sorry.'

I wait for her to catch up. Her wet hair hangs loose in a plait. I've never seen her with her hair down and she appears younger, girlish. Her movements are precise and balletic and she possesses a careful self-constraint as if everything she utters is weighed and measured first. As I've got to know her better, I've found to my surprise that she's not quite the absolute stunner I'd imagined. Of course she's attractive, and in photographs she's made up to be beautiful. I've noticed too that on meeting strangers she always behaves as though she is a lovely woman to whom they ought to be paying court and, somehow, without fail they do.

This afternoon any make-up has been washed clean away by the swim and she seems less contained and for once unself-conscious as she strides through the grass. She plucks the petals from a daisy, scattering them on the verge. There is a tiny streak of mud on her cheek and I don't tell her, knowing that, as soon as I do, she'll seize her pocket handkerchief and scrub it off, self-conscious again. I prefer her like this.

We're to walk to Christopher Lodder's cottage and after-wards back to the Hall. It's a longish walk – nearly seven miles all told – but Edie assures me she can manage it. Also I don't want Jack appearing at the cottage after an hour or whenever he's bored, to collect us in the car. He never can keep time. Things happen precisely when he wishes them to. I make an effort to slow my pace again – I have the itch of excitement I always get when I'm off song collecting.

'When we were boys George pressed leaves, orchids and butterflies between the pages of his schoolbooks so he could take little bits of Hartgrove with him. With me it was songs so I could listen to home. There's nothing better for remember-ing. The songs from a place, the ones that grow there and have been sung down the generations, those are the ones that capture the essence of it. They're like the specific smell of river mud, except that when you're away from the river you can't quite recall it precisely.'

'And Jack? What did Jack take?'

'I don't know. Nothing, Jack never gets homesick, as far as I can tell. Wherever he goes, he's the centre of it all, magnifi-cently present, never pining for anywhere else.'

She makes no reply, knowing it to be true.

'The tunes are often the same but, if you listen carefully enough, you spot a variation in the last verse and the words inevitably change from singer to singer. The best folk songs are living things, shifting with each performance. You can never really catch them.'

'But you still try?'

I laugh. 'Of course.'

Old Lodder doesn't mind that I've brought Edie. In fact, it rather perks him up. He looks right past me but ushers her inside to the coolness of the cottage, seating her in the best chair by the window with a view of the vegetable patch and its row of exquisite green lettuces squatting in the earth. In the distance the river glints and I can hear goldcrests squabbling in the bulrushes.

Lodder is so tall and angular, it's a wonder he fits into the low cottage – he's hunching as he disappears into the kitchen concealed behind a fading curtain. It's cramped and dark in the parlour, the walls painted brown in the Victorian fashion of seventy years earlier and the low beams stained darker still. There's a milking stool, two good chairs, a solid and handsome dresser on which is displayed a hotchpotch of mismatching china. The only picture on the wall is a photograph of a stern, austere woman buttoned into a high-necked gown. I can't tell whether it was his grandmother, mother or wife. The room smells very strongly of cabbage. An overflowing bucket of vegetable peelings and slops perspires nicely beside the range. To my excitement, there is no wireless and I'm hopeful of finding a good song hoard, full of old tunes, not just popular hits. I arrange my manuscript pad on my knee and sharpen my pencil.

'What happens next?' whispers Edie, conscious of Lodder busily brewing tea like a magician behind the partition curtain.

'I'll ask him to sing us some songs. Hopefully there'll be something we haven't heard before and, if there is, I'll write it down.'

'Do you write down the melody or the words?'

'I try to do both. I sometimes get in a bit of a muddle.'

'Let me help. Give me a page and I'll try to scribble down

the words. I don't think I could manage the tune accurately enough. I don't have perfect pitch like you.'

Before I can ask how she can tell that I have perfect pitch – which I do; it's a source of both satisfaction and irritation – Lodder reappears with a tea tray laden with chipped teacups and a saucer of stale biscuits. Dutifully we sip. He sits on the milking stool apparently perfectly comfortable, his spindly legs folded up beside his ears like a daddy-long-legs.

'This one's fer you, missy,' he says, grinning at Edie, and he launches into a rendition of Edie's most celebrated hit, 'A Shropshire Thrush'. I sag and rub my eyes. It was a mistake to have brought her with me. We listen politely. It never does to interrupt.

'That was very pleasant, Mr Lodder,' I say.

'An honour to sing it fer the lady,' he declares, clearly pleased as Punch with himself. 'I never thought I'd see the day. Never thought it.'

'But we'd love – Miss Rose would love to hear one of your own songs. Your nephew told me that you know some Dorset folk songs.'

He frowned. 'What you want to hear that stuff fer?'

Edie leans forward. 'I'd like to hear something. I'd like it very much.'

He pauses, scratches his nose. 'All righty. Fer the lady then.' He refolds his legs and then sings in a clear baritone.

The notes flutter out of the open window and I hear the goldcrests fall silent for a moment as though they're listening too. There's a dignity to him as he sings. He nods once to Edie and then seemingly forgets her, forgets there is any audience at all; he's alone with his song. It's unmistakably English, like the scurry of oak leaves shaking in the rain. As the sound floods the gloomy little parlour I'm filled with a sense of rightness as though he is singing my own thoughts back to me. I've heard variations on this song before. However, it's not its familiarity that is raising the hairs along the back of my neck, but the shiver of loss and longing, and the knowledge that I'm listening to a melody sung down the generations. In his voice I hear a score of other voices converge and there is a shining moment when I can see both forwards and backwards, when time rocks to and fro upon the empty hearth.

Afterwards we stroll outside. I'm as tickled as anything. I have two new songs for my collection. I expect they're probably variants of other more common songs but it doesn't matter. I like the tune of one in particular and I know it will rattle around inside me for the rest of the day. I experience a supine contentment as if I'd eaten a meaty dinner. I want to sit down and have a cold glass of something and smoke a fag. I also want to look over Edie's notes – she's been dashing off pages like a schoolgirl in an exam – but it seems impolite in front of the old chap.

We dawdle through the garden. Lodder lives alone and it's a man's patch – thoroughly practical, stocked solely with things to eat, the only flowers permitted to bloom here being repellents to discourage pests from devouring the vegetables. There's a village of sheds, ugly but useful. Lodder picks slugs off his lettuces between a stout forefinger and thumb, and flings them at the hawthorn hedge with some precision, where they hang on the prickles like wet grey baubles. A skinny and lonesome goat watches us from its tether in a circle of dirt. Edie makes towards it with a coo, but Lodder grunts a warning.

'I wouldn't, if I were yoos. She'll git you something nasty.'

Edie stops short and the goat strains at its tether, horns down.

'Lil' bitch,' says Lodder with a fond chuckle. 'If only I could 'ave kept the wife out here. 'Ere, 'ave a tomato. Lovely 'n' sweet.'

Edie eats her tomato in silence, her eyes wide, and I want to laugh. Lodder's hamming it up for her benefit and I wonder whether she can tell.

'Miserable buggers, them songs. They're all 'bout lost things – sweethearts, youth, maidenhead—'

I shrug, conscious of the late hour and recognising that, although I'm pleased with the songs I've heard, the pleasure is starting to wear off and I'm already wanting something else but I can't properly explain to Lodder what it is since I don't know myself what I'm hunting for. Perhaps it's simply the desire for another song; there's always one more to be found.

Lodder grinds a snail under his boot and then with a grin points to the compost heap. 'Slow-worm,' he says with some satisfaction.

The tiny snake snoozes in the last of the afternoon sunshine, a perfect silver coil.

Edie strides along, her cardigan draped around her shoulders. I fall into step beside her, relieved she doesn't seem tired – I feel guilty about making her walk so far. The sun slinks behind the hill and it becomes abruptly cool, as if all the doors and windows of a fire-warmed room had suddenly been thrown open to the outside. The sky is clear and the earth holds no heat. We pass our former picnic spot. There is nothing to see but flattened grass. The cattle snort in the gloom. The hills are daubed with red for a few minutes and then smothered by darkness. As our eyes adjust we walk in silence, listening to a hurry of blackbirds calling evensong. A mistle thrush sings a counterpoint to their tune. At the bridge

Edie pauses. I move and stand beside her. The black water gurgles in the dark.

'Let me catch myself, just for a minute,' she says.

'Here.'

I pass her some cherries smuggled into my pocket from lunch, wrapped up in the magnolia petals. She eats them, spitting the stones into the river below. She spits them quite a distance and I'm impressed. Singer's lungs, I suppose, lots of puff.

'So you can remember every song you've ever heard?' she asks, not looking at me but out into the gathering dusk.

'I've a good ear for melodies.'

It's true. I remember every song. Well, almost every song. I stare across the flat water meadows towards the shoulder of Hartgrove Hill.

'I discovered a whole crew of musicians this term. It was perfectly wonderful. I was a starving man. I didn't know I'd spent my whole life hungry until gorging at my first proper feast.'

'It is a relief to be amongst other musicians. But then it can also be a relief to be away from them,' Edie says with a smile, and I wonder whether this is one of Jack's attractions.

'I think I'm probably going to fail my exams. I'm afraid that I've ignored my studies and signed up to every music society instead. Orchestras. Quartets. I even play piano for the jazz band. I didn't much like the choirs. Too clean. Too quiet. Too lovely.'

Edie laughs. 'Yes, I've never been fond of choirs. Unless I'm the soloist, of course. I don't mind them harmonising patiently in the background.'

I grin at this sudden and rare flash of the diva. 'My mother used to sing to me. So I'm told.'

'You don't remember?'

I shake my head. 'I was so young when she died. But

sometimes I catch a tune and it feels so familiar that I wonder whether she sang it to me. I know she liked folk songs.'

She stares at me with a look of such wistfulness that I suppose I ought to feel sorry for myself but I don't. Instead, I turn away, embarrassed, conscious of talking too much, and I'm relieved she can't see me properly in the darkness.

'I say, can I take a peep at your notes?' I ask, eager to turn the conversation.

She hands them over, nibbling at her nail as I study them. I produce a torch from my pocket. The battery's nearly spent but it's sufficient to more or less make out the scribbled lyrics. Instantly I know it's quite hopeless and if I want an accurate transcription I'll have to go back and listen to Mr Lodder again, but she's studying me with such eagerness.

'Is it any good?'

'It's entertaining.'

She frowns. 'What do you mean?'

'Well, you see here that you've got "the girl with the cabbage"? It's actually "the girl Will ravished".'

'Oh. I see. Ravished, not cabbage.'

''Fraid so.'

'It's the Dorset accent.'

'Quite. Very hard to understand.'

I'm helpless with laughter and Edie's laughing too, grabbing her notes back and swatting me with them. Before I can stop her she's chucked them into the river. They swirl for a second and then, sodden, are pulled away downstream.

'Oh, what a shame! I was looking forward to those.'

'Beast.'

She pulls on her cardigan, races along the path leading away from the river and scrambles up the bank of the hill towards the Hall and Jack.

We arrive at the boundary of the Hartgrove estate tipsy with laughter. It's been a glorious day and I'm calculating how many more she's likely to stay. I dawdle as we reach the long drive, reluctant to reach the others, but to my surprise Jack and George are walking out to meet us.

'Hello, darling,' says Edie, reaching up to kiss Jack's cheek, but he hardly seems to notice. He stares only at me. I see that George is equally grim-faced.

'Canning has given notice,' says George.

'That is a pity,' I say, not understanding why this news has caused Jack to look quite so bereft. I turn to Edie. 'Canning has managed the estate for thirty years. No, more. He'll be tricky to replace.'

'He's not going to be replaced,' says George.

'No, of course, he's irreplaceable,' I say, irritated now by my brothers' sentimentality. Canning is a decent fellow, a thoroughly good sort who managed both the estate and the General with some determination, but if he wants to retire, it's not for us to make a fuss.

'The General is not going to replace him at all,' says George.

'We're completely out of money,' says Jack. 'The Fox-Talbots are utterly broke.'

'The General is going to dynamite the Hall and auction off the land,' adds George, quietly.

My breath catches. The evening is hushed as if the wind had suddenly died. We've reached the steps of the house. We all sit and look out into the night. I'm shaking, whether with anger or grief I can't tell.

'It would have been better if the whole bloody place had just burned down in the war. To have her back only to lose her again like this. It's beastly,' says Jack.

Edie's sobbing noiselessly into her handkerchief and I'm glad in a way that one of us is able to cry.

'I don't want to see her go up,' I say. 'I couldn't bear that.'

I know that afterwards I'll never come here again. The break must be clean. I can't walk these woods and sneak through these valleys as a stranger trespassing on another man's land. I don't want to stand on the ridge and look down on a handsome new house where ours once stood. No, when she's gone, I shan't come back.

'How long do we have left?' I ask.

'It's all arranged for next week,' says George.

August 2000

I insisted on giving Robin music lessons myself. Clara and I very nearly had a row about it.

'Mrs Claysmore is terribly good. All the mothers swear by her.'

'I'm sure she is, darling. But teaching Robin won't be like teaching other children. We need to be cautious.'

Clara smoothed her already creaseless skirt. We were sitting side by side in the kitchen, both of us resolutely gazing out at the rain-soaked lawns so that we didn't have to look directly at each other. We couldn't possibly have an uncomfortable tête-à-tête while making eye contact. The gardener puttered up and down on the lawn tractor, puffing out black smoke. It made a God-awful racket, leaving nasty gouges in the sodden grass. I wished he'd use the hand-mower as I'd asked but that was another battle I couldn't face – my stomach for petty conflict had dwindled after Edie died. The smaller the task, the less I could bear it.

Clara frowned – a tiny furrow appearing in her forehead – and stared pointedly at the garden, but under the table I could see her knee tap-tapping in irritation.

'I don't want to single him out. Push him. All the books say that's very risky.'

I swallowed my exasperation. As soon as I'd told her that her son had a gift for music, she'd retreated into books, desperate for the reassurance of so-called experts. I refrained from reminding her that I was also considered an expert in music, even if in nothing else. I stared at the black clouds, solid as barrage balloons, threatening more rain, and when I spoke, I made sure my voice was gentle.

'Music lessons with his grandpa isn't pushy. We won't work any longer than he can manage. I want it to be fun. Music ought to be a pleasure.'

'Mrs Claysmore will be most put out. I'll probably lose my deposit.'

I wanted to say bugger Mrs sodding Claysmore but I said nothing and just wrote her a cheque for the lost deposit. The truth is that I wasn't willing to surrender Robin to another teacher. I wanted to see for myself what the boy could do.

It was arranged that he'd come to me three mornings each week. I'd wanted five but Clara had insisted it was too much – whether for me or for him, I wasn't sure. But I supposed, begrudgingly, she was probably right. During the first weeks and months after Edie, I had seemed to drift around the house in a permanent state of tiredness and irritability. Perhaps five days with a young, inexhaustible child in constant motion would have been too much.

I found that I was nervous. I had the jitters in my belly as though I were about to enter into rehearsals with a strange and hostile symphony orchestra rather than tinkle Mozart with my own grandson. I began to fret that, in my discombob-ulated state of mind, I'd over-egged the boy's gift. Perhaps what had happened that day wasn't so remarkable. Or perhaps it was merely a fluke and Robin had no real interest in music. As Clara and I negotiated terms, days and then a week, then two, ticked by and I began to doubt my own memory of that afternoon.

I lay awake all night before our first lesson, wishing that I could talk it through with Edie. When she was alive, I would store up the trivial details of my day to tell her. They hadn't needed to be interesting. After a lifetime together, it's not

69

one's great passions that create intimacy; it's not the mutual love of Beethoven or Italian wine, but ordinary things. Without her, when I heard the first cuckoo of spring I had no one to tell. I found that sapphire earring she lost in '93 and that we claimed for on the insurance. It was wedged inside the lining of a cufflink box. No one else would be interested, nor should they be, but Edie would have been tickled. I didn't mention these things to anyone but the truth is that it's these bric-a-brac moments that make up a shared life. The grand events: the births of one's children, their first day at school or signing my first recording contract with Decca – these shine a little brighter, but they are only a tiny proportion of one's life together; a handful of stars in the night sky. It was the mundane, frankly dull things I missed the most. I missed not talking to her over breakfast. We'd ignored one another over toast and morning coffee with great pleasure for nearly fifty years.

I was adrift those first months. My memories of Edie were like dandelion clocks in the wind, winnowing in every direction. I'd lost all chronology. I missed every Edie at once. The young and terribly glamorous woman I'd met after the war. She was so private about herself. She never spoke about her family or where she'd grown up and whenever she did let a detail slip – how she'd left school at twelve or how she used to queue with her grandmother on a Sunday at the best bagel shop in the East End – I fell upon it, delighted. I'd hoarded those details to myself, feeling sometimes that she was a jigsaw puzzle but I was not allowed to know the picture on the front of the box, and it was for me to piece her together, bit by bit, until finally my reward would be to see her all at once.

When I first knew her I'd thought that she was keeping us from her family. We were too eccentric, an old family clearly in decline, brought sadly low. I didn't discover for many years that it was the other way around. She'd spent years constructing this careful version of herself, Edie Rose, and she kept the other parts of herself scrupulously hidden. Those dreadful wartime hits played everywhere for years and years; one couldn't turn on the radio without being blasted by 'A Shropshire Thrush' sung by England's Perfect Rose. That was the version of her we were supposed to accept.

Next I remembered how she cried for weeks after Clara was born. Just sat curled up on our bedroom floor, clasping this tiny blanketed bundle and weeping. My God, I'd felt useless. No one told you what to do about such things in those days.

And then I'd missed her when I went to the cupboard and found there was no loo roll left. She always wrote the shopping lists and purchased household things in bulk. The knowledge that I must fend for myself, even in the most trivial of matters, momentarily floored me and I'm afraid to confess that I found myself sitting on the loo sobbing – there was no loo roll and there was no Edie. There was no order to anything.

Clara gave me an advice book about grief, which claimed that the peculiar sensation of timelessness, of drifting through days, was quite normal. But why was grief normal? Grief meant that nothing would ever be 'normal' again. Normal was Edie. Without her nothing was normal. She couldn't walk back through the kitchen door, chuck her keys on the table, sink into a chair and smile at me, asking for a gin and tonic. Normality could not be restored.

~

The morning before his first lesson, I couldn't stay in bed and keep my eyes shut against the light. Robin would be arriving in an hour.

I didn't have a plan as to how to actually teach him. I'd never had a regular pupil. I'd given the odd master class to promising students at the Royal College, but they'd always been in composition rather than the piano. I'm a decent pianist – the layman would mistakenly consider me excellent. I am not. I can play most things with the utmost competence, but my playing lacks any real emotion. I play in order to hear aloud the thing in my mind, but then I'm finished with it. It's only when my idea is performed by a real musician that it is called to life. At the end of my fingers, it's merely a blueprint, a sketch of possibility to be realised in its full dimensions by someone else. I have neither the desire nor the patience to play a phrase a thousand times in order to achieve the speckle of perfection.

As I said, I'm not a real pianist. Yet, like most composers, I do become a dictator when it comes to my own work. I may not be able to achieve it myself, but I know precisely how it ought to sound. While I can listen in smiling awe to a recording of Albert Shields perform Rachmaninov, when the great man was rehearsing my own concerto at the Festival Hall I found myself stopping him after a few minutes to insist on a darker rumbling tone and then argued with some heat about his far-too-curvaceous phrasing in the wild second movement. All was well in the end – we're old friends. We fought. We yelled. He performed it as I wished. We reconciled.

But how to teach a four-year-old child? I'd half considered telephoning Clara's blasted Mrs Claysmore and asking for some tips – she did owe me fifty pounds for the deposit. In the end I'd visited a music shop and purchased several piano play-books of varying difficulty.

Robin arrived at eight-thirty. Clara lingered in the kitchen, sipping tea, showing no eagerness to be off. Robin was oddly subdued. He made no dash for my cupboards and didn't remove so much as a single sock, but stood beside the fridge, thoughtfully chewing on a one-eared cuddly mouse and picking his nose.

'Shall I stay?' asked Clara.

'No,' I said, too quickly, seeing then that Clara looked hurt. 'We're not ready for an audience yet. Let us muddle through for a bit together first.'

After she left we went into the music room. The lesson did not start well. I brought out the first book, propped it on the stand and called out the names of the notes as I tinkered through the first rather tedious tune. Robin grabbed the book and chucked it onto the floor.

'Boring,' he announced. 'It's a little tune. It's silly. I want a proper tune. A big one.'

'You have to learn the little ones first. The little ones make up the big ones,' I said and entered into a simple scale.

Robin lay down on the floor in disgust.

'But listen,' I said, aware I was losing him already, 'I can use those notes to build something else.'

I launched into two scales at once, crashing in different directions with thundering noise and a lot of show, and then used it to put together the opening of Saint-Saëns' *Carnival of the Animals*. The piece requires two pianos to be played at once but I did my best alone, although I confess the sheer effort made me breathless and sweaty.

'You see?' I said, wiping my forehead. 'A boring scale can make a lion.'

'I only want the lion. The scale can go in the rubbish bin.'

'All right. I'll show you how to roar like a lion.'

He settled beside me and I watched with wonder as his small fingers bounded across the keys. We made the piano roar with considerable satisfaction for a quarter of an hour; then Robin stopped and put his fingers in his ears.

'Another.'

'Another animal?'

'OK.'

We spent the morning hopping through Saint-Saëns' entire

73

menagerie. We conjured kangaroos and elephants, blue aquariums brimming with fish, wild horses and cuckoos. It was a warm September day, and beneath the music-room window scarlet Michaelmas daisies bossed pale geraniums into submission. I pictured the animals streaming out of the window and landing on the beds where they thumped, bounced and raced amongst the flowers, flattening every one. I was amazed at the speed with which Robin seized upon each new melody. He only had to hear me play a phrase a few times and he could copy with very few mistakes. He possessed at first, however, no desire to improve or perfect his performance. He was greedy for more tunes, more tricks, more animals, and whenever I dared suggest that we try to make the waters of our aquarium a little smoother, he glared at me and folded his arms across his chest.

With some trepidation I reached again for the music book.

'The tunes for the animals and lots of new things are all in here,' I said tapping a page. 'It's like a story book.'

Robin scowled. 'There aren't any pictures.'

'Yes there are. Listen.'

I played a short Mozart piece and when I finished Robin was staring at the open book. He jabbed at the notes on the page with a thumbnail nibbled down to the quick.

'Those dots are a photograph of the tune,' he said.

'Yes. That's exactly it. Do you want to see the pictures the way I can?'

He pursed his lips into a grim little line and gave a single nod.

~

I was astonished at how quickly the boy learned. Within a month he understood the musical notation system – even though he remained quite unable to read or write his letters.

He was a small starving man; no matter how much I fed him – Mozart, a touch of Handel, a sprinkle of Mendelssohn – he wanted more. I suppose I ought to have been more restrained, I was the adult after all, but I was greedy too. I wanted to know what more he could do – the child appeared almost limitless in his abilities.

And yet he was a child. One of the farm cats strolled into the music room and he was instantly down from his seat, crouched on all fours, dangling bits of string and roaring at it. When he was too tired to pick up a melody instantly, or if a complex sequence of fingering required effort and concentration, he'd lie on the floor and sob. With my own fervour interrupted, to my shame I'd huff with irritation and I'd be ready to tick him off, much as I would have done a third-desk violin during rehearsal, when suddenly I'd catch myself. I'd notice the littleness of the creature prostrate on the carpet, the hiccuping sobs. When he got into such a state, I'd try to persuade him down to the kitchen for a cup of cocoa or a walk around the garden, but he never wanted to come. All he wanted was to play the piano. Once or twice he fell asleep mid-rage. I felt ashamed for pushing so hard and forgetting that he was not some impetuous music student from the academy but my own grandson.

~

October was tipping towards November and during our time together I'd kept the poor child inside. I'd told myself it was because the weather had been poor and he liked to spend hours in the music room at the piano but I heard a voice in my mind, Edie's voice, insisting that children also want to watch hours of television and eat chocolate until they're sick, and it's the adult's task to moderate such excess. Guiltily, I recognised that I'd kept Robin at the piano out of selfishness.

During his lessons Edie drifted into the background. Her loss remained a chronic pain, but one blunted by a powerful analgesic. The boy's talent was a luminescence that rippled outwards, and I followed it like a man overboard grasping at a light in the dark.

I still could not sleep but in the long hours before dawn, instead of huddling in the cold, feeling the shape of silence beside me, I made lists of pieces to play for Robin. I'd started with the usual children's tunes – Prokofiev's *Hansel and Gretel* or *Peter and the Wolf* and the candy-cane waltzes that my own daughters had enjoyed, but like the unusual child who prefers olives to sweeties, Robin preferred Bach to Strauss. As I lay awake, dawn crept in at the windows to the call of a woodlark. I decided to start the day with Vaughan Williams and his *Lark Ascending*.

Robin listened to the cadences of soaring sound, his mouth ajar and his eyes half closed – an indication of intense pleasure. He had the same expression when eating vanilla ice cream.

'A lark's a bird?' he asked at the end.

'Yes.'

'Like a chicken?'

'No. Not like a chicken.'

'Like a duck then?'

'A lark is a wild bird. She's nothing like a chicken or a duck.'

He stared at me, puzzled. He didn't understand the concept of a songbird. I was filled with an energy I hadn't felt for months.

'I think we should go out and hunt for a lark this morning.'

'I want to play on the piano.'

He stuck out his bottom lip, which trembled, threatening tears.

'You can't play a lark until you've heard one in our woods.'

'I've been a lion and I didn't heard one of those in our woods.'

I was about to argue further when I remembered Edie's caution – never enter into a debate with a child which you cannot win.

'Let's start by listening for a woodlark. You never know, we might get lucky and find a lion too.'

By the time I'd bribed him into his coat (a clear violation of Edie's rules – but her resolve was always much stronger than mine) and both wellington boots, I was exhausted, almost ready to telephone Clara and ask her to come early to collect him. Sternly, I told myself that I wasn't being fair to the boy. He must know green woods and lost love and a thousand other things, or his music will be an echo without a soul. I glanced down at Robin with his twin channels of yellow snot beneath his nose and his mis-buttoned red raincoat, and wondered whether I was being overambitious. No, I must hold firm. The boy must know more than music. We'd start with a lark.

The ground was wet from the morning's rain, but the clouds had cleared into dirty drifts like roadside snow, leaving glorious streaks of blue sky. The effect of the light made all the colours brighter; the green of the grass appeared to glow, while the huddles of woodland conspiring on the hillside stood out in relief like illustrations in a pop-out book, the treetops glazed in red and brown. I smelled autumn in the air.

'I want a biscuit.'

'In a minute.'

'My legs hurt.'

'Nearly there.'

'No we're not.'

I clutched Robin's hand tightly, and half dragged, half cajoled him up the hill, slip-sliding in his rubber boots. We entered the hush of the woods, the light smeared with a yellowish hue. We'd planted more than ten thousand trees over the last half-century, and the copse that had survived the war had spread long fingers of oak and ash across the shoulders of the hill. Robin sunk into silence and stuck close to my side. He glanced about, alert. Moss and lichen coated the upper branches of the rowans, which twisted in creaking spirals towards the sunlight. I led him deeper into the thicket, past a pile of stones. Robin stopped.

'What's that?' he asked, pointing.

'It's a grave marker. Your great-uncle George is buried there.'

Robin squatted down and scrutinised the stones. An earwig mountaineered across the uneven heap. Rotting leaves coated the topmost pebbles with brown sludge.

'Why isn't he in a churchyard? Isn't that where you're supposed to put dead people?'

'Yes, well, George wasn't much for God. And, in fact, you're quite right. We really oughtn't to have buried him here. They're quite strict about those sorts of things. But they can't really send him to prison now, can they?' I said with a smile – it was a line I'd delivered many times since the small and somewhat illegal funeral in the woods.

Robin did not laugh. 'No,' he said slowly. 'They won't put him in prison. But they might dig him up.'

'I won't let them,' I said with some resolve. 'George liked it here. These woods were his favourite place in all the world. He loved Hartgrove. This was his home and he never, ever wanted to leave it. Now he doesn't have to.' I picked up a fallen stone and slotted it back onto the heap. 'I like coming to visit him. One day, I expect I'll be buried here too.'

Robin wiped his nose with his sleeve, smearing a glistening streak of mud across his face. 'I'll come and visit you,' he announced magnanimously. 'But not often. It's a very long walk.'

'That's terribly kind of you, darling. I'm sure I'll appreciate it,' I said.

'Did you dig the hole for Uncle George?' asked Robin, after a moment.

'I didn't do it myself. Is that what you mean?'

Robin nodded.

'A man dug it for me,' I said, intrigued as to why he wanted the details.

'Good,' said Robin, relaxing ever so slightly. 'I don't think you would have digged it properly, Grandpa, and I wouldn't like it if bits of Uncle George were poking out.'

He glanced about warily, clearly uneasy about the close proximity of George, eyeing the odd twigs lying on the woodland floor with great suspicion as though they were really finger bones.

'There's really nothing to worry about, darling. A dead person is no more horrid than a dead tree.'

'Or a spider.'

'Exactly.'

'I don't like spiders.'

I didn't feel that my introduction to the pleasures of the countryside was progressing terribly well.

'Shall we walk a little, and try to find our lark?'

Robin nodded and allowed me to lead him deeper still. We listened for an hour or more to the music of the wood. We picked out the bright note of a robin, the ever-cheery soul who knows only one song and a jolly one at that. After a while we detected our woodlark.

'Do you hear that?' I whispered.

Robin nodded. 'Can we chuck it bread now?'

He still thought that the woodlark was like a duck in the park. Fat and idle and waiting for scraps of mouldy crusts.

I sighed. This child wasn't as I had been. He was a creature of modernity and suburbs. He was used to fenced-in gardens and rows of uniform houses neatly addressing one another across the street like maiden aunts over the tea-table. He was driven everywhere in an air-conditioned, temperate box that neatly sealed him off from the untidiness beyond.

'I'm cold, Grandpa. I want to go home.'

Subdued and tired, we turned back. The rain started up again, a gauze of drizzle that dripped from my cap and down my neck. And then a gunshot rang out.

Bang. Bang. The echo cracked through the trees. I grabbed Robin's shoulders and pressed him close against my legs, my heart thundering in my chest.

'Get out here and show yourself!' I shouted. 'How dare you shoot in my woods? How bloody dare you.'

I must admit that there's nothing like an unauthorised gun to make me come over all feudal. There was a rustle and then a pause. I could tell he wasn't far off – probably just assessing the level of threat to his own skin. Presumably upon seeing that we were an old man and a small boy, he stepped out from behind an oak and sauntered towards us, stopping thirty yards off. He was short, bundled into a dark waterproof jacket, woollen hat pulled low. He held a rifle. A proper huntsman's gun. This was no local youth taking a furtive pop at a pheasant.

'What the hell are you doing here? I certainly didn't give you permission.'

He studied us for a moment in silence, clearly deciding which version of the truth to recount. 'There's no problem, mister. I'll go. No trouble.'

'Damn right you will. I should call the police. This is trespass.'

He held up his hands. 'Whatever you like. Was an honest mistake. Jon Bentley hired me. I'm out looking for a stray dog that's been worrying his sheep on the hill. Lost twenty ewes this week, he has. I followed it into the woods. I thought this here were Bentley's woods. My mistake.'

'Well, they're not. Twenty ewes, you say?'

'Aye. Them that was killed outright. There was another ten what had to be shot.'

'Good grief. I didn't know.'

'Said he didn't want ter bother you with it. That you had enough on yer mind.'

I was unsettled. Beside me Robin fidgeted and squashed a beetle with his heel.

'Can I carry on now? I wouldn't have hurt you. I heard you a mile off and I were shooting the other way.'

I hesitated. 'A dog, you say?'

'Aye.' He shifted the gun into his other hand.

'Must be the size of a bloody wolf to need that calibre gun. So, no. I'm sorry for Bentley but I don't like it. I won't have a man with a rifle on my land. You need to leave, and if I catch you again, I will call the police.'

The man swore and spat but he turned and headed away, towards the edge of the woods and the open back of the hill. Robin tugged on my arm. 'Come on, Grandpa.'

'Just a minute. I want to make sure he's gone.'

'Are you going to shoot him if he comes back?' For the first time that morning, he sounded enthusiastic.

'No, of course not.'

'Because I won't tell Mummy, if you do.'

I laughed and we started back down the hill, and yet I couldn't shake the sensation that beneath the rain-soaked scrub something crouched, watching.

～

Robin's behaviour improved. With his energy and interest channelled into music, he no longer bit and scratched his sisters or tore the pages out of picture books. He remained a quiet child. Clara fretted that he was withdrawn but I tried to reassure her that he never seemed quiet with me.

'Yes but does he *talk*, Papa?' she asked.

I thought and realised that, while he did speak to me, he mostly spoke through the piano. I felt that I knew him rather well, but through his other voice. I tried to explain this to Clara.

'He does communicate. He has a great deal to say, darling, but he says it using the piano.'

'I can't speak music. Not like you. I want him to talk to me.'

'He is talking to you.' I said. *You simply don't know how to listen.* I succeeded in not saying that out loud. Edie would have been proud.

~

It was the twelfth of December – Robin's fifth birthday – and I was hosting a party. This was the first family gathering since the funeral. I'd asked Mrs Stroud, my housekeeper, to light fires in the drawing room and in the great hall. Usually when the children visited, we never lit one in the vast inglenook in the hall – too dangerous without a fireguard, Clara complained. I decided that all the children were now old enough to be trusted – and I must say that when Clara and Lucy were small, we never fussed about such things. We didn't have central heating then and it was either light the fires or freeze.

Rain was driving against the windows while a gale stole in through the gaps beneath the mullioned panes. Yet it was warm in the great hall – a huge log in the hearth blazed red and spat out orange sparks. As I gazed upon the flames, I could almost believe that the heart of the house was beating once again.

I had Mrs Stroud set out glasses of champagne for the adults in the hall – a party is still a party even if the guest of honour is only five. On the minstrels' gallery, I'd installed a string quartet for the birthday boy. Clara had suggested a magician but I'd ignored her – I knew Robin would prefer musicians. I didn't confide my plans to Clara, choosing to surprise them all.

Lucy was the first to arrive – alone. Over the years, I'd rarely been introduced to Lucy's chaps and they never seemed to last. About ten years ago I'd wondered aloud whether she was a lesbian but Edie had laughed at me, informing me that lots of women nowadays meet a partner later in life and not all unmarried women were lesbians. I thought that was all well and good, but I would have liked Lucy to have a partner of some kind. Well, that isn't quite true. I'm an old-fashioned man. Some may not approve of this, but I would have enjoyed walking Lucy down the aisle to her future husband and I would've liked her to be a mother. Lucy would have been a splendid mother. As the years went by, I was aware that Edie worried she was lonely and had left it all a bit late. When Edie told me that girls often didn't get on with things until their forties, I knew she was reassuring herself rather than me. I think I would have liked Lucy's children.

I hoped rather than believed that she was happy. She had many friends up in London and made it all sound interesting and full but still I worried. She worked as a graphic designer for an advertising company and sometimes sent me cuttings of things she had done that had appeared in the paper. I'd always rather hoped she'd be a painter. She'd made wonderful drawings as a child. Those delicate fingers that were so useless for the piano were skilled at creating pictures. I'd given her the Not-Constable on her twenty-first birthday, but when she'd come to understand that the original painting had once been in the family and been lost, she'd wept; the copy painting had seemed paltry and the gift thoughtless. I hadn't dared confess that once there had also been three Romneys, two Stubbs and a Gainsborough.

'Hello, darling,' I said, kissing her. 'Have some champagne.'

She took a glass and peered about the hall.

'All this is for Robin?' she asked.

'He needed a treat. He's been working terribly hard.'

I glanced around the hall – it was looking super. Mrs Stroud had given everything a thorough spring clean. The flagstones had been swept and scrubbed; the dark panelling had been rubbed with beeswax so that it gleamed; and the room smelled faintly of honey. Soft winter light filtered through the stained glass in the high mullioned windows, forming puddles of green and red on the sandstone floor. From the antlers of the mounted stags Mrs Stroud had draped banners declaring 'Happy Birthday'. I'm sure they'd never been used for such an ignominious purpose before, and I did wonder whether their glass eyes were gazing at me with reproach. Streamers dangled from the still somewhat dusty and unlit chandelier – the thing is an absolute devil to clean. We'd never had it converted to electricity. Too expensive. Now that I thought about it, I ought to have lit five of its candles – but it was too late.

'Hello, Papa. Goodness, you've been busy,' said Clara, sailing across the room, trailing her daughters, Katy and Annabel, in her wake like a pair of small tugboats. Both girls were china-doll copies of their mother, so like her that sometimes I wondered whether their dour and red-faced father had had any part in them at all.

'Where's the birthday boy?' I asked.

'Waiting in the kitchen with his father as instructed.'

'Jolly good.'

I gave Clara a glass of champagne and presented each of the girls with sparkling apple juice in plastic cups decorated with treble clefs and sprays of quavers.

'Where shall I put his cake?' asked Clara.

84

'Oh. I bought one in town already.'

'I told you I was making him a cake,' said Clara.

'Did you?'

'Yes.' Clara did not smile.

'Well, never mind.'

But I grasped as I said it that she did mind very much and I had made some kind of faux pas. I was hit with a gut punch of longing for Edie. Life without her meant navigating family waters without a pilot.

'Well, he's a lucky chap. Two birthday cakes.'

She set hers down on the table. It was a lopsided marbled sponge with a robin stencilled in icing, the red of his breast bleeding into his white feathers. On a whim, I had purchased a gateau in the shape of a piano, the tiny keys slivers of white and dark chocolate, the lid propped open with a spear of chocolate. When you pressed a button on the miniature piano stool, it piped 'Happy Birthday'. Edie never approved of shop-bought cakes, but when I saw this in the bakery window in Dorchester, I couldn't resist ordering one for Robin. Apparently this had been a mistake.

'Shall we call in the birthday boy?' I asked, wishing that I could retire to the music room, put on a little Mahler and abandon all my guests. I'd done it before.

As Robin entered the hall, I signalled to the musicians concealed in the gallery, and they started on a jaunty little Mozart march in D major – one of Robin's current favourites. I conducted from my spot beside the birthday table out of habit rather than necessity – they would have managed perfectly well without me. Robin stood motionless in the middle of the room. He listened with his hands held out before him, fingers spread as though catching notes like snowflakes. The hall glowed with sound. It poured down upon us from the gallery in reds and gold and yellow. I'd forgotten how superb the acoustics were in this room. When they'd finished the piece, Robin remained quite still while the rest of the family clapped with more politeness than enthusiasm. I shouted my approval – I must admit that I can't abide stingy applause after a good performance.

'Jolly good show!' I called.

'More,' said Robin.

'Manners, Robin,' reminded his mother.

'More, please,' said Robin. 'Now.'

The musicians laughed and launched into a Haydn gavotte. I'd given them a playlist consisting mostly of pieces that Robin had been practising on the piano. I wanted him to learn that each performance is unique. The melodies he'd been rehearsing on the Steinway in the music room could be caught and reshaped on a violin or a cello. Music isn't like Plato's world of ideals – there isn't a perfect version of Bach's Sarabande in G, which all fiddle players attempt to emulate. Rather, there is an infinite variety of interpretations – as many as there are Hamlets or Othellos. One might prefer Laurence Olivier's performance to Richard Burton's but, like the words of a play in the mouth of an actor, the notes on the page are conjured to life by the musician and they contain a cosmos of variations.

I was too busy watching Robin to notice the rest of the family. Clara nudged me.

'Papa, let's eat. We've been standing here for nearly an hour. The girls are hungry.'

I looked round to see them studying the cakes and trays of sandwiches. They looked completely bored.

'No,' said Robin. 'More music.'

'Perhaps they can play while we eat,' said Clara.

I opened my mouth to object – I can't bear background music – but I conceded. It could be part of his treat – like having one's supper on a tray in front of the television.

As we sat in the dining room, eating peanut butter and banana sandwiches, strands of Handel fluttered about us, light and bright as garden butterflies. Robin sat between his sisters. Three shining gold heads, like polished coins. The girls nibbled and whispered to each other, ignoring their brother.

Ralph, the children's father, lounged at the head of the table with his back to the fire, a sheen of sweat across his face as though he'd been wrapped in cellophane. I didn't much like Ralph. He was rather clever and so reserved he appeared disdainful of everything and everyone. Edie always told me that he was a nice man – merely quiet. I've often noticed that we're ready to believe the best of taciturn people as though, if they did speak, what they'd say was bound to be pleasant and amusing. I didn't believe it with Ralph. Not for a moment did I think that the words he did not say were amiable. And he'd once declared that he disliked Bach. Cold, he said, and tedious. The accountant of music. That, I could not forgive.

To my bafflement, no one apart from Robin seemed to be enjoying the party. He was suffused with happiness – his cheeks shone pink – but the rest of the family were subdued. Clara and Lucy ate little and spoke less. I had the uneasy sense once again that I'd done something wrong.

Without waiting for Mrs Stroud, I took some glasses into the kitchen. Lucy followed with the dirty plates.

'Darling, am I in trouble? I tried to make the party nice.'

'Oh, Daddy,' said Lucy, kissing me, and I knew instantly that it was worse than I'd thought. 'It's too nice. That's the problem.'

I stiffened, my feelings stung. 'What on earth does that mean?'

'Daddy, you never even gave me and Clara birthday parties.'

'You always had parties. There was a spy party, a witches—'

'Mummy did everything. Mostly you came in for ten minutes. Complained that it was terribly noisy and retreated back to your study.'

'Did I?'

'It's all right. You weren't all bad.'

'Pleased to hear it.'

I placed the glasses in the sink and stared out across the lawns to where the ground sloped down towards the river. The wind buffeted the bare willows, so that the fronds flew up into the air, tangling like a girl's hair. I supposed it was true that I'd sometimes pleased myself. I liked my own children. Loved them. But I never understood those who declared that they adored children as a species. That was like saying one adores people. Children, like people in general, are all different – one prefers some to others. Only a simpleton likes everyone.

Lucy was still talking.

'And a string quartet? For a fifth birthday party? I mean, come on, Daddy. You didn't even get one for my twenty-first.'

'Because you wanted some God-awful disco.'

'So I did.'

'And the musicians are old friends of mine. They'd never ask me to pay.'

This was partly true. They didn't ask but I paid anyway. It's bad luck to cheat musicians or taxi drivers.

I wanted to say to Lucy that it's lonely here. The house is still. Your mother sang until the end and now I find yellowed and silent songbooks strewn around the music room like desiccated wedding confetti. The boy brings noise. Good noise. We hear the same things, he and I.

'Shall we go back to the others?' I said.

Robin sobbed when he saw the train set his parents had bought him. It was a gleaming, remote-controlled engine that raced around an aluminium track.

'I don't want it. I want a piano.'

Clara was trying to be patient. 'It's good to enjoy lots of things, Robin. Pianos are very expensive.'

Katy and Annabel tried to help. They cooed around the train, feigning enthusiasm, and pleaded with Robin to help them race it but he remained sullen, folding his arms and lying face down on the floor. I'd wanted to buy him a piano to practise on at home but Clara wouldn't hear of it.

'He's too fixated already. If he had one at home, I don't think I could ever even get him to eat. I'd have to feed him like a baby bird, dropping titbits into his mouth as he sat at the keyboard. Promise me you won't buy him one?'

I'd promised. Now, I caught Clara's eye as she stared at me over the prostrate, weeping child. I had to concede that he wasn't easy. I didn't see the worst of him, as with me he was able to glut himself on what he loved best. I was like the grandparent who stuffed him with chocolate and then dispatched him back to his mother, only instead of a sugar buzz, I sent him home full of music.

Katy slumped on her chair. 'Why does he always ruin everything? Can we just go home?'

'Come on, old chap,' cajoled his father. 'Get up.'

'You haven't had my present yet,' I said.

Robin lifted up his head, rubbed his eyes. 'Is it a piano?'

'Well, no. It isn't.'

'Can I have yours?'

I frowned. 'You can play it whenever you like. I don't think my piano would fit in your bedroom. It's rather too big.'

Robin paused, considering. 'Can I have it when you're dead then? You won't need it and I'll buy a house big enough.'

I caught Clara's eye and to my relief she was laughing.

'Yes, Robin. You can have the piano when I'm dead.'

'Say "thank you",' said Clara.

Robin shrugged and laid his head back on the carpet. 'Why? He isn't dead yet and I haven't got it.'

I could sense things about to unravel once again, so I pulled out two parcels and slid them towards him. He rolled over and sat up. He rattled the first box.

'Is it a train?'

'Why don't you open it and find out?'

'If it is a train, then I don't need to open it.'

I sighed. Sometimes he was neither an easy nor an endearing child.

'Try the other one.'

He shredded the wrapping paper and held at arm's length a large and battered leather book. He studied it dubiously.

'What is it?'

I pulled over a chair and opened the book for him. 'It's a book of songs I collected from all over England. Most of them from right here in Dorset. I've written them all out in this book. It's like a map but in songs.'

'Can I play them on the piano?'

'Yes, you could, although lots of them have words too.'

'I don't like singing.'

He shoved aside the book and set his face again. I'd been quite silly in thinking for a moment that he'd be interested. I should have bought him some music CDs or a Walkman or something. Quietly, I retrieved the book and put it back on a shelf.

'Why don't you play us something, Robin?' said Annabel. 'Me and Katy haven't ever actually heard you.'

'You must have,' I said.

Annabel shook her head. 'Nope. We're always at school when he comes here.'

I looked at my twelve-year-old granddaughter and felt a ripple of guilt. She was dressed in the usual uniform of the young – a sweater and blue jeans – but like a sapling that had taken root she'd outgrown the spindliness of childhood. Now she studied me with a pair of brown eyes. I didn't know her at all.

'I'm sorry about that. You should hear him.'

Robin had stopped crying but remained lying on his stomach, picking at a hole in the Persian rug.

'That's quite enough, Robin,' I declared. 'You need to decide what to play for your sisters.'

Without hesitation, he stood, wiped his nose on his sleeve and raced across the great hall, into the music room. It had once been known as the morning room, and gentlemen had lingered here after breakfast to read the papers. It faced southwest and even on dark days it was filled with light. Long ago I'd claimed it for my own; it was large enough to comfortably fit a full-size concert grand piano as well as all my other paraphernalia but really I loved it because of the quality of the light. Dusk had crept up on us; the rain-dashed hills had warmed from grey to red and now shoals of rosy clouds drifted across the sky. The white walls of the music room had been temporarily repainted in pink.

I placed several cushions on the piano stool and set Robin on top.

'Do you know what you want to play?'

'Yes.'

'Do you need the sheet music?'

He shook his head and sat quietly, his hands in his lap. The girls had found a spot on the window seat at the far side of the room where they kneeled, tracing their names in the condensation on the glass, only vaguely interested in their brother. Lucy, Clara and Ralph leaned against my desk – a vast Victorian monstrosity in brass and mahogany. The string players from the quartet lingered in the doorway, curious.

Robin gulped a breath, a swimmer about to dive, and then started to play. The change was instant. The girls stopped fiddling with the windows, turned and sat and listened, absolutely still. The string players edged closer, quite unable to help themselves, travellers drawn to a fire on a winter's night. Ralph reached for Clara's hand and gripped it tightly.

Robin played a simple Chopin nocturne; it rippled from his fingers as smoothly as a stream over pebbles, as clear and cool. In those early days, I was still more technically adept than the boy, but I'd never called forth such a tone from the piano. It did what I asked of it, but Robin made it cry out; under his touch, the instrument was a thing that lived. Dusk dulled into evening and the room grew dark but Robin played on.

When at last he stopped, we listened in silence to the slow decay of the final chord. I glanced at Katy and Annabel, their faces pale in the gloom.

'Well, shit on me,' said Annabel.

Everyone laughed, but as I looked at my family I wondered whether they understood, whether any of us understood, what Robin's talent would mean for us all.

~

It was the first Christmas without Edie. There was a cascade of unhappy anniversaries. The first weeks after she died, I'd been awash with grief and yet she was still so close that, if I just reached out far enough, I could still brush her fingertips. I kept her slippers beside the bed, just in case she needed them. She couldn't bear cold feet when she got up for a pee in the night. I didn't cancel her magazine subscriptions – somehow I couldn't bring myself to telephone the call centre, it was too absolute. And suppose she wanted the latest issue of *House and Garden* when she came home? I knew these thoughts were ridiculous and I certainly couldn't voice them aloud to my daughters – they'd cluck in concern and start whispering to one another, convinced I'd gone doolally.

During those early weeks and months, time slid and juddered – nothing was quite real. When I was a child of seven,

I'd had measles and I'd been kept in bed in the nursery for a fortnight with the curtains closed to protect my eyes against damage from the light. In the midst of my darkness and fever, time had stuttered and slowed, and the boundary between wake and sleep had become indistinct and unimportant. The world had contracted to my sickroom and my bed, and the burning itching in my eyes.

Each evening my father would visit. He sat on the edge of my bed; I don't remember him saying a word, but he pressed the cold circle of his gold watch against the hotness of my forehead. It was pleasanter than any flannel or compress. Then he'd remove the watch and wind it up. Ticketty-tick. Ticketty-tick. Like the crunch of the death-watch beetles in the attic beams above. In my feverish state I thought that he held time itself in that watch, and that he released a little for me each evening, the precise quantity that would allow me to manage through the night. And then one evening when I was feeling better and sitting up in bed, he allowed me to rewind the watch. I fumbled, my fingers sweaty and clumsy, but for once he gave no reprimand. It was a great boon – a treat so immense that I could not dilute it by confiding it to my brothers. After I had wound the watch and my father had refastened it on his wrist, he had opened the curtains and time had restarted.

In the first year after Edie, I was still waiting for the curtains to be pulled back and for time to resume. I lived by rote, surviving on habits. I made lists of groceries for Mrs Stroud to purchase. I paid the gas bill. I asked the gardener to plant a thousand daffodils and narcissi along the woodland walk. I declined requests to conduct concerts in London and New York and Bournemouth. But, most of all, I waited. I waited for Edie to come back and, despite knowing intellectually it was quite impossible, I waited.

I tried to write music and failed, and out of frustration continued to keep notes in the exercise book I kept on the bedside table. Discovering it was nearly full, I purchased another in Dorchester. As I scanned the contents, I observed that I was no longer noting reminiscences, rags and scraps of memory, but also recording the events of the last year, of life after Edie. The last year, however dreadful and painful, had its own value. Grief had not yet receded, and yet I could acknowledge that at some point in the future it might. It would be a gradual retreating of the tide, a lessening that ebbed and flowed. I needed to remember the grief itself. The evidence of love.

Robin was the only new addition to my strange and airless world. The mornings that the boy came, we lived in music and there was pleasure in existence. And then he left and the quiet took hold, loneliness leavening it like yeast until it grew and smothered the house. The silence was monstrous. At the moment I needed her most, music deserted me once more.

I worried about Robin. I was concerned that I continued to teach him out of selfishness. I taught him because our lessons were my only respite but I was no piano teacher, especially for a student as brilliant as Robin.

I summoned a few old friends for advice. They arrived with a February gale. The driveway had turned into a series of puddles and a blackbird bathed on a patch of lawn that had metamorphosed into a small pond. Yet my friends braved the foulness of the weather, curious to hear my grandson play. I guessed they all wanted to discover whether grandpaternal fondness had clouded my judgement. I wanted to know it too.

We gathered in the music room, Albert, John, Marcus and I. We were a coterie of grand old men, the elder statesmen of music. Mrs Stroud had stoked the fire to a furnace and turned up the heating. Marcus, at eighty-two, was a little frail and contemplating surrendering his driving licence – although, I noted, he had still agreed to conduct one last performance of the *Messiah* at Easter.

'It will be my last,' he said, eating a large slice of fruit cake with surprising gusto.

Albert laughed. 'You say that each time.'

Marcus shrugged. 'Well, one day it will be true whether I intend it or not. Now, if I should give up the ghost mid-performance, would that improve the crits or not? "Last night's concert at the Festival Hall was a tremendous disappointment. Sir Marcus Albright really let himself down in the final movement of Beethoven's Fifth by turning his toes up—"'

John poured more tea. 'I don't see why you should retire. You can get someone to drive you to Waitrose; you can't get someone to conduct Handel on your behalf.'

'In the spring I might just delve into Beethoven's late quartets,' Marcus added, spearing a stray currant with his fork. 'I never really understood them before. They always seemed a bit strained, uneasy. But then, after my stroke, I listened to them and they made sense for the first time. I'm not sure that they can make sense to anyone under seventy.'

'It's not about age,' I said quietly. 'His late quartets are about suffering. It's acute sadness, a muscular unhappiness that provokes the music. That can happen at any time of life.'

The others paused and looked at me, presuming I was speaking about Edie. I hadn't been directly, but then everything led back to her.

We chatted on for half an hour, debating the nuances of Mozart's sonatas and the narrowness of the car park spaces at the new Tesco, until the door opened. Robin stood there. The men beamed at him.

'Do come in, young man,' said Albert. 'It's probably much too hot in here for you but I'm afraid we old fellows do feel the cold.'

Robin marched in, too young to feel self-conscious or abashed.

'This is my friend Albert,' I said to him. 'You like his recording of the Bach fugues, remember?'

This was an understatement. He had played it so much at home that Clara had limited him to only three times each day.

'I listened to it a hundred and fifteen times,' he declared.

'Why so few?' quipped Marcus.

Robin blinked, not understanding he was being teased. 'I needed to know how it worked. How he put all the bits together. I get it now. It's in my head and I don't need to listen to it any more.'

I glanced at Albert to see how he was reacting to this. His mouth did not betray a twitch of humour; instead he listened with the same thoughtful gravity he would have given to an adult. Robin surveyed the faces of the celebrated men gathered by the fire and scowled.

'I like the recording of Rachmaninov playing his own stuff even better. Is Mr Rachmaninov coming too, Grandpa?'

'He was unavailable this afternoon.'

There was a pause, while we pretended to drink our tea and tried not to smile.

'Would you like to play us something?' asked John.

Robin nodded and moved quickly to the piano, piling up his cushions. The men settled back into their chairs by the fire. Robin hesitated for a few seconds, fingers poised over the piano, and then he began.

'Something a little stronger than tea, I think,' said Marcus after Robin had finished, been collected by Mrs Stroud and taken to the kitchen in search of chocolate biscuits. I produced a bottle of Scotch from my desk. We sat in silence for a few minutes, drinking and somehow still hearing the swell of music swishing through the stillness. Albert was the first to speak.

'I'm sorry, Fox. But you can't continue to teach him piano.

You're simply not good enough. He'll pick up all manner of bad habits from you, thinking that's the way it should be done.'

Miserably, I nodded and took a long swig of whisky. My eyes burned but I hoped they'd put it down to the fumes. It was true. These fellows knew that my playing was serviceable at best.

'What ought I to do?' I asked when I could speak.

Albert wrinkled his brow in thought. 'I can give him the odd master class, but that's really for later on. In a year or so when he's mastered a bit more technique. He has a real instinctive emotionality that needs to be nurtured carefully. His playing is highly personal – and that's rare in such a young player. More often than not, prodigies are miraculous chameleons, borrowing other players' styles but lacking their own voice. Robin is himself.'

He paused and rubbed his forehead. 'You need a teacher who's not only a brilliant pianist himself but experienced in teaching the very young. One mustn't interfere too much. He requires very gentle guidance.'

Marcus glanced at me. 'You'll have to take him to London.'

Albert nodded in agreement. 'It will almost certainly have to be London. Probably every week. Perhaps twice. There needs to be regular lessons and a stringent practice schedule. An older student I'd expect to do eight or nine hours each day. Since he's so young, it will be less but still probably three or four.'

John had said nothing but now he got to his feet, grabbed the poker and started rooting around amongst the coals. I swallowed my irritation – a man's fire is his own. No one should interfere with his host's hearth.

'Are you quite certain that he wants that?' he asked. 'Do his parents? Most child prodigies are washed up by the age of twelve. It's rarely worth it.'

Albert leaned back in his chair. 'I'm afraid John's quite right. The boy is clearly exceptionally gifted. It's remarkable what he can do after a few months with frankly a rather ropy pianist as his teacher.' He smiled but only for an instant and then gave a tiny sigh. 'But the odds are stacked against him. Even with everything we'll try to give him, he will probably never be a concert pianist. It's a shame that his passion isn't for the violin.'

We all grunted in agreement. Even if a violinist doesn't conquer the Everest of becoming a concert soloist and a virtuoso, he can still make a life of music as part of an orchestra. The pianist has no such alternative. His career opportunities are either at the summit, with world concert tours and recording contracts, or giving piano lessons to recalcitrant children. The music departments of most schools reverberate with the spoiled dreams of talented pianists, who came close but not close enough.

'I'll make some calls,' said Albert. 'But in the meantime, you need to talk to his mother.'

~

I asked Clara to come for a walk. It was late February and although the morning's frost still lingered in the shade, patches of snowdrops and hordes of crocuses had emerged in compact puddles of colour. The months of dreary rain and sleet had turned the hillside a muddy brown, the grass uneven and yellowed. The trees remained bare, the fine patterns of branches against the sky reminding me of drawings of capillaries in old anatomy books. The startling purple and vivid yellow of the crocuses adorned the colourless world, reassuring me, just as I was heartily sick of the cold and rain, that spring wasn't far off. I've never been like Edie. I'm a summertime man. I hanker for blue skies and dawns lively with birds.

Clara and I walked briskly across the estate and towards the Wessex Ridgeway along the spine of hills, the trees echoing with the squabble of wood pigeons. As we climbed, the county was spread out below us in miniature, the fields a tone poem in browns and greens, here and there the flooded water meadows catching in the sunlight like molten aluminium. By silent accord we made for Ringmoor, emerging onto the hilltop like swimmers surfacing into the open air. The wind sang in the telephone wires, a perfect C sharp.

No matter how still the day, it's always windy up at Ringmoor. It's a strange place, echoing with millennia of footsteps. Iron Age workings crease the grassy downland like folds in a blanket alongside the raised outlines of a Roman village. At the boundary lie the tumbledown remains of a Victorian cottage, the assorted settlements lying on top of one another as though time has been compressed at a single point, every period in history existing all at once. The wind is loud and the boundary between the ages insubstantial.

We perched for a rest on the ruins of a flint cottage wall and Clara passed me an apple. In a habit inherited from her mother, she never ventures anywhere without pockets bulging with treats.

'Didn't you collect songs once from the shepherd who lived up here?' she asked.

'Yes, you're quite right. So I did. That was long ago. Before you were born.'

We were silent for a while, eating our apples. After a few minutes Clara hurled the core into a tangle of scrub that at some time must have formed part of the cottage garden, and said, 'I liked the story of you coming up here and listening to his old songs. He'd sing them to you only at the right time of year. Wasn't that it? A song for summer? Another for winter?'

I chuckled. 'Yes. Peculiar old fellow. I attempted to hack up here in the snow to hear his winter song. I caught a foul cold. Was in bed for a week.'

Clara studied me for a moment. 'Do you still collect songs?'

I closed my eyes and felt the sting of bright light against my lids. 'Not really. I can't remember the last time I collected something new. It's terribly hard nowadays. The ancient and the wild retreat to the edge of things. The countryside is teeming and too bright at night. I remember coming up here years ago after dark when I was only a little younger than you and it was black. You have no concept of a proper—'

'— a properly dark night. Yes. I know. You've said.'

I smiled. 'I'm sorry, darling. You've heard all my stories before.'

'It just seems a shame that you've given up.'

'There aren't people left any more who sing the old songs. If they do, it's because they've learned them from a book or a CD. There weren't many such chaps around even when I was a boy. I worry that they're all extinct now.'

'Dorset dodos.'

'Exactly.'

'Haven't all the songs been collected in any case?'

'I suspect that's impossible. There's always one more song to be found.'

'So you are still looking, then?'

I laughed. 'You got me. Perhaps I am.'

We sat quietly for a minute, watching the cloud shadows trawl the hillside below, and listening to the melodic hum of the telephone wires.

I talked about Robin. She sat with her hands folded neatly in her lap and said nothing until I'd finished. Then she turned to me and asked, 'But what do you think? Do you think he should stop lessons with you and go to London?'

'I can't teach him what he needs. The teacher Albert's found at the Royal College is experienced with very young children.'

'But travelling to London twice every week. It's a lot. Won't the lessons be awfully expensive? I mean, we'll find the money somehow . . . but what about school?'

'They won't charge for the lessons. Or only a nominal amount.'

This wasn't true. The lessons were indeed expensive, but I'd arranged for the bills to be sent directly to me. Clara never need know.

'And I suppose either his new school will accommodate him or somehow he'll have to be taught at home.' She kicked at a stone with her walking shoe. 'But despite all of that he might never succeed.'

'No. He probably won't.'

'For God's sake, Daddy.'

'You need to know the reality.'

'It sounds like a lot of misery for everyone.' She paused. 'Will it even make Robin happy?'

I told her the one thing I knew with any certainty. 'The boy is happiest at the piano. If he has a chance of making it his life, don't we have to give it to him, even if it's only a little chance?'

Clara didn't answer. The wind buffeted the trees.

June 1947

George wants to know precisely how it will happen. He's like a man whose horse needs to be shot, pleading with the veterinary surgeon for reassurance that the wretched animal won't suffer. He forces us to cycle to Turnworth where they're demolishing the old manor. Apparently it's happening to stately homes all over England. Hardly anyone can afford to keep the damn things going or make the necessary repairs after the neglect of the war years. We cycle to the top of the hill and puff along the ridge. It's a glorious day – the sky a shining cobalt blue, the hedges strewn with dog roses and honeysuckle, and the air brimming with the hum of bees. We sweat in the midday sun, feeling sympathy for the long-haired cattle huffing in the shade of a solitary beech tree beside the road. We pause briefly to fill our water bottles in a stream and pedal on through the swarms of drowsy flies, arriving at Turnworth shortly before the demolition men.

We know the house well. The General and Colonel Winters, the owner, are old pals; before the war we went there to luncheons, suppers and parties, for carol singing on Christmas Eve. It's a grand old place, much larger than ours, cradled in a chalk valley formed by Jurassic seas. It can't be seen from the road; only the curling drive is visible, and if out riding or walking you won't discover it until you're nearly on top of it. The honeyed stone seems to emerge from the hillside as if it had grown there.

I've never really thought about the manor before. It would have been like asking me whether I'd thought an aunt or a cousin attractive. Yet now, standing with Jack and George on the ridge, gazing down at the façade of mullioned windows each reflecting a hundred suns, with the ivy creeping shyly around the porch, I appreciate that it's beautiful. I'm sure that inside the timbers are rotten, infested with dry rot and death-watch beetle, and that the roof leaks whenever it rains, but from up here, on this lazy, sun-filled afternoon, it looks perfect, as if it had always been here and as if, in the years before it was built, the valley was simply waiting for it to appear.

Men carry out the last few pieces of furniture and lay them on the lawns some distance away like corpses removed from the scene of a terrible accident. The three of us remain where we are but below us at the far end of the drive a crowd starts to form. If I squint I could probably make out the colonel, but I can't bear to look for him. Jack reaches into his jacket and produces a hipflask, opens it, knocks it back and wordlessly passes it to George, then to me. A man with a whippet by his side seems to be directing the men. It is the colonel. I've never seen him without his dog. He stores his soul in that creature.

An hour passes. George nudges me and I observe men stuffing sticks of gelly into the boreholes in the hulking outer walls, while other men ferry yet more explosive charges. A sideboard is heaved onto the lawn and dumped there beside a dining table for twenty, as though at any moment the Mad Hatter will show up with the Queen of Hearts to host a tea party amongst the roses and packing boxes. I'm sleepy from the whisky and, in all honesty, a little bored. George passes me a meat paste sandwich. Edie made them for us. She refused to join us, telling us that we were all morbid for coming to watch this spectacle. I can't say that she was wrong – I'm still not quite sure why we're here and yet at this moment none of it seems real. We're watching what will happen to our house in a week or so but we're picnicking in glorious sunshine. A peregrine falcon soars overhead – if he sticks about, he'll have a perfect aerial view of the whole thing.

Then it's time. The colonel and his whippet walk to the far side of the garden. A man in a trilby remonstrates with the crowd, presumably asking them to leave, but they won't budge. We peer down, and I can't help my excitement. The man strides over to stand beside the colonel. By their feet is a plunger with a length of wire running to the gelly. The two men speak for a moment and I assume that the man in the trilby is asking the colonel whether he wishes to press the plunger himself, but he shakes his head. That, clearly, is a step too far.

A moment later, the other man pushes it down, quickly and firmly. Nothing happens for a minute. And then there's a boom, followed by another. And another. They rumble around the hillside and I feel it in my chest rather than hear it. And it's thrilling; blood pumps through me and I'm breathless. There's an awful exhilaration to the destruction, the boyish impulse to knock over a tower of bricks or stamp on a beetle, magnified a thousandfold. The house trembles as though the ground beneath is shaking with a terrible, terrible force. The tiles on the roof lift up, slowly, it seems, like a feather being held aloft by a funnel of breath, and the house appears to pause. For a moment I think it won't fall but then it does. All the windows shatter and the wall furthest from us topples, then the next, crashing down like vast dominoes as the charges go off one by one, until at last the entire house slumps, collapsing in on itself. The noise is catastrophic and the stillness of the afternoon is split open. A cloud of dust rises up, thick as fog, and conceals the ruins.

Jack passes me a cigarette but I wave him away, sickened at the spectacle, at myself. George looks stricken. He's a nasty greenish colour and his skin is coated with sweat.

'Here, George, are you all right?' I ask even though it's perfectly obvious he is not.

He nods, then turns round and vomits on a patch of dandelions behind his bicycle.

'It's the noise,' he says at last, spitting in the grass. 'I don't like the noise.'

'Come on, old chap,' says Jack, holding up George's bicycle, his voice gentle.

We shouldn't have come.

～

Edie produces a box of sugar plums and a record of the young pianist Albert Shields performing Rachmaninov. She waits until Jack and George retreat to bed before placing it on the gramophone. We sit on the worn rug in the Chinese room, our mouths sticky from sugar plums – Lord knows how she found them – and we listen. Except I don't. I only watch her listening – her rapt expression, her eyes lightly closed as though sunbathing, her skin flushed from the warmth of the fire. There is a snowfall of sugar dusting her top lip. I clench my fists to stop myself from leaning over to kiss her.

It takes a force of will not to resent Jack. I stamp on my envy as if on a swarm of wasps. I stare at the blinking embers in the grate.

'Can I tell you something?' I ask.

'Of course,' says Edie.

'If we're really to give up Hartgrove, I'd like to preserve her memory through the songs I've been collecting. At least then this place will exist in music if nowhere else. But the prospect of simply sweeping up the songs into my book and keeping them as some kind of musical scrapbook of ancient England feels wholly inadequate. I have this notion of using the songs as the basis of some kind of pastoral symphony about the loss of home and of an England vanished in the war' – I falter, worried that I'm sounding grandiose, but Edie is listening with patient interest – 'but I don't have an idea for the main theme. I think I'm probably doomed to gathering up songs and pinning them in my wretched book like desiccating moths until I'm falling to bits myself.'

Her mouth twitches in a smile, but she doesn't laugh. 'Perhaps you'll discover the theme in a song you've yet to find.'

I nod but really I'm terribly afraid that I won't ever experience that feverish surge of creativity.

'Most composers have been at it for a decade by the time they are my age,' I say, trying not to sound peevish. 'Think of Mozart and Delius and Mendelssohn.'

'Well, don't forget Vaughan Williams. He didn't get going until he was nearly twenty-five.'

'Oh, yes. So he didn't.'

Despair recedes a touch.

She folds her arms. 'I should think by that reckoning you've at least three more years before we can write you off as an absolute failure and all hope is lost.'

She smiles at me with that funny lopsided smile and even though she's teasing me, I feel a ruffle of optimism.

~

The following day Edie takes the train back up to town for a concert, and George leaves with her, whether for business or out of squeamishness in not wanting to be here so close to the end, I'm not sure. The morning after they depart I'm up before dawn and hurrying across the lawn before the others are awake. Knowing that in a matter of a week – no, less: six days – the house will be gone, I want it over. I'm in a prison cell, counting the hours until my execution. Afterwards, I may not go back up to Cambridge but instead venture abroad for a while. I hear there is a folk-song hoard in the Appalachian Mountains. Perhaps I will travel to the USA and gather up songs over there. And then the thought of being away from Edie makes me feel sick, like having a sudden hangover.

Farmhands have started to empty Hartgrove Hall of the few pieces of decent furniture and stack them in one of the barns. I wonder where the General will go – I presume to his occasional wartime lair, the bungalow on the other side of the hill – but I can't bring myself to ask him. I can't forgive him. He hasn't asked us where we'll go or what we'll do. In fact he carries on precisely as before, taking his breakfast with *The Times* in the morning room, Chivers bringing him coffee and rolls and marmalade from Fortnum's. He clearly intends to spend his last few days in the house as he has spent the previous sixty-eight years, barring the inconvenient interruptions brought by two world wars. For an awful moment I wonder whether he means to go down with the ship, sitting at the breakfast table with his newspaper and his jar of marmalade with its silver spoon as the house falls around him, burying him in the rubble.

I want to be far away and I can't bear to leave. I walk up to the ridge as dawn breaks behind the hill, setting the gorse and the brambles ablaze for an instant. It's cool and the ground is thick with dew; thousands of spiders' webs wobble in the grass, catching the light and looking like the corners of discarded lace handkerchiefs. As I hurry up the steep slope, I realise that I've spent the last few days tramping my favourite walks, bidding them goodbye. The routes I've taken to collect songs in pubs and farm cottages have corresponded exactly with an internal map of the places I love the most. I've been walking the path of my own memories, and, if I think about it, I could trace the last few days by singing the songs I've collected along the way – 'The Foggy Dew' from a gardener unearthing rows of wet brown carrots at the rectory in Belchalwell, through 'The Banks of Sweet Primrose' sung by a pair of labourers burning a pyre of dung at Hedge End, to 'The Spotted Cow' sung by the curate of Woolland, red faced and fastidiously removing his dog collar before he'd sing such an irreverent tune.

I've created an elaborate song-map of Hartgrove, of her hills and barrows and dells and woods. I know that, in years to come, I can find my way here again by singing. Perhaps it's the impending grief of losing our home, but I find myself retreating from the rational and into myth. I hoard songs and stories, visions of a better, older world. I don't know whether they were ever true, these ballads of clear crystal streams and weeping birds, but I wish I could slide inside a song and escape there for the duration of the melody.

Despite the brightness of the morning I feel dreary and grim. My shoelace snaps and I curse, profoundly irritated as I try to knot the frayed pieces back together. I cast about for Max Coffin, the shepherd, and I spy him resting at the top of the field, half concealed by the hedge, but as I draw closer I see that he's not resting but crouched over the bloodied body of a dead sheep. It's been badly mauled and a tangle of red guts spews out across the grass, early flies gathering.

'Dog,' says Max miserably. 'Third bloody sheep lost this week. Sat up all night wi' a shotgun but seen nothin'. Mus' be a dog blacker 'n hell an' quieter.'

'I'm sorry,' I say.

Max shrugs. 'Weren't your dog. See, she's still warm. If we get 'er to the house quick like, I can cut her up and still git sommat for her.'

I grab the forelegs and help Max heave the body into a wheelbarrow he's conjured from somewhere. The sheep's legs stick up in the air, stiff and ungainly. We wheel the unlikely load along the track at the top of the ridge, jolting in the deep ruts so that once or twice the corpse is thrown out and we have to haul it back in. After ten minutes we reach the dewpond marking the entrance to Ringmoor. The air is cool but I'm sweating from the exertion, though to my shame I see that Max isn't even out of breath. He's a slight man, somewhere between forty-five and sixty – his face aged and weathered but his arms revealing tight coils of muscles. His hair was once red but is mostly fading to white.

I sit on the garden wall while he discards his shirt, brings out a knife and starts to butcher the sheep, nimbly slitting the belly and letting the rest of the guts tumble out into a bucket, before starting to peel back the fleecy skin. He works quickly and cleanly, grunting a little with the effort, his hands slippery with blood.

'Right, you can help me string 'er up in the shed.'

Hoisting the remains over his shoulder, he leads me into a small flint shed beside the cottage. It's chilly inside, cold as a larder, with the wind blowing through the holes in the walls and under the corrugated-iron roof. A rope is strung up across the joists from which dangle socks and a few shirts. Max motions to me to make space and we hang the sheep upside down, fastening its hind legs to the washing line. It looks mighty strange, swinging there amongst the laundry.

We retreat outside and I sit on a tree stump as Max disappears to wash. I wonder vaguely where he gets his water – I expect with buckets from the spring. He reappears, clean and proffering a tin mug of tea. I take it, grateful. It's sweetened with ewe's milk and has an odd, sour smell, not unpleasant.

'You're wanting songs, you say.'

'Yes. I'm hoping you'll sing me something.'

'Well, since yer helped me wi' the sheep. Sure yer wouldn't like a few chops better?'

'I'll take them too.'

He chuckles. 'What you going ter do wi' the songs, once you got them?'

I dislike this question immensely and I swallow a sigh. A headache ticks in my temple. 'For now I write them down in a book.' I hold out my pad to him, realising as I do that it's streaked with brownish blood. 'Sometimes I send copies off to London and they add them to a bigger collection there.'

Max frowns. 'If yer lookin' fer new songs, yer bang out o' luck. I ent learned nothin' new fer years.'

'No, no – those are exactly what I do want to hear. I want old songs. Maybe even ones that haven't been collected before.'

'So there are other such—' he pauses, hunting for the appropriate description, 'other such "gentlemen" as yourself?'

He says 'gentlemen' but his tone implies 'perfect idiots'.

'Yes, there are others like me. Not many but a few. We're all folk-song enthusiasts. Song collectors, I suppose.'

'Song collectors?' He nods and slurps his tea to hide a smile. I have an image of how he sees us – as tweed-clad fools, rushing around the countryside with nets like butterfly hunters and specimen jars stuffed with songs.

'Will you sing?' I ask.

He shrugs. 'You can have a song fer summer. A song away from its time and place is jist a purty ditty. Something for little girls ter warble. This is a song calling fer rain ter come before autumn. I need more sun and a bit o' rain or these 'ere lambs will starve out 'ere on the hillside come winter. This ent no parlour tune. My father sang it ter me, and his father ter 'im. And I ent got no son, so I suppose I'll 'ave ter sing it ter you. Collector or not. But don't jist pin my song in a book, so he curls up at the edges like a dead thing.'

'All right,' I say, 'I won't.'

He closes his eyes and starts to sing. He calls to the wind and curses the rain and the sky and the cruelty of fate that leaves him out on the bare hillside while rich men snooze by their fires. His voice shakes with fervour, and there's an anger, raw and fierce, and he is both the singer and the song. This isn't a sentimental lament ruing some idealised past but a personal cry. The sound, which seems to grow from the soil itself, is somehow familiar, as though I've heard it before and forgotten. I want to catch hold of it, to fix this moment, and then he stops and it's lost, but so am I.

'Come back in the snow, and I'll sing yer another,' says Max, laughing, pleased at the effect his singing has had on me and I nod, dazed as a drunken man.

I stumble down the hill, ears ringing with music, both remembered and remade, as Max's melody starts to re-thread its way into another piece, something symphonic, a shout of horns and then the shrill of a flute. It comes to me with a mixture of wonder and relief. I swear I hear a trumpet blasting brightly through the woods. The pleasure is rich and dark. It's almost as I imagined sex would be. I've an idea at last and I think it might be something. I shout at the heather with great whoops of joy. I've boasted to girls in Cambridge bars that I'm a song collector and a composer when I've never written anything other than the odd ditty to amuse my brothers – the musical equivalent of a dirty limerick, not exactly a great symphonic work. But, oh God, this is different.

I shudder. Max's melody moves through me like a pulse, already changing into something else. It has the heart of the shepherd's tune but it catches in the wind and is blown wide. There's a ripple of harps and beneath that a syncopated rumble of strings like river water moving through reeds.

I need to write it down. I run.

I don't see Jack and George until I nearly bash into them. Jack grabs my arm.

'Steady on,' he says. 'Where are you going in such a hurry?'

I shake him off, angry, not taking in the fact that George has returned. 'I have to write,' I say and walk away.

'You can't,' he says. 'You have to wait.'

'Listen,' says George, and I want to tell him that I can't listen, my head is too full of music, there's a crowd in there and there simply isn't room for anyone else.

'Five minutes,' says George.

'Please,' says Jack.

We sit at the edge of the lake. Willows dip their fronds into the water like girls washing their hair. It's cold and a fine film of rain starts to fall but we stay right where we are.

'It's possible we can save the house,' says George. 'We'll certainly have to sell a couple of the larger farms but we must be careful not to sell too much acreage. I've done all the sums. We'll work on the land – all three of us. We can't afford to employ more than one or two other chaps to help. After Canning goes we can't possibly afford a new estate manager so we'll have to do that ourselves. And then we might make the thing work. I talked it through with Canning and he agrees it's possible. Unlikely but possible.'

Canning has never been unfairly accused of being an optimist. If he concedes that it's possible, it must be true. I allow myself to hope. I'll have to change the music. The first movement won't be so dirgelike. There'll need to be something greener in the strings. Instead of a symphonic lament, it will be a portrait of a great house and her family. The melody will be fragmented at the start, and then gradually piece together, a section at a time.

Jack stretches out his legs, kicking idly at a log. 'It's all right for me. I don't really know what else to do. I'm brilliantly inept at most things. I'm far too stupid for the law and too ungodly for the Church. I think farming will suit me.'

Silently I agree. Most things suit Jack.

'What does Father say?'

Jack grimaces.

'We haven't spoken to him yet. We'll do it together.'

This has always been the agreement. We approach the General united. No matter who broke the greenhouse window with the cricket ball, or dared me to jump off the barn roof so that I broke my arm; even when Jack decided to leave Cambridge after a term, we all faced the General as a battalion. George skims a pebble over the smooth surface of the lake. It bounces half a dozen times and sinks.

'You understand what this means, Fox? You'll have to come down from Cambridge. We need you here. We'll all have to work here. It'll be jolly hard. Bloody. There won't be time for anything else.'

I can't meet George's eye. I say nothing. I understand perfectly, better than George does. It means there will be no time for music. They're asking me to choose the life of a farmer instead of that of a musician. He can't understand the cost of what he's asking. I've the idea for my first real symphony, something grand and orchestral, and they tell me there is no time for music.

My brothers are watching me and I know they're bewildered by my silence, my lack of enthusiasm. They want only to save the house. They want nothing else. I see the roof of Turnworth House rise and linger in the air for a moment that stretches and then breaks.

Max's song buzzes in my ears. I've not written it down yet and a headache in shades of purple and white is building behind my eyes.

'And what about Edie?' I ask. I want them to stop scrutinising me with leery disappointment.

Jack colours, a real hot pink. 'We're getting married,' he says. 'She's putting up her money to help save the house. I said I'd let her only if she agreed to marry me.'

And the axe falls. It was always going to but, as it does, I'm winded, as breathless as if Jack had slammed into me full force. I lie back on the wet ground, feeling the earth ooze beneath my fingers.

'Of course I'm game,' I say. Not because I care more about the house now it's to be Edie's home too, but because nothing matters at all.

The melody in my head changes key again. The green in the strings fades to grey.

They slap my shoulders and holler, and I somehow remember to congratulate Jack, but I'm perfectly numb and weightless. As their shouts bounce across the lake like George's skimmed stones, the drizzle thickens into rain, dimpling the surface of the water.

~

Chivers summons us into the study, where he lingers behind the General's chair. He's promised to put in a good word. I watch the two of them as Jack talks. They're perfectly at ease together. This union has been happier and longer-lived than most marriages. It's certainly lasted longer than my father's marriage to my mother.

'And you all agree?' says the General. 'Even you, Little Fox? Always thought you'd do something with music or whatnot. You seem an unlikely farmer. More unlikely than the others, if that's possible.'

I'm taken aback by his solicitation. I nod. 'I want to save the house, Father. I'm needed here.'

'We do need him, if we're to have a hope,' says George.

'And what does Canning say?'

'He believes it is indeed possible, Father. He's hopeful.'

We are careful not to upgrade the dour Mr Canning's declaration too far into optimism or it will cease to be believable.

'Harrumph,' says the General, or at least that is what I think he says. It's possible he's merely clearing his throat.

'Will you at least think on it, Father?' asks Jack.

'This house, this land, it belongs to all of us,' says George, veering dangerously from the script.

The General looks up sharply and settles on George with a grim expression, close to dislike.

'No it doesn't. Don't think that for a moment. It belongs in its entirety to me. And, if there is anything left to inherit, it will pass in its entirety to Jack. And, when he has a son, it will go to him.'

George shakes slightly and there is a tiny tic in the corner of his left eye, but then he swallows. 'My apologies, sir. I misspoke.'

Are George and I quite superfluous to him? Jack is his heir and we are merely insurance policies. The light catches the gold of the General's watch. I can't believe it of him. It's cold in the study. The General never allows a fire to be lit in his room in the afternoon. Warmth breeds softness in a man. And softness, like buggery after Eton, is a sin.

We are dismissed. Chivers opens the door for us, and we retreat to the frigid drawing room, as men are supposed to do, instead of to the cosiness of the kitchen, not wishing to invoke the General's disapproval today at least. We sit. We fidget. I try to write but I'm restless and unhappy and that sense of glorious certainty has dissipated like sunshine into rain. Jack smokes. My jealousy of him ebbs momentarily as I wonder vaguely about how the General will react to the news of the new lady of Hartgrove being a singer and an entertainer. Perhaps her fame will ease the shame.

~

Days come and go. The General gives us no answer. Chivers remains perfectly inscrutable and offers no indication one way or the other. Early one morning I find George burning the corpses of half a dozen rabbits beside the stables.

'It's a sacrifice,' he says before I even have a chance to ask. 'Highland fellow in my regiment told me it's what they do up north. A great house must have a great sacrifice. Thought it was worth a go.'

I cough, spluttering on the stink of burning fur. 'Rabbits? Not much of a sacrifice, though, are they? Stringy little things.'

George looks worried. 'Blast it. You're probably right. I should find something bigger. A deer should do it.'

'Don't you dare,' I tell him. 'If you shoot venison and burn it rather than serving it up to the General, you'll be hindering our cause, not helping it.'

He gives a rueful smile. 'I suppose you're right. Anyway. The old ways of Scotland probably don't hold much sway across the border.'

I make no further comment but study George with some concern. I'm sure that, before the army, he smiled more. At night, I hear him walking up and down in his room above mine, his footsteps creaking along the floorboards.

I wonder whether I should leave. Find somewhere quiet and with a decent piano where I can try to write while I still can. Then Edie arrives back at the Hall and I'm stuck in quicksand.

I make notes for my composition but I can't get even a fix on the main theme. I need a piano to try it out on but the one in the drawing room has finally surrendered to the damp. When I sit down to play, a dozen keys ping off as my fingers touch them and spray onto the floor like an old woman spitting out a mouthful of loose teeth. Disgusted, I close the lid. I'm reduced to sitting at the piano and trying to work through the melody by tapping it out on the lid but it's quite hopeless. I take a cigarette from Jack and watch from the window as the rain moves across the hills.

'Do either of you know the least thing about farming?' I ask.

'The least thing,' says Jack. 'But I have an unwavering belief in myself.'

'George?'

'I thought I might take a course,' he says, emerging from his seed catalogue. 'And I remember some things.'

'Oh God,' I say. And I wonder whether perhaps it would be for the best if the General rejects our plan and the old gal is put out of her misery quickly with a touch of dynamite.

I'm tired. Ghosts of the melodies rush through my dreams, but when I wake and try to pin them on the page, they've gone again. Instead of sleeping, I lie awake and think of Edie. It's a terrible thing to covet your brother's girl. I suppose the only thing worse is to covet your brother's wife. They have not said when they will marry and I do not ask. I tell myself that it will be on some distant date and the wedding may, in fact, never even take place. I try not to watch her, but she's my compass point. When she's in the room, I know where she is and what she's doing – finding a record for the ancient gramophone, hunting for her spectacles so she can sit at the bureau and answer letters.

She sees me fumbling a tune on the piano lid.

'What on earth are you doing?'

I open the piano and show her the ruined instrument.

She sighs. 'What a pity. She must have been a beauty once.'

I'm struck with nostalgia. Edie's right, this piano was young once and couples danced to her music. It's not the piano's fault that she decayed in this damp and mouldering house. I'm frightened that, if I stay, I'll end up like the piano.

'What are you trying to play?' she asks.

Instinctively, I clutch the manuscript pages to my chest. I can't bear for anyone to look until I'm finished but Edie prises them from my grasp.

'It's the main theme for the orchestral piece I'm sketching. I can't get the phrasing right. I just can't hear it.'

'Give me a C.'

I hum it for her and then she sings carefully through the melody. At once I hear the error.

'Wait a tick.'

I mark in the changes.

'Try now.'

She sings again, and I feel a flutter in my chest. Yes.

'That's it.'

I'm taken aback by how good it sounds.

'It's peculiar, plaintive and yet it sticks with you. I rather like it. Reminds me a bit of Butterworth but it's different,' says Edie.

As the others chatter, I withdraw to the chill of the morning room to write. Now, I hear her voice singing the melody and I start to work in earnest.

In the coming days I alternate between writing music and pining for Edie, listening with some resentment to Jack's cheerful complaints about the endless summer rain. I think I would be less miserable about her, I decide, if I wasn't still a virgin. I really ought to drown my sorrows in other women. Cambridge is full of women who're broad-minded about sex. Or so I've heard. I've never actually met such a woman in Cambridge and now, I suppose, utterly depressed, I never will.

Coming into the drawing room, I look out to see that Hartgrove Hill has vanished entirely into the mist but I still feel its pull. Anyone born in its shadow is caught, so they say. I know that during the war years, when I was away at school surrounded by the pretty orderliness of Windsor town, I found myself walking the Ridgeway at night. I wonder whether Jack and George dreamed of it while in Egypt or Poland.

I turn away and sit beside George who stares fixedly at a guide to soil types.

The door opens. The General appears.

'A decision has been made,' he announces as though it were from a committee of twelve rather than himself. We rise like prisoners awaiting sentence.

'You have one year to run the estate.'

George splutters in rage. 'One year? Quite impossible. How can we repair a generation of neglect in a single year? You might as well blow up the damn place right away.'

'Well, if that's what you prefer,' replies the General coolly. 'Otherwise you may have a year. The decision is Jack's. It's his inheritance.'

Jack glances at George, silently urging him to contain his fury. 'We'll take the year, Father.'

Our father turns to look at me. He studies me with quiet interest. 'And you, Little Fox? You really want to be part of this scheme?'

I feel my brothers watching me. I swallow, feeling cold patches of sweat bloom beneath my shirt. 'Yes, sir. I do.'

So this is it then. It's to be the house rather than music. I'm terribly glad and desperately miserable all at once. I wonder whether I shall ever finish my symphony. With a pang, I realise I really shall miss my Cambridge chums. They're decent sorts and one or two of them are decent enough musicians. Perhaps one day I'll tempt them down to wassail the hedgerows.

'Well then.' The General checks his watch. 'Time to dress for dinner.'

We haven't dressed for dinner since the war but no sooner is the General out of the room than a gong booms through the house. I'd forgotten all about it. In the years before the war that gong governed us all. Several evenings each week during the school holidays I was permitted to dine downstairs. The dampening effect of the General's presence ensured it was a rather subdued affair but I always looked forward to it on account of the dining-room puddings –

infinitely better than those served in the nursery. The gong calls again, at once deep and bright, reverberating through the hall, up the stairs and through the attics until I see its sound flying out of the chimney in a volley of crimson sparks. We are here. We are awakened, it cries. I see in the shining faces of my brothers that they believe in its music. I smile and hope for their sakes.

Dinner is jollier than I'd expected. Three of Edie's friends arrive by train and Chivers is forced to re-lay the table for eight. I think they've had a drop of grog in the dining car on the way down, as they arrive pink-cheeked and giggling.

'This is Josie, Betty and Sal,' says Edie, pulling them into the blue drawing room, her arm linked through theirs, a paper chain of girls. They glance about them, ogling the ornate cornicing, the tattered blue silk wallpaper, the plaster birds in flight across the improbably high ceiling. Despite the decay, nothing can hide the elegant proportions of the room, the pleasing symmetry. The floorboards are oak, broad, thick and ancient.

'Delighted to meet you all,' says Jack, kissing each of them on the cheek and making them giggle louder still.

'Yes, quite,' says the General, not looking delighted in the least.

George blinks, nods and retreats to the fire, which to my relief has been lit. The smell of smoking logs now wars with the pervasive odour of damp.

Edie catches my hand and draws me to the trio of girls – their hair is the exact same shade of blonde. As they continue to tremble with laughter, they remind me of a clump of shaking yellow daffodils.

'And this is Little Fox, whom I've been telling you about,' she says with a smile.

'Doesn't look so little to me,' says Josie, though it might be Betty.

'Pleased to meet you.' I offer my hand and they shake it in turn with pious formality. I know they're teasing me.

'You're the musical one. The singer,' says Josie, though again it might be Betty.

'I can hold a tune but I'm afraid that I'm no singer. And you, ladies? Are you also singers?'

'We can hold a tune,' says Sal archly, the youngest of the three and, going by her accent, American. I've not met an American woman before and she's imbued with instant glamour. Her dark eyebrows war with the yellow of her hair.

Edie whispers some remark and the three women are awash with laughter once again. The General clutches his whisky glass so tightly that I wonder it doesn't shatter. Edie, slight, dark, reserved, is nothing like these girls but she seems perfectly at ease and unembarrassed. Although she notices the General's displeasure, it does not concern her and I'm awed. If it's possible, I adore her even more.

'We've performed around the world together,' Edie says, quietly.

'Though I'm afraid we're not such a class act as Edie here,' adds Sal, giving Edie's arm a little squeeze. She surveys the room with frank curiosity. 'I've never been to a house like this before. It's awful big. And awful cold.' She rubs her thin arms. 'Can't you heat it right?'

As the General pales at her American audacity, Jack throws back his head and roars with laughter. 'No, my dear girl, we can't. We're terribly poor.'

'No you're not,' says Sal, with a hint of steel. 'You ain't got enough ready money is all. Don't mistake that for being poor.'

I smile and decide that I like Sal very much. Edie catches my eye and I wink. Tonight isn't going to be as frightful as I'd feared. It might even be fun.

Dinner is a hoot. The girls can send up anyone or anything. They're perfect mimics. Sal, skinny and bright as a polished sixpence, can do a brilliant Churchill. She leans forward and frowns, her shrill, girlish voice becoming the familiar growl, and she wobbles her jowls. I glance at the General, who's quite forgotten to disapprove. George is quiet but he looks happy for the first time I can remember.

The food is pleasant – the best that can be said of anything that has appeared from the kitchen in the last several months – and the wine excellent. That's one thing about the General: he's never mean with his cellar. With a nod and a murmur, Chivers reappears again and again with bottle after bottle.

When the pudding has been cleared away, Edie stands. 'Come along, ladies, let's leave the gentlemen to their brandy.'

Sal pouts. 'I'm very partial to a brandy.'

'Come,' says Edie, more sharply, and they follow her to the drawing room with only a warble of reluctance.

After they leave, the dining room is abruptly silent. All the warmth and humour have been extinguished. We sit and clasp our glasses, feeling dull and uneasy. I wonder how long the General will force us to remain here. Long enough to punish us for the unexpected guests, I presume.

'So you're to marry the little Jewess,' he remarks to Jack.

Jack flinches. I stare at him and then look away.

I didn't know Edie was Jewish. I wonder how on earth the General can tell. I conjure her face in every detail, scrutinising her for hidden exoticism. I can't find any. I'm stung that she hasn't told me herself. I thought we were pals, she and I. Then perhaps she presumed I knew and maybe it's the sort of thing that I ought to have known all along. I feel terribly stupid. Naively, I realise now, I'd imagined all Jews to be like the bearded fellows in tall black hats I've glimpsed occasionally on trips to London. I don't think I know any other Jews apart from Edie. Then I wonder whether I actually know heaps of them and have simply been unaware.

I glance at the General who's redder around the chops than usual. He's clearly furious. For him a Jew is worse than a common singer or even a Catholic. No wonder Jack hasn't uttered a word to him about the engagement. For a moment alarm at our father's rage staunches my jealousy of my brother.

The General laughs. 'Come, come. I've spared you the bother of telling me. See? I'm not quite the fool you all think.'

Jack swallows. A vein ticks at his throat. 'I love Edie and she's agreed to marry me.'

'Then you're the fool. With your crackpot scheme you need a good country girl. Someone bosomy and sensible who knows about running a farm. A nice young girl. Not some little-titted Jewey singer. She looks good, I grant you, but she must be getting on a bit.'

Jack rises to his feet and I think he's going to strike our father but George grabs his wrist and holds him back. 'Don't,' he murmurs. The General is chuckling. His anger is making him spiteful.

'Don't you dare speak about my wife in that way,' says Jack, white as a ghost.

'When she's your wife, I shan't,' says the General serenely. 'But if you do want to save the old place, I urge you to reconsider. She doesn't love Hartgrove Hall; she loves you. And that isn't good enough. A house like this won't tolerate another mistress. She wants all of you. All your money. And your soul. I wouldn't give her mine, and look what happened.' The General points a finger at a florid damp stain blooming in the middle of the ceiling rose.

I don't recall ever having heard the General talk so much. I wonder to whom or to what he gave his soul. The army, I suppose. He drains his brandy, pushes it away and, leaning back in his chair, studies each of us before turning back to Jack.

'And of course it doesn't help that George and Little Fox are quite besotted with the girl too. Can't think why. Not my type at all.'

Jack stares at George and then at me, aghast, and I hate my father. My hate is hot and sharp. He has taken something private that is both painful and a solace – in the dark I retreat to thoughts of Edie – but in making it public, he has made it ugly. George and I both avoid Jack's eye but we catch one another's. Guiltily, we look away. The General rises to his feet, sporting a tiny smug smile beneath the uptick of his moustache.

'Well, gentlemen, shall we go through to the ladies? I believe we've kept them waiting long enough.'

We follow. I am light-headed with anger and humiliation.

Thank God the girls are there. They can tell that something has happened. Edie raises an eyebrow at Jack who shakes his head and goes straight to the whisky decanter, pouring himself a large measure, sufficient to get properly sloshed. Josie and Betty try to draw George into conversation but he hunches in a chair beside the fire, barely seeming to hear them. The lightness and pleasure of earlier in the evening has popped as swiftly as the bubbles in a glass of champagne.

'Some music!' says Sal, clapping her hands. She's right beside me and I hadn't noticed her. I'm as bad as George.

'The piano's bust,' I say. 'And the gramophone's simply awful.'

Sal shrugs. 'We'll have to sing then.'

The three blonde girls conspire in a rustle of whispers and then launch into a medley of caramel wartime hits. We

applaud politely, the General alone with any volume or enthusiasm – his earlier revelation has clearly put him in a splendid
humour. I can't bear these trinket songs – I won't call them
music – but I smile enough not to be rude. Jack is the only one
who professes to enjoy them, but tonight even he is remote
and distracted.

Edie frowns. 'I'm afraid you'll have to try something else,'
she calls at the end. 'Fox just loathes those fancy, feel-good
numbers.'

Sal turns to me, throwing up her arms in mock offence.
'Not smart enough for you, are we? Only Beethoven good
enough for you?'

'Not at all. Where are you from?'

'Texas.'

'Then sing me a song from there. Something your mama
sang to you when you were young.'

Laughing, she rebukes me. 'You've got it all wrong, mister.
I ain't no farm girl and my mama didn't sing to me.'

She studies me and for the first time I grasp that behind her
bluster and pretend indignation she's curious about me.

Jack and Edie feign tiredness and disappear to bed, keeping up a charade of decency by going fifteen minutes apart.
The others vanish soon after until George and I are left alone.
It's some time before we can look at one another. At last I
turn to him.

'So you too?' I say.

He nods, miserable.

I pour him another drink. We never speak of it again.

～

I presume that Jack has told Edie, but she must be a fine
actress because, even when searching for it, I detect no
change in her manner towards either George or me. There is

no hint of pity nor condescension, no coquettish smiles. She's her usual self – lively, friendly and slightly reserved. I can't shake the sense that none of us really knows her, not even Jack. She professes to be thrilled that we're going to save the house – that's how we speak of it, never acknowledging that we've merely been granted a year's reprieve, not a stay of execution. She makes no comment on the fact that we all know she's Jewish and not quite one of us. Since she doesn't acknowledge it, outwardly it makes no difference to things at all. Yet I wonder about her even more than before, hoping for snippets about her family or herself that she declines to give. She plays her part, knocking up aprons and work clothes on an old sewing machine that she lugs down on the train from London and even persuading Sal to stay for another fortnight to help.

I attempt a show of enthusiasm but really I want to steal away and work on my composition. The first movement is sketched and I've a super idea for the second. I long for a cello to try it out but instead I'm walking with the others across waterlogged fields, surveying the estate. Sal strides up the hill in home-made trousers that are far too big and held up with a pair of braces but on Sal they look good, as if she's posing for a shot in a magazine. She pauses below the ridge and scrutinises George's notes.

'This soil is thin. Exhausted like the rest of you. You'd be crazy to try anything but grazing here.' She turns to George. 'But you gonna be crazy, aren't you?'

He grins. Everyone likes Sal.

I study her, thin as a rod of hazel; the garish bottle-blonde of her hair has faded and a ripe catkin brown is showing through. 'You lied,' I say.

'Excuse me?' she asks, hands planted on her hips.

'You said you weren't a farm girl. You lied.'

She throws back her head and roars with laughter. 'You got

me there. Don't like to be put in a box is all. I like to be able to stretch out.'

She stretches her arms high above her head as if to prove her point, revealing a sliver of smooth, freckled belly.

We walk for the rest of the afternoon but I can't shake the feeling that it's a game; we're children playing make-believe. George has his notebook and writes copiously in it but I worry that he knows little more about how to run an estate than Jack or I do. Until the war, our boyhood was spent outside, roaming the hills and woods or fishing in the rivers. We'd helped at harvest time when every man, woman and boy was called out into the fields to gather in the wheat or tidy hay into bales before it could be spoiled by the frost, but it was a carnival where, as the General's offspring, we were indulged, our presence tolerated rather than required.

The General never encouraged us to understand the day-to-day running of the farms. Since he took no interest himself, it never occurred to him that his sons ought to be involved. The tenant farms operated as a series of fiefdoms, each farmer the king of his own onions, sheep or cattle. As far as we were concerned this was a world that would never end. The house and the farms might be run-down but we'd limped along for years and years, untroubled by poorly hung gates and rotting fences. Life would continue as it always had and we had no reason to take more than an idle, pleasurable interest. I suppose I ought to wish now that we'd dangled less for trout and collected fewer birds' nests but helped more with lambing and crop rotations.

For the first few days we discuss our future plans with Canning – George agrees to suspend his dislike. He blames Canning for mismanaging the estate – I'm not so sure. I think the man did the best he could, bustling between the dictates coming from the Ministry of Agriculture and the General, who was away in London for months on end or hunkered down in his bungalow for the odd weekend, shooting rabbits and declining to sign either paperwork or cheques. I'm surprised he lasted as long as he did.

However, after a week of watching Canning suck his teeth and shake his head as he declares, 'No, no, I shouldn't do that, it won't work at all,' I agree with George that ignorance is probably better than Canning. We have neither cash, experience, knowledge nor manpower. All we have is optimism and Canning is running through that at such a lick that we send him off to his retirement in Bournemouth a week early with a bottle of Scotch for thanks.

We agree to leave the tenant farmers alone. We need the rental income and, frankly, we can barely fathom how to cope with the land we do have. There are seven hundred ewes and lambs scattered across the higher ground, while the rest is in a rotation of wheat, barley and grass. The crops are ripening in the fine weather and we are in the lull before harvest, where, if I put my ear to the ground, I can almost hear the grass pushing up through the soil. Beside us an adder bakes in the sun, a smooth hot muscle.

George is determined to use this month of quiet to learn everything he can. He's bemused by the acres of stunted yellow wheat at the bottom of the hill.

'It's unhappy. Wheat doesn't like the wet and it's marshland there by the river. I want to get rid of it all. We should have cows. The vale is supposed to have cows.'

'Where did you hear that?' I ask. 'Why are we "supposed" to have cows?'

He hesitates and Jack senses weakness. 'Yes, George, why the sudden preoccupation with cows?'

George studies his feet. 'It's in Hardy,' he mutters.

'I beg your pardon?'

'Thomas Hardy. *Tess of the D'Urbervilles* to be precise. Hartgrove Hall is slap bang in the middle of the "Valley of the

Little Dairies" in *Tess*. So we shouldn't be breaking our hearts and sowing the hillside with wheat that can't grow properly, when what we ought to be doing is buying three hundred head of dairy cows.'

'George, just to be clear, our reference guide isn't *The Farmer's Almanac* but *Tess of the D'Urbervilles*?'

George plunges his hands deep into his pockets and won't say another word.

'Who's going to milk the three hundred cows?'

George shakes his head, refusing to be drawn, but I can tell from the line of his mouth that he's not finished with the notion.

Apart from us, the only one who knows anything about farming is Sal, but I'm not convinced that her knowledge of Texas cattle ranching is going to be terribly helpful for farming three hundred acres of Dorset clay and chalk.

Warding off despondency, we sit on the top of the ridge, eating stale biscuits and trying to feel restored by the glorious sunshine and the spread of green fields below. A woodpecker hammers for his lunch in a percussive volley of semi-quavers. I stand and find to my disgust that pellets of sheep turd are stuck to my trousers.

'I'm going back to the house,' I call.

'We haven't finished,' says George.

'Haven't finished what?' I ask. 'We've been walking aimlessly. I'm tired of listening to you talk about crop rotations and cows. Sal's right, the soil on this part of the hillside is dreadful. It's only good for sheep. We need more but we haven't any money and no one's daft enough to lend it to us.'

I'm tired and angry and I don't like the fact that Jack hardly speaks to me. He's cordial and as pleasant as a stranger. We've never been polite to one another before. He's not asked me for a favour nor taken advantage of my good nature in more than a week and I can't stand it. I want him and Edie far away. I know I'm being unfair but I can't help it. I want to write. The frustration is making me ill-tempered and miserable.

~

George and I harvest a small field of potatoes. It's a sweaty and filthy task and after eight hours the palms of our hands are blistered, but even with the assistance of two chaps from the village – the only labourers we can afford – our progress is paltry. It's too hot, and the dust and muck dry our throats. My fingertips bleed, the blood running into the mud.

And yet there is a satisfaction to the work. The rhythms come back to me, as familiar as a tune, forgotten for a while and then heard again suddenly, unexpectedly out of the mouth of a different singer. We spent our childhoods in these fields, these woods. I'm ten again, returned to glorious August days, warm and blue. We rise at dawn and fall into bed as the moon rises above Hartgrove Hill. I sing work tunes as we bend and sift. We ignore the gong and we do not dress for dinner.

George never seems to tire. He learns fast. As I watch, he seems to ripen and grow as quickly as a cricket willow, only thicker and more solid. I like to watch him work. He moves through the fields, stooping to fasten bales of hay, and hoisting them up on his shoulders with the smoothness of a dancer, while I sweat and Jack pants in the shade. George is not an elegant man. He's tall and broad, and he fidgets as though his skin is a size too big, but outside under the sky and the broad back of the hill, he's at ease. His reserve fits out here; the starlings and the wood pigeons and the wind through the leaves make enough noise. Lost and uneasy amidst drawing-room small talk, George is the quiet and steady centre here amongst the hedgerows and the winding streams.

In the evenings we all gather with bottles of wine filched from the cellar and laze in the garden, watching the bats drift out of the eaves, listening to George. He knows how he wants the estate to be.

'A house like this should provide work for the village. We should be self-sufficient. The restoration needs to be careful. She needs to be nursed back to health but we have to listen to what she's telling us. And we need money for more sheep.'

'And some cows.'

'Definitely some cows. Lots of cows.' He smiles, not minding our ribbing any more.

The moon is full and high, its light weird and blue, making the lime trees cast shadows on the grass. We all lie back on the lawn, which is now cool and damp. Sal's head rests on my thigh and I see Edie curled against Jack. We smoke cigarettes and whisper. I watch the coil of black woods on the hillside; in the gloom they look like the fur of an animal, crouched and waiting.

'Sing something, Fox,' says Edie, reaching over to me.

I choose an old song about grief and faithless lovers and the foggy, foggy dew. After a line or two Edie sings with me and our voices drift through the dark. When we stop she sings another. It's an unfamiliar tune, and I listen acutely, memorising it. I don't recognise the words but I feel the sadness in the melody, sharp as wild mint.

George shows Jack and me how to drive the aged and cantankerous tractor around the yard. We take on another labourer from the village for the month and, between us, we manage pretty well. I like best to work at night, trundling up and down the fields, the tractor put-putting beneath the stars, the sliced soil glistening like broken glass. The harvest moon is like something from a painting, huge and orange, strung too low. On these nights we need no other light and I drive without headlamps, jolting across the ground, the wheels spitting up dirt and flint, jagged as splinters of bone.

Once we've gathered in the wheat, separated the chaff and baled up the straw, we start to burn the stubble at night, making the darkness crackle and turn red. George gets too close and singes his eyebrows.

The summer fades. As if a great door had been left open, the heat disappears in a rush, and one morning we rise to find the grass powdered with early frost. Golden leaves line the garden paths and freckle the lawns. Next comes the rain, turning the churned soil into mud. Edie and Sal evidently decide that they've had enough: they take a train to London for the afternoon but don't come back. A cable arrives before supper: REDISCOVERED JOY OF HOT BATHS STOP STAYING IN TOWN STOP SORRY STOP.

I should be glad that Edie has gone for a while – without her, Jack is almost his old self with George and me – but I am not. The house is the wrong kind of quiet. When she leaves so does any chance of music. The gates at the top of the hill by Ringmoor are rotten and need replacing but I can't help Jack with them as I promised. I'm a drunkard who needs a tipple.

In desperation I go to church for evensong. Not because I believe that God will grant me a reprieve or the strength to endure these cravings but to listen to the organ. It's a decent instrument, installed by a musically inclined rector at his own expense fifty years ago. The building itself is small, the grey stone smudged with lichen and moss. Part of the wall surrounding the churchyard has fallen down and sheep meander irreverently amongst the tombstones. The grave-yard is crowded with residents past – much busier than the village, which is inevitable, I suppose, as we all finish up there in the end.

If the vicar is surprised to see me, he's sensible enough not to comment, and I slide into a pew in the middle where I hope the acoustics will be best. But after three bars I realise that it doesn't make any difference where I sit, since the organist is astonishingly bad. It takes me the entire piece to grasp what it is that he's attempting to play. I'm desperate to leave. The vicar mumbles a greeting to the congregation and I stand, ready to slip away – but then the choir starts singing the first hymn. They're not really a choir: four large men piped like sausagemeat into straining woollen suits. The hymn is unremarkable although the tune is strange. It's not from the accepted hymnal but something older. Even though the organist tries to keep up, he's the fat boy playing at tag.

'Stop. For God's sake, just stop,' I shout to the organist.

He stops with a crash of chords but the vicar, outraged, scrambles to his feet, opening and closing his mouth like a fish. I ignore him. The choir has faltered, unsure whether my complaint was directed at them.

'Do go on,' I say, with a wave.

They glance at one another and then at the vicar who gives a pained nod. They start again to sing. At first I'm distracted by the trite and pious Victorian lyrics, presumably written by some bespectacled parson in his tidy parsonage, but lurking beneath, like flagstones under linoleum, is a rare Lydian melody with flowing arpeggios. The men sing it well, until I don't even hear the words. I close my eyes, drunk at last.

Afterwards, I retreat quickly, in no mood to listen to the vicar's objections to my behaviour. I hurry to the pub, presuming that the chaps from the choir will be along. I'm quite correct and they appear after a few minutes.

'Drinks for these gentlemen,' I call to the barman.

The choir nod their thanks and withdraw to a corner of the pub to drink in peace, but I pursue them.

'You sing jolly well.'

They grunt in acknowledgement, then wait for me to leave. I do not take the hint.

'Will you sing me something else?' I ask.

The men laugh, perfectly appalled, as if I'd asked them to strip naked. I've had a drink or three and I'm not willing to give up.

'I collect songs. Old songs from these parts. I bet you chaps know some.'

The oldest and fattest of the men looks at me properly for the first time. He releases a tiny sigh – I'm going to be tricky to dislodge.

'Aye. We might know some.'

'Dad's right. We've one or two.'

The son is only marginally less round than his father. Coaxing reluctant singers into performing is an art. I can't push too hard, yet I need to show them how much I want to listen. It's a delicate balance between enthusiasm and patience. These fellows mustn't be rushed. I take out a pipe: I learned to smoke one for precisely this purpose. Slowly I fill it with tobacco and sit back on the settle. I wave the pipe with feigned ease.

'Well, I think you're rather special and I'd love to hear you sing some of your own songs, not those religious bits and bobs, but your own music.'

They glance at one another and I know I've caught them. The fat man breaks out in a grin. 'I'm a cup too low ter sing.'

I signal to the barman to bring another round. They drink in steady silence. I let the smoke from my pipe drift and chew the stem. It's a disgusting thing, but it helps me focus my impatience.

'Now, how do you feel about a song or two?'

'Aye. Best have it now, otherwise we'll be a cup too many.'

The pub is half empty but the other drinkers are quite still, all listening even though they're pretending not to. The rotund

134

man beats a rhythm on the table. They take a breath and they sing. The walls of the pub fall away and we're out on the bare back of the hill, the black trees behind us. I recognise this song and it's an old one, older than Hartgrove Hall. Feet stamping on stone smash through the dark.

'Yes,' I say. 'Yes,' when they've finished. I close my eyes, draining the last drop of sound.

The fat man laughs. 'Yer the youngest of the Fox-Talbot boys, ent yer?'

'I'm afraid so,' I say.

'Knew yer mother,' he says. 'She wis just like yer. Fair hair and potty about music. Used ter play that organ in church.'

I'm still, I can't breathe for listening. 'My mother? You remember her?'

No one speaks of her. Not the chaps I know. The large man nods again and squeezes a hand into his waistcoat pocket. 'Them others are too young ter remember. But I knew her. Nice lady. Good organist. Better than that awful feller we 'ave now. I still miss Mrs Fox-Talbot.'

He looks at me for a moment, slowly recollecting things he hasn't thought about for years.

'She used ter bring you with her sometimes. In a basket like a kitten. Yer'd sleep by her feet while she played. I thought that racket would wake a baby. But no, she said yer liked it.'

I want to know what she played. Every piece. Every note. He can't remember – 'Oh, the usual stuff. Hymn tunes and that.'

This is a picture of my mother I've never seen before. I won't tell it to my brothers. This is mine. I have so little of her and I've been given another piece, an unexpected, blissful fragment.

As I sway home, I warble to myself, only slightly off-key. I kick a tin can, which bounces into the hedgerow. The tunes circle in my mind, round and round in a noisy carousel. I'll go home and I'll write them down before I fall asleep in a pleasant cider haze. And then certainty runs through me, cool as a winterbourne. I have the theme for the third movement of my symphony. These old folk tunes have taken root inside me, and caused something new to grow in my imagination. I hum the theme. Damn and blast – I need a piano. I wonder whether Edie knows where I can find one cheaply. With a hiccup of cider, I realise I haven't thought about her for several hours.

~

'We need a milking machine, not a piano,' says George.

'Why do we need a milking machine? We don't have any cows.' Frustration is making me belligerent.

'We can't afford to buy cows. So we definitely can't afford a piano.'

I swallow my irritation. 'I'm not buying one. Edie's persuaded someone in London to give it to me, but he wants to meet me first.'

I'm tired of the struggle. I simply can't manage without a piano. Jack has remained quiet throughout the squabble. He's torn. On the one hand, he doesn't think I should leave the farm and go off to London, but it's Edie who's arranged the loan of the piano and he can't show disloyalty to her.

'I'll be gone one day and one night.' I glance at George. 'I'll be back before you can say "Dorset longhorn".'

He grunts but doesn't laugh. Jack's trying not to smile. He winks at me.

'I'll nip down to the village and telephone Edie to let her know you're coming up to town.'

Jack knows how I feel about Edie, and yet I'm clearly such a pathetic rival that he's perfectly easy at the thought of my squiring her around London for a day or two. I'm both wounded and grateful, and my gratitude causes a bow-wave of self-loathing to wash over me. After he's gone, I decide to dedicate the rest of the evening and a bottle of Scotch to getting properly sloshed. Two glasses in, I decide with the absolute clarity of a drunk that I simply must persuade George that my collecting folk songs and writing music will be a good thing for all of us.

'The piano's not only for me, George.'

'Thing is, old sport, Jack and I don't play.'

'No, but I need it to play through the old songs I find. I can't transcribe them properly without a piano. The old songs I find are remarkable, George. They're going to save this place.'

'If you say so, Fox.'

'Whenever I'm lost, musically, I listen to these old tunes and they show me the way. They're like route maps.'

George glances at me dubiously over the top of the latest issue of the *Western Gazette*. 'I'm not lost, Fox. I'm in my pleasant, if draughty, sitting room.'

I sigh, take another swig of whisky and try another tack. 'So we don't know what's the best thing for the land on the hill? Well, we simply need to listen to some old songs from around here. If we listen properly, they'll tell us what to do.'

I can tell from his expression that George remains sceptical but I've drunk enough whisky to believe in my own extrapolations.

'The memory is in the melody. If we find songs gathered from right here we'll find out what the farmers used to do on the hillside.'

'So if they sing of sheep, we keep to sheep. If it's a vineyard they mention, we plant grapes.'

'Exactly. Well. Grapes might be more of a metaphor.'

'We'll plant metaphorical grapes, then. White or red?'

'You can rag me all you like, but you say that you want to listen to the land. So listen to the music. These songs are from here and are about here and they've been sung for longer than there've been bloody Fox-Talbots in Hartgrove Hall.'

George surveys me with amusement, which thoroughly incenses me.

'I can't think why you're being so obstinate about it. You're the one trying to find out how everything was done a hundred bloody years ago. Everyone else is tipping on sodding nitrates and maximising yields while we're raking up chicken shit.'

'And cow shit.'

'And pig and horse. But my point is that you don't want to increase mechanisation. You don't want fancy tractors and sprays. You say that the connection to the land matters and without it something is lost.'

'I do,' says George, eyeing me curiously.

'Music is the same thing. The songs are connected to the land. They're all part of the great dance.'

I'm feeling quite pleased with myself when I give an enormous hiccup, which I fear rather undercuts the impact. George smiles. 'I would like to bury that government leaflet on fertilisers and whatnot under the chicken coop.'

I jump to my feet. 'Yes. Let's do it. Let's bury the bloody thing.'

Five minutes later, we're shoving the latest government-issued whatnot into the midst of the vast, wobbling muckheap, a veritable Eiffel Tower of dung. I reach for a match but George holds back my arm.

'Steady on, old thing. Methane. Horribly flammable. Don't need to blow the place sky high after all.'

'No. Perhaps not.'

Swaying, I grasp the whisky bottle. I sip and pass it to George.

'I hear you at night, you know,' I say. 'Your room's above mine and I hear you walking about.'

'Oh, sorry about that, old chap. Always been a bit restless in the wee hours.'

'No you haven't. We used to share a room, remember.' I take the bottle back from him. 'When I can't sleep, I focus on a tune and sing it in my head. Over and over. You should try it.' I warble a simple ditty to George. 'Sing that when you can't sleep. It'll help block out anything else.'

Whether his sleeplessness is caused by thoughts of Edie or something else, I do not enquire.

I don't remember how I found my way back inside. I wake up on the sofa and the fire has petered out but beside me there's an envelope with a little cash. On the envelope George has written, 'Find us some songs then and a piano to bloody play them on. But I'm sure as hell not singing them.'

~

Edie meets me from the train. This version of her is a stranger. In her trim navy suit, curled hair and crimson lipstick she's more like the picture postcards of wartime sweetheart 'Edie Rose' than the girl I'm used to. I'm afraid to shake her hand. She kisses me on the cheek, smearing it with lipstick that she then tries to scrub away with her handkerchief.

'Stop, please,' I say. I don't want her pawing at me like an aunt. This isn't how I want her to think of me.

She withdraws. 'You're not meeting Mr Kenton until six. I thought we could go and have some lunch.'

'Splendid,' I say.

She takes me to Claridge's. It's supposed to be a great treat but I've already decided that I want to pay and Edie's pre-lunch martini costs most of the cash George has given me. I glance down at the menu. I'm hungry but everything is horribly expensive. The room is mirrored, every surface glints and an infinite series of Harry Foxes stare back at me, foreheads glistening. I'm wearing Jack's tweed jacket but it doesn't quite fit; he's slimmer than me with shorter arms and my wrists stick out of the cuffs. By mistake I catch sight of myself in the mirrors again and see that the ill-fitting suit is worn by hundreds of fidgeting Harry Foxes.

'This is one of Jack's favourite places to come when we're in town,' says Edie, with a hesitant smile. 'I thought you'd probably like it too. You boys seem to have very similar tastes.'

I can't tell whether she's being arch but I doubt it. Edie's not that sort of girl. She's brought me to one of their spots and I'm still on Jack's turf even though he isn't here. I'm not surprised that Jack is so fond of it; he'll see only glittering versions of himself laughing back at him in all the blasted mirrors. I stop myself. I'm being unfair. My brother is not vain.

'Do you come here with your family?' I ask, fishing again for titbits.

Edie roars with laughter. 'Goodness, no.'

'Not their scene?'

'Definitely not.'

Her smile is still twitching; I can't think why my question was so frightfully funny. The tablecloths are perfect white snowfields. I want to put on my boots and tramp across them. Somewhere a piano plays. I relax just a little. A waiter appears.

'May I take your order, madam?'

'The soup and then the sole.'

'And for you, sir?'

'The soup.'

'And to follow?'

'Just the soup.'

It's the only item on the menu for less than half a guinea.

'What a good idea,' says Edie. 'Cancel the sole. I'll just have soup too.'

The waiter makes an elaborate crossing-out.

'Would you like some wine?'

'No, thank you,' says Edie quickly.

The waiter disappears. And Edie sighs and raises an eyebrow. 'I wanted to treat you.'

'Does Jack ever let you treat him?'

Edie gives me a look.

'Well then.'

The waiter reappears, clutching a bottle of champagne. 'From the ladies in the corner – "With thanks for keeping their spirits up when the chips were down."'

An elderly woman in a fur coat blows Edie a kiss. Her lavender-haired companion claps her kid-gloved hands in mimed applause.

'That is too kind. Please be sure to tell them "thank you".'

We drink the champagne and eat the soup. It's a consommé, clear as glass. I eat the entre basket of bread but even then champagne bubbles are popping in my head.

'So does this happen often?' I ask, gesturing to the bottle.

Edie shrugs and I realise that it does. I'd forgotten that she's famous. Her cheeks are flushed and I see that she's tipsy too. She starts to giggle.

'Shall we go somewhere else?' she says. 'Something more your scene?'

And at once I wish I had a scene. I wish I knew some down-at-heel dive where as we walked in the black piano player would nod to us without pausing in his Duke Ellington riff while the regulars all slap me on the back and my usual whisky is waiting for me on the bar.

'Yes, let's find another place,' I say. Through the pleasant fog of champagne I've almost convinced myself that my jazz joint does exist.

I call for the bill but the waiter explains that our lady bene-
factors have taken care of everything.

'Blast it,' I say, 'I ought to have had the beef fillet after all.'

Edie giggles. 'So they're allowed to treat you.'

I tell her to shush and she laughs again. I like making her
laugh. Edie goes across to thank the ladies for their kindness,
and after a minute she beckons for me to join her.

'She's so terribly clever and such a pretty girl,' says the lady
with the lilac tint in her hair. She hasn't taken off her fox fur,
even though it is stifling in the dining room.

'Will you sing us a little something?' asks her friend, in a
voice that rustles like dry paper.

'It would be a pleasure. Mr Fox-Talbot will accompany
me.'

She grabs my arm and leads me to the piano, whispering,
'Now you can find out what it's like to sing for your supper.
Well, luncheon.'

'I'm not sure I can play after all I've had to drink,' I murmur.

'Nonsense. Now, we'll have to play one or two of the hits to
keep them happy but afterwards – you choose. Surprise me.'

We play and sing for an hour. The other diners are bemused
the moment we depart from the wartime medley but we
don't care; we're not playing for them. Someone sends over
another bottle of champagne. I've not been near a decent
piano for months and I'm sloppy with joy. We try out variations of the songs I've hunted down. Sometimes I sing along
and sometimes I just listen to Edie. Oh, why did Jack have to
find you first?

We tumble out into the street, happy and brimming with
laughter. Edie checks her watch.

'Goodness me, it's nearly five. We need to sober you up and
get you to your interview with Mr Kenton.'

She tries to straighten my tie but succeeds only in unfas-
tening it entirely, so she drapes it over my shoulder and then

has to lean against the railings, overtaken by another fit of giggles.

'Food,' I say. 'We need to eat something.'

'Soup!' says Edie. 'I'll have the soup. Nothing but soup.'

'Now, soup was once considered by the great French chefs to be the epitome of epicurean excellence.'

'Say that again.'

'Epicurean excellence.'

'I like it when you say that.'

She's laughing up at me, teasing me, and I wonder for a second whether she's daring me to kiss her, but I know that she can't possibly be, and then she's away, running along the street. A street vendor is hawking small orange cakes.

'I want a cake!' she says. 'You have to buy me one.'

I buy her one and she eats it in two bites. I buy her another and she wolfs that too.

'What I really want is a bagel but you can't get those in the posh parts of London.'

'A what?'

'A bagel,' she says. 'They're what we ate at home. The best thing in the world. My grandmother and I would wait for hours in a queue for them at the bakery on Finchleystrasse. During the war I'd take her back nylons and packets of smoked salmon. After the first time, she told me to leave the nylons and bring more salmon. That's what she said she missed about Russia. Proper winters and smoked fish.'

I don't say anything, hoping she'll carry on, but she doesn't, just grins and says again with a groan, 'I could murder a bagel.'

'It sounds wonderful.'

'You're such a classy fellow, you don't even know what a bagel is.'

'A classy fellow who couldn't afford to buy you a proper lunch.'

'You're posh but poor. Poor for now. People like you are never poor for long.'

'People like me?' The champagne is wearing off and I'm a little put out.

'You don't know what it's like to have nothing. To be invisible. Either you'll save your nice house or you won't. If you don't, your father will sell it and Jack will inherit any cash his father doesn't run through. And even if there isn't any left, Jack will end up all right. The Jack Fox-Talbots of the world always do.'

There's a bitterness in her voice that I don't recognise. I wonder whether she's as drunk as she seems, or whether she's using it as an excuse to express how she really feels.

'Is that why you're marrying him?' I say quietly.

She looks at me quizzically, her head on one side. 'What a thing to ask, Fox.'

We walk slowly to the tube, neither of us speaking for a minute or two.

'You don't know what it is, to be someone like me and to be loved by someone like him.'

I want to ask her what the devil she means and then I feel a trickle of hope: she hasn't said she loves him.

I'm more nervous than I like to admit. I really want this piano. The last of the champagne bubbles have burst on the walk to Cecil Sharp House. I've refastened my tie and attempted to smooth my hair, and I take long gulps of cool, late-autumn air but here in the city it tastes gritty and unclean. We skirt Regent's Park. The air-raid shelters haven't been dismantled and squat amongst flower beds brimming with bedraggled geraniums and dahlias. Cecil Sharp House is a large red-brick building on the edge of Primrose Hill; it's streaked with soot and the window frames are flaking, flecks of paint falling to the ground like dandruff. Edie ushers me inside. It's colder inside than out and the place smells familiarly of damp.

'Mr Kenton did say that he'd be here,' says Edie, peering around the brown-painted hallway.

It's deserted. This building is the repository of English folk songs, and I picture them huddled in the library like a vast host of sparrows, all poised to sing. We open doors but the place is quite empty. Edie opens the final door to reveal a vast wood-panelled room with a great vaulted ceiling, again painted in shades of brown. The last of the evening light streams through the double-height windows, setting the walls aglow. A man sits alone at a single desk, manuscript paper spread before him.

'Mr Kenton?' says Edie.

He looks up with a start. 'Yes? Ah, Miss Rose. A pleasure to see you as always. I hope you're well?'

'Very well, thank you. This is my friend, Harry Fox-Talbot.'

He looks blank for a moment and then quickly rises to his feet, spraying manuscript papers in every direction.

'Yes, of course. Mr Fox-Talbot, the aspirant song collector and composer. Please.' He gestures towards a low wooden seat.

'I'm going to find a cup of tea,' says Edie.

Mr Kenton gathers up his papers and settles back in his chair.

'So I understand that you've been collecting Dorset songs.'

'Yes, I have. I've been making transcriptions of local songs—'

'I've looked over the ones you forwarded to the archive. Not the worst I've seen, although you do have a tendency to overcorrect. You need to transcribe what they've actually sung, not what you think they ought to sing or what you believe they actually meant. The older the piece, the stranger it can sound to our ears. Harmony is a relatively modern invention.'

'Yes, sir.'

'And are you a song collector or a composer, Mr Fox-Talbot?'

'May I not be both?'

'Not usually. Composers are always "fiddling" with the melodies, trying to make them sound right to our modern ear. Spoiling them, in my opinion. If a thing isn't broken, then don't turn it into something new.'

I wonder why this resolute, grey-haired man wanted to meet me. It doesn't seem likely from his tenor that he's intending to arrange the loan of a grand piano.

'Mr Kenton, sir. The folk song has stopped evolving in the traditional way. No one gathers around the fire to sing in the evening, coming up with variations on the tunes and lyrics. I have to persuade people to sing the songs and they dig them out like old photographs from a dusty drawer. They're relics. But in the hands of a young composer, the dust can be shaken off. In my hands, folk songs and old melodies can become a real living thing once again. Part of modern life. Music can't be preserved in tissue paper, Mr Kenton, however much you may wish it. Music must be a thing that lives.'

Mr Kenton leans back in his chair and laughs. 'You're very passionate, Mr Fox-Talbot. But I'm surprised that you have much time for either composition or song collecting. I understand from Miss Rose that you and your brothers are attempting to keep possession of your family estate. Surely that keeps you rather occupied?'

I study the slight, harassed figure opposite. He is too thin, as if he chooses music over meals.

'It does. But music is part of the same thing.'

'How do you mean?'

'We want to restore Hartgrove Hall and her estates. The land is exhausted. The soil is poor after years of being sown with the wrong crops. The house has been left to decay. The place needs to be restored. But we want to do it in the old way. George wants cows from Thomas Hardy and to repair the fields with dung, not nitrates and fertilisers.'

Mr Kenton raises an eyebrow. 'You want to wassail the apple trees?'

I smile. 'If we must. It might work. I'd rather sing to a tree in order to induce it to produce more fruit than spray it with all sorts of junk as the government would have us do.' I take a breath. 'I want to restore our patch of Dorset with music as well as cow muck. Folk songs connect us with the land; we've just forgotten how to listen.'

Mr Kenton chuckles. 'All right then. I know of a chap not too far from you in Dorchester with a Steinway. It's a jolly nice concert grand.'

'He doesn't want it any more?'

'No room, I'm afraid. He has to turn his house into flats. He wrote to me asking whether I knew someone who might look after the piano for a while. Doesn't want to sell it in case he can take it back one day. I'll recommend he gives it to you. You'll need to arrange for the transport and pay the associated costs—'

But I'm not listening. I'm getting a piano. A Steinway concert grand.

I walk outside into the cool, yellow dark. Even here in the city, the harvest moon is big and London is lit by its glow, transformed into something less ugly, less broken.

≈

The piano arrives the same day as the first snow. She is to live in the morning room with a splendid view of the white lawns sloping down to the lake and the frozen river beyond. The piano is a beautiful thing of shining black lacquered wood and ivory keys and I wonder what she makes of the shabbiness of her new surroundings. Despite the journey, she is barely out of tune. The tuning required is so minimal that I manage it myself. I smother her in blankets and insist on a constant fire in the morning room. When I'm working outside, my thoughts return to the piano. I feel almost guilty – she's a better instrument than I deserve. A real pianist would bring out all her colours and shades. Instead, I'm using her to batter out my compositions, her glorious tones making them sound, in all honesty, much better than they really are.

It's only November but the ground freezes hard and the hill disappears. None of us has decent gloves and soon we all have painful and throbbing chilblains, which infuriate me as it makes playing the piano almost impossible. The house is never warm. Ignoring the General, we keep the fire in the great hall blazing all day but even so the condensation freezes on the inside of the lead glass. Edie returns to the house after we have a new electric water heater installed above the bath. She's adamant that cold weather outside is enchanting but cold water inside is not. Oddly, I've never seen her so content. Working out of doors in the frigid temperature, she alone never complains. She brings down with her an enormous, luxuriant fox-fur coat and wears it out on the farm to our profound amusement but she ignores the laughter.

'Say what you want, I'm the only one who's perfectly warm.'

'You'll wreck it,' says George.

Edie shrugs. 'Spoiling something through wear isn't anything to be ashamed of. Besides, if it gets too grubby, I shall shampoo it like a dog.'

She's the most glamorous farmhand anyone has ever seen, but as the freeze continues we stop laughing and eye her with envy. When we climb up the hill to Ringmoor to see Max about buying more sheep, he calls her 'the wolf' even though the fur is fox, and tells her to keep away from his flock.

'Sheep can sense big teeth an' it makes 'em act funny. Start doin' stupid things. Drown 'emselves in ponds ter git away. You stay away now,' he tells Edie.

The hilltop is coated with snow several inches deep, which hides the rumps of the barrows, although wiry black grass pokes through the thinner layers like coarse hair through a boar hide. It's much colder up here on the top of the ridge and the wind rushes at us, snatching away my breath until my teeth ache and my face is numb. The ground creaks and snaps, as if restless. I don't know this place. Its unfamiliarity twists its way inside me. The Iron Age grave mounds are transformed into great white humps, like the back and hip of a sleeping giant. A hare sits quite still on top of one with a perfect upright carriage, poised and listening, and then he's off, bounding noiselessly across the ground.

Max brings us cups of milky tea and we sit outside, clutching the mugs to warm our hands.

'You owe me a song,' I remind him. 'A song for winter.'

Max chuckles. 'So I do. You want 'im now?'

'No. Tonight. We'll come up in the tractor.'

I want to listen to him here in the darkness with the big wind buffeting us and the strange cracking in the trees. Up here on the hillside with tracks criss-crossing the snow, that's where the song will hold its potency, not beside the fire at the Hall.

Max nods to Edie. 'Yer'd best come too. Keep 'im from being too foolish.'

Edie agrees.

We leave after dinner. I'm not adept at driving the tractor in this weather. It's ancient and as pernickety as an old man, grumbling and wheezing up the hill. We rattle and bounce.

Edie sits beside me in her fur, small and silent, her lips pursed.

'You don't have to come,' I say.

'Neither of us has to. This is a ridiculous thing to do.'

I don't reply. The truth is that I want to chase this song. I'm not like the others for whom life on the farm is everything. They take a grim physical pleasure in the daily work. To my amazement, George has started to go out for runs, naked, each day, wearing nothing but his old army boots. Some mornings I wake at dawn to spy him at a lick across the ridge, an upright figure moving amongst the trees and scrub. At least Jack hasn't joined him in this particular pursuit.

George and Jack spread their delight at life out of doors like the clap, but I haven't caught it. I find it tedious and repetitive. For a day or two there is some pleasure to be had in hard manual work, the acid ache in my arms and back in the evening. The tearing, animal hunger in my belly, followed by the satisfaction of baked apples and slabs of roast pork with jugs of thick, jellied gravy. I'm aware of my body as a piece of machinery that gets easier with use, but after a few days boredom seeps in. Every day the work is the same.

The landscape changes; the gorse blooms yellow and clashes with the brush of purple heather, while a barn owl watches us in the afternoon, his feathers dirty against the iridescent snow. Yet even these delights are insufficient to stop my restlessness and growing irritation. I think of my Cambridge chums. I even miss the jazz band. If only I could have the college orchestra for a day, a week. But each day as I'm coated in mud and sweat and slime, I promise that tonight, tonight I'll write. Every night I'm too tired and slide into bed, sore and exhausted, while the piano sits silent in the morning room, covered in her rugs and hot-water bottles like an old woman. The work takes everything and I'm scraped down to the marrow. I've not written a note for a week. I need a song to fill me up. I want a song to open that door that leads down and down into the dark and unknown.

Before me, all I can see is white and I can't tell whether the ground is rising or falling. The moon and stars shelter behind a blanket of clouds. I steer the tractor around a tree stump and straight into a ditch.

'Blast,' I say, and then again, 'Damn and blast,' when it doesn't seem enough. 'Are you all right?' I ask.

'I'm not hurt. I'm cross,' says Edie.

The tractor is at a strange angle, two of its wheels in the ditch. Foul smoke chugs out of the chimney. I leap down, land-ing in a heap of wet snow. It's not freezing tonight and the tractor is sinking into a wall of sludge. I'm relieved it has not overturned.

'Here, ease your way out and I'll lift you down,' I say.

Edie wriggles forward and I wrap my arms around her. I'm engulfed in the warm, animal smell of her fur coat. I hold her for a moment, feeling the weight of her in my arms, before setting her down on the top of the rise.

'Go back to the house. I'm going to dig the tractor out.'

She nods. I'm grateful that she hasn't repeated that this was a foolish idea.

'And, Edie, don't tell them, will you?'

I can't bear the thought of my brothers descending into the sludge with their good cheer and riotous teasing.

'It'll take you all night to do it by yourself. And look, you're wet through.'

'I don't mind.'

'What about Max's song?'

'It'll have to wait.' I try to keep the disappointment from my voice but clearly I don't manage.

'Here. I'll give you one. Are you ready?'

'Yes.'

I pull my notebook from my coat along with a stub of pencil. She wraps her arms close around her and starts to sing. It takes me a moment to realise that I don't know the song. I thought I knew her entire repertoire but not this. It's not in English and I don't even recognise the language she's singing in. Her voice sounds different, raw and fierce. She doesn't look at me while she sings, but out past the house to the blackness of the hill beyond. When she stops, I see that she's crying. Quickly, angrily, she wipes away her tears, using her sleeve with girlish inelegance. I offer her my handkerchief. She snatches it and, after blowing her nose, stuffs it into her pocket.

'Did you get it?' she snaps.

'I think so,' I say, still writing feverishly.

'You can never show this song to anyone. I mean, no one at all. Not ever. Do you understand?'

'I promise.'

'I'm not Edie Rose. She's just a song that I sing.'

'I have only the melody. I couldn't catch the words. What language were you singing in?'

'Yiddish.'

'I've never heard it before.'

'Well, now you have.'

'What's the song about?'

She gives a low laugh. 'It's a folk song, Fox. What are they all about? It's a song of love and sadness and a lost homeland, a land of milk and snow.'

I've never known her quite so irritable and I daren't ask for a proper translation.

'Can we please go now?' she asks, lighting another cigarette, her hands trembling.

I lean against the tractor. Beside me I hear the uneven sound of her breath. I want to know who taught her the song. She stubs out her cigarette on a mound of melting slush and hums the same strange tune. It suits the dark and the cold.

'Have you ever sung that to Jack?' I ask when she's finished.

'No. Just to you.'

She looks at me with an expression that I can't read, then turns away. 'I'm going back to the house. You should come too. You'll catch cold out here like this.'

'I promise I won't.'

~

I catch a cold. I can't shake it off and it goes to my chest so that I cough and spit like an old man. Jack buys me special cigarettes in order to smoke out the infection but they taste awful and I throw them away. I struggle to work outside, having to stop every fifteen minutes to hack and wheeze, leaning against the barn or a gatepost. I'm not hungry and I can't sleep and I'm never, ever warm. The dankness has seeped inside me, and even in bed under an army of blankets I cower and tremble, too cold and too miserable to sleep. In contrast my brothers flourish with farm life. As I shrink and my skin takes on a nasty waxy sheen, they grow broad-shouldered; their faces a bright, wind-whipped red. When I rise at six, cursing the hour, they're already in the kitchen, having returned from their first round of happy chores on the hill. They eye me with concern and quickly look away. Jack passes me tea and congealing porridge that I can barely eat.

'Are you sure you shouldn't visit the doctor?' he asks, as I set the bowl aside.

'I'm fine. Give me a few days and I'll be all right.'

He and George exchange glances but say nothing. We know the General's decree that 'Only women fuss over trifles'. The more wretched the illness and the more stoically we bear it, the greater the General's opinion of us. I'm aware that this chasing of his regard is foolhardy but I'm unable to stop myself. As I cough my guts out, bent over the kitchen table, and Jack and George carefully look away, I know that they at least understand.

Edie does not.

'For God's sake, man, go back to bed and I'll send for the doctor.'

'I'm perfectly all right,' I say, sweating and feeling vomit rise in my throat. I swallow it back down and meander out to the yard. I focus on the cobbles. They need to be sluiced. I wobble over to the tap there and fasten the hose. Triumphant that I've managed this without falling over, I turn the stream of water onto the ground. Edie screams.

'You're pointing it at me! I'm soaked.'

I croak an apology and aim the hose a little higher, then higher again as she continues to yell. I can't understand why she's still making such a fuss as I seem to be watering the sky, which, I decide, is rather pointless as those clouds look very much like rain.

'For pity's sake,' says Edie again, and snatches away the hose. 'You've fainted. I'm calling the doctor.'

'Nonsense. Men don't faint,' I tell her, curtly.

'Very well, what would you call it?' she asks from a great height, her head swimming amongst the clouds, and I'm worried she's going to yell again and I really hope she doesn't as my head is pulsing red and black.

'I went flop.'

'Yes. Much more manly.'

Jack and George help me up to bed. Despite being aware of the General's well-known contempt for afternoon naps taken by anyone other than grandmothers and infants, I sleep.

It appears that not only have I a lung infection, I also have an ear infection that has caused my eardrum to burst. My hearing is damaged and unless I rest and allow it to heal properly, the loss may be permanent. Edie comes to see me and sits on the edge of my bed. She doesn't take my hand. She's not the kind of girl to be comfortable with casual intimacies.

'You need to stop being stupid. All three of you boys are stupid. But you're simply not allowed to be stupid about your hearing. Your ears are your work tools, and you're going to be a great composer one day. If you risk your hearing I won't ever speak to you again.' She looks terribly serious and gives a tiny, irritated sigh.

'I need to do something. Jack and George need me,' I say, mostly because it sounds good. I'm not sure that the others would notice if I'm not there for a week or even a month.

Edie says nothing but she gives me a look to show that she at least isn't fooled. With a pang of guilt, I conclude that I'm actually relieved at this forced break from days spent out in the soggy fields but I'm disgusted by my own antipathy. My family comes from old country stock. I spent my boyhood barefoot in icy ponds, plunging for the gob and slime of tadpoles, luxuriating in their ooze between my toes. There was joy in it then and I wonder what has changed within me. Have I indeed grown soft? I imagine the General's snarl of ready disapproval, then the same look from Jack and George, and I shrivel.

I close my eyes and remember how, even as a boy, I'd tire sooner than the others of filching frogspawn or hunting rabbits or building dens deep in the woods. I'd leave them and tear through the trees to chase a nightingale or else return to the house to play the piano. Or, if the General was at home, I'd line up rocks and ribs of kindling, and mime playing tunes upon an impromptu keyboard. Of course I want to save the old place but I want to do it through music rather than with my bare and chapped hands. Still I want to do something significant, something that makes them all notice, makes Edie notice.

~

155

I have an idea of what I might do. The first day that I'm well enough to sit up, I write to the leader of my old college orchestra, asking them all to visit for a week before Christmas. I have a proposal for them and I hope they're game. While I wait, I rest and eat and sleep and slowly recover.

The morning of their arrival dawns cold and bright. Too impatient to wait in the house, I set off for an early walk. I'm still convalescing and I pick my way down the hill back to the Hall more tired from the effort than I would like to admit. As I reach the edge of the lawn, I notice a small crowd gathered on the steps of the house. I see them only a moment before I hear them, a light and crisp baroque refrain reaching out to greet me. There's a joyful march of strings and then a pair of flutes, wrapping around one another as easily as a couple of wagtails in song. I wait for the cello, but when it finally comes it's a semitone sharp. This is what strikes me, so it takes me a moment to acknowledge that there is a small orchestra sitting on the steps of Hartgrove Hall, playing, not well but with enthusiasm, Bach's fourth orchestral suite.

'You're a bar late,' I say to the cello. 'Everyone, go back to the repeat at the top of Section A.'

I break off a switch of hazel for a baton and count them in. The second time through is better, although the cello is still sharp.

'Shall we go inside and rehearse the folk-song suite? The cold can't be helping your tuning,' I say, once we've played it through for the third time.

It's jolly nice to see my old chums. The flutes – both girls and both remarkably accomplished – a clutch of violins, a double bass, a French horn player and the rogue cello. I like the cellist very much but not when he's playing his cello. I rather wish he hadn't come. Without him the Bach would have been quite acceptable.

I set the musicians up on the minstrels' gallery in the great hall. I pass around the sketches of my composition. They're all handwritten, some a little smudged and bleary with crossings-out. I haven't written out the part for double bass at all.

'If I give you the piano score, can you make do?' I ask the bass player.

He's a thick-set chap from Aberdeenshire, a laird of some kind, and a miraculous jazz player. If you close your eyes, you'll believe he's from South Carolina. But then, I suppose even Scotsmen get the blues.

He nods and starts to play my chords. He improvises a little and it's better.

'Yes,' I say. 'Mark those changes on the score, please.'

I turn to the leader of the little band. 'Edward, are you happy?' One always has to pay court to the first violin.

'Yes. Is that a B flat? I can't make it out.'

I scrutinise the score. 'Neither. It's a bit of biscuit. It should be a rest.'

He makes an elaborate mark with a pencil. I turn to the cellist.

'Colin. If you're going to play, you need to retune.'

Edward plays a long C while Colin fumbles to correct his tuning. It's a slight improvement. I raise my hand and they wait, poised upon the upbeat.

'Again.'

After the fifth time through, they don't wait to be told. They listen to my notes, make changes to their scores and are ready.

'Again.'

Somewhere between the twenty-fifth and twenty-sixth play-through, the General emerges from the library to bemoan the noise. We ignore him. During the thirtieth and penultimate run, I'm aware of an audience. This time Colin doesn't stumble as the flutes pass him Max's melody; he picks it up and runs with it, neat as a runner in a relay. It rumbles through the strings, deep and rich, and I remember why I love the cello. I look up and see Edie in the hall below, leaning against the great oak mantelpiece.

'Again,' she says.

Edward and the string players raise their instruments, but I wave at them to stop. 'There's a voice part. Will you sing?'

I chuck the page over the edge of the gallery and it flutters to the ground, Edie picks it up and reads it quickly.

'All right. But it's a little low for me.'

'No, it's not,' I say. 'Trust me.'

She laughs at my audacity. 'Very well then, maestro.'

～

It's Christmas Eve. A soggy, rain-soaked evening – nothing picture postcard about it at all. The snow recedes, leaving brown damp earth in its place. Because the woodshed leaks, all the logs are too wet to burn, and nothing dries properly – not us, not our clothes, not the clammy walls of the house – but still people come. Some are curious. They've heard whispers about young Fox chasing over the countryside naked, hunting for songs – regrettably George's penchant for nude running and my song collecting have become inexplicably combined in the minds of our neighbours. Frankly, we don't mind what they say about us, as long as they come and pay their five shillings for the concert. All proceeds are to go towards purchasing George's cows.

The whole county is here, along with most of the village. It's an unusual social mix. The farmers, carters and labourers linger with their own kind on one side of the hall, silent and uneasy, still buttoned stiffly into their coats, while the county set shudder in elegant but chilly frocks, wearing paste copies of the jewels they sold to pay inheritance tax a generation back, and they discuss one another in too-loud voices. Jack and George move through their ranks, topping up drinks and complimenting the ladies, guffawing at the gentlemen's jokes and attempting to push tickets for the raffle. It's an unsavoury but necessary task. None of us has much cash, but I'm grateful to see people buying tickets.

I notice Colonel and Mrs Winters amongst the crowd. I last saw him the morning Turnworth House was destroyed. I've heard they're living in a flat in Bournemouth with a sea view and central heating. I scrutinise his face and decide it's lost the grim haunted look from that day. Central heating and promenades along the pier suit him. I wonder what it must be like for them to be back here, swigging sherry with the ghosts of Christmas past. The General struts towards them like a prize rooster and accepts their compliments on the evening as if it has all been his doing. Mrs Winters glances about her and her expression is fixed, stricken. She at least would trade her sea view and warm towels for these old, damp-riddled walls and a fire that smokes.

Edie lingers beside me on the minstrels' gallery. 'Who are you looking at with such intensity? Is it a girl?'

'Just the crowd. A jolly decent turnout, isn't it?'

Edie turns to me and smiles. 'It's simply terrific. I never thought so many people would come. You've done a good thing, Fox.'

'They've not heard a note yet. It might all go horribly wrong.'

'It won't. And if it does, what does it matter? They've already paid.'

'You'll be splendid,' I say. 'You always are.'

She frowns. 'Don't say that. That's what Jack always says regardless of whether I was any good. "Marvellous, darling. Simply marvellous." From you, I demand honesty.'

I grin, pleased. 'All right. Not a word of flattery. And you don't have to sing those awful popular numbers, not if you don't want to. Sing what you like.'

Edie laughs. 'What is it you call them? My "old tat songs"?'

I nod, a little ashamed.

'I'm afraid I do have to sing them. It's not at all what I want. I have to please the audience too. That's something you still have to learn, Little Fox.'

'You never have to try to please me. I liked your Yiddish song. I think I like it best of all.'

She's wearing a deep evergreen dress the colour of fresh yew leaves, with sleeves, a little cape on the shoulders and a pair of grey silk gloves. A tiny gold brooch in the shape of a bird is pinned to her breast. I've never seen her look so lovely. I feel light-headed as though I've had too much to drink, which I haven't, not a drop. Not before a performance.

'You look very pretty tonight, Edie.'

She smiles and a dimple appears in one cheek. 'Thank you, Harry,' she says. She's not called me Harry since we first met and I like it. For a moment she studies me and then she seizes my hand and squeezes it; her small fingers have surprising strength.

'We're good friends, you and I, aren't we, Harry? Tell me that we're good friends. The best of them.'

Her eyes are glassy with tears and she blinks them back.

'Of course,' I say. 'The very best of friends.'

She still doesn't release my hand and I stare at her, thrilled and somewhat puzzled. She looks as if she wants to confide something and my heart thumps, my blood pulses with electricity. She loves me too. I'm sure of it. At once I feel bad for Jack, but not too bad. For Jack there's always another girl, and besides, I don't want to think of him at this moment. I want to think only about Edie. Edie and me.

She loosens her grasp on my hand.

'Good luck, Harry.'

She leans over, kisses me on the cheek and walks across the gallery to the bedroom serving as the dressing room for tonight's singers. I don't follow her. I'm in no hurry. Luxuriant warmth suffuses my body, more effective than brandy or the hottest of baths. In a minute I need to go and speak to the leader of the orchestra, that utterly pompous lead violin, but not yet, not for another minute. Amongst the local gentry and the villagers lurk critics from the *Morning Post* and the *Western Gazette*. I ought to be nervous but I feel only a smooth calm. I know the concert will go well.

And it does. I guide the orchestra through Edie's standards without so much as a grimace. And when I steer them out across the less familiar refrains of my folk-song arrangements, the audience comes with us. Edward Bishop might be an arrogant fellow but he's a damn fine fiddler, and he leads the orchestra with total confidence, his sound as sweet and rich as Dundee cake. We play 'The Foggy Dew' and 'The Seeds of Love' and I have to swallow a lump in my throat as Edie sings of lost summer love and the violet and the pink. My Symphony in G minor, *The Song of Hartgrove Hall*, inspired by Max's theme is the last and best of it. We perform the first and third movements (the second relies too heavily on the cello, who simply isn't up to it, and the fourth isn't finished).

Time is relative in music. The composer sets a time signature, the number of beats in each bar and a guide to the tempo at which they should be played. Yet every performance is unique, and each lasts for a different amount of time. The conductor guides the orchestra through the piece, dictating the speed of this particular journey through the music. As I raise my arm and the orchestra takes a breath, waiting on the upbeat, I hold time in my hand. Max's melody blows through us all. It swirls above the heads of the listeners and around the panelled hall. This symphony is a small world and as long as the music plays, we're all held within it: audience, musicians, singers. As I slow the pace, time expands and shifts. I feel it shudder. Max's melody is old. I hear the wind on the top of Ringmoor in the dark, and out of a churning void, indistinct, cold and filled with musical dissonance, rises a melody, the shepherd's song held aloft by a glorious and bright soprano. The world begins with Edie. The hall is awash with light and colour. I'm a magician.

Her voice falls like spring rain and I want her to understand that I've written this part for her. I know what her voice can do, how best to release that sound. She's been fastened into those silly patriotic songs like cheap costumes, and at last she's dressed in silk. I see in her face that she knows it too, and as she sings, a pure iridescent sound that reverberates through me, I catch her eye, wide with surprise. Listen to what you can do, I tell her through the music. Listen. You are the nightingale but not the one they think.

I don't notice the applause. I only hear time restart. We're no longer suspended within the music and for a minute I'm adrift, uneasy.

'Hello.' A small hand slides into mine, and I hold it tight. I'm steady again. 'Bow,' she whispers.

'Thank you,' I say to her. 'Thank you.' I squeeze her hand. This time she doesn't let go.

We persuade the audience outside into the damp air. The rain has petered out into a light drizzle that wraps around the hill. Pads of cloud squat on the ridge, turning it into a soft mountain. This part of the evening was George's idea. I worry that George is turning into a bit of a green man. At least tonight he's wearing his clothes. We lead the concert-goers across the sodden lawns to the orchard. I can hear irritated huffs from the ladies in their smart shoes as they sink into sucking mud. Fingers of mist probe the bare trees. George moves to the front of the crowd. This is his idea, so I insist that he introduce it. He clears his throat and shifts from foot to foot, awkward and unable to look directly at the throng.

'We're bringing back an old custom tonight. We're going to wassail the apple trees for a good harvest next year. Max, if you would.'

The shepherd, dressed up for the occasion in a borrowed suit, slides out from amongst the trees. He didn't want to sing but cash banished his reluctance. The audience are torn between amusement and being charmed by the spectacle. Jack passes around cups of cider. Edie slips in beside me, strokes my arm, rests her head on my shoulder.

'This is fun,' she says. 'It's nice just to listen.'

'And now at least we can drink.'

We toast but I'm clumsy and I slop cider all over her glove, soaking her.

'I'm sorry,' I say.

'It doesn't matter a bit.' She peels off her glove and something catches in the beam of a torch. There's a ring on her finger. I grab her hand.

'You're wearing a wedding ring.'

She recoils, holding her hand to her chest. 'Yes. We were married this afternoon. Neither of us wanted any fuss.'

I'm a fool. An absolute fool. It's a moment before I can speak.

'For Christ's sake, Edie. When were you going to tell me? Does George know? Does Father?'

I fire questions at her as she twists her finger, fiddles with her ring. She doesn't look at me.

'We haven't told your father. Jack, well, he thought it was best to tell him after the event. We didn't want any further unpleasantness.'

She pauses and meets my gaze for a moment, silently asking me to understand. Sweaty with anger, I look away. She gives a tiny sigh and continues, her voice pleading.

'Jack wanted to tell you himself. He'll be dreadfully upset you found out like this.'

'Christ.'

Jack hasn't told me in order to spare my feelings, since he knows perfectly well how I feel about Edie. I'm both desolate and utterly mortified. Edie reaches out to touch my sleeve but I pull away.

'Don't.'

I can't bear her pity. I walk away through the trees. I think I might be sick. Behind me I hear Max's voice rising through the dark and Edie softly calling.

I'm dazed with cider and misery. I can't stay here, that much I know. I can't see them together. Happy at the breakfast table. Happy in the garden, reading the morning papers. Each of them watching me with that awful blend of pity and concern.

Hurriedly, I go back to the house where I unearth a suitcase and fill it with my manuscript pages, then pack the book containing the folk songs I've collected. I'm about to leave when I realise that I might need some clothes and a razor and such. Gathering them as quickly as I can, I toss my belongings into the car. I help myself to a bottle of burgundy from the cellar and a little petty cash, and I walk out onto the driveway. The first guests are leaving now, drifting in twos and threes into the night. I hear singing and laughter from the orchard.

I start the car and drive away. The suitcase rattles and bounces. I wind down the window and take a long swig of burgundy. I don't know where I'm going. The freedom of this thought is a relief and I take another hit of wine. I shall drive and drive. The air is cool. I shall find somewhere quiet and write. Exhilaration surges, then falls. Nothing can compensate for what I've lost. Except that she was never mine to lose.

March 2001

It had been a year since Edie died. Statistics suggested that I should have been grateful that I'd made it through at all – many of the bereaved die within the first few months and since I had survived for a year my own death was supposedly not imminent. On the other hand, the fact that my body had decided to continue did not mean my life would suddenly become easier.

For the first year Clara and Lucy rallied around me. Our lives orbited the void Edie's absence had created, that black hole at the centre of our universe. Yet piece by piece my daughters inched back into their ordinary routines. There were setbacks. Clara telephoned a week before Edie's birthday, distraught that she'd purchased a card for her, remembering only once outside the shop that it was horribly unnecessary. I told her to write the card and post it to me. I received it and dutifully informed Clara that it was very touching, but the truth was that I couldn't bear to open it at all. I shoved it into Edie's bedside drawer where it sat with her spectacle case and the last, never-to-be-finished novel she'd been reading when she died, none of them to be opened again.

I understood that the girls' loss was different from mine. Their sudden tsunamis of grief were brought on by the realisation that for a minute or an hour or even half a day they had not thought about Edie. They'd been caught up in everyday life – buying chops for supper or attending a school parents' evening – and had briefly forgotten that their mother was dead. This was as it should be. We cannot be so utterly desolate at the death of a parent that we are unable to continue with our own lives and those of our children. If we did, then the human race would cease pretty sharpish. I watched them slip back into the rhythms of their busy lives with regret but also with relief.

It was not the same for me. Edie and I had been married for too long and were too much part of one another's worlds. We were trees with a shared canopy, grown and shaped to fit one another. When one tree is lost in a storm, the other remains, ugly and distorted. I lingered at the edge of things, an observer, never quite managing properly to engage in any conversation.

To my immense sadness, at the end of a year I started to lose that sense of Edie being just around the corner. Until then, I had almost been able to persuade myself that she was making tea in the kitchen or had popped to the loo and was coming back any minute. I missed that magical self-delusion and felt, as each week and month passed, that Edie was sliding further and further away from me. Instead of easing my loss, time increased the distance between us. I tried to accept the grim fact that the best parts of my life were behind me. I now had to be nourished on memories alone, but, treacherous, they slithered away. I retreated into my notebooks, recording thoughts of her – early and late – and also scrutinising my more recent jottings, analysing my own grief.

It came in waves. Sometimes for hours or even days I'd function perfectly well. Then, something would trigger it. The knowledge of an anniversary – 'Today a year ago was the last time we walked around the garden together' – or not leaping to turn off the blasted radio quickly enough before I caught her singing. Then in the sudden silence, grief would catch me and bear me off on grey tides. I was helpless until it receded once more and despair dwindled into ordinary unhappiness.

I still couldn't write music. Not a note. I wanted to write Edie her symphony but after a year I had nothing. It had to be a symphony and not a requiem – much too sad, not like

Edie at all. She was full of melodies and always reminded me that, as a composer, it was my duty to please the audience as well as myself. She used to sing endless nursery rhymes to the children when they were small. I found most of them horribly tedious but when I dared to complain, Edie wouldn't hear of it.

'I don't only sing for myself, I sing for my listener, who in this case is three and a half with a sore tummy. She wants "Three Blind Mice", not Bartók.'

It was always her Yiddish songs that I wanted to hear. She rarely sang them and when I pressed her, she refused. They reminded her too strongly of her own childhood and of things she preferred to forget. Once, she confessed that soon after the family had arrived from Russia, there were times when they didn't have enough to eat, and went to bed hungry. If she woke in the night, restless and with an empty stomach, her grandmother would pull Edie into her own bed and sing her songs to fill the hole. Later, Edie's mother found a job at a bakery, and there were always yesterday's bagels to eat, even if there wasn't enough cream cheese or fancy things to put inside them. Occasionally, I overheard her singing them instead of nursery rhymes to soothe the children. I'd sneak in and listen in the doorway, frightened of disturbing her and making her stop. Heard melodies are sweet, but those overheard in stolen snatches, I discovered, are sweeter still.

I'd wake some mornings with a surge of energy, full of determination: this was the morning I'd start to write Edie's symphony. I'd shower and as the hot water rushed over me I'd feel a sense of vigour and eagerness. Sometimes I'd scrub it away as I towelled myself dry and had to sit down on the edge of the bath, already drained, fighting the urge to slink back to bed. Other times my enthusiasm lasted as far as the kitchen, where I'd brew myself a cup of bad coffee, always too weak or too strong – it was Edie who understood the quirks of the rickety coffee maker. I couldn't do the sensible thing and buy a fancy new espresso machine, the sort Lucy was always marvelling over, because this one was another object that Edie had touched. So, I'd take my revolting coffee to my desk or to the piano and I'd sit ready to start sketching. Here, if it hadn't already, inspiration invariably left me. I couldn't settle. The house was too quiet.

Edie's study door was open across the hall. I never closed it. For forty years we'd popped in and out to chat, to listen to an idea, to agree it was time for lunch – a cheese sandwich or should we treat ourselves and go to the pub? I rarely ventured inside her study any more. Her desk was exactly as she'd left it. I had Mrs Stroud dust it every week but I forbade her from tidying. Edie hated to have anyone touch the things on her desk. It was always a terrible mess – I couldn't have borne to work in such chaos – but Edie maintained everything was exactly where it was supposed to be. The open door taunted me. It signalled that everything was all right, when I knew perfectly well that it was not. I'd wonder whether I ought to close it, and with that any tentative inspiration I might have had inevitably fled.

The only time my imagination was teeming with music was when Robin came to the house to play the piano. Those days were circled in red on the calendar and in my mind. Perhaps it was because of those red days that I didn't die of a stroke or flu or any of the ailments of the bereaved, but found myself waking three mornings a week with a thrill of impatience. Robin came around to practise on Saturdays, Sunday afternoons and Wednesday evenings.

We'd agreed that for the time being it remained best that Robin used my Steinway rather than our purchasing a piano for him to have at home. Clara still fretted that if there was a piano in the house Robin would do nothing but play it. It was already enough of a struggle to deliver him to school on the days each week when he attended.

Family life now revolved around him. On Mondays, Clara and Robin would drive up to the Royal College of Music in Marylebone, leaving Dorset at five in the morning (the only time that Robin did not object with fury to getting out of bed was when he knew it meant piano lessons). Clara and Robin would spend the night in London and not return until nearly eleven o'clock on Tuesday evenings. On Fridays, Clara and Robin would rise again at dawn and drive to London and back before lunch. During the days each week that their mother was in town, Ralph would take the girls to school, where they had to stay late until he could collect them after work.

The schedule was exhausting for the entire family. Katy was not doing as well at school as she had been, and her teachers worried that no one was supervising her homework. Despite Robin's rages and passionate objection, I think Clara was probably correct in forbidding the presence of a piano in their house. On the nights when Robin stayed with me, I'd discover him playing at three in the morning until I was forced to lock the music-room door before I went to bed.

One Sunday I had been anticipating his arrival with considerable pleasure. I'd purchased his preferred brand of chocolate biscuits and was looking forward to hearing the Brahms again. He arrived in a flurry of noise, hurling himself through the kitchen door, yelling somewhat unnecessarily, 'Grandpa, I'm here! I'm here!'

Clara looked worn out. She sat down in the kitchen and reached for the teapot. I noticed that there were stripes of grey in her hair and, seeing me look, she ran her hand through it self-consciously.

'I know, my hair is dreadful. I never seem to have time to get it done any more.'

'I brought you something,' said Robin, profoundly uninterested in his mother's personal regime, thrusting a tatty piece of paper at me.

It was a splodge drawing. I squinted. Robin sighed and rolled his eyes.

'It's you playing the piano,' he said, clearly exasperated at my stupidity.

'So it is. It's wonderful,' I said.

It wasn't. The figure was crude and barely recognisable as a person, but we'd been told to praise Robin when he showed interest in anything other than the piano. His school wanted to encourage balance and if possible to dampen his enthusiasm for music. It seemed a futile task to me, akin to trying to empty a pond with a teaspoon during a rainstorm, but I'm only a grandparent and so I did as I was told.

'I'll come back early today. To give you time to get ready,' said Clara.

'Ready for what, darling?'

She frowned and looked concerned. 'This afternoon is Mummy's stone setting. Did you forget?'

'No. I hadn't forgotten. I'm not going.'

Clara looked aghast, as though I'd finally lost it. I had forgotten, or rather I'd successfully put it out of my mind.

'You go, if you want. I'll stay here and mind Robin. He won't want to go and he'll have much more fun playing music with me.'

'Yes. Please. That,' agreed Robin.

Clara continued to stare at me with the same appalled expression. 'Robin, go and play for a minute. I need to talk to Grandpa.'

Robin shrugged and disappeared at a run. Twenty seconds later the sound of 'The Flight of the Bumblebee' came cascading along the hall.

'Papa, how can you not go to Mummy's stone setting? I don't understand.'

I shifted unhappily on my chair. I wondered whether sons were easier than daughters who constantly demanded explanations and needed to be told in unpleasant intimate detail the minutiae of one's feelings.

'I don't wish to go. It's a religious ceremony. They make me uncomfortable and listening to a stranger recite prayers in a foreign language has nothing to do with the woman I knew and loved. She wanted prayers and all those knick-knacks. But it has nothing in the least to do with me.'

I sounded angrier than I intended.

'You're really not going?' Clara's eyes filled with tears.

'No, darling. I'm not. I'm sorry to upset you.'

'It's what Mummy wanted.'

'Yes. But it's not what I wanted. And I'm the one still here.'

I started to clatter cups in the sink to signal that I didn't wish to discuss the matter any longer. Clara gathered herself. 'All right. Very well. I'll leave Robin here with you then. We'll pick him up afterwards.'

I watched her leave, aware that I'd disappointed her, but I was unable to behave as she wished me to. While Edie was alive she always acted as a buffer between the girls and me, persuading them to leave me to sail my own ship, not to make too many demands, especially those that might interfere with my music. After she died, the girls stole closer like players in a game of 'Grandmother's Footsteps' and while I often took solace in the intimacy, wondering why I'd kept them at a careful distance for so long, at other times I wished they'd allow me some privacy. A man doesn't always wish to discuss his marriage with his daughters.

Wearily, I trailed across the hall to the music room. I lingered in the doorway watching Robin, feeling my spirits lift. With utter focus he was playing a Schubert sonata in G major. His eyes were almost closed and, although the music was open on the stand, he did not so much as glance at it. His teacher had suggested that he should see whether he could learn the music by heart, explaining that just as actors don't walk around on the stage or on television shows holding their scripts but learn their parts, so musicians need to do the same. It's only when one has memorised a piece that one can disappear into it, understand the music from the inside.

I watched Robin as much as listened to him. It was apparent from his posture that he was wholly within the music; the piano was an extension of his body. His shoulders swayed and rolled with a dancer's grace, his fingers running over the keys. His immersion was an intensely personal thing, and I felt I was an intruder. At the end of the piece, he opened his eyes and, noticing me, grinned.

'I like that one,' he said. 'It feels nice under my fingers.'

'It feels nice in my ears, listening to it,' I said. 'You're getting better.'

'Good.' He stretched like a cat. 'I'm going to play the piano for, like, I dunno, ten years.'

I smiled. Ten years, to a five-year-old, was akin to for ever. I sat at my desk and listened to his practice. It was no longer my task to offer a critique. While he played I never did anything other than listen. I did not answer the phone nor drink a cup of tea nor read letters nor turn on the computer. My attention belonged wholly to Robin.

Yet on that Sunday, I found my thoughts straying to Edie. I was distracted by thoughts of the stone setting. I'd never been to one and I didn't know how to picture it. I'd never been to a Jewish funeral before Edie's. I certainly hadn't expected that the first Jewish funeral I attended would be my wife's. When Edie started visiting the synagogue, she didn't tell me. If I'm being quite honest, mostly I forgot that she was Jewish. When I had to fill in one of those bureaucratic tick-box forms, I'd mark 'White, British' without a thought. On one of our trips shortly after I'd had a cataract operation and couldn't see terribly well, Edie had filled in the form. I noticed that beside the box asking for 'ethnicity' she'd ticked

'Other' beside her name and had written 'Jewish' next to it. That was probably the only time I gave it a second thought. She was just Edie.

Neither of us had much time for God. No, that's not quite true – I didn't have much time for God and I simply presumed Edie felt the same. The first I knew about the synagogue trips was a few months before she died, when a rabbi came to the house and rang the bell. When I opened the door and saw the man in the tall hat and the black coat, I thought he was from some sort of cult and was either going to try to convert me or sell me dictionaries.

I said, 'Not today, thank you,' and he said quietly, 'I'm here to see Edie. Edie Rose.'

That had startled me. Edie hadn't been 'Edie Rose', except on CD covers and in tribute concerts, for forty years. She was Mrs Edie Fox-Talbot.

Edie never publicly discussed her Jewishness. Yet all our Jewish friends seemed to know without being told. I remembered a dinner with Albert and his wife thirty years ago. We probably served them sausage cassoulet. Even Edie ate pork after we were married and, truthfully, it would never have occurred to me that it might be tactless to serve pig to Albert and Margot. They were contemplating a trip back to Berlin. Albert had been asked to perform and was inclined to go, but Margot was appalled at the thought of returning. Albert turned to Edie and solicited her opinion.

'Would you go back? Have you been back to Russia?'

Slowly, she shook her head. 'No. I've not been back. I'm not sure I would go. I was so young when we left. And, suppose, you know. Suppose it still felt like home? What would I do then?'

I'd looked at her, aghast. All this shared life, and yet a part of her still hankered after something else. I'd made light of it then, silently resolving never to accept a job to conduct in

Moscow, and wondered aloud, 'How did you know Edie was Jewish? Do you chaps have a secret handshake like the Masons?'

The three of them stared at me as though I were drunk or mad or both.

'Of course she's Jewish,' Albert had said with a shrug, and total assurance. I'd felt that they were all quietly laughing at me, and it was an uncomfortable sensation being the odd man out.

Sometimes, in later years when she agreed to the occasional interview, a piece might mention her Russian ancestry and the fact that she was 'of Jewish descent' – a vague phrase; after all, most of us possess a dash of something or other in our genes. Yet, after she died, every single obituary stated that she was Jewish as though everyone had always known, which was utter guff. I liked the piece in the *Guardian* the best. The head-line was 'England's Winter Rose Dies'. Edie would have rather liked that.

I'd been disconcerted when the rabbi had appeared on the doorstep, and in all honesty I'd not been thrilled to discover that she'd been making trips to the synagogue. Even after I found out, I never went with her. I don't know whether I would have gone if she'd asked, but then she never did. I wasn't pleased about Edie returning to her Jewish roots. We were to be parted by death, and I thought that was a sufficient division. I resented the further separation. I didn't want her to be buried in a cemetery in a grotty suburb of Bournemouth miles from where we'd spent our lives together. George was comfortable in his spot in the woods. I fully expected to lie beside him at some point, and I'd always presumed Edie would be there too. I wanted to think of her on the hillside amongst the snow-drops or trudging through the bluebell woods, not lying in a box surrounded by strangers and the hum of traffic on the roundabout near Ikea.

After her funeral, I swore I would not go back to the cemetery. She might want to be buried there but I did not have to visit. I preferred to remember her in my own way. I could not understand why after all this time together that at the very end she'd insisted on turning away from me.

'What do you think, Grandpa?' asked Robin and I realised with some surprise that I hadn't heard a single note.

'Play it again,' I said.

Happily, he returned to the keyboard and with a struggle, like closing an overfull suitcase, I pushed all thoughts of Edie from my mind.

Later in the afternoon we listened to CDs. I might not have been able to teach Robin the piano but I was still permitted to further his musical education.

We had a pleasant routine. Robin built himself a nest of cushions on the Persian rug and wriggled in amongst them. He always asked for the heavy damask curtains to be closed: he liked to transform the music room into an auditorium. I had to introduce the programme giving the title of the piece. I flashed the electric lights to signal the programme was about to start and Robin dutifully applauded the imaginary conductor while I pressed 'play' on the first track. I'd invested in better speakers; one of the sound engineers I'd worked with on my last couple of albums had come to the house and put it all together. It sounded simply marvellous – akin to sitting right in the centre of the stalls. Whether it was in imitation of me or because he felt the same, Robin refused any snack or refreshment while the music played. Instead, we had an interval after the first piece where we'd both eat chocolate biscuits and I'd have a cup of tea and Robin some milk while we discussed the performance with great earnestness.

For the concert that Sunday I'd selected Delius's *On Hearing the First Cuckoo in Spring*. I enjoyed observing Robin as he listened. He sat amongst his cushions, never once slouching, always alert and taut with concentration. He reminded me of a hare I once saw in the snow on the ridgeway, its long ears upright, perfectly still, every atom poised as it listened for the tiniest sound across the snowfield. When the Delius ended, we both clapped politely.

'Well, what did you think?' I asked, turning on the lights.

This was our routine. I liked to know Robin's thoughts before I gave him the précis about the piece. He needed first to learn his own mind and feelings.

'Shivery,' said Robin.

He'd had a cold a couple of weeks before and had learned that the word elicited almost instant sympathy from his mother and sisters.

'All right. Why?'

Robin screwed up his face. He didn't enjoy having to put into words how music made him feel.

'Try to tell me. And then I'm going to make milkshakes.'

Robin gave an elaborate sigh. 'It's shivery like when I get out of the bath at your house.'

The radiator in the bathroom that the grandchildren used didn't work very well and it was always a good idea to hop in and out of the bath at speed, dressing and undressing smartly.

'The music sounds cold?'

'That's what I said, Grandpa. Shivery.' Robin fidgeted and huffed. The moment the music ended, so did his miraculous concentration. He started to pick at a loose thread on the cushion cover.

'I think you're quite right,' I said, trying to engage him. 'The music does sound cold. It's about the first cuckoo in spring but it's very early spring and still chilly. It makes me think of green things shooting.'

I opened my desk drawer, pulled out a typed sheet of paper and handed it to him.

'Here. These are the programme notes for today's music-room concert. I thought you might like them to be typed up like at a real concert.'

Robin took them from me and stared at the piece of paper reverently, even though he couldn't read it. He glanced up at me with a look of mild reproach. 'Grandpa, if it's a proper concert you have to give me the programme at the beginning and I have to pay money for it and it has to be folded and not like that.'

He flapped the single sheet at me.

'I'll give it to you at the start next time. And you can pay me a penny.'

'A pound or it isn't real.'

'A pound for the subscription for the whole concert series.'

He looked dubious.

'I'm giving you a special rate because you're an excellent customer and come to all the concerts,' I explained. 'It's what the proper concert halls do.'

He stared at me for a moment, blue eyes big with suspicion, and then acquiesced with a nod.

We traipsed along the passage to the kitchen to make milk-shakes. The kitchen was rather old-fashioned with green Formica work surfaces rather than the modern taste for gran-ite or marble, and I'd kept the ancient range even though it didn't work. We sat at the oak table, scrubbed white over the years, and drank banana milkshakes, Robin slurping his happily through a curly straw. The piano had curbed some of his naughtiness. However, if, God forbid, a lesson was cancelled or he couldn't practise during his allotted time, the entire family suffered. His tantrums were Wagnerian and lasted nearly as long as the entire *Ring* cycle.

He watched me over the top of his glass, blowing bubbles

with his straw. I didn't want him to spend the whole day in the music room with the curtains drawn. Boys also require dirt and fresh air. I feared the consequences of suggesting such a thing but I would not be a coward in small matters. My father had instilled in us as children a deep-rooted fear of being what he termed 'a drip'. It was a sin and a failing so hideous that for some years I had believed it to be a fatal and infectious disease that one could stave off only through cold baths, tedious walks in the rain and endless evenings without the respite of a fire.

'Robin, at the end of the concert we shall go for a walk. We can take the fishing nets down to the river and hunt for tadpoles.'

'Are they slimy?'

'Absolutely. Covered in the stuff. Perfectly disgusting.'

'OK, I'll come.'

'Oh. Good,' I said, relieved.

After the second part of our concert – Mahler – we put on wellingtons and waterproofs and strolled down to the river. I felt a little guilty about the Mahler; it seemed adult and inappropriate – as if I'd shown him a film containing love-making – but his teacher had apparently mentioned Mahler's piano quartet and, not having a recording of that, I'd ended up playing him Mahler's Fifth. He'd sat, rapt as ever, and afterwards didn't seem any the worse for it.

The grass was slick with dew and a flush of yellow celandine had unfurled in the spring sunshine, speckling the ground beneath the willows and blackthorn in the wild part of the garden. Daffodils and narcissi bobbed in the wind, studding the verge with colour. The earth smelled of fresh, growing things. Even before we reached the river, I could hear the trickle of the groundwater beneath us, seeping through the soil. Our progress was slow as Robin had to investigate the tiny, bedraggled corpse of a mouse, and sluice his boots in every puddle. When we arrived at the riverbank we dangled for tadpoles in a slow-flowing bend. I'd brought jam jars and Robin ladled phlegmy gobs of wriggling ooze into them. He surveyed the tadpoles writhing in the water, gloriously revolted.

'They're crotchets,' he announced. 'But when they wiggle their tails, they turn into quavers.' He rubbed a filthy hand across his face, streaking it with mud or goodness knew what. 'I shall write them a sonata. A tadpole sonata.'

'What an excellent idea,' I said. 'And how will you create the musical effect of slime?'

Robin scratched his nose and considered the matter. Crouching on his haunches, he was silent for a moment. 'There's something I'm not supposed to tell you, Grandpa.'

'Who said you're not supposed to tell me?'

'Mummy.'

This put me in a bit of a quandary – I was more than a little curious to know something that Clara had insisted Robin conceal. On the other hand, I didn't want to land the poor fellow in hot water with his mother.

'Oh dear. Then I suppose you'd better not.'

Robin scowled. 'I'm going to tell you and you can just not tell Mummy that I told you.' He glanced up at me. 'You're very old, Grandpa. You should be good at keeping secrets. You might even die before you have a chance to tell.'

I wasn't quite sure how to respond to this. 'I'll do my best to keep the secret. Hopefully my death won't be necessary.'

Robin avoided meeting my eye. 'Some people want me to play piano on the telly.'

Anger threaded through me. 'What people?'

'I dunno. Some people. Daddy knows them. I'm not supposed to tell you. Mummy said, "Grandpa won't like it.

Robin George Bennet, you mustn't tell Grandpa because he won't like it one bit."'

'Bloody right,' I said. 'For God's sake. What are they thinking? Ruddy fools.'

I was almost shouting and Robin looked as if he might start to cry.

'Oh, darling. I'm sorry. I'm not angry with you.'

'Don't you like the telly?'

'I don't like children on the telly.'

'Never? Then you couldn't have kids in any of the shows. Even the ones for kids.'

'That's different. I don't think that bright young chaps like you should perform in front of people. Not till you're older.'

We pottered about by the river for a little longer, but I kept checking my watch, wanting to return to the house and wait for Clara. It grew cold and we headed back. Exhausted, Robin struggled to walk and whined for me to carry him. I heaved him onto my shoulders, invigorated that I was still strong enough. There's life in this old dog yet, I declared silently. I hummed an old tune as we trudged back to the house. Robin was so tired that I laid him down to snooze in the drawing room, tucking him under the ancient horsehair blanket, which he insisted upon and then complained was itchy. I poured myself a Scotch and waited.

I heard the rumble of wheels on gravel. A few minutes later voices echoed in the passage. Lucy and Clara appeared in the drawing room. I pointed to Robin and put my finger to my lips. Clara turned round and waved at her daughters to be quiet. Katy and Annabel crept in, tiptoeing elaborately, and lay down beside the fire. Ralph followed a moment later and, after helping himself to a slug of the good Scotch, stretched out in the chair nearest the fire. I stiffened.

'Well, how was it?' I said quietly.

Lucy shrugged. 'Short. Sad.'

I didn't know what to add to this. I was sure that there was some kind of pleasantry invented for the occasion but not knowing what it was I said nothing. The girls looked very smart. They wore dark skirt suits and I thought how pretty my daughters were. Such things shouldn't matter but they do.

'Darlings, would you like a drink? Gin and tonic? A glass of wine?'

'Gin and tonic,' called Katy from the hearthrug, making her sister giggle.

I opened a bottle of wine, found some crisps and we settled back beside the fire. The children sipped lemonade. Katy eyed me with interest.

'The rabbi wondered why you weren't there. He thought you were poorly. He said we could have done it another time when you were better.'

'I'm not poorly,' I said.

'No,' agreed Katy.

She was fishing for information. I couldn't understand how these women learned such tactics so young. I glanced at my son-in-law, occupied with his whisky and filling in the cross-word on my copy of *The Times* (another habit I can't abide – what sort of chap does another chap's crossword with-out checking first?) I was outflanked by women, and the men who ought to be on my side were either aged five and fast asleep or, in the case of Ralph, unhelpful and hostile. I decided it was time to change the topic of conversation.

'Robin tells me that you want him to go on some television show.'

'Blast it, Clara. I thought you'd told him not to say anything,' snapped Ralph, no longer making an effort to be quiet.

Clara looked anxiously from her husband to me, wonder-ing how to placate us both. 'I did tell him not to say anything.' She turned to me. 'Of course we were going to discuss it with you, Daddy, but I didn't think today was the right time. And nothing is decided yet.'

'I should hope not,' I said, cross all over again.

'It's a tremendous opportunity,' said Ralph, fixing me with a look of ill-concealed dislike. 'I don't really see why it's a matter for the whole family.'

I glanced over to the sofa where Robin was sprawled, still asleep. I wished for the thousandth time that Edie were here. She would have defused the situation, mollified Ralph and quietly persuaded them both that having Robin perform in public at such a young age was a ghastly idea. I tried to think what she would have said, although inevitably I was incapable of presenting it with much tact.

'Your mother sang as a child and loathed it. Her lifelong stage fright was a consequence of having been forced to perform when she was so young.'

Clara stiffened. 'She never said that to me. And no one is forcing Robin to do anything. He loves to perform.'

I felt a pulse tick in my temple. 'He loves to play, not to perform.' I glanced at Ralph who was rolling his eyes at Clara. 'No, Ralph, it is not the same thing. At present Robin's enjoyment of music is a very private matter. He plays for himself. If we happen to listen, then all to the good. He likes to please us – we're his family, after all. But he does not play for us. He's a charming and selfish little fellow who plays solely for his own pleasure. And at five years old it's absolutely right that he should. Performance, on the other hand, is about presenting oneself to an audience. It necessitates self-awareness, which Robin doesn't have and, frankly, oughtn't to have.'

I sat back on the sofa and steadied myself with a sip of whisky. My heart was beating wildly like a panicked bird, a most unpleasant sensation. Katy and Annabel stared at me, mouths agape. I didn't think many people dared to contradict their father, but I confess that, when it comes to matters of music, I'm afraid of no man.

Clara shot a pleading look at her sister. Next to Edie, Lucy was considered the best person to reason with me. Lucy was always the peacemaker. When they were girls she'd confess to Clara's crimes simply to get the unpleasantness over with. We never believed her, leading, inevitably, to Clara complaining that, in my eyes at least, darling Lucy could do no wrong.

Lucy cleared her throat. 'Papa, you keep telling us how difficult it is to succeed as a pianist. Isn't this a wonderful opportunity for Robin?'

Ralph seized his moment. 'It is. I showed the producers a tape of him and they were astounded. They've never had a kid his age on the show. They're desperate for a prodigy.'

I winced, unable to abide that term. 'Child prodigies are circus animals. Remarkable because they're freaks of nature. Brilliant but freaks nonetheless. They want to put him on television so that people can gawp at him.'

'Oh for God's sake, Fox. There is no need to be so melodramatic,' said Ralph, helping himself to yet more of the good single malt. 'It's a fantastic opportunity. He works hard. We all do. The lessons and travel are bloody expensive. It all mounts up.'

I thought this was a bit of a cheek, considering that I'd surreptitiously paid for Robin's lessons.

'And yes, Fox, I know that you've been paying for the lessons. That has to stop. It's humiliating. I'm his father and it's up to me to foot his bills.'

He dared me to contradict him but I threw up my hands. What he said was true: it's a man's right to pay for his own son.

Clara frowned and looked at her daughters. 'Wouldn't you prefer to go and play or watch a video?'

They shook their heads in unison. Watching us squabble was clearly much more interesting than any other kind of entertainment.

Lucy frowned and coughed. 'Has anyone asked Robin what he would like?'

'For pity's sake,' I exclaimed, quite exasperated by these trendy parenting notions. I've never given two hoots for what a child proclaims he wants. 'He wants to eat chocolate instead of vegetables, wipe bogies under the dining-room table and play the piano twenty-three hours each day. We decide what's best.'

'No,' said Ralph, 'Clara and I decide.'

I grunted, too angry to talk, and looked over at Robin, snoozing on the sofa. His eyelids flickered. The rascal was only pretending to be asleep. I hoped the argument hadn't upset him. On the other hand, I dreaded that there was worse to come.

∼

The television show was one of those ghastly talent contests. I'd never watched it before but Clara lent me some videos that the production company had sent through and I dutifully endured a few episodes. I fast-forwarded through most of the first few, which I considered to be the worst kind of freak show. Some of the contestants appeared to have some kind of mental illness and in my view should have been referred to a doctor instead of being given an opportunity to share their delusions with the nation. It was a pitiful spectacle. It never ceases to bewilder me what people find entertaining. There are so many marvellous and talented individuals – musicians, actors, ballerinas – all of whom are eager to transport us with their remarkable skills, and yet many of us prefer to watch the twitchings of the asinine and the damaged. It's the modern equivalent of the gallows. Sterile and sanctioned, but a gallows nonetheless – we applaud while they dance in the air.

I digress. These things infuriated and frustrated me but, as Robin never stopped reminding me, I am very old.

It was the first of Robin's meetings with the producers in London and Clara and Robin wanted me to go. I did not bother to ask whether Ralph felt the same way since it was perfectly clear that he did not. The meeting was in the afternoon and, although we had time beforehand, for once I did not invite Clara and Robin to lunch with me at the club. I could feel Clara waiting for the invitation, but while I did feel rather bad about it (despite everything, I do very much enjoy my daughters' company and taking them out to luncheon is a father's great pleasure), on this occasion I'd arranged to meet Marcus and Albert. I found myself once again very much in need of their advice. Clara and Robin disappeared to John Lewis to purchase new school shoes or some such, and I took a taxi down to Pall Mall and my club.

I enjoy playing the part of the old gent when I come to town. The pavement along St James's is strewn with elderly chaps much like myself, like white anemones. They all wear similar suits: good hard-wearing tweed, never in fashion but also never quite out of it. We fellows are an endangered breed in general, but the clubs along Pall Mall are stuffed with us. They are places where jackets and ties must be worn, where burgundy and cigars are encouraged, while denim and women are frowned upon.

My club is the RAC. Nothing to do with the automobile rescue service any longer; it is instead one of those last bastions of civility or old fogery, depending on your point of view. Being an old fogey, I am fond of the place. It's very comfortable – a little too comfortable after yet another shiny refurbishment. I preferred the worn leather, the slightly gloomy bar and the atmosphere of regretful yet elegant decay, but with members dying off at quite a rate, the club needed to encourage the enemy – young chaps of merely forty or fifty – to join.

A porter in a red uniform greeted me at the desk.

'Mr Fox-Talbot, Sir Marcus and Mr Shields are waiting for you in the bar.'

I walked across the chequered floor to the new bar, ablaze with the light from an array of chandeliers.

'Morning,' said Marcus a little sadly. 'They've cleaned out all the nooks and repapered the crannies. I don't like it at all.'

'No,' I agreed, glancing about. 'It's beastly. It feels like a gentlemen's club in drag.'

'Well, I like it,' said Albert. 'I think the new bar is splendid.'

'You always were a bit of a modernist,' reproached Marcus, and Albert laughed.

'I'm not sure that liking art deco lamps and polished brass makes me a modernist exactly. Shall we order drinks?'

This was another thing that I liked about my old chums. There was never the slightest hesitation about pre-luncheon drinks. Clara and Lucy, even Ralph, inevitably objected on the grounds that they'd really better not since they had work to do in the afternoon. I've always considered that a paltry excuse. If I'm honest, some of my most innovative works have been achieved as a direct result of a Negroni, a dozen oysters and a bottle of lunchtime Chablis.

We settled down with our drinks and, after a few minutes of chit-chat, Marcus turned to me with a 'Well? What's up?'

I told them as succinctly as I could about the television business, which wasn't succinctly at all, since I succeeded in getting het up and furious all over again. They listened without interruption and only when I slowed, reaching for my glass, did Albert raise an eyebrow.

'Are you quite finished, Fox?' he asked.

'Yes. I think so. The whole business is dreadful. It's a terrible thing for the boy.'

'Quite so,' agreed Marcus.

Albert sighed. 'Whether it is or it isn't, you are not a musician in this situation. You're a grandfather. If you've made your point, which, knowing you, old chap, you probably have several times over with decreasing politeness . . .' He glanced at me and I nodded: it was perfectly true. The last time I'd said my piece, Clara had left pretty quickly without saying goodbye. 'Then I'm afraid,' Albert said, 'it's time to shut the hell up.'

'I'll have to pick up the bloody pieces afterwards when it all goes wrong,' I said, signalling for another snifter.

Albert shrugged. 'Then you do. You're the boy's grandfather, not his father. It's not up to you to make the decisions. If you keep sticking your nose in, you won't change anything but you will thoroughly annoy Clara.'

I turned to Marcus. 'You're very quiet.'

He frowned. 'It's a quandary. I agree with you that the boy is far too young to perform in public. It's a horrible idea.'

'Good. At least I have one ally,' I grumbled, giving Albert a sharp look.

Marcus waved his hand. 'Oh do be quiet, Fox. Albert's perfectly correct. Don't piss off your daughter. It won't end well.'

I stared miserably at the melting ice in my glass.

'Do you remember in the early days when I used to advise you on your orchestration?' asked Marcus.

'Good grief, do I remember? "Too thick. Too much cello. No pianist could play that unless he had four fucking hands."'

Marcus looked extremely smug, an unusual expression for a man of eighty-two. 'Ah, yes, but was I ever wrong?'

'No.'

He looked even more smug. Positively Cheshire cat. 'Well, Albert and I are equally correct about this. You've said your bit.

Now shut up and cheer at the sidelines. If it does all go wrong, then be glad that you're around to help pick up the pieces.'

'Don't upset them all, Fox,' said Albert, more gently this time. 'You seem better. You've put on a bit of weight and you smile. The boy's doing you good. You don't want to lose him by being rude to his parents.'

This wasn't the advice that I'd wanted. I'd rather hoped that the three of us would blaze into the production company's offices like the ageing cowboys in *The Magnificent Seven* and call a halt to the whole thing. Unfortunately, I had a disagreeable, churning feeling in my guts suggesting either that the oysters were off or, more likely, that my friends were right. I decided to voice no further objections to Clara and Ralph – or, as Edie liked to say, 'For once in your life, Harry, keep *schtum*.' I wished she could have been here to see it. Harry Fox-Talbot, keeping *schtum* at last.

~

The meeting wasn't held at the television studios but in cramped offices in Soho, plastered with posters of previous talent-show winners – at least I presumed they were winners due to the number of exclamation marks after their names. Robin, Clara and I perched in a row on a leather sofa, while Ralph prowled the waiting room, pretending to read the industry magazines. On the opposite sofa a doll-faced girl of eight or nine, wearing a pink T-shirt and a glittery Alice band, sat with her mother, a large stuffed bear with a matching Alice band between them. She smiled at Robin, who grimaced and started to pick his nose. My grandson had not yet developed charm.

I was already irritated. I didn't think children ought to be kept waiting like this. It only exacerbates their anxiety. But then I wondered whether perhaps that was the point. To see how they managed under pressure. Robin clutched his music on his lap. He didn't need it to play, but its presence comforted him.

A barrage of overly solicitous assistants kept offering us a surprising variety of waters. 'Still? Sparking? Chilled? Room temperature?'

'Tea, please,' I said. 'Hot.'

Clara shot me an anxious glance. I sighed. Robin had promised me that he would behave and in turn Clara had extorted the same promise from me. After twenty minutes or so we were called in to see the producers, ahead of the girl and her mother.

A cluster of chairs had been set out around a coffee table. The walls were lined with yet more posters of aspiring and perspiring young men and women, most of them mid-song, eyes screwed up, pink mouths open as wide as starling chicks' waiting for worms to be popped in. Three people stood up to greet us as we entered, two women and a man. All of them were much too young – everyone seems young to me but even the man, who was the eldest of the three, was barely out of his twenties.

'Hi, I'm Mike,' he said. 'This is Ellie and Jocasta.'

The two women smiled and waved in bubbly unison, like synchronised swimmers. Ellie, a sparkly blonde who looked as though she ought to still be in school finishing her geography homework, grinned warmly at Robin. 'We're so excited to meet you, Robin. We loved the tape your dad sent in. You're very talented.'

Robin said nothing, only stared. There were a few minutes of chit-chat about the weather. I've observed over the years that this is the way that one can distinguish meetings in the various parts of the world. In England one starts with a discussion of the weather, usually commiserating about the rain, occasionally marvelling at an outbreak of sunshine, while in Los Angeles every meeting begins with at least fifteen minutes spent complaining about traffic. Meetings in Dorset inevitably start with discussions on compost and the progress of one's vegetable patch.

The other woman, Jocasta, leaned over and whispered something to Ellie, who nodded.

'You're the grandfather?' said Ellie to me as if it were a role for a play.

'I'm Robin's grandfather, yes.'

'And you're the composer?'

'I am a composer.'

'And it was you who discovered Robin's gift?' She glanced down again at Jocasta's clipboard.

'I realised that he had an affinity for music, yes.'

'And you're a well-known composer, is that right? And you run a series of summer music concerts at a country house?'

'Well, at my house,' I said.

Ellie frowned and looked at the clipboard in Jocasta's lap. 'Oh. So you actually own,' she ran her finger down the page, 'Hartgrove Hall in Dorset?'

'I do.'

'Oh.' She appeared momentarily stumped and then shrugged. 'We like to reflect the audience's world back at them and so perhaps Hartgrove Hall is a bit' – she hesitated, reaching for the right word – 'rarefied for us.'

I thought this was a bit much since it was quite clear to me that both Jocasta and Ellie had been educated at Cheltenham Ladies' College or some such establishment. They had the gleam and shimmer of the expensively educated. The three of them stared at me, clearly making a reassessment. Jocasta produced a flourish of fresh notes.

'But you teach him? That must be a wonderful experience.'

'I don't teach him any more. I'm afraid I'm a limited pianist. He comes to my house to practise.'

Three sets of eyes now swivelled eagerly to face Clara and Ralph. 'You can't afford to buy Robin his own piano? That's fantastic.'

They wrote copious notes.

Ralph coughed. 'No, that isn't it at all. We could. We decided that Robin is so hooked on the piano it was better not to have one in the house.'

'I'm the same with chocolate,' said Jocasta, smiling at Robin. 'Can't have it in the house. I just can't resist.' She giggled.

I felt deeply uneasy. My instinct was that these people were much, much smarter than they were pretending to be. There was a careful plan here and simply because we couldn't see it didn't mean that it wasn't laid out meticulously around our ankles.

I cleared my throat. 'May I ask what is the purpose of today's meeting?'

'Of course!' said Ellie. 'I'm so glad you asked. Thank you.'

Mike, who hadn't spoken yet, leaned forward and addressed himself directly to Robin. 'We simply want to have a friendly chat. Our researchers have told us a bit about you but we'd like to hear it from you. Then if we're all happy – you most of all, Robin – we'll put you up tonight in a nice hotel in London and pay for you and your family to go out for a nice dinner, and then tomorrow you'll show us what you can do on the piano.'

Clara frowned. 'He's auditioning tomorrow? I thought the auditions for the new series weren't for months.'

Mike shook his head. 'The open auditions aren't till August. This is a special pre-performance. It's not an audition at all.'

We must have looked utterly confused as Ellie smiled indulgently at Mike. 'We like to have a few really special performers, some absolute gems of talent dotted amongst the public auditions. We want to see if Robin might be a good fit for one of those spots.'

Jocasta took over. 'So, if all goes well, Robin would go along to the open auditions in Bournemouth or, if you prefer, here in London, but he'd already know everyone and he'd almost certainly be guaranteed a place on the live show.'

'He does well tomorrow and then he'll be on the show?' asked Ralph.

'Very probably. Nothing is ever absolutely certain in live TV,' said Mike.

'So tomorrow is a pre-audition audition?' I asked, trying to keep the disdain from my voice.

'I wouldn't call it that,' said Ellie, brightly.

'No, but I wouldn't be wrong if I did,' I said and Clara shot me a filthy look.

I bit my tongue but I was troubled. This wasn't how things ought to be done. When I asked a musician to play to secure a spot in the festival orchestra or for a new recording, then I jolly well told them it was an audition.

'We shouldn't really be discussing any of this just yet,' said Mike. 'The behind-the-scenes stuff of television is very boring but we do need to keep it secret or the magic is spoiled.'

'If Robin does decide to play at the pre-performance tomorrow, we will need all of you to sign a confidentiality agreement,' said Ellie with a particular nod in my direction.

I glanced at Clara. 'I'm here to do what I'm told.'

For some unknown reason this seemed only to infuriate Clara and she looked away, refusing to meet my eye.

Jocasta returned to her clipboard with its kaleidoscope of neon-pen highlights. She spoke softly, her voice sticky with sympathy. 'I understand it was the passing of Robin's grandmother that brought the two of you together.'

I stiffened. I would not discuss Edie.

She tried again. 'I understand that Edie – it was Edie, wasn't it? – was a singer?'

Clara shot me an anxious look, clearly unhappy herself at

the line of questioning. 'Yes, my mother's name was Edie. Her maiden and stage name was Edie Rose.'

The three producers nodded with enthusiasm. 'Yes. The famous wartime singer. "A Shropshire Thrush." Amazing. Robin has such talented grandparents,' said Ellie in reverent tones.

'Musicality often runs in families,' I said. 'The Bach dynasty is the most famous, perhaps. But there was also the Strauss family, and Wolfgang Mozart's father Leopold was an accomplished pianist as well as a composer. And of course there's the Von Trapp family. One mustn't forget them. Without them, lederhosen wouldn't be nearly as popular as they are today.'

Mike didn't smile. 'Your dad's funny,' he said to Clara.

'He is a talented man,' she said dryly. 'But I'm afraid, in our family, musical ability skipped a generation.'

'In any case, the grandparents make for a compelling backstory. It's great stuff. Really great,' said Jocasta.

I winced. 'It's not a back-story. It's my life,' I said.

'Of course,' said Jocasta quickly. 'We're not trying to diminish you.'

Ralph snorted. 'Oh, don't worry about that. Fox is never knowingly diminished.'

Clearly sensing a family squabble brewing, Ellie turned to Robin who'd remained silent throughout the entire conversation.

'How about you, my love? Is there anything you're worried about?'

Robin shook his head.

'Good! That's how it should be!'

I sighed inwardly. These people littered their conversation with exclamation marks. It must be exhausting to maintain such a fever pitch of enthusiasm.

'Do you have any questions, lovely?'

'Yes,' said Robin. It was the first time he'd opened his mouth except to slot in one of the cupcakes that had been set out on the table.

'What is it, my love?'

'When can I play the piano?'

They all laughed uproariously, perfectly delighted with him.

I did not join in.

~

The budget apparently didn't stretch to putting me up in a hotel too, so with considerable relief I took a room at the club. I was exhausted. I'd been grilled on my career and my routine with Robin. They were evidently thrilled when I described our music-room concerts and asked whether they could come and film us if, as they hoped, Robin appeared on the show. However, they confessed with an air of obsequious confidentiality, we'd need to film it at Robin's house, Hartgrove Hall being 'a little out of the mainstream'. I'd spent a lifetime avoiding publicity. Edie despised anyone prying into our personal lives, while I've always hated talking about my music – everything that I want to say is in the piece. Either you can hear it and it works, or you don't and it doesn't. There's not much to discuss. The idea of having a film crew watching us was very unpleasant.

I was ruminating on all this in the bar when Marcus appeared.

'You're staying tonight too?' he asked, evidently pleased to see me.

I nodded miserably and told him about the afternoon.

'For God's sake, say no to any filming!' he said.

'But you told me to be amenable,' I said. 'This is me pretending to be amenable.'

'We said stop arguing with your daughter. That's all.'

'Oh,' I said, more miserable still. 'I have to go with Robin to an audition tomorrow that isn't an audition.'

'That definitely calls for brandy,' said Marcus firmly, gesturing to a waiter.

'That is a splendid idea,' I said, perking up a bit.

We chatted for a while with pleasant ease and familiarity. Then, sometime after the second nightcap, Marcus turned to me and asked, 'Are you writing again, old chap?'

I shook my head. 'No. Nothing. It's all quiet up here.' I tapped my temple.

'Give it time,' he said.

'That's all very well. But I'm not quite so young as I was. I can't wait for ever.'

We sat for a while, pleasantly discussing mutual acquaintances, orchestras past and present, conductors come and gone, and then Marcus cleared his throat.

'I wasn't sure whether to tell you. But what the hell. I've got cancer. Now don't get all upset. It's not a tragedy. I'm eighty-three next birthday but the doctors have told me that will probably be my last. I'd better have a jolly good party.'

'Oh God, Marcus, I'm so sorry.'

I was sorry. More than I could say, but not just for him, for myself too. Marcus Albright was my closest and dearest pal. His sense of fun and mischief remained undimmed. That was the peril of old age, to outlive one's great friends.

'I don't want you to die,' I said, as a result of having drunk rather too much brandy.

'No,' agreed Marcus. 'I don't much fancy it myself. I know that as one gets older, one is supposed to be dignified and peacefully resigned but I don't feel like that at all. I'm downright pissed off. I was just starting to get somewhere with the Beethoven sonatas and now I might not have time to finish. And death isn't really a deadline that I can push.'

'It's terrible timing,' I agreed.

'To terrible timing,' said Marcus, raising his glass.

We clinked.

'And to death,' he added ruefully. 'May he come in his pyjamas while I'm sleeping.'

I raised my glass again, swallowing with some difficulty.

'I keep thinking of George,' said Marcus. 'He was so brave at the end. I don't want to be brave. I don't want it to be the least bit necessary. I want to be a wimp to the finish.'

We were both silent for a moment, considering George's grim stoicism through his final illness.

'Edie took wonderful care of him,' said Marcus. 'I wish she was still around to take care of me. On second thoughts, I'd prefer a young Errol Flynn.'

I was desperate to go upstairs to my room. I had an unpleasant feeling that I might cry and I didn't want to do that in front of Marcus. It seemed tactless.

'What sort of cancer?' I asked because I thought I should.

'Do you really want to know? Does it make a difference?'

'No. I hope you're not in pain.'

'I'm not. Not yet. When I am, I shall take all the drugs. All the exciting new ones that weren't available when I was young enough to really take advantage.'

'Excellent plan.'

My chest was starting to ache and I had a lump in my throat that I couldn't swallow. Marcus reached out and clasped my hand. He was surprisingly strong. He gripped it, stroking my knuckles with his forefinger.

'I loved you, Fox,' he said.

And I saw him again as he had been, twenty-nine and sunburned, diving off the rocks and vanishing into the waters as I yelled at the empty sea, only to see him pop up a moment later, spluttering and laughing, as I shouted, furious that he'd frightened me.

He looked frightened now. I was filled with helpless fury. I leaned over and kissed him. His cheek was wet with tears. He clenched my hand more tightly, almost hurting me, and he did not let go for a long time.

I did not sleep well. I dreamed of Marcus and Edie. We were sailing in a boat off the Isle of Mull, which was quite wrong as Edie hadn't been there. We were young again or rather we looked young; I was my present self, yet with my memory of everything that had happened since. It was a sunlit afternoon and I felt unbearably, unconscionably sad. There was no sound except for the slap of water against the wooden hull of the boat. Then they were both gone, leaving me desolate and alone in glorious sunshine.

I woke up with a headache, feeling thoroughly sorry for myself. I attempted to pull myself together with a hearty breakfast of coffee and kippers in the club restaurant. Cowardly as it might seem, I couldn't bear to see Marcus. I ate quickly and left, hoping to avoid him. I spent a quiet morning drifting along St James's, ordering another half-dozen Oxford shirts from my tailor, and afterwards walked up to Hatchards where I bought a few books that I felt I ought to read but knew I wouldn't. I still found it terribly hard to concentrate on anything longer or more involved than a newspaper article. Still, the act of purchasing the books made me feel better, as though by owning them I would be better informed, even if I never opened their covers.

I ate a lonely lunch at a dreary restaurant and returned to the club for an indulgent snooze. I thus managed to dawdle through the hours until Robin's not-audition, and at three o'clock climbed in a taxi to take me to the television studio. I'd been before, back in the days when classical performances were

198

still occasionally televised, but, to my shock, I calculated that I'd not been for nearly twenty years. Everything had changed. I barely recognised the building and thought for a moment that the driver had brought me to the wrong place. Inside everything was white like in an upmarket dentist's surgery, while a barrage of television screens displayed the shows currently being broadcast. I'd never watched any of them.

I gave my name to a girl behind the reception desk and on receiving a plastic identity pass was herded along a maze of neon-bright corridors to a studio. It was much larger than I'd been led to expect after yesterday's meeting, and I was surprised to find an audience of more than fifty people milling along raked rows of seating. The technical crew were busy with lighting and cameras at the front. A grand piano stood at the centre, a constellation of lights, cameras and electrical cables all around it.

I felt distinctly apprehensive. I glanced about for Robin or Clara but couldn't see them. Noticing a girl with a headset, I introduced myself.

'Hello, I'm Robin Bennet's grandfather. I'd very much like to see him before the – well, the whatever this is,' I said.

The girl smiled at me and mumbled something into her headset.

'You're the prodigy's grandpa?' she asked after a moment.

I winced, then nodded.

She mumbled again. Clearly the invisible voice gave her some instruction, as she turned to me, saying, 'Will you come with me, my lovely? You must be thrilled. Gosh, it's so exciting.'

We hurried along yet more white corridors – God knew how people found their way around such a place – until we reached a black door and I was shown into Robin's dressing room. I ruffled his hair and shook his hand. He was always very particular about not being kissed by anyone other than his mother, who was permitted to on special occasions.

'Have you asked to speak to one of the three musketeers from yesterday about all of this?' I asked Clara.

'No? Do you think I should?'

A child-sized dinner suit hung from a clothes rail.

'He's supposed to wear this.'

Robin looked from the suit to his mother with growing horror.

'Yes. I think you should speak to someone,' I said. 'This is a bit much.'

Before I could gather whether or not Clara agreed with me, Ralph entered, holding paper cups of coffee and a carton of juice for Robin. 'Well, isn't this exciting?' he announced with too much bravado.

'Grandpa?' said Robin.

'What is it?' I asked, pulling up a chair beside him. 'You can play if you want to, but if you've changed your mind that's perfectly all right.'

'I want to play,' said Robin. 'I really, really want to play.'

'Well, that's settled,' said Ralph, practically rubbing his hands.

'Is there lots of people out there?' asked Robin.

'Yes,' I said. I'd never seen the point in lying to performers. They'd see for themselves soon enough and it was always better to be prepared, either way. 'I think there's more than fifty in the audience and then, with the crew, it might be nearly a hundred.'

He looked terrified. In hindsight, perhaps I ought to have fibbed – he probably wouldn't have been able to tell the number under the glare of the lights.

'You don't have to play,' said Clara.

'I do. I do,' shouted Robin, looking as if he was about to cry.

I noticed that he'd developed a large stye on his left eye, which was puffy and bloodshot. He blinked and rubbed it.

'Stop it, darling. I've told you not to touch it,' said Clara.

He nodded and rubbed it again, smearing yellow ointment all over his sleeve. My grandson was not looking his best.

Clara found another headset-wearing young person and asked to speak to one of the producers. Ten minutes later Mike appeared.

'How are you all feeling? Excited?'

'Itchy,' said Robin, rubbing his eye again.

'We have a few questions,' said Clara. 'There seem to be a vast number of people. More than we were expecting.'

'We like to have quite a few bums on seats. It adds to the atmosphere of the test,' said Mike.

'So it's a test now,' I said, feeling cross. 'Not an audition but a test.'

'A screen test,' corrected Mike. 'But really it's just a fabulous opportunity for Robin to play in a different environment without the pressure of performing on live TV.' He turned and grinned at Robin with too-white teeth. 'The thing to remember is that everyone out there is on your side. Most of them all work right here. They all want to love you, OK?'

'Is it only Robin who's performing?' I asked. It seemed unlikely they'd go to all this trouble for one child – no matter how precocious.

Mike hesitated a moment too long. 'There's a blind opera singer, and a bus driver who plays the bassoon. And there's also Keira, the little girl from yesterday. I don't know if you guys got chatting? She's also a pianist,' he added brightly.

I smelled a rat. I drew Mike to one side. 'I can't imagine that you've room for two young piano players on your television show?'

Mike smiled his white smile and did not meet my eye.

'Nothing is decided yet,' he said, glancing at his phone. 'I'm sorry. I've got to dash. See you out there. You'll be great, Robin.'

We lingered in the sweltering dressing room, listening to the ineffectual roar of the air-conditioner. Clara helped Robin into his dinner suit. The sleeves were too long and the cuffs dangled below his wrists.

'That's no good at all,' I said. 'They'll get in the way of him playing.'

I sat down so that I was eye to eye with Robin. 'Can you stretch your arms out for me? How does your jacket feel?'

He wiggled about and shrugged.

I sighed. 'This is perfectly ridiculous. He needs to try the piano. And see whether this awful get-up interferes with his playing.'

I glanced down at him. He'd now succeeded in getting yellow eye-ointment all over the dinner jacket.

'Robin, darling,' I said. 'You don't have to do what they say. I think you should simply play in your jeans and your T-shirt. You'll be much more comfortable and it will be terribly hot out there under the lights.'

He frowned. 'Can't. I have to wear this, Grandpa. This is what proper piano players wear. If I do good, then I'll get to play in Carn Higgy Hall.'

Clara smiled but I only felt tired. 'Well, you've already played at Hartgrove Hall and I think that's perfectly good enough for the time being.'

This was everything I'd been dreading. For the first time in more than a year, Robin was anxious and self-conscious. Silly ideas about outfits and appearances at concert halls were distracting him at a time when he ought to be playing at home or with his teacher for the simple joy of discovering music. Instead he fidgeted in his shiny suit, hopping from foot to foot like a circus ringmaster who needed to pee.

Another young person muttering into a walkie-talkie appeared.

'Hiya, Robin, all set?'

He gave a small, formal nod.

'I'm going to take your family out front now but they'll all be watching, cheering you on.'

Clara and Ralph hugged the small figure who stood stiffly, receiving their good wishes with quiet acquiescence.

'Forget everyone,' I said. 'No one matters. It's just you and the piano like at home. Afterwards we'll go for milkshakes.'

'OK.'

As we walked away, Clara close to tears – I'm afraid I was for once rather out of sympathy with my daughter – we heard the woman say to Robin, 'It would be lovely if you could run up and give the presenter a hug before you play.'

I glanced at Clara and shook my head in exasperation. Robin really wasn't a casual-hugging kind of child. Demonstrations of affection were rare, spontaneous and limited to immediate family or, after playing Beethoven, his piano teacher.

We were allocated seats at the front of the raked section. A table for the judges had been set up but the famous people from the television show were not there at all. Instead, three stand-ins sat in the chairs with signs round their necks, stating the names of the celebrities they were supposed to represent. I found the whole thing perfectly ridiculous. Mike, Ellie and Jocasta lurked near the cameras, chatting intensely. Clara sat between Ralph and me, pale with anxiety. Even Ralph appeared tense, his foot tap-tapping on the floor.

Mike came to the front and spoke to the audience, informing us when to clap. We sat and we waited. Then Robin appeared, blinking against the lights and rubbing his sore eye. He did not hug anyone. Neither did he smile. He looked serious and grim-faced. Clara had slathered some dreadful junk into his hair, supposedly to smooth his curls, but instead it made it appear greasy and unwashed. He walked straight over to the piano, piled up the cushions on the leather stool and sat down. I realised immediately that they were far too slippery. Before he had even started to play, it was quite clear that he was struggling not to fall off. He hopped down, picked up the cushions again, and rearranged the pile as the audience laughed indulgently. The laughter was kind, but Robin was obviously unsettled.

He sat at the keyboard, shifting and trying not to slide off again, then closed his eyes. I knew that he was trying to shut out the world and will himself back to the hush of the music room at Hartgrove Hall, to conjure the vast mullioned windows with their view of the lawns and the grey lake, and the smell of cedarwood and dust. I watched his shoulders soften. Perhaps he would be all right. He raised his hands to the keys and started to play, more hesitant than usual, but after a few bars he relaxed and Brahms's Rhapsody in B minor rippled across the audience. I felt the collective intake of breath, the sense of wonder that this small person was producing this sound. In a minute or two they would forget that too and simply listen, lost.

But then Robin's sleeves slithered down over his hands. He fumbled with a crash of chords and stopped. The audience giggled. Ralph swore and Clara went so white that I thought she was going to be sick. There was a dreadful silence while Robin sat, fumbling with his cuffs, but while the boy was a marvel at the piano, he couldn't manage a stiff button under duress. This was simply ghastly. I couldn't bear it.

I stood and strode over to the stage. A large man in a black T-shirt tried to block my way.

'Move aside,' I snapped in my best conductor's voice.

The man drew back in surprise. I climbed up onto the stage and stood beside Robin.

'Hello, old chap,' I said softly. 'Having a spot of bother?'

Robin was trying valiantly not to cry. 'I think I'd like very much to go home.'

'I quite understand. But perhaps we should play something since we're here.'

I knew that we couldn't leave just yet. I wouldn't allow him to feel that his first appearance was a total failure. Since we were on a stage beneath the lights and before an audience, he needed to experience the pleasure of performance, of weaving a spell over his listeners, even if only for a minute.

'Let's take your jacket off.'

Meekly, he allowed me to remove his jacket and roll up his sleeves so that they no longer interfered with his playing.

'Now play a couple of scales, just to be certain that you're quite comfortable.'

He did as I suggested and nodded. Mike appeared at my elbow.

'Everything OK, folks?'

'Leave us alone,' I snapped. 'We'll play when we're ready.'

He left, muttering something under his breath.

I succeeded in raising the piano stool and found the least slippery of the cushions.

'Will you stay with me, Grandpa?'

'Of course.'

'And will you do the pedals?'

'All right.'

His legs were too short to reach the pedals, and he liked it sometimes when I sat beside him and managed them on his behalf. I squeezed in beside him and waited for him to begin.

He played well – remarkably well for a child of his age – but usually he played well for anyone and no caveats mentioning his tender years were necessary. His playing was extraordinary, not so much for his technical skill but for the emotion he conveyed. I always felt that Robin played from inside the music. But that afternoon, in the television studio, he did not. His performance was self-contained and inhibited. Before the audience he neither felt the same emotions nor conveyed anything much to his listeners beyond the bare notes. The audience was appreciative and applauded with abandon – but I knew that they were clapping a circus act. They would have done the same if a dog had thumped out 'Twinkle, Twinkle' with its paws – they could not tell Robin was an astounding musician. I understood the problem. Robin usually played for himself alone. Until that excruciating afternoon he'd had no interest in communicating his music to anyone else. He had never experienced an audience before, only eavesdroppers, and he was not ready to let anyone else in.

As the applause faded, Robin was led back to his dressing room. I followed but, after his parents arrived, I returned to the studio and hovered at the back behind the cameras. The young girl from yesterday was waiting to perform. She looked terribly pretty, a nodding peony in a flouncy pink frock, her black hair plaited into pigtails. In one hand she clutched her teddy bear – dressed in an outfit matching her own. As she was given her cue, she rushed over to the stand-in presenter, hugging her tightly.

'Would you like to see me play the piano backwards?' she asked the pretend judges, smiling, two perfect dimples appearing in the middle of each rosy cheek like a clever magic trick.

'Yes, please,' said one of the judges at the table. Mike and Jocasta gave a thumbs-up.

I noticed that a special raised piano stool had been brought in – no tumbling off cushions for this child – and she perched carefully with her back to the keyboard. Reaching around, she played a ditty. It was a neat trick. Silly but the audience roared its approval.

'How about upside down?' she asked.

The audience applauded as she lay on the piano stool and stretched up to tinkle on the keys. It was the sort of thing I'd have done in years gone by to entertain my own brothers, but it was a trick for other children, not a display for adults. But again the audience whooped. I felt unutterably drained. This was not my world.

Mike stepped forward, clapping. 'That was great fun, Keira. Now, will you play us something?'

'I'd love to,' she replied, dimples reappearing like cherries on a Belgian bun.

This I was interested to witness. She sat down carefully at the piano and, after a studied pause, launched into Chopin. Her teacher had chosen well. The piece was fast and her technical ability was reasonably good, masking the coldness of her playing. Everything lay in neat rows, tidy and characterless. At the end of the first movement, I had no more knowledge of her personality than I had at the start. Yet her performance was accomplished. She smiled and swayed as she played, creating an elaborate illusion of engagement. She chattered sweetly at the end of the piece and, when she dropped her music during her curtsey, let out a little 'Oops-a-daisy' and giggled, to the audience's delight. She wasn't half the musician that I knew Robin to be, but she was a consummate performer.

As she made her teddy bear bow to the judges' table, I knew with quiet certainty that the producers would not choose Robin to be on their television show.

I was correct in my assessment. After an hour Mike popped by the dressing room to inform us. Robin was devastated.

'But I'm better than her,' he sobbed after Mike had left. 'I heard her before and I'm better.'

'You are better,' I said. 'But you don't want to play on a silly television show.'

'I do want to play on a silly show. I do. I do.'

He lapsed into hiccuping sobs as Clara rubbed his back. Ralph sat at the dressing table in the corner, saying nothing at all.

'You play the piano wonderfully, Robin,' I said. 'But you don't know how to play the audience.'

He gazed at me blankly through a fog of snot and tears. His swollen eye streamed.

'Will you teach me?' he asked.

'No, I won't,' I said and he began to cry again.

'Oh for goodness' sake, Daddy,' said Clara, which I thought was a cheek, considering all I'd put up with.

'Let's go and have some ice cream,' I said.

'I think you were marvellous,' insisted Clara, rumpling his hair.

I took them to Claridge's. Ralph had a supper meeting, or so he said. I suspected he wished to avoid me and my disapproval. We sat in an elegant salon amongst ladies taking late-afternoon tea. Robin looked happier after his second chocolate ice cream while Clara looked happier after her second glass of Chardonnay. I was exhausted by it all and desperate to go home to Dorset. Clara chattered on soothingly about how it was all good experience and how of course he'd play Carnegie Hall one day. I wished she'd stop. I knew it was all kindly meant – she wanted to comfort him, but she offered promises that were not hers to make. When she declared that she was certain he'd play all the great concert halls and that he would, in time, love playing before an audience, she meant only that she wished it. None of us knew; we merely hoped.

I remained cantankerous and thoroughly out of sorts. I worried that they'd stolen something from Robin, something that I'd need to work hard to help him recover: the simple and unconscious joy of playing for one's own pleasure. I watched as Robin shook his head politely: no, he didn't want more ice cream or any more pop to drink. He didn't want to stay up late and watch cartoons or any of the cornucopia of treats Clara offered him. I looked at my grandson and understood. He had an ache inside, but ice cream wouldn't ease it.

'Come,' I said, standing and holding out my hand.

Robin took it and trotted out of the room with me. I led him through the glitzy ocean liner of an entrance hall, past the reception desk with its fleet of uniformed staff, and ushered him into the restaurant. It was not quite six o'clock and there were no diners. The glittering room had that empty, expectant air, like a concert hall before the arrival of the audience. Waiters checked place settings. The sommelier sailed towards us.

'My apologies, sir. The dining room is not yet open. If I could make you a reservation for later on?'

'Another time perhaps. May we borrow the piano for a minute or two?'

He studied us for a moment and then smiled. 'Of course, please.'

I led Robin over to the grand piano. I avoided coming here if I could. It reminded me too much of Edie. This was one of our places and it had not altered very much since our first visit. The grand dining room remained an art deco delight; every wall was mirrored so that the room twinkled and glinted. Waiters flitted from table to table, lighting candles so that in the dozens of mirrors each flame became a constellation.

'Sit down at the keyboard and close your eyes.'

Robin did as I asked.

'Now, pretend we're at home. It's only us.'

He opened his eyes and glanced at the gliding waiters in their black and white.

'Don't mind them. They're not in the least bit interested in you.'

He closed his eyes again.

'Let your mind drift. Let music drift into you like water.'

Apparently unaware of what he was doing, Robin raised his hands to the keyboard and, after a minute, began to play. He played as if he were in a dream. Beethoven's *Little Appassionato* seeped into the room, filling it with drowsy colour. The waiters stopped fussing around the place settings and paused, unable to do anything but listen. The door opened and I saw Clara slip inside. I noticed two guests peer into the room after her, drawn to the music like moths.

I walked over and said quietly, 'The dining room opens at seven,' shooing them away. I did not want them to see that it was a child playing the piano.

Firmly closing the door behind them, I turned to Clara. 'One day we'll open the door and he can hear the applause. One day, but not yet.'

February 1948

I want to be in a place where no one knows me, preferably drunk. I can't bear polite enquiries and sympathetic smiles. Defeated and humiliated, I want to lick my wounds in peace. I end up in London, simply another face in the crowd. I head east because it's cheap and I'm perilously low on funds. This part of the city, battered and broken, suits my frame of mind. There are no new buildings pushing up amidst the bomb craters and grime. No one here even notices the wreckage any longer. I find a nice old pub near Brick Lane, the only building left standing in a sea of rubble, moored amongst the craters like a lone ship, where the landlord lets me play the piano during opening hours and keep any tips. It's a rickety, irritable instrument and I like it. The bar was frequented by black American soldiers during the war. When I find drawing pins pressed into all the tiny hammers inside the piano, I realise it must have been used for jazz. I wonder what happened to those Yankee jazz players and shake off my wretchedness long enough to wish I could have heard them.

I feel the odd twinge of guilt about taking the car. I'm careful not to use the word 'steal'. I did not steal, as it was mine to begin with – at least in part. I estimate that a third of the rattling, decrepit Austin belonged to me. The steering wheel and the broken hubcaps must be mine. In any case, they'll have bought another by now – there was plenty of money from the concert. A nagging internal voice reminds me that the concert cash was supposed to be George's cow money.

I edge away from thoughts of George. Awkward, taciturn, noble George who pines for Edie without complaint. George, who ploughs his unhappiness and longing into furrows along the side of the hill. The muddy ridges and ruts carved into the eastern slopes of Hartgrove Hill are the only sign of George's sorrow.

To hell with George and his silent love. I don't want George as my companion in this. It makes us both ridiculous. And I won't pity him. I couldn't bear to be pitied myself and I won't insult him with sympathy. I tuck away all thoughts of Hartgrove Hall and the green expanse of the hill, the way the field slopes and curves beneath the church like the smooth hollow of a woman's back. And yet, in my sleep, I walk Ringmoor in the dark. I hear the ring of ancient feet, of boots on stone, the whisper of the larch trees in the rain. I follow Edie's footprints in the snow but somewhere amongst the rustling woods, I lose her and wake, empty and adrift.

I have grandiose plans of using my melancholy to fuel my symphony but I'm too miserable to write. I'd always thought that sadness was useful for an artist but either I'm the wrong sort of artist or it's the wrong sort of misery. A dreary flat-ness settles over me, thick as fog, and nothing penetrates. Nothing except for gin or whisky, even beer – as long as I drink enough of it, which I do assiduously. My cash runs out and I make no more than pennies playing the piano so I take a job behind the bar. At the end of each week there is precious little left once my drinks have been taken out of my pay and I take to sleeping in my car. I'm torn between wishing that Edie could see what she's driven me to and being relieved that she can't.

Weeks turn into months. Still I don't write and tell them where I am. At first I'm too mortified. I'm scraped out and the hollow inside is filled with anger at Edie, at Jack. While the heat goes out of my rage, like a sun-baked stone cooling at dusk, the hurt never disappears. Besides, too much time has passed and now I can't write. I begin, in my mind at least, a dozen letters but I can't think of what to say, so I say nothing at all. I alternate between wanting to know how they are battling with the farm and profound relief that I never hear their names.

Winter sinks into spring, warm and grubby. It is not the same here amongst the grey ruins and smoke-filled skies. There are no curlews nor snowdrops. There is no hawthorn blossom nor crocuses. I feel only the easing of the cold. When I wake one morning my car windows are not smudged with frost. I wake with the first light, which comes later now. I trudge into the pub to wash – the landlady kindly lets me use the outside toilet and allows me to bathe twice a week, all for a few shillings. Afterwards I walk the streets, breakfasting on a bagel and trying not to think of Edie. She's a wound that I pick at. Even though today was a bath day, already I feel grimy, my skin covered in grit and a sprinkling of smuts.

On the pavements, hawkers peddle their wares: old clothes, broken or mended kettles, mismatched cutlery, cauliflowers, potatoes, bottles of milk, bottles of nothing, snatches of sheet music, penny-dreadfuls, dried fish, fresh fish, rotten fish. Bare-legged children weave amongst them, dawdling on their way to school or to skip school. Mothers push babies or heave shopping bags or squabble with the traders. I toss my bagel to a gaunt-eyed girl of about seven or eight who snatches it, and clutches it close, uneaten. If I came here believing that it would help me to understand Edie better, to be closer to her, it doesn't and I'm not.

I return to the pub in time to open up. The regulars are queuing outside. I pour them drinks and hide my own behind the counter. That's the landlord's only rule. I mustn't be openly drunk and I mustn't have a drink set out on the bar. A girl walks in. She's blonde and too nice-looking for a place like this.

'I'm sorry, miss,' I say. 'I'm afraid you're lost.'

'So are you,' says Sal in her soft Texan accent.

I'm caught between indignation and embarrassment. She shouldn't be here and I'm put out that she is.

'What can I get you?' I say. I don't want to quarrel.

'Gin and lime.'

I pour it for her. She sips it slowly and shudders, raising a perfectly pencilled eyebrow. I notice that her hair is that garish daffodil yellow again.

'Well?' she demands.

I shrug and pretend to be occupied behind the bar.

'Well, how're you doin'? You don't look so good. What a dive.' She wrinkles her nose delicately and I hand her a cigarette.

'Here. To mask the smell. I suppose Edie sent you.'

There's a burning sensation in my chest. I haven't said her name aloud since I left.

'Afraid not, Fox.'

No one's called me Fox for a while. Here I'm simply Harry.

'One of Jack's pals spotted you. It was Jack who asked me to look in on you.'

Humiliation blooms. I'm not a recalcitrant child. Another part of me is hurt he didn't come himself. His concern clearly has limits.

'I'm not going back.'

'Never said you should. I've come to take you to a concert.'

She places a flyer on the bar. *St Matthew Passion*, St-Martin-in-the-Fields, conductor Marcus Albright.

'So you can report back to Jack, I suppose.'

'Is that so dreadful? To have people who mind about you?'

I've a filthy headache brewing, and I want desperately for her to leave.

'I'm busy.'

'Well, get un-busy.'

'I'm sorry, Sal. It's jolly decent of you to drop by and all that but I'm afraid that I really can't go.'

'I'll pick you up at six. Wear a clean shirt.'

She gives me one last hard stare, then slithers off the bar stool and stalks out.

~

At six-thirty we're sitting side by side on the bus to Piccadilly. It's crammed and I hastily relinquish my seat to a mother and her green-nosed tot with considerable eagerness as it means I can't talk to Sal. I'm feeling grim from the lurching by the time we climb off the bus near Piccadilly.

'Let's find a pub,' I say. 'I could do with a drink.'

'No,' says Sal. 'No more drinking. You can take me to the Lyons' Corner House for an early supper.'

I find myself being propelled along the Haymarket and into the restaurant where we have a dubious meal of potted ham, sloppy potatoes and wet vegetables. I don't eat much, but watch as Sal wolfs down everything. She's rake thin but has the appetite of a teenage boy. If I were in a less foul frame of mind, I'd say that it's oddly attractive.

'Do you know Marcus Albright?' she asks, wiping her mouth with her napkin and setting down her cutlery with a sorrowful little sigh.

'No, not personally. I admire him of course.'

'Well, you should know him. I'm sure you'll like him. Let's get dessert. Shall we get dessert? I love English puddings.'

Before I can answer she's summoned the waitress and orders two spotted dicks and custard, a pudding I've loathed since school. She eats hers and then embarks on mine.

'I have four brothers back home,' she says. 'You learn to eat fast with not much talking or someone will scoop it right off your plate.'

Even Sal is too full for coffee. We hurry to Trafalgar Square. I used to come here to lunchtime concerts at the National

Gallery during the war. I liked to hear Myra Hess's piano recitals. It was always a strange experience – the gallery bereft of pictures, and music taking the place of the missing paintings. I'd come up once in a while during the school hols and there were always queues crocodiling along the street – servicemen were allowed to skip to the front while I always had to wait ignominiously in line with the women and children. I'd longed for the day when I too would be able to stroll to the front in my uniform, the ladies urging me forward. I'd not hankered after much in those days except for a green army jacket and the whiff of adventure. At the thought of my earlier self, I recoil, discomfited.

The queue is still here but this evening it wriggles along the other side of Trafalgar Square, outside St-Martin-in-the-Fields. Vast banners billowing on either side of the church doors advertise 'Marcus Albright' and I experience both admiration and huge, gut-piercing envy. He's the youngest conductor ever to perform with the London Phil and it's rumoured that the Americans want him for the New York Symphony. We join the end of the line and wait. All around us couples chatter and laugh. We are silent. After a few minutes of quiet shuffling, I can bear it no longer.

'I must find a loo. Give me my ticket, I'll see you in there.'

I'm not being very gallant but Sal gives in without a fuss, surrendering a ticket. I hurry around the corner, looking for a gents. I consider slipping into a pub for a swift half before the concert – Lord knows I could do with one – but guilt gets the better of me and after using a particularly unsavoury public lavatory I hurry back to the church. The queue has evaporated and from the open doors I can hear the sound of the orchestra tuning up, which always fills me with the tingle of anticipation; it's better than any aperitif. It's not quite seven-thirty and I still have time to find my seat. For the first time this evening I'm glad that Sal has hauled me here.

'Ticket please, sir.'

I reach into my pocket and, scrabbling, find nothing. To my dismay I realise it must have slipped out in the gents and is now probably lying on the floor beside a urinal.

'I'm terribly sorry. I seem to have misplaced it.'

The usher notices me properly and recoils slightly. My dishevelled appearance doesn't match my voice. I probably still smell of booze and my shirt is not as clean as it ought to be.

'That's a pity, sir. That there is the line for returns. Doesn't seem likely now but you might get lucky.'

I glance to where he's pointing and see a queue of twenty people, fidgeting and checking their watches. None of them is going to see this concert and neither, by the looks of it, am I.

I try to jostle past him. 'Please. I really did have a ticket. My friend is inside. At least let me tell her what's happened. I don't want her to worry.'

The usher is surprisingly solid. 'Thing is, sir, I've heard all the tricks. I want a quiet night. Why don't you do us both a favour and just eff off?'

On balance this does seem like the best option. I leave and go to sit in the square. I could easily go to a pub, but somehow I don't. The fountains are filled with water for the first time since I can remember. It's another kind of music and it reminds me of the winterbourne streams that break across the fields after heavy rain. I'm struck with a pang of homesickness so fierce and sharp that it's like a hunger pain and I momentarily double up.

I smoke five cigarettes and watch the traffic curl around me. Big Ben chimes the half-hour. I wonder whether Sal will try to find me during the interval, so I hurry back up the steps and linger near the doors but the beastly usher is there and I can tell he's still got his eye on me. Sal doesn't come out. I should probably leave but I can't face going back to the dingy pub, and I don't want Sal to think that I've stood her up, so I return to the fountain and wait.

The traffic quietens and I can hear wisps of sound from the concert but it's underwater music, distorted and unpleasant. The sun sinks behind the Thames and it suddenly gets cold. A mizzle of rain starts to fall, spotting the pavements. I shiver and wrap my arms around myself, cursing my carelessness. I could be sitting in a warm church and listening to fine music instead of freezing out here. I could also do with a decent mackintosh. Ruefully, I picture for the umpteenth time the smart mackintosh hanging on its peg in the gunroom at Hartgrove Hall.

At last, concert-goers start to file out. I nip across the road and force my way inside against a tide of large women smelling strongly of rosewater, lavender and lily of the valley – I'm elbowing my way through a bosomy herbaceous border. They mutter crossly. I catch a glimpse of yellow hair and see Sal disappearing through a side door off the chancel. Ignoring the ladies' angry mutterings, I push my way through the ample hordes. Reaching the door, I discover it's locked and hammer on it with my fists. A musician appears, his bow tie dangling loose, violin in one hand, glass in the other. He looks me up and down.

'I suppose you're a pal of Marcus?'

'Yes, that's right,' I say, with barely a moment's hesitation, and follow him into the vestry.

A party is well under way. I notice Sal in close conversation with a man whom I recognise as Marcus Albright himself. He spots me first and stiffens, like a cat spying a robin. It sounds ridiculous but I hadn't appreciated how young he is. I'd read in all the papers the lists of his grand achievements before the age of thirty, feeling rather envious, but I'd consoled myself with the fact that twenty-nine was almost middle-aged and that I had heaps of time to do something marvellous myself before I reached such an age. Now, looking at the slender, boyish figure conspiring with Sal, I realise that he seems hardly older than me. I decide I don't like him at all. He smiles and waves me over. Imperious so and so, I say to myself. Thinks he's so high and mighty.

'Did you like the concert?' he demands with an easy smile, confident of my response.

'No,' I say. 'I was too cold to like anything.'

His face falls and I feel almost bad but really I'm pleased that my opinion matters at all. Sal elbows me sharply in the ribs.

'Ignore him, Marcus. He's having you on. He skipped out on me and didn't hear a single note. What the hell happened to you?'

I try not to laugh. Sal's a different breed from the reticent English gals. She always says exactly what she thinks, often in somewhat coarse language. I'd forgotten how much I approve of Sal. However, she looks genuinely cross, her hands planted on her hips.

'I'm terribly sorry, old thing. Must have dropped my ticket on the floor of the lav. Wretched usher wouldn't let me in.'

'You should have used my name,' says Marcus, still looking at me appraisingly. I'm uncomfortable under his scrutiny.

'Well, might have been a bit tricky. I didn't know you until five ticks ago.'

'No. But now we're going to be excellent chums, I'm sure of it.' He slips his arm through mine and steers me to a table where a bar has been set up with gin and sticky bottles of lime syrup.

'We'll stay here for one and then we'll go on to the Langham. I expect that's more your scene.'

'Oh, yes please,' says Sal, appearing at my elbow. 'I'm starving.'

I look at Sal with wonder and then survey the grubby vestry with some regret. I'd much prefer to stay here, swigging gin with the second violins, than sip champagne in a smart hotel.

But then I discover that everything with Marcus is fun. Despite my present gloom, I find myself laughing. It feels strange and unfamiliar. Marcus discreetly pays for everything without condescension or show. We drink champagne and eat oysters although oddly, for the first evening in God knows how long, I don't feel drunk.

Sometime after midnight, Marcus turns to me, his eyes bright.

'So you're a composer?'

The gloom returns. I feel all the candles in the shining Langham bar gutter out one by one. I shake my head.

'Want to be. I'm stuck. And I'm not sure whether I'm really good enough to bother about getting unstuck.'

'The *Morning Post* and the *Western Gazette* seem to think you are.'

'You read the reviews?'

Marcus shrugs and slurps another oyster. 'Sal showed me. I like to keep track of all my rivals.'

I perk up, delighted, but Marcus laughs, putting me back in my place. 'You're not a rival yet, but I like to be prepared.'

There were two very short reviews of the concert at Hartgrove Hall. It's only because of Edie that the critics took any notice at all. They mostly commented on the eccentricity of the occasion and weren't terribly complimentary about my own piece.

'"Muddy orchestration. Overcomplication in the string section,"' I quote in my best 'man from the papers' voice.

'They were nice about Edie,' counters Sal. '"Edie Rose never sounded better. A different style for the young lady but very satisfactory nonetheless."'

'A singer's only as good as the song.' Marcus grins, a frank, open smile. He is a hard fellow to dislike.

'There was a decent photo of you too,' he adds, reaching for the last oyster, only to find Sal already taking it. 'Good grief, girl, I pity the husband that's going to have to pay to feed you,' he says, surrendering.

Sal laughs, but I can tell she's hurt.

We talk for a while longer, or rather they talk and I listen. To my relief they don't mention Edie again. It's a grubby thing, to love your brother's wife. It's biblical and hopeless and thoroughly unpleasant. I wonder whether Edie has told Sal. I expect not. She's horribly discreet. And even if she had, why would Sal tell Marcus? I'm fooling myself to think that the world is concerned about my own small miseries.

'So you're really coming?' says Sal, her eyes bright.

I've not heard a word. 'I beg your pardon?' I ask.

'Of course he is,' says Marcus. 'It's all decided. We'll stay up till dawn, and catch the first train.'

'The train to where?' I ask, with the feeling that it has already left the station.

'Scotland,' says Marcus.

~

Marcus has rented a small house on the Ardnamurchan penin-sula, purportedly to find some peace and quiet to write music and study next season's scores. However, he has also invited a ragtag assortment of pals to visit, so there never is any quiet. I see Marcus neither write nor study.

The sheer beauty of the place catches me off guard. We're at the westernmost tip of the mainland but it feels like an island. The sand is moon white, the waters are as clear as glass and, when the sun shines, they shimmer, a bold Renaissance blue that is Mediterranean and distinctly un-British. Sheep meander through coarse marram grass that sprouts stiffly along the beach. The dunes run for miles, sand spraying like mist in the wind. At low tide the sea recedes to the mouth of the bay, leaving shallow pools of glinting water. For days on end we spy no one but each other and the teeming birds – gulls, cormorants and even, now and again, a vast, red-dashed sea eagle.

In the stillness, I consider unhappily whether my leaving Hartgrove was entirely due to Jack and Edie. Disliking myself, I wonder whether part of my desire to leave was ambition. Those few horrid months of farming showed me how much I despise it. Staying at Hartgrove and working the estate would be the right thing to do, the moral choice, yet I simply can't do it. I have to write. It's ironic, then, how stuck I am. Now with peace and time to compose, I stutter and flail. I contemplate, grimly, the possibility that my inspiration comes from Hartgrove. Like Antaeus, my strength flows directly from the soil and, when separated from it, I stultify.

I'd understood that in Scotland it was always raining, but for the first week we have nothing but glorious sunshine. The cottage is a whitewashed stone croft on the edge of the beach. At high tide the waters lick around its garden of heather and at night it's like being adrift on a boat, the sea echoing through the dark. It's too big for me. The rhythm of the waves and the grind of the sand push out my own thoughts, showing them to be silly and small. Nothing but twiddles and trifles.

Each tide carries new visitors to the cottage and takes others away. After a few days I stop attempting to learn their names; they never stay more than a day or two before the small striped fishing boat ferries them away again. Marcus, Sal and I are the only visitors who remain day after day. There's a prevailing carnival, last-day-of-term feeling amongst the others but I feel like an actor in a play, saying my lines but knowing it's all hopelessly pretend. Marcus and his friends rise late and wander out into the garden to sit on the small terrace overlooking the water, draping themselves in blankets or beach towels against the cool, northerly breeze. The talk is rambunctious and incessant: of music and sex. Usually I'd delight in such conversation but I can't quite bring myself to join in. As the others pad outside to the terrace with mugs of coffee, I disappear off to the beach to pace the strand and watch the surf. I tell Marcus that I'm working on something – it's a fib but I need to be left alone.

To my relief, the air smells different from at home. There's a smell of salt and as the tide withdraws, leaving a green ooze of seaweed and slime, there's the stench of decaying fish, but beneath that there's the scent of heather and of wild herbs I don't recognise. The birds are different too. The dawn chorus is full of other voices, awash with strange songs. I'm far away from everything I've known and the relief is enormous.

The sharp sea wind catches me off guard, and as I gulp greedy lungfuls, I feel a space opening up inside me. For months there's been nothing but a void filled with self-loathing but as the salt air rushes through me it drives out the image of Edie. For a moment I feel stillness inside myself, like a pause between concerto movements. After a minute the restlessness returns but it has changed tone. I need to do something. I'm fed up with drifting, afloat on misery and self-pity. The unfamiliar songs of the birds give me an idea – perhaps I ought to collect a few songs from here. I've not collected anything for months. I question whether that, as much as unhappiness, has blocked my writing. I've stopped mixing paint for my palette, yet I'm complaining that I don't have any interesting colours.

'You look cheery this morning,' says Sal, striding towards me in her green slacks, straggles of hair whipping out like yellow ribbons behind her.

Sal is the only person whom I don't mind meeting on my walks. She knows when to talk and when to be quiet.

She stops a couple of yards from me and prods a shell with her toe, then yawns and stretches, showing her smooth midriff, the sunlight catching the fine down on her belly. I want to reach out and stroke it with my fingers. I can't tell whether she's teasing me deliberately. I realise that I'd very much like to sleep with her. I've still not slept with a girl. I feel embarrassed and backward about the whole thing. The chat amongst the others brims with misadventures on tour – tales of furious landladies and slamming doors, and while I doubt how much of it can possibly be true, I listen with apprehension, dreading the moment when I'm called upon for my own dubious anecdote.

'I'm going collecting today,' I say.

'Jolly good. We're short for lunch. Crab or scallops?'

'Songs.'

'Oh?'

She studies me for a moment, shading her eyes against the glare of the morning sun. Her feet are bare, the sand white against her toes, almost like snow. I notice that she's wearing a navy-blue sweater knotted around her waist, the coarse-knitted island kind that's supposed to repel water. I've seen the other chaps stare at Sal and make clumsy attempts to flirt, but she bats them away like moths, barely seeming to acknowledge their interest. I don't much like my own chances. She isn't pretty, not like Edie; her mouth is too wide and her brown eyes too far apart, but there's certainly something attractive about her. Perhaps it's the bold, American confidence. She smacks of the new world, of fresh possibilities. Her clothes are bright and unfaded. Even when she wears drab utility trousers and a man's sweater, on Sal it looks like a costume or a pose, a decision instead of a defeat.

'You can come with me, if you like,' I say. 'You can try to write down the words of the song if we find a singer.'

'All right.' I reckoned she'd come, but I find that I'm pleased, more pleased than I'd expected.

'We should probably try one of the local pubs. I wonder whether Marcus knows if there's a singing pub near by.'

I'm being optimistic. The nearest village is a huddle of dwellings somewhere between cottages and hovels, all of which are in unfortunate states of repair. The war has not been kind to this part of the highlands. The men left and the younger fellows mostly chose not to return. The place contains widows, old men, children and fish. When we venture into the village to raid the shop for supplies, they watch us, unsmiling and mistrustful. However, I admit to myself with a prickling feeling that I don't mind if the excursion is a wild-goose chase. I like the prospect of spending a drowsy early summer's day with Sal. She glances at me and grins, revealing a small gap between her front teeth. It's odd, I decide, how these assorted collections of small flaws in a face can make someone terribly attractive. It dawns on me that I want to sleep with Sal with considerably more urgency than I wish to collect traditional Scottish songs.

We return to the cottage to find the others have dragged the furniture onto the beach and are lazing on an armchair and a sofa at the top of the strand. It looks quite peculiar, as though the little sitting room has simply been transported, the shoddy oil seascape that hangs on the cottage wall being replaced with the beach itself. I half expect to see the matted rug and the oil lamps on their side tables. I don't expect the landlord will be too pleased but Marcus doesn't seem to bother about such things. He sits with his legs dangling over the armrest of the chair, wrapped in his dressing gown, humming.

'What-ho?' he calls.

'Fox is taking me song collecting,' says Sal.

'I am indeed,' I say, trying to keep the note of satisfaction from my voice.

'Oh yes?'

I join them in the sitting-room-on-the-beach. 'Do you know of any singing pubs? Or someone I could ask about singers?'

Marcus wrinkles his brow. 'You could ask Mrs Partick.' When I gaze at him blankly, he adds, 'The rather sweet old thing who cooks for us and cleans up our dreadful mess. She'll be here ten-ish.'

'It's nearly twelve,' I say.

Marcus laughs uproariously. 'Gosh, laziness is thoroughly exhausting.'

But he's already up and moving. He's a man always in motion, like a metronome. If he's still, it's only the rest between notes. Clasping in his hands a stash of manuscript paper, he jogs into the waves with it, still in his dressing gown, pyjamas and slippers. In a second he's thoroughly soaked but he takes no notice. With a shout, he throws the papers up into the air and the sheets flutter down to the surface of the water to float like a shoal of dead fish, belly up.

'What are you doing?' I call, hurrying down to join him, although I do remove my shoes and socks before crashing into the surf.

Marcus lights a bedraggled cigarette and wistfully surveys the flotsam and jetsam bobbing around him. 'I was up writing all last night. Utter tosh. I told myself that I should carry on regardless. If I decided it was still drivel in the morning, then I'd burn the whole thing.' He smiles at me ruefully. 'I think I should have burned it after all. We're awfully low on kindling and this gesture wasn't quite as dramatic as I'd hoped.'

Wads of sodden paper stick to our legs while some wash up on the sand. The others are all laughing; it's a bit of a lark – a daft story to tell about Marcus Albright when they get home. He chucks his cigarette into the ocean, half smoked, and crashes back up the strand. Beneath the jovial banter, he's furious, enraged by his own creative impotence. He reaches out and grabs my arm.

'Can I come with you? I need a change of scene.'

I'm torn. The chap looks stricken but I was anticipating with some considerable pleasure a day alone with Sal, wondering how I could conceivably combine song collecting with a swim. It might be tawdry, but I'd very much like to see Sal in her brassiere and knickers. Marcus senses my hesitation.

'I won't get in your way, old chap. Pretty thing but not my type at all. Think you might be hers, though.'

At once I'm overcome with gratitude, as though any tenderness Sal might feel towards me is entirely owing to Marcus. I shake his hand warmly.

'Yes, of course you must come. Be glad to have you.'

It's a relief to leave the others behind, carousing. They're a motley gang of musicians who've played with Marcus over the years, jovial and raucous fellows who've spent so long on tour that they've lost all notion of and desire for home. Providing they have their instruments and a cold glass of something, they're quite content or so it seems. Decent as they are, I'm glad to have Sal and even Marcus to myself. As we walk along the snaking path through the dunes, in companionable silence, I sense their relief too.

I turn to Sal.

'Do you miss Texas?'

'Yes. But as soon as I'm there, I'm desperate to be anywhere else.'

We check inside the cottage for Mrs Partick but she has already left. Opening the larder, we spy two poached salmon and a salad for supper under a mesh.

'Damn it,' says Marcus. 'Suppose we could walk into the village and knock on a few doors. Hope for the best.'

'It's Sunday. We could catch them after church,' I say. 'I've found chaps that way before. We ought really to go to the service and listen out for any likely singers.'

'Church it is,' declares Marcus, rubbing his hands.

We set back off across the dunes. We're not really dressed for church. Sal insisted upon changing out of her slacks into a green cotton dress, which, I can't help but notice, clings intriguingly to her bare legs. Marcus and I swelter in wool jackets and unironed shirts. I try to hide the worst of the creases with my tie, but, looking at Marcus who's attempted the same, I concede it's not terribly successful.

The church is a low building with harled white walls and a plain grey roof. It squats alone amongst the gorse, solemn and standoffish. The haze of the morning has burned off into a warm blue day but the doors of the church are firmly closed. It's apparent that we're late and the service has already started.

'Let's go back. We can talk to Mrs Partick tomorrow,' I say, ready to suggest a swim instead.

'Not at all,' says Marcus, grabbing both our arms and propelling us towards the church.

'We should wait until they come out,' I say.

'We can't go inside in the middle of a service,' says Sal, trying to shake Marcus off, but he laughs, quite undeterred, and urges us forward like a father with recalcitrant children.

'Don't be such spoilsports. I'm in the mood for God and then a song.'

Ignoring our grumbles, he thrusts open the doors of the church with a bang. Marcus has a penchant for the dramatic whether it's Beethoven at the Royal Albert Hall or Sunday morning in Ardnamurchan.

Forty pale faces beneath forty dark hats swivel to look at us, open-mouthed and agog. The minister splutters, outraged. He's aloft in the pulpit, arms held wide, and we've clearly interrupted a grand moment. The congregation look torn between shock and profound interest. A small child in pigtails is forcibly made to face the front by her mother, who hisses a reprimand. Sal has the grace to be embarrassed. She smiles blushing at the ladies and gentlemen who turn away, appalled.

Marcus strolls up the centre aisle and slides into a pew near the back.

'Don't mind us. Do carry on, my good man.' He waves cheerfully at the parson.

The minister, a small man with nimbus clouds of white hair, stares at us with fixed horror as though Satan himself had strolled into his church, arm in arm with the whore of Babylon and rattling a cocktail shaker. He's evidently quite lost his train of thought. I sit beside Marcus, who settles himself, smiling expectantly. The minister fixes us with a look of profound dislike and then, stirring himself and clasping both sides of the rostrum, he resumes his sermon with a great revving throttle of phlegm and spittle.

'*Sinners repent or you will burn. Burn. Bu–rrn!*' he exclaims, rolling his Rs with an impressive, percussive rumble.

At the conclusion of twenty-five minutes of sin, hellfire and fury, he pauses, spent and breathless. His white hair is plastered to his cheeks with sweat and his countenance is as red as the fiery pits he's described in such thrilling detail. The congregation nod and murmur their approval. This isn't sufficient for Marcus who's clearly enjoyed the whole performance immensely.

'Hear, hear!' he shouts from the back, rising to his feet, clapping loudly. 'Splendid.'

'I do like a bit of passion,' he whispers to Sal and me, not at all quietly. 'I liked the bit about buggery. Very rousing.'

Sal hushes him. 'No one applauds sermons.'

'You're American. Things are different here,' says Marcus.

'No. They don't applaud them in England either,' says Sal, firmly, trying to shush him.

'It really isn't done,' I agree.

'Well, it is by me,' huffs Marcus, unabashed.

While I'm amused, I think it rather doubtful that any of these people will sing for us now. The service is concluded.

There is no music nor singing of any kind. We join the throng and follow them out into the brisk sunshine. It's a glorious day, hot and cloudless. A fat seagull basks atop the war memorial and the threatened hellfire seems unlikely.

'Splendid service,' says Marcus, clasping the minister by the hand.

The minister grimaces, muttering begrudging thanks while trying to extricate his hand. The parishioners circle, curious.

'We're looking for some singers and musicians,' says Marcus, beaming round at the crowd. 'We'd like to hear some old songs of Scotland.'

The minister quivers and closes his eyes. 'Today is the La-rd's day,' he declares.

'Yes, jolly good,' says Marcus, his smile becoming fixed and tight.

'We do not make music on the La-rd's day. It's a day of prayer. Prayer and contrition.'

'Oh, I'm terribly contrite,' says Marcus. 'But we must have music, mustn't we, Fox?'

I nod. I'm always on the side of music, whatever the argument, whatever the consequences. 'I'm afraid so.'

The minister can take no more. He turns to his parishioners, blazing with righteous fury. 'No immodest songs. No sinful songs filled with lust. No songs for these' – he reaches for a word sufficiently damning – 'English gentlemen.'

The parishioners shake their heads – they wouldn't dream of it, not at all. Sal takes Marcus's hand and gently draws him away. I follow, finding myself both amused and irritated. We meander back to the cottage.

'I'm not sure that you have a future as a song collector, old sport,' I say. 'The trick is to coax it out of them.'

'Bugger them. Sod the lot of them,' declares Marcus and I realise that he's filled with a bright anger. I can almost see it bounce off his skin like the glare on the surface of the water in the bay. 'We're having music on the bloody beach tonight,' he announces.

He stops walking and turns to face Sal and me, squinting in the harsh midday sun.

'Are you Christians?'

I shrug and shake my head. 'Sorry. Pagan agnostic,' I say, not because it's really true but because I heard someone say it once and I liked the sound of it. Religion to me means dull mumblings in a frigid church while my stomach gurgles in expectation of Sunday lunch. I associate God with tedium and the anticipation of Yorkshire pudding.

'I'm a Christian,' says Sal.

'And so am I,' says Marcus. 'And I'll be damned to hell before I let any dead-hearted Presbyterian shit of a minister tell me that God doesn't like music. God is in the music. Any savage knows that.'

We reach the cottage garden where the gang are still lolling on the furniture on the beach.

'Rehearsals, Vivaldi's *Gloria*. Twenty minutes,' snaps Marcus.

The assorted guests pause for a moment, watching him, and then, grasping that he's transformed from affable host to conductor, they rise and return to the house, metamorphosing themselves from idle sunbathers into musicians, albeit reluctant ones. Sal and I do not have instruments, and I'm not quite sure how we fit into all this. I'm just starting to wonder whether perhaps this might be a good moment for us to slope off together and go for that swim when Marcus turns to us, cool and unsmiling.

'You'll sing treble,' he says to Sal. 'And you,' he says, looking at me, 'are the tenor.'

With a sigh, I accept that even though the part is hopelessly beyond me, it's pointless to refuse.

Marcus conjures scores from a trunk in his bedroom. I understand now why all his clothes are so crumpled and

231

grubby. He has brought only a couple of shirts with him; the remainder of his luggage is taken up with music – not merely the score but parts for each instrument in the orchestra. A dozen of us are staying at the cottage – in addition to Marcus, myself and Sal, there are five violins, a viola, a clarinet, an oboe and a cellist. Marcus bemoans the lack of flutes and absence of a double bass.

'And it really is too bad that there isn't a harpsichord.'

None of us dares to remark how ludicrous this is. I picture a harpsichord strapped to the lurching fishing boat, and want to laugh. The moment Marcus picks up his baton he gains gravitas and power. He holds instant authority, and we obey him instinctively and immediately as though he were wielding a pistol as opposed to a switch of wood. The piece also requires a full choir, not a single soprano and a tenor of limited skill, but I don't question him about that either.

He thrusts a score at Sal. 'Here. Go and practise. Help Fox. Come back in a couple of hours to play it through with the orchestra. We'll have the *Domine Deus* and the *Qui Sedes*.'

Now as Sal leads me away, I follow her with a feeling of utter dread; all my delicious excitement has been thoroughly trampled. I'm furious with Marcus for inflicting this upon me and furious with myself for not pointing out to him that I'm quite incapable of singing such a part. Even if I had a month to prepare, I wouldn't be up to it.

Sal, sensing my despondency, slides her hand into mine.

'Don't worry. Ignore the bluster. It's only for fun.'

'For you perhaps. The rest of you are professional musicians. I'm—'

At this I'm lost. I don't know what I am. I'm a composer with a single, unfinished symphony. We reach the far end of the strand. Disjointed snatches of Vivaldi curl around to reach us.

'I don't want to make an utter fool of myself,' I say eventually.

'You won't do that,' she says with a smile. 'Let's walk a while first. It's hopeless trying to learn something when you're tense.'

To hell with Marcus and his ridiculous game, I decide. 'Never mind walking. Let's swim.'

Sal raises an eyebrow. 'It's gonna be really cold.'

I shrug. 'Well, if you're chicken . . .'

She laughs and punches my arm with surprising force. 'Never.'

I strip off with considerable eagerness before Sal can change her mind. Naked except for my shorts, I hurry down to the water's edge and turn to watch her with frank interest. She blushes under my scrutiny, but I don't look away. She's thin but strong and lovely like the slender stem of a young hazel. I can see the sharp ridge of her hipbones beneath her skin, and yet as shyly she turns away from me, I can't help noticing that her bottom is nicely rounded. She races down to the sea and crashes into the water, leaping into the waves belly down with a tremendous splash, and gives out a great scream.

'It's freezing!'

'Well, it is the North Sea,' I say, smug in the safety of the shallows except that my feet are slowly growing numb.

She paddles closer, grabs me round the waist and, hauling me off balance, with strong arms drags me deeper into the waves. I cough and choke, winded by the sheer cold. I'm plunged into ice and my skin burns. I cry out as I surface to find Sal treading water and laughing at me.

'Told you it was bloody cold.'

'Bloody goddamned cold,' I say, between chattering teeth.

Her blonde hair has turned dark and sticks smoothly to her scalp, giving her an instant shorn crop. She looks like an awfully pretty, snub-nosed boy. I swim over to her, pull her close and, fumbling, attempt to kiss her. I'm out of my depth in every sense. Our teeth clink. Spluttering, she pushes me away but I grip her more tightly and try again. For a second she lies passive and lets me kiss her, inexpertly prodding her mouth with my tongue. She ducks down and wriggles out of my grasp, bobbing up a few feet away, appraising me.

'You're not very good,' she says, pleasantly. 'Honestly, I thought you'd be better.'

I don't know what to say to this. Feeling pretty ghastly, I start to swim back to shore.

'Don't go,' calls Sal.

I ignore her and clamber out, shivering. The sun isn't strong enough to warm me and I rub uselessly at my arms. She's nothing but a tease, I tell myself. A nasty little tease – always Jack's worst insult. At the thought of my brother, my humiliation deepens. No girl has ever criticised Jack's amorous abilities, I'm sure.

'Oh, don't be sore,' says Sal. 'You just need some practice.'

'Well, unless you're going to oblige,' I snap, still cross.

'Oh, well. I suppose I could,' she says, her head on one side, watching me with steady brown eyes.

I pause, tempted and intrigued but still affronted.

'I'm sorry,' says Sal. 'I was surprised is all. You seem like you've had lots of girls.'

'I do?'

My vanity marginally appeased, I soften and turn back to her. She's trembling in the shallows, clearly frozen. Sand sticks to her legs and is plastered in her hair, which is poking up in tufts around her face like feathers. She looks ridiculous and I feel marginally less inadequate. I step back towards her, drape my sweater around her shoulders and pull her close, clumsily trying to warm her.

'Yes, you look like you've been with dozens of girls,' she says dryly.

'Hundreds, more like,' I say.

'Here,' she says, pulling me down onto the wet sand to lie beside her.

I'm terribly cold and I want to dress and get warm more than I want to kiss her again, but I know this is feeble. She places a cool, damp hand behind my neck and draws me towards her. I let Sal kiss me and for a moment I wonder how many men she must have kissed to be this accomplished and then I don't think at all.

She spends the afternoon resisting all my attempts to make love to her, pushing me away gently but firmly, whispering, 'Later,' both a promise and a reprimand. I have no sense of the timescale of 'later'. Later tonight? Next year? Never? She has succeeded, however, in alleviating my concerns about singing tenor in the Vivaldi. I'm utterly preoccupied by persuading Sal to turn 'later' into 'sooner' or 'right now' and the Vivaldi is a mere inconvenience. I've never felt like this before about music. Usually it is the trivial inconveniences of life that get in the way of music.

Sal sits in the sand, wearing her thick fisherman's sweater, white knickers and nothing else. Her brassiere is draped over the marram grass to dry. She peers at me primly over her copy of the Vivaldi score and attempts a different course of instruction. I know that she's naked under that awful sweater and I can't concentrate at all on her recommendations about where to breathe.

'You're hopeless,' she declares, exasperated.

'I'm afraid so,' I say and, catching her, kiss her again, sliding my hand beneath her sweater to touch her small, cold breasts. To my delight, she doesn't remove my hand immediately but allows me to fumble, inexpertly yet with enthusiasm.

'But a decent student in other things,' she says, flushing and shoving me away, with some determination.

'Only decent?'

'Promising.'

'Bloody hell, that's worse.' I lunge for her again but she shifts away, placing the wretched score between us.

'Now, Fox. The *Largo*.'

'Oh God,' I say, lying back in the sand and closing my eyes. I have a towering erection. I curse Marcus.

I sing the damn piece through to placate her. It's pretty ropy, but I'm no opera singer.

'I suppose that'll have to do,' she says, not satisfied.

'I suppose it will,' I say. 'I told you. I'm not a real singer. And, anyway, how come you know so much about choral technique? I thought you only sang show tunes.'

'One day you'll have to stop being such an awful snob about popular music.'

I shrug. I don't really see why I should, and all the other musicians here – especially Marcus – are as entrenched as I. Sal traces the lines on my palm, which tickles like hell, but it seems churlish to ask her to stop.

'I trained to be an opera singer,' she says. 'But I'm not really built for it. My chest is too small, so it doesn't have the resonance.'

I register that she's confiding some great disappointment, but I can't help staring at her small bust. She notices my gaze and swats me.

'My ribcage, you horrid thing,' she says, and swats me again.

'Opera's loss,' I say.

I glance at her, bright yellow hair drying in the sun, long, thin legs brushed with sand. Freckles like biscuit crumbs are starting to emerge on her nose. She looks perfectly charming, the prettiest I've ever seen her.

'I'm afraid I can't really see you as one of Wagner's Valkyries.'

'No,' she agrees quietly. Although I'm only ribbing her, I've touched upon real sadness. She looks lost and gazes out to the horizon where grey swirls of cloud are gathering. The tide is coming in, swallowing the beach in greedy gulps, the water licking doglike at our toes.

'I wish you'd write something for me like you did for Edie.'

Her name flutters between us in the sunlight like a butterfly.

'I'm not writing much at present,' I say eventually, my voice cheery and false, like that of a stranger. 'Shall we go back to the others? See how they're getting on?'

Sal stares at me for a moment and then starts to pull on her clothes.

~

We build a bonfire on the beach, dragging fallen branches from the oak woods. Amongst the trees the air is cool and moist; the filtered sunlight, dappled and green, paints our faces. Even the trunks are smothered in lichen. Back home the woodland floor is a palette of colours, a blend of brown and yellow leaf litter but here even the ground is carpeted in plush emerald moss, so dense that we seem to spring from foot to foot as we pad amongst the trees. The young leaves of the ash are ribbed like the tender belly of a water snake. In fact I feel almost as though I'm strolling along the bottom of a sea bed, which I suppose I am – albeit one that existed a hundred million years ago.

At this thought, I'm pierced with a pang of homesickness. Walking on Hartgrove Hill as boys, we'd race out to scour the chalk for ammonites after the rain had prised them loose. These hard, round objects like cricket balls, imprinted with long-dead sea creatures, seemed like messages from another time when our hill had been submerged beneath the deep, dark ocean.

'Here, Fox, give me a hand with this,' calls Marcus and I run to help him with a large branch, glad of the distraction. I mustn't think about home.

We haul it along the ground, grunting with the effort, and emerge from the wood with some relief. It's cooler now but bright with an evening glow that will not fade for hours. We're far enough north that the days stretch on and on, each one seeming to last twice as long as smog-filled ones in London. The light ignites the top of the stone hills overlooking the beach and illuminates the distant small isles across the water.

The tower of wood on the beach has reached several feet. I drop my end of the branch.

'Come on, Fox, no slacking,' grumbles Marcus.

'No. Leave it for now. We need to start the fire small and slow. Too much, too soon, and it won't light properly.'

Marcus chuckles. 'I forget that you're a country boy.'

I smile, gratified. 'Here, does anyone have a match?'

Sal passes me one and I crouch, lighting the fire, which blooms in an instant. Sal's changed into a skirt, her fisherman's sweater tugged low over the waistband, but her feet are still bare. She slides up behind me and slips her skinny arms around my waist. I can feel the others watching us surreptitiously, their conversations suddenly growing louder as they pretend not to notice. I preen in the imagined envy of the other chaps. We stand, wrapped in one another, and watch the flames catch, first in the dry leaves and moss and then in the wood, which starts to burn with a hungry snap. I toss on a driftwood log and it blazes blue. It's still light but all the heat has gone from the day, and the low sun lingers above the horizon, as if reluctant to leave.

'Come,' says Marcus, clicking his fingers.

Reluctantly Sal and I break apart and follow the musicians who've dragged the sofa and chairs nearer to the bonfire. I notice that the woodwind, like spaniels, have claimed the spot closest to the blaze. They look supine and ready to nap. The cellist perches uncomfortably on the edge of the sofa, his cello's pointed stand sinking into the sand like a high-heeled shoe. He swears loudly and complains vociferously to Marcus about the damp spoiling the woodwork.

Marcus takes no notice. He's built himself a podium out of wet sand at the furthest point from the fire. The violins flock around his feet, gazing up at him with something close to adoration. His hair has grown in the weeks we've been here and, uncombed and straggling, in the light from the flames it gleams wild and red, making him appear at once like Moses and the burning bush. I'm torn between wanting to laugh – the notion of a performance of Vivaldi cobbled together on a beach is ludicrous – and finding myself being drawn in, seduced by Marcus's seriousness. He stands on his makeshift podium with his eyes closed, baton at his side, and bows at the sea as if it were a vast, unseen audience. He motions to Sal and me. She takes my hand, leading me to a pair of hard, upright chairs to the side of the musicians. The tide has begun to retreat, leaving a wide ribbon of smooth sand, pristine white and gleaming in the fading light. I feel dusk fall, the shift between day and night.

Marcus raises his baton and the orchestra starts to play the first movement from Vivaldi's Concerto in A minor. And to my wonderment they are an orchestra, not a ragtag assortment of odd musicians, but parts of a whole, the rowers in a single boat, Marcus the coxswain effortlessly piloting them through. I've heard the piece a hundred times on the gramophone at Hartgrove Hall and once or twice in concert by orchestras grander and more illustrious than this motley crew, but I know that I'll never hear it like this, with the wind rushing through the marram grass, and the grind of the tide pushing against the sand. Sal squeezes my fingers and I experience a rush of blood and warmth in my chest. Music feels much like love.

It's Sal's turn to sing. The oboist stands and calls out the *Domine Deus* from the *Gloria*, melancholy as the cry of a greylag goose. It flies across the water and, as Marcus nods to Sal, she echoes it, her small, sweet voice wrapping in and under the note of the oboe. Beneath them, the strings tiptoe up and down. Sal's voice is girlish and pretty, and it lacks power. But somehow Marcus forces her to find a depth and sadness I've not heard before. She'll never sing this solo before a real audience or in a concert hall, and that unhappiness and discontent seep into the melody, infusing it with melancholy. Sal sings of her disappointment at not being a great singer, and somehow becomes a better one.

Then it's my turn. To my amazement, Marcus coaxes a passable performance even from me. I decide to trust him and lean back into the music, to find that he catches me and leads me through, deft and sure. I listen to my own voice pouring out into the gathering dark. Marcus is a magician. For a night he can turn fragile warblers into singers. I want to hear what he can do with a full symphony orchestra. I curse myself for dropping my ticket on the floor of the gents. We finish, the notes slowly decay, and we all sit and listen to the sudden hush. The slap of the waves on the shore. The spit and hiss of damp wood on the fire.

We wait instinctively for the applause that does not come but we hear it anyway in the rhythmic boom of the surf. It's dark now and late. A paring of moon glints, casting a corridor of light upon the black water. I look at Marcus and can see even in the darkness that he's drenched in sweat, as though he's been running for miles and miles at full tilt.

'Let's swim!' he calls, his voice giddy and loud.

'No fear,' I say to Sal. 'Too bloody cold.'

'Don't tell them that,' she whispers back with a giggle.

Taking my hand in hers, she leads me away from the others and up the beach, past the dunes and back towards the oak woods. We hesitate on the boundary between the strand and the trees. The night woods are so dark that something primitive and instinctive buried inside us makes us pause, uneasy. It's the frisson of strangeness that I feel at the top of Ringmoor at dusk, the sense of shadows, the echo of ancient footsteps, and at last something nameless and older still that watches us from the blackness. I take the first step, and tug Sal behind me across the threshold. She cries out in pain.

'Ouch, my foot.'

I glance down. She's still not wearing shoes. Concealed in the cushions of moss are roots and stones and pine needles. I pick her up and, panting with effort, carry her, laughing, into the thicket. She's heavier than I expect, but she wraps her arms around my neck and I can smell the sandy, heather scent of her skin. I sense my advantage. For the first time today, I don't feel inept. Sweating now, I bear her deeper into the wood. The trees become less dense; beeches and moss give way to bluebells and wild garlic. Their fragrance is stronger at night, so potent that I can taste it at the back of my throat. As my steps crush the flowers, they release still more perfume, thick as smoke. The white blooms of garlic are stars littering the woodland floor.

The smell of the place confounds me. It's the very essence of Hartgrove copse in spring – but here the bluebells are mixed with something else, peat and salt carried in from the sea. I hear the creak of the trees like old bones and the distant wash of the tide. I set Sal down and she tries to walk but falters, the rough ground hurting her feet. She's pinned. I smile and kiss her.

'Come sit,' I say between kisses, trying to tug her down beside me.

She flutters, undecided.

'Come on.'

She allows herself to be drawn to lie beside me. We're both dishevelled. My shirt is filthy and I've lost a button. I slide my hand up her thigh and beneath her skirt. She trembles, I hope in anticipation. The stink of garlic is too much, sickly and overwhelming. The ground is moist. I flick away something with a multitude of legs scurrying across my cheek. This time Sal lets me roll up her jumper and with clumsy and too-eager fingers I find her nipples, hard as beads. I want her but I'm also filled with profound relief that I'm no longer going to be a virgin. I think of Edie but only for a moment and only from habit. I've thought of doing this with Edie a thousand times but it's a picture from a book, static and unyielding, and Sal's breast is soft and warm under my fingers. It starts to rain but we do not stop.

≈

Marcus sends the others home. Only Sal, Marcus and I remain for the summer. We're a comfortable threesome. Sal cooks and sings and sleeps with me at night. And sometimes in the afternoons when Marcus goes for a walk – we suspect for the very purpose of allowing us time alone. Music and sex. Even as they pass, I know that these are halcyon days.

Mrs Partick informs us with some delight that we've been labelled 'the fornicators' and that our souls are prayed for every Sabbath – whether for our rehabilitation or our eternal condemnation, she declines to say. She lingers in the garden with us after she's finished cleaning, smoking her pipe and, to my great delight, singing bawdy songs in Old Scots. I can't understand the half of them but I can tell they're lewd by her cackles and winks. One evening she conjures a bottle of thirty-year-old Macallan, and we all sit outside amongst the heather, drinking and listening to her sing. She leans close to me, confiding her song like a filthy joke, her breath like shortbread.

I've had no news of Hartgrove since I left; I daren't hope that George and Jack have managed to extend the stay of execution. I still can't bring myself to write and I won't ask Sal to enquire on my behalf. Each week I scour the copies of *The Times* and the *Telegraph*, which Marcus has sent up and which arrive a full fortnight out of date, brimming with old reports. Here and there is a mention of an ancient house that has been felled like a diseased tree. I read with dread but either Hartgrove Hall is safe or it is insufficiently grand to merit a mention. The loss of the place might be a blow to us but not to the nation. It would not signal the end of a great dynasty, only of a family. In my mind, the piece I'm trying to write becomes both an elegy – the Hall's destruction seems inevitable – and an apology. I should not have left as I did. My running away seems childish, my subsequent silence cowardly.

One morning the boat arrives and, along with the newspapers and post for Marcus and Sal, is a package for me. I'm bewildered as no one knows that I'm here. At breakfast while we pick kipper bones from our teeth I unwrap the parcel. Inside is the Not-Constable painting of Hartgrove barrow. I stare at the murky colours and sniff the canvas, conscious of the familiar smell. I shake the wrappings but there's no message to say who's sent it. I suppose it must be either Edie or George. To my shame, I hope it's Edie. I turn to Sal, who's studying the picture with curiosity.

'It isn't very good, is it?' she asks.

'No,' I agree. 'But I'm fond of it anyway.' I retrieve another kipper bone. 'Did you tell someone I'm here?'

Sal shrugs, glances away. 'Only Edie.'

'Did you ask her about the house too?'

'No. I only dropped her a line to tell her that you were here. I didn't want them all to worry. You ought to have done it yourself. Don't be cross I told her.'

I smile, taking her hand. 'I'm not,' I say, discovering that it's true. It must have been Edie who sent the painting. I drift through the morning, cheerful.

I prop the Not-Constable upon my makeshift desk and gaze at the view from Hartgrove barrow. I pinch one of Mrs Partick's melodies for my composition and for the first time in months I write. I don't know whether it's the proximity of the view of Hartgrove, Mrs Partick's tune or the emancipating effect of regular sex with Sal that finally liberates me from my block.

Marcus studies his scores while I write and I turn my pages over to him so that he can dispense voluminous criticism. He's relentless, uncomplimentary and, I remonstrate, needlessly cruel. We shout. He mocks and laughs and tells me that if I know so much then I should simply leave. Go back to Hartgrove Hall. And yet, I stay. I know that he's making me a better composer, and somehow I understand that I can't leave until the piece is finished. I can't return without it even though George and Jack will be united in their indifference. They'd much rather I came back with a tractor or fifty pounds or a cow – not a perfectly useless piece of music. But I have to finish nonetheless. I try not to consider what Edie will think of it. I try not to think of her at all.

'No,' says Marcus, drinking coffee and flicking cigarette ash onto the already criss-crossed page of my manuscript. 'You play the piano, don't you?'

'A bit,' I say.

'Well, either you're the most brilliant virtuoso or an idiot. I don't know anyone who could play this. Do you?'

'I don't know many piano players. Not great ones,' I say, wounded.

'Well, there aren't any I know who could play this piffle,' says Marcus. 'Albert Shields might. But even he'd struggle.'

He's crumpling the pages in his zeal and I resist the impulse to snatch them back.

He frowns and studies the manuscript again.

'It might work for two pianos. Could you tease out two parts? Make sure they work in counterpoint or it's pointless.'

I spend days puzzling and show my efforts with some satisfaction to Marcus who grunts and dismisses them.

'No. Doesn't work at all. You're not hearing the instruments distinctly enough. You have an ear for melody, that's clear. But you don't understand what each instrument can do, and equally what it can't do. You need to compose within its range. That way you show off an instrument to its best advantage. You're like the director of photography of a film whose job it is to make Greta Garbo look absolutely cracking.'

He has a gramophone brought over on the little fishing boat and we sit around each evening, listening to records again and again, different orchestras and a cornucopia of conductors performing the same piece, Marcus pointing out the subtle variations. Slowly, painfully, I learn to listen better and then to hear better as I write.

Marcus allows me to study the scores with him. He's accepted a position as conductor for the Bournemouth Symphony Orchestra. I'm frankly baffled that he chose it over the New York Phil.

'Ah,' says Marcus. 'You read that piece in *The Times*? Where I said that I hadn't yet accepted the New York Phil?'

'Yes, that was the one.'

Marcus chuckles. '"I haven't yet accepted" as they never actually offered.'

'I can't believe it. I'm sure I read it several times—'

'There were lots of rumours, most of them started by me,' says Marcus happily. 'If I suggest myself enough, they'll realise what a jolly good idea I am. But until they do, I'm going to play nicely with the BSO. They're pretty damn good. I can make them better.'

I agree without hesitation. I'm quite certain he can.

'Hello, now I've an idea. How about me taking you on as my assistant? I won't be able to pay you terribly much, but it would be useful for you.' His tone is casual, but something about the way that he won't meet my eye makes me wonder whether he's been rehearsing this for a while.

'Bournemouth's a little close to home,' I say, reluctant.

I can't see them yet. Not until the piece is finished. Jack or George or the General are all highly unlikely to turn up to a concert. Edie, however, might.

'We'll be on tour for most of the first year,' says Marcus. 'It'll do you good to see a bit more of the world. And while you're at it, you can learn to orchestrate properly. No more of that muddy, thick sound you're currently so enamoured by.'

I glare at him. It's typical of Marcus to offer a gift with one hand and an insult with the other. He beams at me, quite oblivious.

'What about Sal?' I ask, not because I actually feel guilty but because I should.

He shrugs. 'Oh, bring her along. I'm sure we can find room for her somewhere.'

He glances at me shrewdly and then carefully stares out of the window to watch a flock of greylag geese wheeling above the dunes, honking gloriously.

'Are you in love with her, old chap?'

'I suppose so,' I say.

August 2002

The school holidays came as a relief. Clara and Ralph no longer had to tear around, taking Katy and Annabel to and from school while shuttling Robin up to London for his piano lessons. The only one who was not thrilled at the respite was Robin. His lessons were reduced to once a fortnight during August, an outrage he could barely endure. As a sop he was allowed to come to the Hall to play the piano as often as he wanted. Consequently, we spent most of the summer together as somewhat unlikely playfellows.

I was troubled that he appeared to have almost no friends. Flattering as it was, a fellow of seventy-odd is no companion for a six-year-old. Even though I spent much of my time as a boy hankering after music, plotting how I could slope away and bash out a tune on the decrepit piano or listen to a concert on the wireless on the sly, mostly my proclivity was frustrated. Consequently my summers were spent pinching apples, attempting to drown my brothers in the lake, being drowned in turn and, one notable holiday, watching circus elephants bathing in the Stour at dawn. With the benefit of hindsight I concluded that being forced to play outside, listening to cuckoos and larks, and watching for badgers in the dusk, had enriched those boyhood days and I desperately wanted the same for Robin. While the elephants might prove elusive, I was determined that he would experience a boyhood summer of muck and mischief.

When Robin finished his Schumann sonata and closed his eyes in pleasure, I chose my moment.

'James and Paul are coming round tomorrow for a picnic by the lake. We're going to fish and Paul's daddy is going to row us across the lake. If we catch anything, we're going to cook it for lunch on a bonfire,' I said.

'What if we don't catch anything?'

'We'll draw straws and decide whom to cook instead.'

'You can't eat people.'

'You certainly can. They had a lovely recipe for braised child with garlic in this month's Waitrose magazine.'

At this Robin laughed, which I took as acceptance.

The following morning we walked through Hartgrove's once-formal garden, the lawns and herbaceous borders now brimming with geraniums, vast wobble-headed hydrangeas and blowzy poppies, as well as nettles and bindweed. I'm afraid that my interest in keeping the gardens up to their usual standard wavered after Edie. We reached the wilder part of the garden where mown paths sloped down to the lake. Buttercups, dandelions and lady's smock trembled in the tall, uncut grass, the air thick with the rhythm section of the crickets and the melodic warble of a blackbird.

We walked in silence for a while until Robin turned to me and asked, 'You used to have musicians stay here every summer, didn't you?'

'Yes, we did. For many years.'

'Why did you stop? I would have liked that. Better than boating anyway.'

'You haven't tried boating, so you don't know what you think about it yet, Robin,' I reminded him, sounding prim, even to myself. 'And I found the festival a bit much after your grandmother passed away.'

'Why? Did she do all the cooking or something?'

'Something like that.'

I could not explain to him how Edie had been at the heart of it all. She hadn't sung at the festival for many years but somehow it was her warmth that put everyone at ease. She knew how to calm the nerves of the novice performer and soothe the egos of the distinguished stars unused to the indignities of shared bathrooms and damp bedrooms. Everyone said that while the Hartgrove Festival might not be the smartest nor the most exclusive – we were no Glyndebourne – we had the most character. The character was Edie's own. The easy friendliness, the charm of home-baked scones, tea-bread and our vintage cider in the dressing rooms made up for the antique plumbing and the shared loo along the corridor. It was Edie who saw to all these little touches and a thousand other things. Without her, even if we laid out the scones and provided the cider, the character would be lost. I couldn't bear to put on the festival and overhear the whispers of how it wasn't as charming without Edie. Of course it couldn't be. Nothing could.

To my relief we were interrupted by the arrival of Paul Bentley and his father, Jon. They grunted their good mornings in the Dorset way, Robin and Paul eyeing each other warily.

'Do you like cars?' asked Paul at last, producing a blue police car from his pocket. 'It has a remote control and I can drive it and everything.'

'I don't like cars,' said Robin, hunching his shoulders. 'I like pianos.'

The two children retreated into silence and stared at one another with bewilderment and regret. I stifled a sigh. As adults, one thrusts children of similar ages together in the belief that they must surely get along, which, I supposed, was terribly unfair. However, I reminded myself sternly, the aim of today was to introduce Robin to children with different interests and attempt to broaden his horizons.

'Well, I think your car looks marvellous, Paul,' I said. 'I should very much like a turn driving it later on.'

Paul smiled but Robin shot me a look of concern and disappointment. I feared it was to be a long morning.

Soon, young James joined us and we set off with the three boys down to the lake. James and Paul ran ahead, leaping across stones and whacking the heads of dandelions with huge energy so that they shot across the fields like fuzzy cannon balls. Robin watched with interest but remained at my side. For once, I was saddened by my grandson. I wanted him to run and holler like the others. James and Paul were both suntanned and grubby – a reliable signal of a summer well spent – while to my dismay I noticed that Robin was pale and far too clean.

We reached the edge of the lake. We'd always called it that even though in reality it was midway between a very large pond and a very small lake. It was wide enough to row across and in hot weather a mud island emerged in the middle. Jon pulled out three penknives and solemnly handed one to each boy, showing them how to slice the rods of hazel sprouting along the banks.

'Cut careful, like, don't cut yerself. I ent got no plasters and I don't want to drive yer to Dorchester to have yer fingers stitched back on.'

The boys listened open-mouthed and, to my delight, even Robin seemed happy as he hacked away at a hazel spear. Jon helped them attach lines and flies to their home-made rods and they settled contentedly on the bank at a short distance from us, dangling for fish. Jon carried a cooler with him and as he opened it, passing me a beer, I noticed a bag of fish from Tesco hidden at the bottom. He saw my look and grinned.

'Thought it were best we didn't trust to finding fish in your big pond.'

'Didn't you write a book on foraging?' I asked, trying to remember.

He chuckled. 'Aye, that's right. *Eating the Hedgerows and Foraging the Forests*.'

'Isn't this cheating?'

'Not a bit of it. The trick ter successful foraging is knowing when it's bloody useless. Nothing you'd want ter eat in that muck-hole,' he said with a dubious glance at the lake.

It was drowsily warm and I lay back on the grass, feeling the heat of the earth beneath me. The sun crept higher and higher, while gnats spun overhead in frenzied patterns. We sat in silence – Jon, like most Dorset men, had no use for small talk – and listened to the happy chatter of the boys. To my profound relief, I heard Robin's voice mixing with the others.

'Think it's about time they caught a fish, don't you?' said Jon with a smile, reaching into the grocery bag and unwrapping a large trout from its plastic wrapper.

He slipped it naked into his jacket and slid noiselessly along the bank, smooth as an otter. A minute later I heard squeals of joy.

We ate the fish baked in nettles that the boys gathered and on a fire Jon helped them to build. I heard George and Jack in their carousing until I was dizzy with nostalgia. It was the smell of the wet mud mingled with woodsmoke and the pain in my burned fingers. As a boy I could never wait for food to cool, and my sudden greediness as I tore into the trout reminded me of another piece of myself. It was the hottest time of the day and the sun gleamed on the smooth surface of the lake. A petrol-blue kingfisher swooped for his lunch, while the water oozed and trickled around the trailing branches of the willows. It was warm in the shade, and feeling full I fancied an indulgent snooze. Hearing the joyful shouts of Jon and the boys, I allowed myself to drift off for a minute or two.

I woke suddenly to find Jon shaking me.

'Is he with you?'

I glanced about, still half asleep. 'Robin?'

'Yes. He was playing with the others in the boat and then suddenly he wasn't there.'

I saw utter panic in the countenance of the other man, and I was instantly wide awake. Everything went quiet and still.

'My God, I hope he isn't in the lake,' said Jon, his face white.

'He's a good swimmer,' I said, sounding calmer than I felt.

I noticed the other boys lingering beside the willows, looking frightened.

'I'm going to circle around and look for him again. You go and call for help. We'll probably 'ave found the rascal before they get here but best be on the safe side.'

'Right,' I said, relieved to be told what to do.

I forced myself to run back to the house, my legs abruptly feeble and slow. I heard Jon instructing the other boys, his voice already receding. 'You two check in the woods just here, don't go far now, stay together. You got that?'

Where had Robin disappeared to? I felt light-headed with fear. Oh God, I couldn't call Clara and tell her I'd lost her son. He had to be all right. He had to be. The scamp had wandered off mid-game and lost his bearings. Clara had lost him in the supermarket when he was two and she'd nearly had a heart attack. This wasn't any different. But it was. I'd heard about the supermarket story only after Robin had been safely found beside the frozen peas. I started to bargain with him in my head. If I found him in the next ten minutes, then he could play the piano as much as he liked. I'd buy him a damn piano. I found to my horror that I was close to tears. I reached the lawns and, breathless, was forced to slow. It took me a moment to register that, along with the ragged gasp of my own breath, I could actually hear a piano. Chords fluttered across the grass.

I felt relief roll over me, cool as seawater, but after a moment or two it warmed into anger. How could he wander off like that? It was selfish and thoughtless behaviour even for a child. My father would have given him a good thrashing and, in that instant, I could see the merits of such a thing. Then, three strides later, my rage dissipated like smoke. I recognised what he was playing.

I'd never given Robin any of my own work to practise, even avoiding all recordings of my music during our afternoon CD concerts. I hadn't admitted to myself the reason why. Now I understood. At the age of seventy-four, after a full career and a cuttings folder brimming with reviews – some complimentary, others not – I was worried about rejection. Not the considered rejection of some stranger but the instinctive and gut-felt refusal of a child. I couldn't bear the prospect of Robin's casual and simple dislike. Even if, in time, he learned to appreciate my style, my innovation of the old modal forms or the surprising orchestration, I knew that I would never recover from that first, unthinking recoil.

Then, on that summer's afternoon, I heard my own music calling to me across the lawn. God, what a child. Nobody had ever understood me as this boy did. He played the piano solo from my Symphony in G minor, *The Song of Hartgrove Hall*, right out of my own imagination, as though it could not be played any other way. Always I would have to give the soloist a little note here, a tactful suggestion there – but not with Robin. The music reached out across the garden.

I could hardly breathe. He heard the music as I did. For the first time since Edie died, I no longer felt alone.

~

Jon discovered us in the music room three-quarters of an hour later, somewhat surprised that I hadn't come to tell him that I'd found Robin. Abashed, I apologised and pleaded age and incompetence – the truth was that I'd quite forgotten Robin had been lost. I forgot everything except Robin and the miracle of his playing.

That night I couldn't sleep. I lay awake, my heart beating wildly, sending too-hot blood pulsing through me. I used to feel like this before a big concert or on the eve of a new recording or when I had an idea for a new piece of music. Although it was after midnight, I was surprised to find that the house was reverberating with music. I was perplexed. Automatically, I checked the radio alarm clock beside my bed but it was switched off and the music I could hear was full and symphonic, with a richness in the strings – not the tinny warble of the ancient clock radio. I must have forgotten to lock the music-room door. Robin was probably playing along to some record.

I slid out of bed and, seizing my dressing gown, hurried along the corridor. The door to the guest room where Robin slept was open, the curtains fluttering, and the blue light of the full moon shone on the neatly made bed. I'd quite forgotten that he wasn't staying here tonight and had gone home with Clara. Puzzled, I padded into the music room. The sound grew louder. The melody was familiar and yet I was fairly certain that I hadn't heard it before. The room was perfectly empty except for the swell of sound. It crashed and crescendoed about me, breaking like waves, and, with a surge of joy, I understood. The music was internal. I could hear it again.

I sat down at what I'd come to see as Robin's piano, and the melody tumbled from my fingers. I couldn't play with the ease or passion of my grandson, but as I rummaged for a shock of manuscript paper, I knew that I had something. I wasn't sure of the shape of it – it might be a sonata, or a song, or the opening theme for a larger work – but it was definitely something.

Outside my window the moon cast skinny shadows of the aspen trees across the lawns. It was so bright that I was reluctant to turn on a side lamp and wrote in the strange half-light, reaching down into the dark for the melody that was immediately so familiar that I wondered whether I was remembering some remote childhood thing rather than conjuring it. I wrote and played while dawn snuck up behind Hartgrove Hill, a thin line of light drawn along the ridge that grew and stretched, smearing across the row of trees, and then was absorbed into the sky like blotting paper. The birds woke; their noisy chorus was rowdy interval chatter that interrupted my rhythm. I paused, drank tea and listened. When it was fully light, I slunk back to bed, exhausted and exhilarated, and I slept and did not dream.

March 1950

I loathe Marcus Albright. I loathe him with a fury. He's a bloody good conductor and a bloody infuriating man. Absolutely bloody. I tell Sal that we're leaving and to pack our bags, but she sits on the bed, smoking a cigarette, and doesn't move as I rant. She's heard it all before: I'll rage and then complain to Marcus who won't apologise. We'll stay anyway. We always do. The landlady bangs on the ceiling with her mop handle to signal me to be quiet. I slump beside Sal and flop back on the bed.

'You should dress,' she says. 'You'll be late.'

'What's the point? He never lets me do anything. He won't notice if I'm there or not. No one will.'

Despite my protestations, I'm pulling on my shirt and Sal adjusts my winged collar. She's already dressed in a fetching blue dress, velvet and sumptuous. I'm pinched with guilt.

'I'm sorry, darling, I'm being beastly.'

She wrinkles her nose and bestows a kiss on my forehead.

'It's all right. I know you don't mean it.'

'Not to you, I don't. But Marcus—'

She turns and disappears to the bathroom before I have a chance to finish. I'm not sure whether she really needs to freshen up or simply wants to escape. Now that she's gone and I don't have an audience, my fury peters out into dreary resentment.

The hideous hall clock cuckoos the half-hour – a present from the landlady's equally ghastly sister that chirps maddeningly day and night – and reluctantly I jog down the stairs, calling to Sal that I'll see her during the interval. The landlady presumes we're married. She's slovenly in her housekeeping but not in her morals, and she'd never permit us to live together in that fetid little room otherwise. We've never explicitly told her that we're not married, so it's a sin of omission concealing a greater sin. I suppose I really ought to marry Sal, make everything tidier. If she falls pregnant, then of course I shall. None of these thoughts makes me happy, only weary, as though the course of my life is meticulously timetabled like a Swiss railway line.

It's a Friday night and as I hasten along the pavement, bent against the wind and drizzle and fumbling for my brolly, I pass Hassidic men and boys in their black hats and black coats, strolling to the synagogue without an umbrella between them, apparently impervious to the rain. These fellows are how I'd imagined all Jews to be until I'd met Edie.

I try not to think of her. I'm embarrassed when I recall our last conversation. I wish I could simply forget it, but when I wake in the night I play it over in my mind, wincing at my silliness. It's ludicrous to call all that mooning and pining 'love'. 'Infatuation' is more apt. I can admit this now that I'm nearly twenty-two. A composer with a published and professionally performed symphony who posts home cheques with nice round figures. I preen, rather pleased with myself. One day I shall return to Hartgrove Hall. I'll apologise to Jack and George for leaving in the manner in which I did, and we'll laugh and toast one another, putting it down to the behaviour of young men sowing their wild oats, and all will be forgotten. The cheques will enable it to be forgiven.

As for Edie? Well, we'll shake hands and I'll be struck by how she's not as pretty as Sal, never was. My goodness, she must be over thirty now. I smile at the very idea that I could love someone as old as all that.

I turn the corner and reach the Winter Garden. Its charming name belies the drab brick building at the end of a long suburban street. Looking more like a bowling alley than a concert hall, it's an unprepossessing home for what is now, under Marcus's severe leadership, a splendid orchestra. For the last two years he has vowed to find them more salubrious headquarters. Vast posters with a flattering photograph of Marcus are plastered on every wall. I can't understand how the orchestra can stomach the ego of the man but they do. They are hopelessly devoted to him. I find the whole thing profoundly irritating.

It's nearly six and I'm late. The box office clerk nods to me and I force myself not to hurry as I walk along the mildewed corridor towards Marcus's dressing room. I don't knock.

'Hello, Fox,' he calls, cheerful as ever.

My latest work is strewn about him, the pages covered with a swarm of red ink. His dressing room is an absolute mess, littered with empty coffee cups, ashtrays, papers and endless scores, as well as several tailcoats and a regiment of shirts dangling over a hanging rail that needs to be mended. He notices none of this. He's absolutely fixed on my score.

'This bit is dreadful,' he says, happily.

I clench my jaw. Why didn't I insist upon Sal packing up our things?

'But this section I rather like. The entire orchestra is shaking its fist. Splendid stuff.'

The compliment catches me off guard as it always does and for a moment he's forgiven.

'Now, would you pop back to my digs? The shirt I want isn't here.'

'What's wrong with one of these?' I say, pointing to the array of starched laundry.

Marcus stretches his arms wide, signalling with a flourish to an imaginary orchestra. 'All too tight across the shoulders. I need more room for the Beethoven.'

I sigh and try to retrieve my spoiled score as I leave, but Marcus slaps at my wrist with his baton, an abhorrent schoolmaster's trick. 'Leave it. I'm not finished commenting yet.'

I slam the door and stride up the corridor, hearing Marcus shout behind me, 'Don't despair! We'll elevate you out of mediocrity yet! Oh, and fetch me a cheese sandwich, would you, there's a good fellow.'

Cursing him, I hurry out of the Winter Garden and back onto the street. I walk quickly up the hill towards Marcus's digs in one of the handsome Victorian villas in the more elegant part of town. The Bournemouth Musical Society is inevitably low on funds but some appearances must be upheld and the maestro's residence thus possesses a soupçon of dilapidated grandeur.

I glance at the sky. It's between rain showers and, as I reach the top of the mount, a vista of the sea opens up below. Black clouds rush in from the horizon and slices of yellow light glint sharply between the gaps, catching the surface of the water, which flashes and gleams. The air smells of salt spray and fish and chips. My stomach gives a loud rumble and I realise I'm famished. Bugger Marcus and his shirt and his cheese sandwich. A few minutes later I'm strolling along the front in my white tie and tailcoat, eating chips from a fold of newspaper. I perch on a bench and watch the lightshow over the sea, licking vinegar and salt from my fingers and sniffing the metallic tang of more rain to come.

'Fox? Is it really you?'

I turn and there she is.

Edie Rose.

No, Edie Fox-Talbot.

'It *is* you.'

She steps forward as though to embrace me and then, thinking better of it, stops short.

'I was coming to the concert and thought I might see you. And here you are.'

'Here I am,' I agree, momentarily stuck for anything to say.

I reach out to shake her hand as I've been practising in my thoughts, only to find my fingers coated in chip grease. I resist the urge to wipe them down my dress trousers. Instead, I offer her a chip.

'No, thanks,' she says, with a shake of her head.

I notice her hair is shorter. She looks uncertain but then she smiles and I'm reminded how pretty she is. She sits beside me on the bench. Her perfume is just the same. There is too much to say and so we say nothing. The threatened rain falls in a sluice wash. In a moment the pavement is awash. We splash along the front, searching for somewhere to shelter, but everything is closed this early in the season. I grab her hand and propel her onto the pier where we duck under the striped awning of a candyfloss stall. If we stand with our backs pressed against the locked shutters we can stay dry. I glance sadly at my shoes, which are wet through, as are Edie's. Her stockings are sodden and stained with water. The rain drums on the tin roof, which magnifies the sound to a roar.

I notice I'm still clasping her hand. I release her. I'm going to ask her why she's coming to the concert, and about Jack and George and the house, even the General, and I want to know whether George managed to buy his cows, and I'll tell her how I've been greedy for news, any stray snippet, and that I hear she's been singing again and that I wanted to come and listen, but I knew I couldn't simply sneak in and then go quietly away, so I thought it best that I didn't come at all, and that I'm with Sal and I'll probably marry her, and I'm sorry I didn't write as I ought to have done, but I hope the cheques helped a little, and soon I'll be able to spare a bit more, and that I miss Jack and George and the dark woods, and that she mustn't worry, I didn't miss her at all, but I'm not sure whether that's true or not.

'Dreadful weather,' I say.

'Isn't it just.'

~

We sit in a pub, drinking whisky and hot water, steaming gently beside the fire. It's seven o'clock and I am not at the concert and Marcus does not have his preferred shirt. Or his cheese sandwich. I ought to go and meet Sal in the interval but I know I shan't. I bat away a nudge of guilt as if it were an irksome bluebottle. Edie stares into her glass. Her eyes are such a peculiar wintry grey. She glances up at me and gives a tiny smile.

'I heard your symphony. *The Song of Hartgrove Hall*.'

My heart thump-thumps. I wonder that she can't hear it. It dawns on me that it's Edie's opinion I've been wanting all along. I know Sal's delight in the piece ought to be enough but it isn't. It's Edie's voice that I hear as I write.

'You were at the concert?' I manage to say at last.

'Yes. And then like a coward I crept away.'

'Did Jack—?'

She shakes her head. 'He never goes to concerts.'

From the way she says this, I understand that he's still angry. I'm too apprehensive to ask whether she liked the music.

'It's changed a fair bit from the version you and I performed,' I say, wishing instantly I hadn't brought up that last evening. I hurry on. 'The second movement with the piano worked well, but I wasn't terribly happy with the singer. She wasn't a patch on you.'

'I thought Sal might have sung my part.'

'So did she,' I say dryly. 'I wasn't popular, let's say. But what could I do? Her voice isn't right.'

'Brave man,' says Edie, 'choosing music over your girl.'

'Or a foolish one.'

'That too.' She's laughing at me and I find that I like it. 'I'd hoped you'd be conducting.'

'I wanted to. Marcus insisted he have the first shot at it but I loathed it. Marcus gets in the way of everything. He has to be the star, when it should be the music. I've refused to let him conduct anything of mine since.' I sigh and rub my head, which is starting to throb. 'But he won't let me conduct anything at all until I do. We've reached a sort of stalemate. It's all rather unpleasant.'

I can hear how miserable I sound. How miserable I am.

'Can't you leave?'

'His notes are jolly good. Nasty. Smug. But, regrettably, useful and I'm getting better.'

We talk carefully, stepping around the gaping holes of what is unsaid. Edie licks her lips and I realise that she's nervous.

'I'd hoped choosing music would have made you happy,' she says.

This surprises me and I want to ask her whether she thought that was why I really left, but we're edging towards dangerous ground.

'Music does make me happy,' I say instead. 'It's merely the nonsense that comes with it that I can't bear.'

We drink quickly, as it is easier than speaking.

'Thank you for sending the painting of Hartgrove barrow,' I say at last.

Edie smiles. 'How do you know it was from me?'

'Wasn't it?'

'Yes.'

'Well, it was very kind.'

'Not really.' She looks down at the glass in her lap. 'I hoped it might make you homesick. Silly, really. But I don't want you to think it was done out of kindness. It was selfish. I wanted you to come back.'

She pauses, chewing her lip, and I look at her, unsure suddenly whether her interest in my return is purely sisterly.

'Come home, Fox,' she says abruptly, her colour rising. 'Just for a visit. To see Jack and George. They miss you. I know they do. We all do. Even the General.'

At this I laugh. I can't imagine the General missing anything or anyone.

'He does. Jack wanted to give your room to one of the cranks George has to stay and the General absolutely forbade it. Wanted to know where you'd stay, should you chance to come home that week.'

I'm oddly moved. To my shame, in all my thoughts of home I've pictured again and again the hills and the woods and the sloping fields and my brothers, but I've hardly thought about the General. At this moment I'm caught with a longing to see him, to see all of them.

'Well, it's good to know that the house is still standing in any case,' I say.

Edie sighs. 'For the present. Oh, do come home. I'll go away while you're there, if that's any easier – not that you even care for me in the least any more, I'm sure.' She's blushing now, a full and furious pink to the tips of her ears, and if I wasn't equally embarrassed, I'd want to laugh.

She takes my hand in hers. To the rest of the drinkers in the pub we must appear like lovers.

'Jack won't let me put any more money in, but the truth is I don't have much left. I'm singing again but even that's not enough. They can't possibly manage for more than a season or two. George is full of ideas but they aren't very practical and Jack can't talk to him, and the General sits in his library and reads the paper while everything goes to hell around him.'

She releases my hand and leans back in her chair.

'Oh, for God's sake, Fox, please, please come home.'

She holds my gaze. And I know instantly that I'm lost once again. I love her. Always will, even if she is over thirty.

～

I can't return to Hartgrove, not yet, I tell her, but we agree to meet again in London for dinner at Claridge's. The orchestra is playing at the Royal Albert Hall and we're staying in fairly gruesome digs dotted around the grottier parts of Knightsbridge. For once I'm by myself: Sal has a horrid cold and has stayed in Bournemouth, victim to the doubtful ministrations of our landlady. At least the old so-and-so likes Sal better than me, I reassure myself, guilty about leaving her. But it's not leaving Sal behind I'm ashamed of – no, it's that I'm pleased she isn't here. I'm glad I shall have Edie to myself.

It's nearly midnight and it's taken me over an hour to escape from Marcus, who has a bloodhound's nose for the scent of mischief. He allows me to leave, and leave alone, only when finally I confess whom I'm meeting. Then he raises an eyebrow and asks, suddenly serious, 'Do I need to worry for Sal?'

'No,' I say with a laugh. 'Don't be perfectly ridiculous.'

I wonder, as I sit waiting for Edie, whether his concern is indeed ridiculous. A shameful part of me hopes it isn't. Then Edie walks in. She's wearing a grey silk dress that matches her eyes, and, even in her high-heeled shoes, I notice how small she is. In her bare feet she'd hardly reach my shoulder. Her face lights up as she sees me and hurries over, apologising for being late. Fumbling, I kiss her cheek and squeeze her hand. She smells wonderful.

'It's simply heavenly to see you, Edie, darling.'

'You too, Fox,' she says and unthinkingly glances about her. I wonder whether she's anxious about being seen with me.

The thought thrills me. Surely there's nothing in the least to be ashamed about in meeting her brother-in-law?

'Have you eaten?' I ask. 'I know it's horribly late but on concert nights I never get the chance to have supper until a ridiculous hour.'

'I haven't eaten,' says Edie, 'but I'm not hungry.'

I discover suddenly that neither am I. She's staring at me with an odd look, at once wary and eager. I'm not sure that I understand but on impulse I reach out and take her hand. It's so small, almost a child's hand. She does not pull away, merely looks at me, her expression terribly sad. I can't bear it, I want to make that ghastly look disappear, and at first, more out of a desire to distract her than actual desire, I kiss her hand and stroke her knuckles, and then to my delight, she shivers and squeezes my fingers. We stare at one another, each trying to read the other. Is she? Is this? Are we?

'What brings you to town?' I say, eventually, still holding onto her.

'I'm in town for a day or two each week. I'm helping a friend who's planning the Bolshoi's first English tour. You know I speak a little Russian.'

'Of course.' I didn't know.

The silence stretches again, threatening to engulf us both.

'Who was the soloist tonight?' she asks at last.

Her knee encased in water silk is touching mine and I'm almost giddy from wanting her, hardly able to think at all.

'Albert Shields. The pianist.'

'Oh yes?'

'He's a pal of Marcus.'

She slides further away from me so that we're no longer touching, and instantly my head clears.

'I like Albert very much,' I say. 'He doesn't stand for any of Marcus's usual guff. They argue vociferously over the score but Albert stands up to him. I came into rehearsal yesterday to find them both shouting at one another so loudly that, this morning, the dispute continued in whispers, both men having shouted themselves hoarse.'

Edie laughs, and perhaps it's the alcohol, but she looks a good deal more at ease. A rosy flush suffuses her cheeks. Good God, she's attractive. I order another round of martinis.

'Why do any of you put up with him, if he's so dreadful?' she asks.

'Well, I asked Albert that. I mean, he's the star pianist of the moment, he can play with any conductor he chooses. And he said, "The man's a blighter, but he's a brilliant blighter. Afterwards I'll tell myself that it wasn't worth it. But it is. I'll decline to play with him for six months or a year but after that I'll start hankering to sound like that again." And the thing is, Edie, he's right. Marcus is a perfect genius at coaxing genius out of other people.'

'You have a knack for it yourself.'

I'm desperate to ask what she means, but I don't want her to think I'm fishing. She shifts on her seat, and then looks up at me.

'I liked the way I sounded when I sang with you conducting. I want to sound like that again.'

She swallows and her hand darts to her throat. She reaches into her bag, pulls out a cigarette and, after fumbling with a match, puts it away again, unlit.

'I'm trying to stop. It plays havoc with my voice. But if I'm not singing your songs, I'm not so sure that it matters.'

'Don't be silly. Of course it does.'

I study her, perspiration trickling down the small of my back. She sips her martini and then places it back on the bar, asking with sudden resolve, 'Why won't you come home?'

'I will soon. It's simply—'

She waves at me to be quiet. 'The thing is, I'm not even sure if I want you to come.'

'Oh?' I say, hurt.

'No,' she says steadily. 'I like the thought of seeing you every day. I like that. But everything else—'

I take her hand again, running my fingers across the ridge of her knuckles.

'You are so horribly young,' she says, half to herself.

I recoil, offended. 'I'm twenty-one.'

She laughs. 'God help me. It's thoroughly absurd. Do you even know how old I am, Harry?'

I shrug, feigning nonchalance. I want to appear knowing, but I also don't wish to offend her. 'Twenty-nine? Thirty?'

'Thirty-two.'

I'm surprised. I'm still a novice with women and I can't hide it. She laughs at my discomfiture but I can tell she's wounded by the way she won't meet my eye.

'It doesn't matter in the least,' I say.

'Of course it does.'

'I'm only glad that you told me. I like it when you tell me things.'

Finally she looks at me. There are faint shadows like bruises beneath her eyes.

'I really ought to go,' she says.

She doesn't move. She frowns and I lean forward to kiss her but she turns away. 'Not here.'

But somewhere.

My heart raps against my ribs. I've wanted her so much for so long. Then I'm stricken with the intrusion of practicalities. I'm trying not to think of Jack but, of course, by trying not to, he's already here. Besides, I can't possibly afford a room at Claridge's, and I certainly can't have Edie back to my digs with its typed sign declaring 'Absolutely NO overnight guests by order of the Management', but she's tugging my hand and I'm leaving cash on the bar and following her out into the street where, to my immense surprise, she runs to the kerb, places two fingers in her mouth and whistles loudly for a cab. One pulls up and she slips in.

'Come on! I don't know where we're going.'

Neither do I.

Somehow we end up outside my Knightsbridge digs, which to my relief are perfectly dark. Giggling, we creep up the stairs, Edie in her bare feet, trying not to make a sound, which is tricky as we're both sloshed. And then we're alone in the dingy bedsit with its nasty, none-too-clean linoleum floor that sticks to our feet and the thin, faded curtains flapping. The only decorations on the walls are mounted jigsaw puzzles of London landmarks. I shut the door and tuck a chair beneath the handle as I don't trust the landlady's assurance that I possess the only key. The room smells faintly of old soup.

'May I get you a drink, madam?' I say, producing a bottle of whisky from the bedside table.

'How kind,' says Edie with an arch smile.

As I watch her, I feel again how little I know her, as though she's a broken mirror and I glimpse her image only in fragments.

She sighs and looks perfectly wretched, saying, 'I keep telling myself that you're just a boy. That this is the silliest of crushes. That if perhaps we make love once, then we'll get it out of the way and we won't ever need to do it again. Things will simply go back to how they were.'

'Do you believe that?' I ask.

'No.'

I splash some whisky into a mug that smells a little of toothpaste and hold it out to her. She pads closer, but ignores the proffered mug and instead reaches up on tiptoe to kiss me. I'm tentative, but for no more than a moment. The whisky spills over the floor. Our teeth clink but we don't care and we don't stop and I wrap my arms around her and lift her up onto the bed, vaguely aware of my relief that in the dark she won't see the dubious cleanliness of the sheets. She lies on her back, propped up on her elbows, dress rucked up to show the smooth whiteness of her thighs above her stockings, and I lean over her, but she holds me back.

'Wait, Fox. Wait. Are you sure? Are we sure? We can't take this back. It's a terrible thing to do.'

'A terrible thing,' I say, sliding next to her, quite unable to stop.

She kisses me.

'It's unforgivable, Fox.'

'Yes.'

She looks so sad and I know I should stop but I don't.

August 2002

'I want to know whether it's something or nonsense,' I said. Marcus sat across from me on the terrace and laughed. 'If you don't know . . . then it's probably nonsense.'

'It isn't,' I snapped.

'Well, there you are,' he said, reaching for a biscuit. His hand was thin, the skin papery and yellow revealing the bones beneath, fragile as a bird's.

'I don't think it's nonsense but it's the first time I've written anything in a while and I'm worried my radar's off.'

'All right. I'll take a look after luncheon. There is luncheon?' He glanced about, pretending concern.

'Yes, of course.'

During the previous week, I'd lived off sandwiches and Pot Noodles – a young man's diet that had played havoc with my insides, but knowing Marcus's fastidiousness I'd asked Mrs Stroud to cook for a few days. Until I'd finished writing the opening theme, I'd been quite unable to do anything else. Even poor Robin had been banished, rationed to an hour a day at the piano while I had an afternoon snooze.

We took lunch on the terrace. I'd invited John and Albert to join us and it was a pleasant, lazy affair. I brought out rather a good Chablis and another when the first turned out to be insufficient. It was nearly September and the hill had ripened to a dull gold; the flower beds in the garden were studded with lurid pink and yellow dahlias while the sticky, sweetshop scent of late summer roses drifted across the terrace. A squadron of wild ducks squabbled as they flew in formation overhead, managing to fire white squirts of shit across the paving stones on the terrace.

'Ah, countryside delights,' said John, helping himself to more blackberry fool and another glass of wine. 'I must say, you look better, Fox. More like your old self.'

'I feel better.'

I couldn't express the relief that, after two years of silence, my head was once again full of music. I hadn't appreciated how much I'd missed it, how appalling its absence had been. I felt as if I'd been freed unexpectedly from solitary confinement long after having abandoned any hope of release.

'How's that rather wonderful grandson of yours?' asked Albert.

'Brilliant. Tricky.'

Albert smiled. 'That's the way of it, I'm afraid, with these young musicians. It's much easier to be like me – a late bloomer. I had my first lesson at ten. Wasn't really much cop until I was twenty.'

'And now you're past it,' said John with a grin. 'Short window.'

'Indeed,' said Albert, unperturbed. 'Still, I can listen to recordings and marvel at myself.'

'Right then,' said Marcus, who was beginning to look tired. 'Shall we all listen to your latest efforts?'

I hesitated. After Edie, Marcus had always been my second pair of ears but he inevitably made me nervous. No one was more brutal than Marcus.

'All right,' I said. 'It's just sketched for now. You'll need to imagine the melody played by a pair of flutes.'

'Are you going to play it for us?' asked Marcus.

I shook my head. 'I'd rather not. Albert? Will you do the honours?'

They followed me into the music room, arranging themselves on chairs with much shuffling of cushions. I went to the piano, set out the pages for Albert and then, before he'd had a chance to start, I slipped out of the room. I paced outside in the corridor, anxious as an expectant father. If they were horribly tactful and kind at the end, I'd know it was rubbish and I would be done with composing. But I'd not had a bad run. I was a jolly decent footnote in British musical history. My footnote might even have to run into a second column.

The playing stopped. The door didn't open. I heard mutterings. I was filled with dread. There was shuffling and a moment later the door opened. Marcus beamed at me.

'Bloody hell,' he said at last. 'You've found your second wind.'

~

They all decided to stay for a few days, which stretched into a week and then longer. Marcus usually lived alone and ill health had forced his retirement, but the speed with which Albert and John, who were both married and still working, cancelled their plans both surprised and gratified me. By good luck, neither had any professional engagements until the end of September and they seemed perfectly unconcerned at the prospect of missing the lunch parties or drinks or garden visits their wives might have organised. But by then both women were much like ship's widows, resigned to a life where their husbands' watery mistress called them back time and again. Music could be as much of a temptress as the sea.

Mrs Stroud arrived each morning to cook for us all. I wrote and showed pages to Marcus, who offered suggestions and, for old times' sake, the odd complaint about the thickness of my orchestration. Mostly he slept. I realised that over the last year, he'd grown frail. He pretended to still have his vast appetite but the heap of potatoes he'd help himself to would be pushed around his plate and thrown away, uneaten. At night, I could hear him pacing, restless and in pain. His laugh remained the same, filthy and undimmed. John and Albert lazed in the garden and played through snatches of what we all agreed was the opening movement to a symphony. Their suggestions were always interesting but inevitably it was Marcus to whom I really listened.

Robin was thrilled by the influx of musicians. I didn't have the heart to tell him that this was a pathetic imitation of festivals past. This gathering was more like a summer camp for the geriatric. Yet, for the first time in as long as I could remember, I was perilously close to happiness. It was tinged with loss and I often slept badly, but there were moments of stillness and peace. I took pleasure in walking around the garden, Marcus's arm in mine as he prodded at the geraniums with his stick. Later, as I sat at the piano, not writing but watching bands of mist and rain roll down the hillside, I experienced a ripple of contentment. Up till then I'd lived on memories of Edie and better times but now I could see that there might be a possibility of enjoyment in the present; in smaller and fleeting doses perhaps, but spoonfuls of joy all the same.

Along with endless advice on composition, the cooking of pears and the steeping of sloes, Marcus also brought with him a prodigious quantity of pot. Marcus liked to share good things – whether a restaurant recommendation, a new recording of Beethoven or, in this case, some astounding grass given to him to help with his pain by a forward-thinking and kindly GP. I'd smoked a little back in the 1970s, but not since. Albert, we soon discovered, was the best at rolling joints. As a pianist he had tremendous dexterity in his fingers.

One morning I telephoned Clara and, pleading a summer cold, asked her not to bring Robin round to the house. She was irritated – informing Robin he could not play the piano for a day was a ghastly task – and she was suspicious because I sounded insufficiently unwell.

'Are you sure it isn't just a touch of hay fever? I could bring him later on, and you wouldn't even have to see us.'

I forced a cough into my handkerchief, feeling a buzz of exhilaration at my subterfuge. 'No, no. Best not. Wouldn't want the little chap to catch anything.'

I rang off quickly before she could make any further helpful suggestions. I could tell that she didn't believe me but I knew she would never suspect the real reason – I wanted to get absolutely blotto with my old pals. I certainly didn't want Clara stumbling by with her drab disapproval and prim tut-tutting.

It was a warm day, stray licks of cloud only further setting off the bold blue of the sky. A tractor grunted along the slope of the hill, baling hay, and the air was filled with the scent of cut grass and wild flowers. I wished the farmers had a stronger sense of the picturesque and would stop parcelling their bales in black plastic – the effect was less Bruegel and more giant black bin bags littering the hill. Yet nothing could really disturb the gleam of the morning. A flotilla of white butterflies, wings like tiny sails, skimmed across the lawn as though part of a miniature regatta. We lunched late and then, having thanked Mrs Stroud, we gathered on the terrace.

John perched on the edge of a deckchair, peering at Albert, who, on his second attempt, was succeeding in rolling a fat and firm joint, as pale and long as one of the young slow-worms I sometimes discovered basking in the vegetable patch. John frowned and I knew that he was struggling to hold back from offering advice. John, I was utterly confident, had never even smoked a joint before, much less rolled one, but like Marcus he was a conductor to his soul and had advice to bestow on all matters. He dispensed it as he would nicely rotted compost, shovelling it liberally everywhere.

'Are you quite sure that's how it's supposed to be done?' he asked at last.

Albert shrugged. 'Well, it's how I've done it. You're welcome to have another go.'

'No, no,' said John, who preferred to instruct others, not risk failure himself. 'I'm sure it will be splendid.'

'How do you usually do it?' asked Albert, turning to Marcus.

'I don't. The girl who cleans for me rolls a nice supply in exchange for taking one or two home with her. She also brings me excellent Cornish pasties.' He put on his reading glasses and inspected Albert's attempt with the air of a connoisseur. 'Not bad for a beginner. Not bad at all.'

Understanding from watching films that we might be hungry afterwards, I'd ensured that Mrs Stroud had left us a good supply of cheese scones and a Dundee cake. There was also a leftover cold salmon and some potato salad but I was unsure whether that was appropriate fare.

Albert struck a match and took a long suck on the joint, as though it were a cigar. Marcus chuckled. 'Not like that. You have to breathe in the smoke. Here, give it to me.'

Like furtive and decrepit schoolboys, we all watched the more experienced Marcus with considerable interest. He puffed away, blowing elegant smoke rings and smiling, a little smugly, at John. The two men had been cheerful rivals for nearly half a century, meticulously sending one another copies of any poor reviews they claimed to have chanced upon.

I knew, certainly in Marcus's case, that this claim was quite untrue. After John had conducted a concert in New York, I'd sat with Marcus in a hotel room, watching while he pored over every single newspaper, discarding with contempt the praise and effusions, until with a shout of triumph he came across the single line of measured criticism. I had watched with astonishment as he'd carefully cut it out from the surrounding compliments and placed it happily in an envelope to post to his friend, declaring, 'It's always good to know what people are saying about you.'

275

I'd pointed out that mostly people were saying jolly nice things and Marcus wasn't sending those to John.

'One learns only from one's mistakes,' he'd said, humming with pleasure as he affixed the stamp.

Albert absolutely refused to perform the same pieces with them – he had a repertoire he played with Marcus and another with John. He complained that, otherwise, his performance was a tug-of-war – each maestro trying to yank him into a different interpretation, more dramatic than his rival's.

As I was predominantly known as a composer, and any renown I had as a conductor was mostly for interpretations of my own work, I was exempt from their competition. In fact, the one thing that both John and Marcus agreed upon with any unanimity was that they were both far superior in this field to myself, viewing my talents with benevolent disdain. I had my revenge, though, in politely declining them permission to publicly perform my works – however much they cajoled and pleaded over the brandy.

John had evidently decided this was a choice moment for renewing his petition. 'When are you going to let me at this latest piece, then, old chap?' he asked.

'Precisely when I let you at the others.'

He perked up and shot a glance at Marcus to see how his rival was taking this promise. Marcus chuckled. 'Don't be so chirpy. He means that he won't let you. We're both barred.'

'Don't be such a spoilsport,' grumbled John. 'If you give it to me, I'll show you how it should really sound.'

'That's the problem,' I said. 'I already know how it's supposed to sound. It doesn't need added bombast.'

Albert was rather quiet. We looked over to find that he was lying back in his deckchair, grinning emptily at the clouds. 'Very nice,' he said. 'Very nice. Very, very nice.' He giggled and then gave a sonorous fart. 'F flat,' he declared and giggled again.

'Told you it was jolly decent stuff,' said Marcus proudly.

He passed the joint to me and I inhaled tentatively, then coughed and retched, wondering why on earth I was attempting something so undignified.

Marcus handed me a glass of water. I took a sip and then, taking the joint, tried again.

'Just a little, not a ruddy great lungful,' advised Marcus.

This time, I managed. It was jagged and sore, much as I imagined inhaling glass to be, but then came a wave of green calm. I tried another, and felt soft and boneless.

'Off,' I said to John, gesticulating vaguely at his deckchair. He moved aside and, gratefully, I lay down.

The afternoon passed in a pleasurable jumble. Time jumped to and fro. Someone suggested we fetch the Dundee cake. Then it was gone though I couldn't recall ever eating it, but the crumbs and raisins on my lapel suggested otherwise. I heard the warble of the garden birds inside my skull and the thrum of the earthworms beneath the grass. The leaves on the climbing roses and the wisteria vibrated with revolving colour like the patterns in a child's kaleidoscope.

'You should have a revelation for the second movement, Fox,' said John, jabbing a finger too close to my face. 'That's what you're supposed to do. A drug-fuelled revelation.'

'Yes,' said Marcus. 'I agree with John so it must be true.'

'Irrefutably,' agreed John, kissing Marcus's hand.

'I think I'd rather have something to eat,' I said. 'Just a little nibble.'

'All right. A snack first. Then a revelation.'

'Go and see if there's anything else in the fridge, Fox.'

Thus I found myself searching in the refrigerator for a revelation but succeeded only in finding half a poached salmon. Then I was sitting back on the terrace with the others, gazing at the picked bones of the fish, unable to remember either returning from the kitchen or consuming the salmon. Albert and John were fast asleep, snoring gently. Marcus reached over and took my hand.

'You can conduct the new work. You and not John,' I said.

'Now, now, that sounds perilously close to pity,' said Marcus. 'You've rightly not allowed us close to your work for nearly fifty years. Don't break your rules now.' He gave me a rueful smile. 'Besides, when you hear how wonderful I make you sound, you'll only regret those wasted years when I could have been championing you to millions.'

I laughed. Even at eighty-three and dying, Marcus had the ego of a true maestro.

~

The pot did not provide me with great inspiration, only constipation. Fellows of my advanced age simply can't spend afternoons feasting furiously on all manner of things and then expect no digestive consequences. A day and a half and a packet of Alka-Seltzer later, I returned to the music room, dawdling through various ideas while trying to banish a faint headache. My flood of inspiration had dwindled to a paltry trickle and I wondered where I'd gone wrong. I fumbled at the keys, unable to hear the next passage. There was the thump, thump of Marcus's stick along the corridor and the next moment he entered the music room, sitting down heavily in a chair.

'What did you used to do, when you reached this section? Every piece has a thorny bit. What was your trick?' he asked.

I frowned, trying to remember. 'Well, sometimes, I'd try it in a different key. Some variations.'

Marcus thumped his stick. 'No. Have I taught you nothing? No padding. No unnecessary passages.'

I laughed at his imperious tone. 'I went out song collecting.

Always helped, whether it was the walk itself, or discovering an unexpected melody.'

Marcus clapped his hands. 'Very good! Let's get going then.'

I sighed. 'There's nothing left to find. The older singers are gone and their tunes with them. It's all pub fiddlers and careful revival now.'

Marcus wrinkled his brow. 'I don't believe that. You just don't know where to look.'

'No,' I agreed. 'But anyway, I don't think that will help this time. It's something else that's wrong. Something's missing. Something terribly, terribly obvious.'

Marcus left me and I sat alone in the music room. I was irritated with myself and frustrated. I read and reread the score I'd written so far. I was pleased with it, and a little terrified – I knew this was as good as anything I'd ever done, but what if all I could produce was this unfinished movement, this fractured symphony? Perhaps this was it – the last rush of inspiration like the final rallying of a dying patient.

I laughed aloud at myself. I was being overdramatic. The truth was that it had been some years since I'd produced anything really good. My more recent works were perfectly decent and had been kindly received – the critics became more benevolent as I'd neared seventy – but I knew myself that they were ordinary. Not much more than echoes of ideas that had been fresh and exhilarating when I was in my thirties and forties. This new work was no echo. It had snuck up on me in the shower and haunted me as nothing had done for years. I was finding myself impatient with the conversation of my good friends and I longed to slope off after dinner to be alone to listen to my thoughts. I played through the theme, frustrated at the inadequacy of my playing, and trying to imagine it on a pair of flutes. The pedal on the piano was sticking and, as I peered at it, I discovered, wedged underneath, a small bouncy ball belonging to Robin. With some difficulty, I eased myself onto my hands and knees and, groping about, managed to slide it free.

'Grandpa?' said a voice in the doorway.

Instantly I raised my head, cracking it on the underside of the instrument, and swore. Robin slipped into the room and crept under the piano to sit beside me. Tucking his knees under his chin, he peered at me.

'I like to sit under the piano too,' he said. 'It's my thinking place.'

Wordlessly, I handed him his ball. He remained crouched beside me in silence for a moment, and then said, 'Grandpa? I want a go at the thing you were playing.'

Painfully, I eased my way out from under the piano and settled back onto one of the armchairs. I hesitated, unsure whether I wanted Robin to play. It was too soon. The piece was unfinished and it was the opinion of this child that really mattered to me, more even than the esteem of my celebrated friends. I wanted him to understand it. I didn't want to be alone again.

Before I'd entirely made up my mind, Robin was sitting at the piano and playing through the sketches with more fluidity and nuance than I ever could. I grasped at once what my difficulty had been. I'd been fooling myself. The melody wasn't for a pair of flutes. This was a piano symphony. And I had to write it for Robin.

~

I wrote at white heat, hardly pausing to eat the meals that Mrs Stroud sent up to the music room and which Marcus insisted I finish. I was exhilarated by my work. The approbation of my chums was satisfying but most of all I was elated by the feeling that I was in the midst of writing the best music of my career. It's all very well to be praised and acknowledged at fifteen or twenty-five or even forty, but afterwards there is the maudlin sense that one is on a downward slide.

That was why I was apprehensive for Robin. It is a terrible thing for someone to reach their peak as a child. If one scales Rachmaninov before the age of twelve, then what other mountains are left, either critically or intellectually? I believe it is worst of all for trebles, those astounding boy singers with a dizzying purity of sound who dazzle the world for a brief season before their voices crack and break. I pity those children most of all. They lose not only their career but also their instrument. They are like piano players who have lost their hands.

I didn't want Robin's gifts to take quite so long to mature as my own. I decided that I was like a pre-war brandy – remarkable both in flavour and for the sheer bloody length of time it had to reach its best. I wrote with the fervour and vim of a young man. Sometimes, too exhausted to write, I would draw the curtains and lie back on one of the vast armchairs in the music room, prop up my feet and listen to my early recordings. I found it eerie, akin to watching my life flash before my eyes.

I suppose that must be how an actor or actress must feel. I spared a thought for Elizabeth Taylor, bloated and old, watching *Cleopatra* or *National Velvet* and seeing her own radiant beauty – a desperate experience, I would imagine. For me, however, it was disconcerting in a different way; I was not struck by the sense of youth lost, more that another man was conducting those pieces. In my mind I no longer heard them that way. When I looked at photographs of my younger self, I somehow imagined I could remember more or less how I'd felt when the shutter had clicked and that in essentials I remained very much the same – a little worn around the edges, the digestion less reliable and with markedly less hair, but otherwise unaltered. On hearing myself conduct Mahler at the age of thirty, it occurred to me that I was quite wrong. This earlier Fox was as different from Fox at seventy-odd as he was to another conductor entirely. It was an uncomfortable and dislocating sensation.

Clara brought Robin around several evenings each week to play through the latest pages. As he played, the following day's passage seemed to be suddenly illuminated like the safe course picked out by the beam of a lighthouse.

As he finished, he gave a small huff of satisfaction. 'I like to be the first to play your stuff.'

I laughed. In this, Robin reminded me of his grandmother – the first to run across the snow, or to play across a page.

Later, when Robin had gone home, we all sat on the terrace drinking brandy. The marigolds had been nipped by an early September frost and the hydrangeas had started to burnish. This would be the last evening outside until next year. Miserably, I wondered whether for Marcus this would simply be the last time. We sat in silence, a heaviness in the air between us. Our content had dwindled as the warmth of summer gave way to the nip of autumn.

'Come, come, this won't do at all,' said Marcus at last. 'Surely you saw that list in *Music Maker* of twenty-first-century greats? I was listed higher than the lot of you.'

'I was only one place behind,' grumbled John.

'See! I knew you'd seen it,' said Marcus, triumphant.

'And when Fox's piano symphony is performed, he'll be higher than all of us, even you, Marcus,' said Albert.

'No doubt,' said Marcus, smiling. 'No doubt at all.'

Albert cleared his throat. 'It's quite something you've done, Fox. I've read the score. I've heard the snatches Robin's been playing. And I'd say that it's the music of a man thirty years younger – it has such energy and passion but it also has the depth and sadness that come with age.'

Marcus chuckled and shrugged. 'Well, the last Rembrandts were the best, the last Titians the most surprising.'

∼

When I reached the end of the second movement, I hesitated. I wanted to introduce another theme. As I sat in the dusk, watching the pale underbellies of the poplars' canopies shiver and shake in the wind, I found myself thinking of Edie. She adored those trees, calling them the winter trees; even in summer their silver leaves appeared to be perpetually frosted.

I closed my eyes and, for the first time in many months, I allowed myself to remember her singing. I listened to her sing a Yiddish refrain, a lilting, rhythmic tune of swaying bodies and sliding notes. I pulled out a sheet of manuscript paper and started to sketch the melody, varying it here and there, writing the song for Robin's piano instead of Edie's voice. I knew both instruments so well. They could share this symphony, grandmother and grandson. I'd call it Piano Symphony in G: *Edie and Robin*.

In a year or two, he wouldn't remember her. He'd been so young when she died, but through this music he would discover her. I'd write a breadcrumb trail for him to seek out his grandmother, a song path leading through the hills and barrows of Hartgrove and then eastwards towards the cold, the Russia of long ago. He'd find her there, singing in the snow.

June 1952

The entire country is eager for music and we spend the year touring, performing to packed houses. At least Marcus is allowing me to conduct. I take several rehearsals and even the odd performance at the lesser venues. He's so exhausted by the regimen that he puts up only a token resistance. Wherever we go it's the same: queues of shining, eager faces. Everyone's caught coronation fever. The entire country has been put through the wash one too many times and is a dreary shade of grey; the exchequer is flat broke, but at last we have something to celebrate. A new Elizabethan age is coming and we're overcome with fervour for Elgar.

The programme varies very little from city to county town: Vaughan Williams, Handel, Elgar, Elgar, Elgar and 'Jerusalem'. There's something very English about the fact that our national hymn isn't called 'London' or 'Hastings' or 'Cambridge' but 'Jerusalem'.

Edie is once again at the apex of national sentiment. If Queen Elizabeth is the face of a nation, then Edie Rose is its singing voice. In something of a coup, Edie is touring with us. All the orchestras want her, but inexplicably – to the outside world anyway – she's chosen the Bournemouth Symphony Orchestra. It's delightful and excruciating to be in such extended proximity to her. After two years of snatched moments in grubby digs and the occasional provincial hotel, here she is with me. But as always, there's Jack. And Sal.

The guilt is monstrous. Each time we tell one another it is for the last time. We shan't meet again. But we do. Sometimes I wonder whether Sal suspects the affair, but in reality I know she doesn't. I'm fooling myself. If I can tell myself that she knows and hasn't left me, then I can pretend that I have her tacit consent. I know Edie's remorse is as agonising as mine. We both try to buy it off. Edie is making money again, lots of it, and I know without needing to be told that it is all being poured into Hartgrove Hall. My royalties, although less hand- some than Edie's fees, are split between my twin shames: Jack and Sal. I send money home and I've bought Sal everything I can. Everything except that which I know she really wants: a wedding ring. It would be the final hypocrisy and I simply can't do it, even when I hear her weeping at night when she thinks I'm asleep. It's a dreadful thing I'm doing. I must stop. I must. I shall.

I don't. I watch as Edie wearily pulls on her stockings. We're in her hotel room. Bristol, I think. It takes me a moment to remember – there have been so many hotels, so many cities. I've told Sal that I'm running errands for Marcus. I'm exhausted with the lies.

'We have to end this,' I say.

'Don't,' snaps Edie. 'We lie about everything else. Let's not lie to each other about this. We're never going to stop. I can't imagine not seeing you, not sleeping with you. Can you?'

I shake my head. I never knew that love was so terrible.

'Then let's stop pretending. We simply have to live with knowing the kind of people we really are. People who can do this to people they proclaim to love.'

I know that Edie still loves Jack. I don't know what kind of love it is and how it differs from her love for me. I don't ask. She doesn't ask about Sal. It's harder for Edie, I suppose, since she has to see Sal. Eat luncheon with her and see her in the theatre and chat about pleasantries, all the time knowing. At least I don't have to face Jack. It's much easier to betray him in the abstract. Every now and again, I have unconscionable fantasies, where he's killed in a car crash or in some desperate, tragic accident, and I can weep and mourn for him and recite a heartfelt eulogy, and then, quietly, respectably, marry Edie and everyone will admire our fortitude, and he will never discover our betrayal.

But even that still leaves Sal. I'm terribly fond of Sal. It's a quieter affection born of familiarity and habit. I like her. I'm grateful to her and I don't wish to hurt her and that cowardice propels me further into moral stagnation.

I anticipate my liaisons with Edie as much for the moments after making love as for the act itself. Ordinarily she remains so guarded, but during those minutes or hours as we lie together in damp sheets, staring at the tattered hotel wall-paper in Brighton or Didsbury or Stratford, I find that she will grant me scraps of herself. Perhaps it is simply that she finds talking easier than contemplating the rottenness of what we're doing.

I run a finger along the hollow curve of her back. She shivers and reaches for her slip.

'We'd better not. You should go.'

'In a minute. Don't get dressed yet, darling.'

She nestles her face into the pillow and allows me to trace the fine down at the base of her spine. She shivers again, but not from desire.

'Are you worrying about the concert tonight? You'll be splendid,' I say, lying down beside her, trying to make her face me.

She gives a wan smile, but she looks drawn.

'I can't help it. I think I might be sick.'

She clambers out of bed and vomits in the wastepaper basket.

'It never gets any better.'

'Are you sure it's jitters? You're not pregnant, are you?'

She shakes her head, momentarily stricken. 'No. It hasn't happened after all these years with Jack. Or with you. I think I must be barren. Never mind. It's probably for the best.'

With that, she's sick again. I gaze at her, dizzy with love, and think: so this is how our affair has progressed – from making love to watching her stark naked and vomiting into a wastepaper bin.

'Can I get you something? Water? A dry biscuit?'

She shakes her head. 'No. I'll be all right after the perform-ance. Talk to me. Distract me. It's the only thing that helps.'

'Has it always been like this?'

'Talking about stage fright isn't really a distraction, Harry.'

'Tell me anyway. I want to know.'

She sighs, resigned. 'You know that my parents were poor?'

'I know.'

'There was nothing picturesque about it. We lived in a grubby and nasty little flat near Brick Lane. There's this idea amongst the English that one doesn't talk about money. That's true only if one has it. When one doesn't have money, that's simply all one talks about. How we don't have enough. Where we can get some. What we'd do if we had it. My mother worked in a kosher bakery but it didn't pay much. My father, well, he dabbled in schemes. I remember one summer he made soap until the flat reeked foully of animal fat and violets, and the walls and floors were constantly sloppy with grease. Eventually my mother put a stop to it. Other times, he cycled around the suburbs with a trailer, buying up tat for a penny, tarting it up somewhat ineffectually and trying to sell it on for twopence. Anyway, it was never enough. We were always fret-ting about rent and worrying about the coal bill and trying to find out which stores might give us credit.'

I don't want to interrupt her, fearful that she'll stop, so I say nothing while she reaches for her robe, knotting it loosely around her waist. She fumbles in her bag for a packet of gum, which she has taken to chewing in an attempt to give up ciga-rettes. She settles back on the bed, picking at the chipped crimson nail polish on her toes.

'My parents went out during the day and I stayed at home with my grandmother,' she says. 'I adored her. You would have loved her, Fox. She sang and cooked and told me terrifying stories about life in Russia that utterly thrilled me. I dreamed of beetroot and Cossacks. The two always seemed to go together in my mind. I used to sing with her all the old tunes she could remember. One afternoon my father came home early – I must have been nearly six – and found us singing together while doing the laundry. He started to cry—'

'He must have been terribly moved by your voice, darling.'

'No. Not really. He proceeded to shout at my grandmother, swearing and berating her furiously in Yiddish and Russian.'

'Why?'

'He was outraged that she hadn't told him that I could sing. Here had been his meal ticket all along, sitting idly at home in pigtails, when I could have been out earning. He took me with him that first evening. We traipsed round all the pubs. I'd perch on the bar and sing. We didn't do too badly but my father was cross, feeling we ought to have done better. The thing was, people were charmed by my youth and littleness, but they didn't care much for the songs themselves. Yiddish was too foreign and I seemed too much like a gypsy child. Those songs were all I knew, so my father invested in some sheets of popular songs. He shoved them at me and told me to learn them. Of course, I couldn't read music and didn't know what to do with them. He was furious when he found out.'

'Did he hurt you, darling?'

She shrugs. 'Oh, not too much. I'm sure you were given the strap when you misbehaved.'

'Well, the General never believed in sparing the rod.'

'No, I can't imagine he did. Neither did my father.'

'How did you learn to read music? Did he teach you?'

'No, he couldn't read music either. A neighbour taught me. He had been a violinist. I learned quickly; fear is an efficient sharpener of wits.

'Anyway, we did better after that. But I hated it. If I did well, then my father was happy and bought me an iced bun or a pretzel on the way home. If we didn't, he sulked or raged. I became more and more anxious about performing, dreading every night. It's better now but it never quite goes away.'

I hold her tightly to me but she wriggles away. 'I'm fine. Really I am. You asked, so I told you.'

'I'd like to meet your father, tell him what I think of him.'

'Well, you can't,' she says. 'He's dead.'

'Oh,' I say, taken aback. 'I'm sorry.'

'Are you? I thought you wanted to give him a piece of your mind.'

'Yes, but—' I'm flummoxed and she laughs, kissing my cheek.

'I'm teasing you, darling. I'm not sad about it. He wasn't all bad but he wasn't a happy man.'

'And your mother?'

'Still in Brick Lane. I see her occasionally. We're not close.'

She starts to dress, then sits back on the bed in her slip, one leg dangling over the edge. She chews on her finger and then glances at me. When she speaks again, her voice is shrill and pleading.

'Do you see now, Fox? Do you see how it was for me when Jack loved me? A man like that?'

She doesn't elucidate on what she means by 'a man like that' but I understand precisely. Growing up with Jack, I felt rather like one of the shoddy copies of the old master paintings in the great hall, displayed unflatteringly beside the original.

'I'm sure your mother is extremely proud of you,' I say, wanting to change the subject. I can't bear talking about Jack. Especially when Edie has just risen from my bed.

'She is. Although she wishes I hadn't changed my name.'

I stare at her, bewildered.

'What do you mean?'

She laughs. 'Edie Rose is my stage name, darling. Surely you knew that?'

'No, stupidly, I'd never thought about it. What was your real name then?'

'My surname is Rozanov. I couldn't possibly have got along as I have with a name like that. Much too Jewish. And foreign. Simply wouldn't do. If you're going to sing for the troops, they want to know that your soul is red, white and blue all the way back to bloody King Alfred.'

'Rozanov?' I say, trying it out like a strange new dish.

'Yes, Rozanov.'

I stare at her. In that moment I feel as if I don't know her at all. To my dismay, it has never occurred to me that before she married Jack her name was anything other than 'Rose'. Rose is the quintessential English surname; a delightful accident, I've always thought. Edie was clearly destined to become the forces' favourite singer, their sweet English Rose. I understand now that it has not been an accident at all, but a careful arrangement.

'And "Edie"?' I ask her, my mouth dry. 'You haven't always been Edie?'

She shakes her head.

'No. My real name is Iskra.'

'Iskra?'

She nods and smiles. 'Iskra Rozanov. A pleasure to meet you.'

She stretches out her hand to shake mine as though it's a game, and I take it, playing along, but it's not funny in the least. My lover is a stranger to me.

⁓

The concert goes off well. Despite her fears, Edie's marvellous. I wonder whether Jack knows about Iskra Rozanov. I suppose he must. It's her maiden name after all. Thinking about Jack causes my guilt to break out, itching like a rash that has flared up in the heat. I find it hard to concentrate on anything else.

Marcus offers to let me conduct Edie's popular wartime songs, knowing perfectly well that I will decline. My love for Edie has not extended to her hits. Instead, I'm given Delius's *On Hearing the First Cuckoo in Spring*. It's the music of hope and fresh green shoots but all I can think is that the cuckoo is the lying bird, pretending to be something it is not.

Afterwards, Marcus slaps me roundly on the shoulders. 'Jolly good show, old thing. Didn't think you had it in you. You found something in there that I'd not heard before. Clever you.'

I should be proud, but I'm not.

Marcus carouses with the string section in the bar. I slip over and join them. Drinking with Marcus and some rowdy violins seems like a good method of forgetting. Marcus has a copy of the vocal score of *Messiah* and is calling out the orchestration from memory, conducting a ghost orchestra with a fury. He hums the tune loudly and wields a paper straw as a baton.

'Brass!' he yells. 'Violas!'

Each time that he brings in a section correctly, the string players take a drink.

'Oboe solo!'

'No!' shouts one of the viola players, pointing at the score. 'You're a bar early. Drink! Drink!'

Gamely, after confirming his mistake, Marcus drains his glass.

I wonder how Handel would feel – his masterpiece as the basis of a drinking game. I feel a hand on my back and, turning, see Sal beside me.

'May I tempt you away?'

'Of course, darling.'

I order her a 'gin and it', and we begin one of our usual discussions about when we will go to America and see her family. The unspoken agreement is that we must be married before we depart.

'I don't see how it can possibly be before next summer,' I say. 'Our touring commitments are absurd. We're booked up for months and months.'

'We could take a leave of absence. I'm sure Marcus would hire you back afterwards if that's really what you want.'

I know she's right and I'm searching for a reason why it can't possibly work when I hear Edie calling my name. She rarely speaks to me in front of Sal. We keep a friendly distance. Not too cold – that would be strange – but reserved.

'Fox,' she calls again.

I turn around and see her arm in arm with Jack.

We're sitting in the bar with a bottle of champagne between the four of us. Jack's arm is around Edie and mine is draped around Sal. I wish I were drunk. I feel sick. To my surprise, I'm also overwhelmingly glad to see Jack. I have missed him hugely. His feelings are simpler. After an initial hesitation, he embraces me.

'Good God, Fox. It's bloody good to see you. Do come home. Even just for a visit. It simply isn't the same without you.'

'I'm sorry. So terribly sorry. I wish that—'

My apology is heartfelt, but it is for something other than leaving in a hurry and a lack of letters, and I want the relief of saying it aloud. Edie is staring at me, pale and wary, but he's already forgiven me or believes he has, and cuts me off before I've hardly started.

'Never think of it, old chap. Things are different for you now, I can see,' he says, smiling warmly at Sal. 'It's splendid to see you again. You're looking perfectly charming, Sal. When are you two young things getting married? You must do it at Hartgrove church. Edie and I didn't, just sloped off to a damned registry office, and I've always regretted it. I simply won't allow you to make the same mistake. We can have a nice party at the Hall afterwards.'

While Jack gets carried away with the jollity of his plans, Sal's face is suffused with pleasure and she squeezes my hand. I feel perfectly vile.

~

We return home the following week. The roof has collapsed on the Winter Garden concert hall and while Marcus disappears back to Bournemouth to survey the damage, the four of us retreat to Hartgrove. Jack drives, Edie in the front beside him, his hand resting on her knee. I'm tense with dread. I also want to remove his hand and clout him one, hard, but I keep reminding myself, it's he who has the right. He's the cuckold.

The closer we get, the more despicable I feel. I can hardly bear it and there's a queer pain in my stomach. I can see Edie's face in the mirror. Behind the enormous Bette Davis sunglasses she's pale and a tiny muscle at the corner of her eye is starting to tick. Sal and Jack are oblivious. In their happiness they chatter on and on, hardly seeming to pause for breath. I'm irritated and relieved in equal measure.

We stop for lunch at a little pub in Somerset, and as we carry glasses of shandy back to the girls, Jack places his hand on my arm, reassuring me.

'Don't worry, old chap. I know you feel pretty grotty about the whole thing. It will be all right. You know George can't hold a grudge for long. The General's already quite forgiven you. He thinks your running off was quite our fault.'

His kindness, if it's possible, makes me feel even worse. I can't look at Edie through lunch. She barely eats, only smokes, sitting as far as she can from me, her face turned away. It's a perfect June day, the sky a painter's rich blue, the sun blisteringly hot. Dog roses speckle the hedgerows, while the verges foam with cow parsley, flecked with the bright pink of ragged robin and red campion. High scribbles of birds mark the sky, while a woodpecker rattles on an elm for his lunch, his scarlet plume like a party hat. It's idyllic and beautiful, and Sal is smiling with delight, and I feel an utter cad.

Yet as Jack turns along the drive to Hartgrove, even my melancholy lifts. There, at last, is the hill, spotted with sheep, and then the Hall itself, elegant and serene, nestled beneath the ridge. I remember that other homecoming at the end of the war, which seems now so simple and unsullied. I don't think the house has ever looked more charming than it does today. Wisteria clothes the façade, its leaves softening the stonework, while around the windows white roses unfurl, blowzy and heavy, half obscuring the panes. Peonies droop in the borders like drunken girls in upside-down taffeta dresses. Daisies and yellow buttercups spread thickly across the unkempt lawn, climbing here and there into the flower beds with spurts of yellow. Battalions of foxgloves stand to attention on the fringe of the garden, where, in a deckchair, the General is asleep.

'Hello, Father,' I say, walking over.

He starts and then rises, looking pleased and cross at once. He detests being discovered asleep at his post, which he sees as a weakness, implying age and infirmity. I observe that the General, like the house, has gone to seed. There are sagging pouches beneath his eyes, which, although blue as ever, are bloodshot.

'Yes. Good. About time,' he says, which is as close as he can manage to saying that he too is bloody glad to see me. _

Chivers serves us all drinks on the lawn. He looks so frail that I wonder he can carry the tray. We stand and wait as he edges towards us, glasses rattling horribly, convention forbidding us from helping – he'd view any attempt as a dreadful insult. He greets me with excruciating politeness, indicating that he at least has not forgiven my absence. The gin is warm and there isn't any ice. Our chit-chat is awkward and subdued. I try not to catch Edie's eye. She looks perfectly miserable.

After an age, George appears. He's in his overalls, and my first thought is that he's vast. He can't have grown taller but his shoulders and chest are broad and strong, his arms ridged with muscle. When he shakes my hand, his fingers feel as rough as dried grass. I find that I'm nervous around him; we're as polite as strangers at a cocktail party.

We all move to the loggia, half of which has further collapsed so that we huddle at one end, as though on the lone, dry stretch of deck on a sinking ship, carefully ignoring the inevitable. When I slip into the house, desperate to escape for a minute or two, the symptoms of decay are worse. Pieces of plaster have fallen from the ceiling, exposing the horsehair beneath, so that when I look up, the flaking ceilings seem to be suffering from some grotesque skin disease. On the outside, the true state of the Hall has been masked by the cacophony of summer flowers, its dilapidation transmuted into picturesque dishevelment, but once on the inside, I see that it is teetering on the verge of ruin. I can't imagine how they manage with any comfort during the winter. Then, ruefully, I consider that Edie's eagerness to come on tour might have been less to do with my charms than those of hot water and a warm bed.

~

In the evening Jack and I walk through the orchards. Tiny green apples are forming on the trees, and as I peer closer I notice something lodged in the hollow of a trunk. Reaching up, I retrieve a piece of toast. How on earth did it get there? Glancing around the other trees, I spot that each one has a piece of burned toast in the same place.

'George,' says Jack. 'George does it.'

'Whatever for?'

'He read it in some old farming almanac. Apparently in the Middle Ages they put toast in the trees to scare away fairies. And I've not seen any, so I suppose that makes it a triumph.'

Beneath the easy smile, Jack looks troubled. I've been too preoccupied with my own discomfort to notice his.

'The house isn't in tip-top condition,' I say at last.

'It's ghastly. If it weren't for Edie we'd have gone under ages ago. And you of course,' he adds politely. 'I'm afraid after you left things went from pretty bad to absolutely rotten.'

'I'm not sure that they would have been any better if I'd stayed. I wasn't much help.'

'That's true.' He grins, and he's the old Jack once more. 'At least the General's stopped threatening to blow the place up. I expect he thinks that if he just waits a bit, it will simply fall down and he can save the expense of demolition. In any case, we can't go on as we are. Even with the money from you and Edie, it's not enough.'

We've reached the edge of the orchard where the grass grows thickly, a deep glossy green as it slopes down to the lake. On its smooth surface a swan drifts, its neck a white question mark. I sit on the edge of the bank. Jack settles beside me, picking at a blade of grass.

'George is determined not to use anything modern. None of the chemical fertilisers that would make things so much damned easier. If it were up to him, we'd be using bloody horses instead of a tractor. He just says that he wants to listen to the land and do what it's telling him. But it's sure as hell not saying anything to me.' He's nearly shouting and looks close to tears. 'You have to talk to him, Fox. George is going to ruin us all. That means something to me, even if it doesn't to you.'

'Of course it bloody does,' I say, cross.

'Then you'll make him see sense,' says Jack, lying back and closing his eyes, his face serene now that he's safely passed the buck.

～

'It's all part of the great dance,' George explains slowly for the third time. 'You're recreating Jerusalem through English music and I'm rebuilding it with the earth herself.'

'And cow muck.'

'Which is very beneficial to the soil. Like music.'

George is nothing if not committed. He wassails the apple trees, wards off pests with toast and would perform rain dances if the dampness of the climate didn't render it unnecessary. We're sitting on the loggia, waiting for Chivers to call us in for dinner. I'm already buttoned into my dinner jacket, while George fidgets in a tweed jacket that is evidently too small. He looks like a farmer dressed for a wedding.

'But George, old thing, you're not making any money.'

'You're as bad as Jack. He thinks this is nothing but muck and mysticism.'

That seems to me a pretty tidy way of putting it.

'I don't think that at all. I'm not Jack,' I say, trying to placate him.

I listen for a while as George rumbles on about the building of a rural Jerusalem under Hartgrove barrow through ancient farming methods and how we must merge the rhythms of the Church year with those of the pagan festivals.

'I'm not sure the vicar will really embrace fertility rituals on Sunday mornings,' I say at last.

'I know. He's being thoroughly unpleasant about the whole thing.'

To my amazement, I gather that George has already asked poor Reverend Lobb about it. I wonder whether George hasn't gone a little dotty, but on the other hand he appears to be in obscenely good health: tanned from a life outdoors, his brown hair bleached gold by the sun. If only the house and estate looked half as well. George sighs and closes his eyes against the glare of the evening sun.

'You told me a few years ago about the importance of songs,' he says. 'You were right, you know. Only it's not just folk song but folklore too. It's all there. People simply don't listen any more.' He turns to me, his face glowing from the sun's rays but also lit by his inner fervour. 'You could help. You could write music. For the harvest. For the planting. Workers are more productive if they sing. But it's more than that. The music is a gift for the land itself.'

'I know, George. I wrote it a ruddy symphony.'

He grins and stretches his huge arms, cracking the joints, and peers up at the sky where the first early bats, emerging from the eaves, are whizzing in rapid circles.

'You see, then? You know I'm not a crank, Fox. I've not lost my marbles. Jack thinks I'm a hopeless eccentric.'

'Actually he called you much worse.'

George chuckles. To my relief he has not lost his sense of humour.

'I hear all the chit-chat from Westminster – the country's near bankrupt and hungry. We need higher caloric yields and so on but I don't like their methods, Fox. I don't want to get rid of labourers and increase mechanisation. If we replace farmhands with machines, what will disappear is our countrymen. I believe Englishmen are also a crop worth producing and protecting.'

As he speaks, his voice trembles with the passion of the convert and, while I'm embarrassed by it, I can't help admiring him.

'I'm supposed to talk you out of it.'

'I know.'

The light sets fire to a pack of running clouds, scarlet as the hunt as they chase along the ridge, and turns the whitewashed cottages pink. I hear the distant bleating of the sheep, and watch the flock of late lambs dash across the fields, twisting and jumping together at the sheer joy of a summer's evening. I accept that I didn't leave Hartgrove only because of Edie, but also because I wanted a different life. A life of music. But now that I'm here, listening to the wind shake the larches and watching the weather form above the hill, I know that I don't want to leave ever again.

～

Dinner is an uneasy, subdued affair. The General has not lost his talent for dampening the mood of any party – although this time he cannot be held entirely responsible. Edie's gaiety is too much, too forced, while I'm distracted and dispirited. We sit in our dinner suits, the girls in their smart frocks, and sip wine while Chivers spoons out Irish stew and greens, his hands trembling from the effort as we all watch. Even the candlelight can't disguise the state of the dining room. The paper is peeling off the walls and the smell of mould is overpowering. I feel as if I'm in a lousy and unfunny play.

Afterwards, I escape for a walk. In the gathering dark, I hasten up the hill towards Ringmoor. The effort makes me perspire and I rather regret not having changed out of my dinner suit. I perch on a stile and inhale lungfuls of cool fresh air, knowing that I really ought to go and rescue Sal. I've an idea forming. I can't tell whether it's perfectly ridiculous or jolly clever. I need to talk it over with Edie. I find more and more that I don't know quite what I think until I've said it aloud to her. I hasten back to the house, in the hope of finding her, only to be met by Sal.

'They've gone to bed. Everyone's tired, I think.'

She leads me upstairs, eager and happy, but I find that I can't make love to her, knowing that Edie is so close. It's remarkable how treachery has its own standards. Sal is so horribly kind about my inadequacy that I lie awake for hours in the dark, listening to the rattle of the death-watch beetle and the hum of my own conscience.

~

It's Edie who finds me, late the following afternoon. She's wearing a fetching yellow cotton dress. I'm startled by how young she looks. I'm alone on the loggia, trying to look through the accounts.

'Come for a walk,' she says.

We fall into step but keep a respectable distance between us until we're out of sight of the house, then I feel her small fingers slip into my palm.

'This is horrid, darling,' she says, 'simply horrid.'

I nod because she's right, it is, but there's another part of me that's fearfully glad to be home. The last few years have been a self-inflicted exile and along with the guilt – whose perpetual grinding in the background, like chronic pain, I'm now accustomed to – there is also relief. Greedily, I inhale the scent of damp grass and honeysuckle.

'I telephoned Marcus and the Winter Garden's roof is in a desperate state. The orchestra's presently homeless,' I tell her.

'Oh dear, I am sorry. Thank goodness you're all still on tour.'

'Yes. But afterwards. What do you think about the orchestra coming here? Everywhere I go, I hear about Glyndebourne. They make a heap of money. I think we should put on a music festival at Hartgrove Hall.'

'Wouldn't it be terribly expensive?'

'Don't see why. We'd need to tidy up the great hall a bit, but you know how wonderful the acoustics are in there. The orchestra is used to seedy digs as it is.'

'Darling, I think it's a splendid idea.'

She kisses me, delighted, and I'm suddenly excited at the prospect. We chatter for an hour about the possibilities. It strikes me that Edie understands the Hartgrove finances far better than anyone else.

'Do you still have that friend at the Bolshoi?' I ask.

'Yes. Why?'

'Well, I wondered whether they'd consider doing a few performances here as well. It would be a super thing for the orchestra. Marcus is a horror, but he's brought the orchestra on wonderfully. Do you think the Bolshoi might do it?'

'They might. Yes. I'm sure they would. You'd put the orchestra in the minstrels' gallery, I suppose?'

We've been walking for nearly two hours and now we turn towards the house, but before we reach the garden Edie pulls me back.

'Not yet. I'm not ready to put my face on yet. It's such a relief not to pretend.'

We sit in the shade of an ancient chestnut, her head on my shoulder, neither of us talking. We do not kiss nor make love.

We want to be with one another for the pleasure of conversation and of silence. We commit our greatest betrayal: not sex but intimacy.

~

The drive to the station is ghastly. Sal's eyes are so swollen from crying that she looks as if she's been beaten.

'Is it her? Is it Edie?'

'No.'

For once, I'm lying out of kindness. Knowing that I betrayed her won't help.

'You simply "can't marry me".'

'No.'

'I don't understand.'

I'm not surprised. I'm desperate to confess and unburden myself, but I recognise that any confession would only be a further act of selfishness. I might feel relieved, but Sal undoubtedly would not.

'How can you simply stop loving somebody?' she asks, reaching for her handkerchief. She gives her eyes another dab.

'I'm sorry.'

My apologies only infuriate her. I give her ten pounds – slipping it into her handbag when she's not looking – and put her on the train. I drive back to the Hall, and as I climb out of the car my legs are shaking.

~

Edie corners me in the drawing room before dinner.

'What did you do?' she asks, her face pale.

'I broke it off with Sal. I can't lie any more.'

'You're not going to tell Jack?'

She's so white that I'm frightened for a moment she might faint. I pour her a gin and press it into her hand.

'I am tired of lying, Edie. I love you. I want only you.'

'I can't tell Jack,' she says, quietly. 'I simply can't.'

I sit down on the edge of an easy chair with my head in my hands. I notice on the floor by my foot a tear of butterfly wing, like a tiny scrap of patterned wallpaper.

'Idiotically I'd hoped you'd be inspired by my resolve.'

'It's not the same. You weren't married to Sal.'

God knows what the consequences would be of telling Jack but it has to be better than this. The guilt has become an earworm, a tedious tune that I simply can't stop humming. I suppose I never shall.

'I'm sorry,' she says. 'I'm a coward. I can't do it. I don't want to hurt him, Harry.'

'Stop it.'

I can't bear it when she talks like this. I'm silent for a minute, thinking. Finally, I look up at her and reach for her hand.

'I shan't say a word. I shall lie and accept the guilt and the cost of those lies as the cost of loving you.'

Edie stares at me, her face still paper white. 'Tell Jack – tell him I'm not feeling well.' She turns and hurries from the room and I hear the sound of her footsteps running up the stairs.

Ten minutes later, Jack and George appear from the garden.

'Where's Edie?' asks Jack, pouring drinks.

'She has a headache,' I say. 'I don't think she's coming down for dinner.'

March 2003

At half past six on Sunday evening, Lucy's car appeared in the driveway. I watched from the kitchen window as both girls climbed out, Lucy wrapping her arms around Clara who was clearly crying. I hurried to the back door and ushered them into the kitchen. Clara sat down at the table, her head in her hands, and hiccuped with sobs so violent that I couldn't understand what she was trying to say.

'What is it, my darling? Is it Robin? Is he all right?' I asked, panicked.

'Robin's fine,' said Lucy.

Clara looked up, her face streaked with tears. 'You always think everything's about him.'

I waited quietly for her sobs to subside.

'Ralph's left me,' she said at last.

'Oh darling, I'm so sorry.'

'Are you? You never liked him.'

'No. And I like him even less now. He's an execrable man. I'm terribly sorry.'

She looked so desperate, so unhappy, that I felt something crack in my chest. I'd never wanted her to marry that beastly, smug man. His interest in music was mercurial, a sinister failing in a person. I rummaged through the cupboards and poured three very stiff gin and tonics.

'Where are the children?' I asked.

'Staying with a friend,' said Clara. 'We haven't told them anything yet. I don't even know what it is that I am going to tell them. I need some time to think.'

Her eyes were puffy from crying and she wiped them with a scrap of hankie.

'He's sleeping with someone else. Says he's in love with her and wants a divorce. Never meant it to happen. He's so fucking sorry—'

Here she started to sob again. Lucy rubbed her back and pressed the gin and tonic upon her.

'Oh Clara,' I said, sitting down in the chair beside hers and clasping her hand. 'You'll be all right. You really will. We're here to help you. Anything you need. Money. Lawyers.'

'An assassin,' said Lucy grimly. Evidently, now at least, she disliked Ralph as much as I.

Clara didn't seem to hear. 'An affair. With some woman in Accounting. It's humiliating. It's such a bloody cliché.'

I wished Edie were here. The longing was so fervent it was like a physical pain. Edie would have known what to do. She would have gathered Clara to her, taken her weeping daughter into bed with her, as she did when the girls were small and sick with a fever. Edie sang away all their sorrows, easing them into sleep. With a grimace, I accepted that, even if Edie had been here, this was a sorrow that could not be sung away.

Clara rubbed her eyes, making them redder still. She'd cried so much that her eyelids looked bruised and her skin had a waxy translucence.

'Things haven't been right between us for – oh, I don't know,' she said. 'We barely see each other. He's always working and I spend half my life driving Robin to piano lessons in London. And some time while I was stuck in traffic on the A303, Ralph was talking about sales invoices and year-end returns and falling in love with a woman called Angela.'

'It's not Robin's fault,' I said.

'No, of course it isn't,' snapped Clara. 'Ralph and I drifted apart, so far apart that there was space for bloody Angela in Accounting to squeeze into the gap between us.' She sighed and rubbed her forehead, a tiny crease appearing, a perfect copy of her mother's. 'I knew things weren't right but somehow I was always too tired or busy to do anything about it.'

'Stop it,' said Lucy firmly. 'You're making it sound as if it's your fault and it isn't.'

Clara nodded and swallowed, holding back the tears. She slid her empty glass across the table. 'I want Mum,' she said and began to cry again.

I found the pain of seeing her visceral unhappiness quite unbearable. One thinks it must become easier as one's small, pigtailed daughters grow into self-reliant women with families and smart careers, but it doesn't. Not a bit. I reached out to pat her hand and then withdrew, unable to offer any solace.

'I'll run you a bath,' I said at last. 'I always ran your mother a bath when she was upset. Gin and a hot bath make everything a bit better, she always said.'

'Yes, do,' said Lucy. 'And I'll come and chat to you while you soak, Clara darling.'

I left the two of them colluding earnestly in the kitchen and went to draw a bath upstairs. I sat on the edge of the tub – chosen of course by Edie – a cast-iron, clawfoot design, positioned so as to have a splendid view of Hartgrove Hill and the copse. It was dark and a yellow slice of moon dangled low above the ridge.

I thought of Sal, for the first time in many years. Was I a better man than Ralph? I usually tried hard not to think about Sal. I had behaved too badly. That period of my life had exposed the very worst of me and, as an ordinary coward, I preferred not to dwell on such things. I secreted Sal deep down inside my conscience and did my best to forget about her. I'd never told Clara or Lucy about her. There had never been occasion to. For the first time in decades, I was stricken about the affair – if I ever confided in them, could they forgive me?

It didn't matter, I told myself. There would never be a reason to tell them. And yet, as an owl hooted at the back of the hill and the water thundered against the side of the bath, I knew that it did matter. I didn't merely want their love, I wanted their absolution.

Clara came downstairs in Edie's old dressing gown, her face flushed from the bath, and curled up in the chair beside the fire in the drawing room. The firelight and the rosiness of her skin made her look closer to fifteen than forty. She tucked her knees beneath her chin and stared absently at the flames. The two of us had sat here together much like this the night before her wedding. I hoped she didn't remember.

'We sat here just like this the night before my wedding,' she said.

'You were dreadfully nervous,' I said.

'With good reason, it turns out.' She sighed. 'I asked you whether you were nervous before marrying Mummy and you said, "No." That you'd never been less nervous of anything in your life. Only the thought of not marrying her had ever frightened you.'

'Did I really say that?'

'Yes.' She turned to me, her eyes glistening once more. 'You don't know what it's like, Papa. I wanted what you and Mummy had. You made it look easy. No, not easy, inevitable. That's it. I thought my happiness in marriage was inevitable. And it wasn't.'

'I'm so sorry, darling. We didn't mean—'

'Of course you didn't. It's not your fault that you were happy. It was wonderful. Just quite a lot for us to live up to. It's why Lucy's never bothered to marry, you know.'

'What on earth do you mean?'

'She's not as silly as me. She wants what you had and won't

settle for anything less. She always knew it wasn't easy or inevitable.'

I felt a horrible gloom descend upon me. I never imagined that my own happiness would compromise my daughters'.

'Stop it,' said Clara.

'Stop what?'

'Looking so bloody dejected. I told you, it's not your fault. You and Mummy were terribly lucky. Anyone else's bad luck is not your fault. It's nothing to do with you at all.'

This was an opportunity for confession, for me to confide that, yes, some of the unhappiness inflicted over the years had been entirely due to me and to Edie. Clara gazed at me with such frank love, such sadness and exhaustion, that I couldn't bear to tell her. There was no need for her to know that her father wasn't quite the man she'd thought. That he wasn't worthy of such esteem.

∽

Robin spent even more time at Hartgrove than before. While his sisters flocked around their mother, proffering both anger and consolation, Robin retreated. He wanted neither comfort nor conversation. He wanted music. I allowed him to play the piano for longer than usual, and I temporarily lifted the ban on Beethoven – accepting that Robin needed to play through his loss and his fury. His childhood had slipped from a major into a minor key.

I tried not to listen to the music swilling through my own thoughts. I was drained from writing and needed to pause; I no longer had the stamina I once possessed. Nonetheless, melodies nagged at me, calling for me to come and play, much as my daughters had done when they were children and I was trying to work. Then, I had turned from the girls, irritated by their plaguing, and I had shut the music-room door, retreating into music. Now, I attempted the reverse. I ignored the tunes pulsing in my forehead like a headache and attempted to focus solely on Clara and her children. I invited them all around for supper after Robin's piano practice, taking care to choose the seat between Annabel and Katy, much to Robin's surprise. I attempted to engage them in conversation, but I had scant idea of what to say. I didn't recall struggling to engage with my own daughters but my granddaughters remained little strangers – polite, pretty and distant as dollies.

I hacked at a roast chicken and distributed plates.

Annabel shook her curls. 'I'm a vegetarian, Grandpa.'

'You are? Since when?'

'Since, like, for ever.'

Both girls stared at me with wounded bewilderment.

'Oh, there's probably some cheese or smoked salmon some-where in the fridge. You can have that if you want.'

'I don't eat fish. Is it vegetarian cheese?'

'I really wouldn't know, darling. I can't imagine it eats many steaks.'

I glanced across the table at Robin who smiled at me with some sympathy. Perhaps supper had been a mistake. Discussing Brahms with Robin was infinitely less taxing than being inter-rogated on the contents of my fridge by two visitors in pink-and-white-striped jeans and fancifully coloured trainers. I tried gamely to ask the girls about school and clubs and netball practice but the unpleasant truth was that I wasn't terribly interested in the answers.

Afterwards Clara and I washed up the dishes.

'It's good that you made an effort with the girls. They'll appreciate the attempt.'

'Will they? Seemed rather futile to me. I'm afraid we don't have a great deal in common. I don't know what to say to them. I've become one of those tedious elderly relatives I dreaded as a child.'

I did not add that I found the girls somewhat tedious myself.

Clara looked at me oddly and then gazed out of the kitchen window, where clouds glowed crimson like a coal fire, improbably beautiful.

'Half the time I don't know what to say to Robin. He's my own child and yet I sit there in the car with him on these endless drives to and from London and I don't know what to say.'

'You can talk about music.'

'I can't. I don't know how. Not in the way that he does or that you do. I'd sound like an idiot. And, anyway, I don't hear music the way the two of you do.'

She fumbled with a cup and dropped it so that it smashed on the tiled floor with a xylophone crash.

'Damn it.'

She began to cry. Those days, Clara's tears were always close to the surface.

'For goodness' sake, Clara. It's only a cup. Here.' I dropped another, which shattered on the tiles with a satisfying tinkle.

She laughed. 'It's not the stupid cup, Papa. It's Robin. You don't know what it's like, not knowing what to say to your own child. I don't know how he's coping with it all. He must be missing his father. He saw Ralph last week and afterwards he wouldn't talk about it.'

'I think he's all right. He's angry. Lots of Beethoven at first but he's returning to Mozart again and I think that's a good sign. As long as he's not reaching for Schoenberg, I think we're in the clear.'

She gave a weak smile. 'You see? You get him. I can't decipher him at all and he thinks I'm an idiot.'

'Of course he doesn't.'

'Last week I told him I liked the Debussy he was playing. He gave me a reproachful look and said, "That was Delius. Don't you know anything, Mummy? You have very stupid ears."'

'That was very rude of him.'

It was also true. Clara did have stupid ears. It wasn't her fault but there it was.

She bent down to pick up the fragments of china.

'He's supposed to love me most. He's supposed to want to share things with me. I'm his mother. It's lovely that the two of you are so close. But sometimes it's hard not to be a little jealous.'

She stood up and stared out across the lawns at the sky, fading from red to black, her expression unconscionably sad.

~

Marcus died in the spring. He sloped off to a hospice to die, surrounded by strangers. He refused to see me. We spoke regularly on the telephone but he did not relent: he would not allow me to visit.

'No, dear boy, I want you to remember me as I was. Strikingly handsome and debonair.'

I admired him immensely: eighty-three, dying and vain till the end. During our telephone calls we discussed music. Marcus liked to play games, asking me to choose between two pieces: 'Which should I die listening to if it's a choice between Prokofiev's *War and Peace* or Shostakovich's Fourth? Quick, quick. First answer.'

Invariably, I selected the wrong one.

'Really? That. Well. Goodness. I thought you were a man of taste. It's a good thing that this friendship is shortly coming to an end.'

I was not permitted to ask whether he was in pain. 'Dying's not much fun, Fox. Take my advice and don't ever try it yourself.'

We spent a good deal of time planning his funeral. Marcus was terribly concerned about both the turnout and the programme.

'John Godbolt had better come and he'd better look bloody sad about it, even if the New York Phil have just offered him my old position. I think I'll have the Bach fugue before the first prayer. And at least one of the Beethoven sonatas. They're about death but not too depressing, which is important for a funeral. I'm not sure who should conduct – someone competent, or the audience won't be able to lose themselves in the music and remember me as fondly as they ought. But he mustn't be *too* good, as I want the audience to be reminded of my superior talent. Hello, now that's a thought. Will you do it, Fox?'

'With such an invitation, how could I refuse? And, technically, they're not an audience, Marcus. They're mourners.'

'Oh yes, so they are. Jolly good.'

After that we spent a good deal of time considering the selection.

'I think a little Rachmaninov or would that be too sentimental?' he wondered.

'One's allowed a little sentiment at a funeral, Marcus. We will all be very sad.'

'Of course you will. I can hardly bear thinking about it. Now, will Albert play the piano or will he be too overwhelmed by grief?'

'He'll be terribly upset, but he'll manage – through the tears of course – since it's what you really want.' I could tell by the ensuing silence that he was satisfied.

'And I do want a little Mozart. *Don Giovanni*, I think. Perhaps Don Pedro's statue coming out of the tomb to cart Giovanni off to the underworld. Playful or too macabre?'

'It simply isn't you. You should have Don Giovanni's list of lovers.'

'Of course! Perhaps we could alter the libretto . . . pop in one or two of my *liaisons amoureuses*.'

'Certainly not. Some secrets must be kept.'

I heard Marcus smiling in the pause.

I said nothing and, after a moment or two, Marcus started adding another half-dozen pieces to his programme until at last I cried out, 'This is ridiculous. Your funeral's going to require a full symphony orchestra, a choir, two tenors, a pianist and an intermission. It isn't a funeral, it's a concert.'

'What a splendid idea! A memorial concert.'

I hoped that planning the concert distracted him from the nastiness of those last days. We bickered agreeably over the programme and he insisted on dispensing endless notes as to how he wanted the pieces performed, until I'd had quite enough. I was steeling myself to tell him that if he wanted me to conduct, then I really must do it in my own way, for better or for worse, only to be informed by the duty nurse when I telephoned that he'd died that afternoon.

'Just slipped away at ten to three, listening to his CD player,' she said.

'What piece was it?' I asked, when my voice was steady.

'I'm really not sure. I could try to find out for you.'

'Yes please, if you would.'

She called me back after a few minutes.

'It was Mahler's Fifth.'

'And the conductor?'

'Sir Marcus Albright.'

Of course. How could it have been anybody else? I wanted to share with someone my sorrow and amusement over the aptness of Marcus Albright, great maestro and egotist, dying while listening to himself conduct, but the two people who'd find it the most diverting – Edie and Marcus himself – were now both gone.

I hung up the telephone, sat down on my bed and cried.

July 1954

The hall table is set with a hundred vases of flowers. The house smells like a florist's shop. We discovered during last year's festival that it's quite remarkable how many allowances will be made for shabbiness and sporadic hot water when every room is filled with flowers. Edie similarly insists upon splendid food – most of the produce coming from the estate itself – starched sheets aired with lavender and fires lit in every grate on chilly days. George tends the flower seedlings in early spring, mixes a special potting mixture and plants them out in May in the cuttings garden, so that now Edie has enough pink and white sweet peas, striped dahlias the size of dinner plates, scented stocks and roses.

I hear the grind of tyres on the gravel outside.

'The first lot are here,' I say.

Minutes later, members of the Bournemouth Symphony assemble for lemonade and gin on the front lawn, yawning and stretching and picking clean the plates of sandwiches that have been set out for twice their number – it's always a marvel how much an orchestra can eat. I don't think the biblical plague was one of locusts, merely a symphony orchestra.

It's the first performance of the festival and the première of the heavily revised *Song of Hartgrove Hall*. I'm all a-fidget with excitement. I've rewritten the second movement for a solo piano and to my delight (and Edie's, who's in charge of the box office receipts) Albert Shields has accepted our invitation to perform. The chaps from Decca fiddle with cables and microphones, ready to record the performance for release as an LP. My first recording contract. The advance and any royalties will inevitably be ploughed back into the estate. It's peculiar how a piece of music imagining the loss and destruction of Hartgrove Hall has ended up helping to save it instead. I suppose that now, rather than a farewell, it's become a portrait. I picture the notes seeping into the soil, rich as dung.

The General and Chivers retreat to the library and close the door against the gaiety of the musicians, put out by all the noise and kerfuffle. The two old men are perfect curmudgeons, profoundly annoyed by the invasion of strangers and conveniently ignoring the fact that those strangers are enabling us to keep possession of the house.

Two hundred concert-goers picnic upon the lawns, eating cold salmon and strawberries and drinking champagne. I notice the General and Chivers peeking out from the library, barricaded inside against the evening sunshine and the onslaught of other people's pleasure. I meander amongst the picnickers, nodding greetings but avoiding conversation. I spot Edie in the flower garden, cutting yet more sweet peas, a basket brimming with candy-coloured blooms resting on her hip. She smiles to see me.

'Hello, darling.'

We have few moments alone during festival season, so those we do share are heavenly. I no longer ask her when or if we can confess to Jack. I suppose that this is to be our lives – a furtive *ménage à trois*.

'I'm looking forward to tonight. The rehearsal sounded wonderful,' she says.

'It wasn't bad. Albert's a super pianist but' – I reach for the words, trying to explain – 'it doesn't sound right. It sounds good. Very good, but somehow it's not quite how I imagined it.'

Edie glances over her shoulder, then draws me into the shadow of the greenhouse and kisses me slowly. She smells of garden flowers and sunshine.

'I ought to go,' I say at last, reluctantly.

'Give Marcus my love. Tell him I'll see him after the concert.'

'I will. And have you met that new chap, John something or other? Wants to come to the festival and conduct next year. Frightfully pushy. Keeps cornering me to talk about Bach.'

Edie laughs and brushes a leaf from my shoulder. 'I'll keep an eye out for him. Is he any good?'

'Marcus can't stand him, which is always a good sign.'

We edge towards the lawns and see Jack move easily amongst the guests, as handsome as a film star. Even the young girls watch him, eyes wide. He's the perfect host – friendly but dusting glamour upon the evening.

'Righto. I'm going. I need to talk to Albert,' I say.

'Good luck,' says Edie.

The concert has started – Brahms – conducted by Marcus. We still need the draw of his name to pull in the crowds. I'm not on until after the interval. I see George walking through the orchard, tending to the beehives. He wears only the lightest of masks and long gloves, insisting the bees know him too well to sting. As he moves amongst the hives he croons in a pleasant baritone. The tunes are familiar folk songs, ones I've heard all across the country. I sit on the gate and watch him. He reaches into one hive, and I'm concerned that he'll be stung, but I stay silent and watch. He sings a song that I've not come across during my travels and yet it is familiar to me, one I so nearly remember, that I feel he's singing back to me a piece of myself. The bees drift about him, as though drugged by the music, allowing him to retrieve a piece of honeycomb and place it in a bowl. He spots me and stops singing.

'Do carry on, George,' I say. 'Sing me the chorus.'

'I don't remember any more,' he says and for some reason I think he's fibbing.

I worry about George. He remains on the edge of things, uncomfortable amongst so many people. Out of obligation he attended last year's concerts but, seeing how ill at ease it made him, we quietly suggested that he was much too busy with the farm and the bees to be distracted with such trifles and he retreated, relieved.

'Sit there and keep quiet and still or you'll upset the bees,' he says.

I do as he says and listen while he sings again. This time he chooses a German Lied from Brahms and the bees grow sleepy once again, as though his voice is smoke. I'm intrigued. He reaches into the hive and pulls out another slab of dripping honeycomb, never ceasing his song.

'I know that one,' I say.

'Didn't I tell you to be quiet?' he says.

'I thought you'd finished thieving.'

'Yes, well. I suppose I have.'

He busies himself around the hive. 'The profusion of flowers have made the honey particularly good this year. The bees are blissful.'

'How can you tell?'

'They're producing lots of honey and I can hear it in the sound of their hum. It has a purr to it. Like a cat.'

It takes me a moment to realise that he's teasing – he does it so rarely – then he throws back his head and roars with laughter.

'Gosh, we always could get you to believe anything, Little Fox.'

I smile. I've not been called that for a long time, but, next to the great mountain that is now George, I suppose I am Little Fox.

'I do know where I've heard that last song,' I say, sliding down from the gate. 'It's one of the Lieder from the Brahms suite that Marcus has been conducting. I didn't know you'd been going to the rehearsals.'

George flushes. An ungainly red like sunburn splashes across his neck.

'I didn't. I haven't.'

I'm embarrassing him, but I'm his brother and I want to know. 'Then where did you hear it?'

'Marcus taught it to me,' he snaps.

I stare at him. 'Oh, I didn't know you were friends.'

'Well, we are,' he says.

George watches me steadily, his colour subsiding. I'm aware of the bees starting to hum all around us.

The hum reaches a crescendo and changes key.

'I think you should go,' he says. 'The bees are upset.'

I find Marcus during the interval. I ought to be looking through the score, but I'm perturbed. He's holding court on the lawn, a glass of champagne in his hand and laughing loudly.

'I take it that the first half went well,' I say with a smile.

'Yes, dear boy, I'm afraid you have a great deal to live up to.' He nods to his admirers. 'If you'll excuse me, ladies, gentlemen. I must offer some words of wisdom to my protégé.'

He slides his arm into mine and leads me away. 'You see, I intend to accept compliments for your performance too. But if you cock anything up, you're quite on your own.'

He catches sight of my expression. 'Oh don't be silly, Fox. The piece is marvellous. You're a distinctly average conductor but a fine composer. And a decent-looking fellow, which helps a good deal.'

I'm sweating a little and I'd like to change my shirt before the performance. If I hurry, I'll just have time. I must be more anxious than I'd thought.

'Are you all right, Fox?'

I look at him carefully. I've never asked Marcus outright if he's queer. I've simply presumed. There are things one doesn't mention. Until now, it's never really been any of my affair.

We reach the walled garden where a chorus of roses in oranges, yellows and reds fills the air with perfume.

'Perhaps it's none of my concern. But George—?' I say, hoping that's sufficient.

Marcus's face darkens, but only for a moment. Then he leans forward, catching my shoulder, kisses me hard on the mouth and releases me in an instant, before I even have a chance to shove him away. I'm speechless with cold indignation.

'You were correct before, Fox. It is none of your concern.'

He smiles serenely at me before turning and walking out of the garden, while I stand amongst the roses, outraged and none the wiser. I'd always believed that George had once loved Edie, and it's possible I was mistaken. Yet, I'm sure that he did love her in his own way. I watch Marcus's upright figure disappear around the corner. I suppose one can never really see into another man's heart.

～

The flowers wither in their vases, spewing pollen and petals across every surface. The compost heap is piled high with them, the smell of summer's decay. A legion of girls from the village come to help with the great clean-up, supervised nominally by Chivers but really by Edie. They're either too young or too old and mostly they're interested only in having a good nose around the house, but still, we need any help we can find. Every bed must be stripped and the sheets sent to the laundry;

the floors must be washed and swept, the grates emptied, the bathrooms scrubbed. Finally there is the melancholy task of shrouding the guest bedrooms and the principal rooms until next year's festival.

I despise this part. It's thoroughly depressing, imbuing the house with that awful, last-day-of-summer-hols feeling one used to dread as a boy, knowing that the following day one would be packed off to school. That was one of the few times when I was glad not to have a mother. Those first days of each term at prep school, watching my pals pine for their mothers, was frightful, and I'd been profoundly relieved not to have to endure such a thing myself. Being separated from Jack and George at the end of each summer had been torment enough.

Edie and I are the only members of the family to assist in the great clean-up. After several weeks playing host, striding through the house and garden in his dinner jacket with a 'Black Baccara' rose in his buttonhole, Jack has now declared he's indispensable on the farm and, having changed into his overalls, has disappeared. I long to play the same trick – I can hear the rumble of the tractor making silage on the hill – but I feel bad about leaving Edie alone to face the dreary part. Not that I'm much help. I dodge a broom and narrowly miss slipping on a sopping-wet floor. I suspect that someone has merely upturned a bucket rather than washed the blasted thing.

Yet I can't find Edie anywhere. I scour the house from top to bottom, even asking the less sloppy-looking girls whether they've seen her, and I get nothing but shrugs. She's not in the flower garden – the sweet peas are dropping and turning into pods on the willow wigwams now, and the lilies fade, uncut. I can't see her on the lawn and I'm about to give up when I hear the sound of weeping. It's an ugly sound. Uninhibited, animal grief.

I find her crouched in the potting shed, amidst a citadel of broken flowerpots and last year's mouldering compost.

'Darling, what on earth's the matter?' I say, bending down and trying to hug her to me, but she pushes me away and continues to sob. Uselessly, I reach for my pocket handkerchief, which she takes and does not use, only twists around her finger.

'Please try to breathe,' I say. 'Tell me what's wrong. Are you ill?'

She stares up at me, her face puffy and swollen, her cheeks sodden and her nose running. I wonder how long she's been hiding here.

'I'm having a baby.'

She starts to cry again.

'Oh, Edie.'

This time she lets me embrace her, and I hug her tightly to my chest, hoping that her tears will subside. But I can't help asking.

'Is it mine?'

'I don't know. How could I possibly know?'

'I thought women could tell these things.'

'Oh, Fox. Don't be ridiculous.'

I hold her close, not wanting her to see that I'm wounded. It's beastly knowing that she's still sleeping with Jack. Again, I'm not permitted to be upset about it, not being the husband. I guessed she probably was but I discover that's quite a different thing from knowing for sure.

'What do you want to do? I can try to find a doctor to, well, you know, put a stop to the thing, if that's what you want,' I ask, as gently as I can.

She sits back on an upturned flowerpot, rubs her eyes, smearing dirt across her cheek, and offers me a look of disdain.

'It's not a thing. It's a baby. I'm going to be a mother.'

She sounds absolutely certain and, for the first time since I found her in the potting shed, she stops crying.

321

'The baby's going to have a family. A proper one. Even if it's just him and me.'

She looks at me again, her expression grave and defiant.

I kneel beside her, uncomfortably aware that I'm not party to this decision at all. I study her, wondering exactly how long she's known.

'What do you want to do, Edie? I don't suppose we can carry on as we are.'

She shakes her head. 'Of course we can't. The whole thing is a ghastly mess but we have to tidy it up before the baby appears. It's not his fault.' She sounds irritated and distant. 'I have to do the right thing. It's a bit late for it, I know, but there it is. I've been a coward long enough.'

Dread gathers in the pit of my stomach. She doesn't know who the father is and so I suppose she could discreetly cast me off. No one else would ever know. The possibility of this makes me crippled with anxiety. I suppose it's the least selfish course but I don't care.

'Don't leave me,' I say. I try to keep the note of pleading from my voice. 'I love you.'

'What if the baby's Jack's?'

'It doesn't matter.'

I'm not sure that anything matters much other than that Edie doesn't leave me. I'm vaguely aware that I ought to be considering the child in all this but it's a tiny abstract, not yet a person. I try not to resent the ramifications that its very existence is causing in adult, fully realised lives.

'We'll get married. I'll look after you both,' I say.

Edie studies me, saying nothing but nibbling on a fingernail.

'I have to tell Jack,' she says quietly.

'Tell him what?' I ask, trying to keep my voice steady. 'That you're leaving him? That you love me?'

'Oh, Fox,' she says.

Her eyes fill with tears and with horrible clarity I understand that she doesn't know what she will decide. I suppose that in one way or another she must love him too.

'Well,' I say, standing and drawing back from her.

I look down at her, still perched on top of a terracotta flowerpot, my bedraggled handkerchief clutched in her hand. With her eyes bright from crying, she looks frightfully young.

'Well,' I repeat, 'I'm not going to be dignified or magnanimous. I love you. Always have, I'm afraid. Expect I always will. I'm not entirely sure that I could manage without you.'

She swallows and nods but does not speak.

We find Jack reading the newspaper in the morning room, squinting against the sunlight streaming through the windows. He smiles with simple pleasure at seeing us both.

'Jack—' says Edie.

I can't bear to watch as she tells him. We have done this, she and I. Like a coward, I look away, scrutinising the clouds ballooning across the sky.

When she has finished, with an evident force of will, like an injured man scooping his guts back inside, Jack gathers himself, moves to sit on the window seat and looks out at the garden. It's tactlessly beautiful: the lawns in perfect stripes, the borders purple with lavender and late summer bees. I see our three faces reflected in the glass like ghosts. This room will always be haunted for me now. I will never enter it without the guilt of remembering what I've done.

Edie sits on the high-backed settle and sobs.

'Please stop,' says Jack, quietly.

She stops.

'I wish we could take it back,' I say.

'No you don't. It's carried on for years, so you say. And you love her?'

'I do. Very much.'

'Then don't say you'd take it back. That makes it worse. Makes it some little affair. Is that all it was?' His voice is very soft. He's white with anger. A muscle in his forehead pulses.

'No.'

He turns to Edie, his face blank. 'And do you love him?'

'Yes.' Tears are streaming down her face now. 'But I loved you too. I still do. I never meant to hurt you.'

'Well, I'm afraid you have.'

I wish he weren't so calm. I wish he'd rage and hit me. His eyes are wide with incredulity. The shame is overwhelming.

'You've hurt me. Humiliated me. Sheer bloody betrayal is what it is. I'm not as clever as you or Fox. I simply don't have the words to express what it is you've done to me.'

Edie sobs again and this time she can't stop. I want to go to her, but know I mustn't. Jack pours us all a drink. Edie's hands are trembling so badly that she can hardly hold the glass. Jack sits across from her, eyeing her steadily.

'Please look at me, Edie. I'd like you to look at me while I'm speaking to you.'

She raises her eyes. She looks so full of shame, so distraught, that I can hardly bear it. Even Jack is shaken.

'Well, here we are,' he says gently.

He reaches out and takes her hand. Grateful at this apparent sign of forgiveness, she clasps it in both of hers. Despite everything, I feel an unconscionable spurt of jealousy. Jack sighs.

'You are pregnant. There is no way to know whose child it is. Most likely Fox's, since you and I aren't quite the honeymooners we once were.'

Edie looks down at her lap and instinctively tries to withdraw her hand but Jack holds onto it.

'I'm sorry, Edie darling. I'm not trying to embarrass you, merely tell the truth. That's what we're trying to do, isn't it?'

She nods, unable to speak.

'Now. I shall try to forgive you and raise the child as my own, if that's what you want. Or you may divorce me. We can arrange it in the usual way. I'll be discovered in Weston-super-Mare with some two-bit whore and you'll be free to marry Fox here. But' – and now for the first time Jack sounds angry; his voice wobbles with held-back rage – 'but if you'd hoped that I would simply leave you so that you didn't have to make a decision, I'm afraid that you're quite mistaken.'

Edie gazes at him in shock, a round spot of colour on each cheek.

'We're good men, Fox and I. We won't make it easy and walk away from you, so you'll have to choose.'

'I'm so sorry—'

'Don't be sorry. Choose.'

He speaks with some force. Edie looks from Jack to me, her eyes wide with alarm. I'm frightened. Terribly frightened that I might lose her. I feel sick. Blood rushes in my ears. Choose me. Oh God, choose me. A fly batters against the windowpane.

'Fox,' she says. 'I choose Fox.'

My heart hurries.

Edie turns to Jack, eyes big with guilt. 'I'm so sorry.'

'Well. There we are,' he says and stands. He brushes some imaginary muck from his trousers and straightens. He glances from Edie to me, daring us to pity him. We don't dare.

'I'm sorry,' I say. 'This is the worst thing I've ever done in my life. The worst thing I'll ever do.' I offer him my hand, but he shakes his head and steps back.

'No. I shan't shake your hand, Fox. It isn't all right and I don't forgive you. Because I'm not eloquent and clever, you thought I didn't love her as you could. You are wrong. I did and I do.'

I'm shaken by the unhappiness and anger spilling from him. 'I'm so sorry. Edie and I will leave this afternoon. You need never see us again.'

Jack smiles sadly. 'Leave or stay. Do what you want. I'm afraid I simply don't care in the least what you do. But I shan't stay here. Not for another minute. Not after what you've done. Everything at Hartgrove will remind me of you. Every path we walked together. Every bloody tree. I can't look at what you've done. And I can't forgive you.'

I stand there, dumb.

He shakes his head. 'You've taken everything. My wife. My home. Perhaps even my child.'

He walks to the window and stares out. A pair of swans swoop above the lake, their necks stretched out in flight like spurts of lightning. The sun catches on their wings, making them glint gold. I would prefer it to be raining, so that he left Hartgrove in soggy ugliness and not this sublime beauty. He looks away but if he sighs, I do not hear him.

He pauses at the door. 'Goodbye, Edie. Goodbye Fox.'

And then he's gone.

October 2003

I found the loneliness piercing. I'd begun to find a rhythm after Edie; altered, of course, but I'd started to believe in the possibility of pleasures here and there. After Marcus, I lost my footing again. Sleep eluded me. Frightened that the silence might return, I forced myself to write a little in the afternoons, but everything I produced seemed inadequate and thin.

One Saturday morning, I read a grisly review of a new piece I'd been writing in the *Telegraph*. It had been performed at the Cheltenham Music Festival but I'd had a horrid cold and been unable to conduct, so John had stepped in at the last minute. I had never liked his style, but I'd been in quite a pinch. Uncharitably, I considered how much of the critic's rudeness could be put down to John's interpretation. Mostly the critic seemed put out that someone old had dared attempt something new. John telephoned to apologise. I wouldn't hear of it.

'Don't be ridiculous. Of course it wasn't your fault. He simply didn't like the piece. That's all there is to it.'

There was a pause. Then I heard John sigh. 'It's the first time I've had to find a lousy review on my own. Usually Marcus has faxed the damned thing over to me before I've even woken up. You'd think I'd be glad but I'm not. I miss the old bugger.'

'It's the miserable thing about getting to our age. One starts to outlive one's friends. It's a lonely business.'

After he'd rung off, I reread the review and, thoroughly depressed, asked myself whether, as well as outliving my friends, I'd outlived my era.

Ten minutes later Robin sprang into the music room, while I was still bathing in self-pity.

'Hello, Grandpa!' he said and came to sit beside me at the piano, where I was reviewing a concerto I'd been attempting. He'd shot up in the past few months, and to his utter delight could now reach the pedals.

'Can I give it a go?' he said, glancing through the pages.

'Perhaps later. I'm too cross to think at the moment.'

'Ah. Are you growing too? I get cross when I grow, Mum says.'

'I'm certainly not growing. Shrinking perhaps.'

'Shrinking? Poor you. No wonder you're cross. Well, if you can't reach the pedals any more, I can do them for you, like you used to for me when I was little.'

I laughed despite myself. He'd managed them alone for a mere matter of weeks.

'I'll bear it in mind, Robin.'

I surrendered my chair to him and listened for nearly two hours while he practised without pausing for so much as a pee or a glass of water.

'You're really coming on, darling.'

'I played in school assembly on Monday.'

'So I heard. Did it go well? They can't have known what had hit 'em.'

I'd finally agreed with Clara that it would be a good thing for Robin to perform in front of his school. All the children learning musical instruments did so, apparently, and, according to Clara, the fact that Robin did not was odd. She also insisted that if the children could hear Robin, they'd understand why he was sometimes a little different – why he always chose piano practice over football or cricket. Perhaps she was right, but privately I suspected that a primary-school assembly was a very good place for him to play – the audience would not distinguish in its enthusiasm between a rendition of 'Twinkle, Twinkle' wheezed out on a recorder or a distinctive interpretation of Tchaikovsky's Piano Concerto in D.

'Well, what did they make of it then?'

'I was fantastic,' he said, with the straightforwardness of the young. 'I was told by Mrs Morgan to play for only ten minutes because the little ones in Reception and Year One couldn't manage any more, but at the end of the first movement they clapped so hard that I played the second. And then I did the third even though she was waving at me to stop. I closed my eyes and pretended I couldn't see her.'

'Did they like those too?'

'Oh yes. I played for over half an hour. Everyone was really late for first lesson.'

'And even the little ones sat still?'

'Yes. But when they went out, there was a puddle because Mark Stanton in Year One had done a wee on the floor.'

'Oh dear. That's a shame.'

'Not really. He told me at break that he didn't want to miss anything. That's why he didn't go to the loo even though he couldn't hold it in. I thought it was a really nice compliment, actually.'

'Yes, you're quite right. I don't think my music has ever made anyone pee on the floor.'

Robin grinned. Clearly I'd underestimated the discernment of young children: they were perfectly capable of recognising extraordinary talent.

After orange juice and chocolate cake in the kitchen, Robin turned to me. 'Please can I try your new tune now? I've not been the first to play anything for ages.'

In hindsight, I ought simply to have refused. I knew the piece wasn't ready and I was in quite the wrong frame of mind. We returned to the music room, and I gave him the first few pages. I was surprised at how well they sounded. It was astonishing how the boy could sense what I was trying to say and tease out the intention, making it elegant and lyrical. He overheard my thoughts, even as I had them.

'It's not at all bad! Much better than I thought. You're an absolute marvel,' I said, and Robin's ears pinked with pleasure as he continued to play.

And then, inevitably, it went wrong. Our ideas diverged and it was no longer the piece I'd imagined but something else.

'No. Stop. You're not hearing it. Try again.'

He faltered and then had another go. It was worse. It didn't sound anything like what I'd envisaged.

'Stop. No. Again.'

He tried once more, but this time I stopped him after only a few bars.

'It's all off. Why can't you hear it? Is there something wrong?'

'You're shouting, Grandpa.'

'I'm sorry, Robin.'

I tried to control my rising sense of panic. If Robin couldn't hear it, then no one could and I'd be alone.

'Try again. Go from the top. The first bit was wonderful.'

Only this time it wasn't. He played it differently and it was quite wrong. Not how I'd heard it at all.

'No! For Christ's sake, Marcus, just stop,' I said, slamming the piano lid down.

Robin snapped back his fingers just in time and turned to look at me, his mottled face now streaming with tears. 'I'm not Marcus. I'm Robin.'

I was instantly filled with remorse. 'Oh darling, I'm sorry. It isn't your fault. It's mine. I'm not myself.'

I tried to hug him, but Robin pushed me away. 'I think I'd like to go home now,' he said with trembling dignity. 'I'm sorry I didn't play it how you heard it in your head. I played it how I heard it in mine.'

'Of course you did. I'm so sorry.'

I telephoned Clara who came straight away. Shamefaced, I told her what had happened, while Robin stayed close to her, staring at me in wounded puzzlement.

She sighed. 'Hasn't he got enough to cope with at the moment, Pa? I know you're feeling pretty wretched, but you have to try. You're supposed to be the grown-up.'

'You're quite right,' I replied, feeling rotten. 'I'm sorry, Robin,' I said for the umpteenth time. 'I'm not myself just now.'

I offered him my hand, and he hesitated for a moment before shaking it.

After they'd left, I went to lie down but I could not sleep. I listened to the wind rustle through the beeches and breathed in the sickly scent of the last honeysuckle. I heard the sound of the doorbell, shrill and insistent. I ignored it but it rang a second time and then a third. Thoroughly put out, I hastened downstairs to find a young woman on the doorstep.

'I'm sorry, Mr Fox-Talbot, you did say three o'clock, didn't you?'

'Three o'clock for what exactly?'

Had I forgotten the chiropodist again?

'I'm Emma Livingstone from *The Times*. We were going to talk about the Marcus Albright memorial concert?'

'Oh, yes. So we were.'

She stared at me, glancing down at my feet in their socks, part inconvenienced journalist and part social services concern. 'We can reschedule if you like but it might end up being too late to run the interview before the concert.'

'No. No. Mustn't risk that. Come on in.'

A little later, we were safely ensconced in the music room, a tape recorder and two cups of tea between us. She looked to me to be about Clara's age. She wore black-rimmed spectacles, her dark hair was threaded with grey and she had that tired, smudged look of women in their forties with small children. I noticed a little trail of jam on her T-shirt. Her linen trousers had not been ironed. I supposed most women didn't bother with such things nowadays.

'So, you met in the 1950s?'

'I'm so terribly sorry. I met whom?'

Still agitated after the upset with Robin, I realised with some alarm that I was finding it difficult to concentrate on the young woman's questions.

'Did you meet Marcus Albright in the 1950s?'

'No, it would have been earlier than that. Forty-eight or forty-nine.'

'You often describe him as your collaborator, which intrigues me because, famously, you never let him conduct your work.'

'I did once. Terrible mistake. Sounded bloody awful. But he was my first listener. After Edie, that is. Edie, my wife. She was like my own ears. I didn't know what I thought about something until Edie told me. Now with them both gone, I feel rather as if I'm going deaf. I'm unsure half the time whether what I'm hearing is any good or not.'

I glanced down at the tape recorder. 'Leave that bit out, would you? Makes me sound a bit doolally.'

'I don't think it does. It makes you sound like a man who's lost people he loved.'

'Now I sound pathetic. An emotional squeeze-box. I've always loathed the accordion.'

She stared at me. 'I'll leave it out.' She scribbled something in her notebook.

I fidgeted. The business with Robin was itching away at me like a nasty woollen vest. Although I wanted to call Clara and find out whether he was all right, I supposed I ought to leave them in peace for a while.

'And you and Marcus were very close.'

'Yes, we were. For more than fifty years.'

To my utter shame and horror, I had the dreadful feeling that I was about to cry. At that moment I could think of no indignity worse than sitting in an interview with a jam-speckled woman from *The Times* and sobbing. Perhaps that's why I found myself blurting out, 'Marcus was family essentially. He was my brother George's lover on and off for many years.'

I took momentary glee in the look of sheer surprise on her face, then felt a twinge of anxiety about how thoroughly inappropriate this admission was. On the plus side, I no longer felt in the least like bawling.

'I'm afraid you can't possibly print that,' I said. 'Sorry.'

She removed her spectacles and gave a tiny, school-mistressy sigh. 'Fine. But you do realise that you're waving candy bars under my nose and then telling me that I can't eat them?'

'Oh dear. But it's quite out of the question. Marcus wouldn't have minded in the least – indeed, I was always begging him for more discretion over his affairs, but George was a very private person. I miss George. He was a good egg.'

'He was your middle brother?'

'Yes. And terribly attractive, according to Marcus. He always complained that George had a hard time of it. Said people noticed me and, of course, Jack. Everyone noticed Jack. But old George got rather left out of things.'

George who never reproached me or Edie about what we had done, who'd simply sat and listened when we told him. He did not blame us even when it transpired that Jack had left without saying goodbye to him. I'd thought that was callous; after all, George, good old George, was not to blame but then, I'd supposed, I could hardly complain about my brother disappearing and cutting off contact. He had far better reason than I had ever had. Latterly I had begun to view it as an act of kindness. Perhaps George would have tried to go with him to God knows where and Jack had known that would never do. George needed Hartgrove. He could not leave the Hall and be happy.

George missed Jack dreadfully. George's loss was pure while mine was edged with relief. No longer having to face Jack, I did not have to face my guilt daily. I could pack it neatly away and try not to think of it in the quiet and the dark. Jack's absence was soon filled with Clara, who wriggled into the void he had created, noisy and vital, until soon we didn't notice any hole at all.

The General took Jack's absence at first as a joke, some farcical, bed-swapping fun.

'Well, there's no need for you two to marry, is there? She already has your last name.'

He'd started to call Edie 'Bathsheba' until George quietly, tactfully, put a stop to it. Later, in his dotage, when the General persistently called me Jack, I thought that this was probably his way of telling me that he did not forgive me.

The journalist leaned forward and adjusted her tape recorder. I wondered uneasily how much I had said aloud.

'Who was Jack, Mr Fox-Talbot?'

'My eldest brother.'

'Is he still alive?'

'We're not in touch.'

The queasy feeling returned. A yellow haze clouded my vision, and once again I was close to tears. This really would not do.

'Are you all right, Mr Fox-Talbot? We can always do this another time.'

'No. No. I'm perfectly fine. Perhaps you'd be so kind as to fetch me a glass of water from the kitchen? I think I've had rather too much sun today.'

The woman glanced over to the window. The drizzle had settled into heavy rain. Still, she did not contradict me and trotted off to the kitchen while I furiously attempted to gather myself. I riffled through the CDs in their rack, trying to find something rousing to distract me. Every bloody one seemed to be conducted by sodding Marcus. He grinned at me from the covers, smugly gratified by my distress.

The next CD was one of Edie's. I'd conducted the Bournemouth Symphony as she sang the soprano solo for one

334

of my arrangements of Dorset folk songs. It had not been a hit. No one else liked it much when Edie dared to sing anything other than her usual wartime drivel. I'd loved this record – I'd not been able to bear listening to it since she'd died. It was odd: I could come face to face with photographs of her and revel in a masochistic nostalgia, but I could not listen to her recordings. Even after several years the sound of her voice was too much.

'Your water, Mr Fox-Talbot.'

'Thank you, you're most kind.'

As I took it from her, I discovered that I was still holding Edie's CD. Her photograph mimed a song at me, her mouth open like a bird's.

~

After the lady journalist left, I retreated into the garden. Usually I avoided interviews, and while I'd wanted to promote Marcus's concert, I had an unpleasant feeling that I'd given away far too much of myself without saying anything useful about Marcus or the music. I surveyed the flower beds. The last of the Michaelmas daisies were black from frost, and the foliage was all dying back, leaving expanses of bare brown earth. Ours had always been a summer garden.

I was worried about Robin. Knowing I'd upset him felt ghastly, and I was filled with shame. I'd relied too much on the boy. He'd given me a ball of string to help me find my way out of grief's labyrinth. Now after Marcus I'd propped myself up on him once again. He wasn't quite eight years old. Dizzy, I sat down on a rain-dashed bench, soaking my trousers. I hoped he'd forgive me. Children were more tolerant and more merciful than adults, weren't they? If not, I'd buy him a box of chocolates and a piano. That ought to do it.

I heard his voice ringing across the empty garden: *I'm sorry I didn't play it how you heard it in your head. I played it how*

I heard it in mine. He was no longer a musical savant playing by instinct. He now wanted to interpret for himself. He was no cipher but an independent artist. I felt a belly-punch of nostalgia for the baby musician he'd been – happy simply to listen to what my music told him. I supposed that this was how mothers must feel when their dimple-kneed toddlers metamorphose into skinny schoolboys. I felt horribly unnecessary to him. The charms of the old Steinway and cake with Grandpa would ebb, and one day he wouldn't want to come and visit at all. I would be a duty, not a necessary pleasure. I registered with some disquiet that, for me, Robin had become inadvertently and dangerously essential.

Tired and out of sorts, I was unable to resist the melancholy ruminations I usually told myself sternly to avoid. I'd lost a good many people over the years. It made me sound very careless. But it happened at my age. One missed them all. The Christmas card list became shorter and shorter. Each year one crossed off another few names. Saved a fortune on stamps.

It began to drizzle and I returned to the house. I headed for the music room, but then I veered into Edie's study instead. I'd still not emptied it. Mrs Stroud had finally tidied away Edie's things into the desk but the room itself remained untouched. The pink damask wallpaper. The pretty writing desk and the hopeless kitchen chair she used instead of a proper desk chair. The photographs of the children were spread out in a ring around the blotter. Clara on her wedding day – all white gauze and smiles; Lucy at graduation, looking tense and with an unflattering haircut. The grandchildren were pictured as they had been before Edie died: Annabel and Katy in matching polka-dot, little-girl dresses; Robin a serious-faced infant, wielding a rattle like a club.

The room no longer contained the sense that Edie had just walked out for a moment, soon to return. It was a museum.

The memories had been mothballed. I fumbled through her drawers and pulled out a mouldering pack of mints and an ancient packet of cigarettes, half empty. Edie always claimed that she'd stopped – but once in a while, I knew she'd sloped off to the potting shed like some elderly schoolgirl and had a quick fag behind the roses. I could always tell, but she preferred it if I pretended not to. I hadn't thought about this for yonks, and it shook me. How many other aspects of her had I forgotten? She was vanishing, piece by piece, and I hadn't even noticed.

Delving deeper into her drawer, I found a copy of the Torah, which I hastily set aside. Any souvenirs from her religious endeavours served only to remind me that this was something we had not shared. It annoyed me, this defiance not only of logic but of us – she and her chum Jehovah wilfully excluding me.

I yanked open the drawer with more force than was necessary and succeeded in spilling the contents all over the carpet. Swearing, I lowered myself painfully onto my knees and started to dump back into the drawer biros, paperclips, packets of tissues, letters and old Christmas cards. An elegant and familiar script caught my eye – I examined the picture on the card. A robin on a beach. A trifle vulgar and at odds with the beautiful handwriting inside, which I recognised even though I hadn't seen it for many years. It was very similar to my own, only taller, more masculine, more graceful. My dizziness returned. I sat back, wondering how on earth I was going to get up.

My heart crescendoed in my ears, its tempo quickening from a steady *adagio* to a furious *allegrissimo*. I was suddenly frightened that I would die right there of a heart attack on the not-terribly-clean carpet and no one would notice for days. Mrs Stroud would discover me as she prodded my corpse with the hoover. A pain bloomed across my chest and in my gut. I forced myself to breathe. I pretended my heartbeat was the pulse of the orchestra, and I its conductor – no instrument dare disobey the maestro. I tapped a slower rhythm in my head, and, sure enough, compliant and meek as a desk of second violins, my own heart obeyed my command of *ritardando* and slowed to a steadier pace. The pain subsided.

Calmer now, I read the inscription:

'To Edie, Happy Christmas, love, Jack. The Lotus Club, Long Boat Key, December '98.'

I turned over the card. There was nothing else.

~

I couldn't sleep. I sat up in the dark with a glass of whisky, listening to the creak and shudder of the house. Jack had been quite clear: he would not forgive us. And yet there was the Christmas card – did it reveal a softening of his resolve? Or perhaps he had forgiven Edie and not me. For Christ's sake, why hadn't she told me he'd sent it? Why, of all things to send her, did he choose a bloody Christmas card? Or were there other cards, a letter even?

I rifled through her desk, taking it apart drawer by drawer, leaving an armada of papers strewn across the rug, but I couldn't find any others. Had she tossed them out? Hidden them? Or was this the only one? I might never know. Anger flared with the whisky fumes. I'd not been angry with Edie for a long time. It was a queer feeling. Before, when I'd been angry, I'd tell her and we'd have a jolly good row. This anger had nowhere to go and it trickled through me like melt water.

I'd never attempted to find Jack. He knew where to find us. He'd asked us to leave him alone and it had felt like the very least I could do, considering. Yet the card suggested other possibilities. Perhaps I ought to search for him. Perhaps he'd been waiting for me to do so for years. Bloody Edie. I could always stuff the card back in the drawer and forget about it, but that was silly talk. I knew it was there, and so a decision must be made.

An owl hooted through the stillness and at a distance another answered. I sloshed another finger of whisky into my glass, satisfied to find that I was buoyant with alcohol, bobbing most obligingly upon waves of fifteen-year-old Macallan.

Had Edie ever seen Jack, I wondered. She'd certainly had the opportunity to, during her various concert tours. A lustrous spark of jealousy flared deep inside me, long dormant, suddenly and uselessly rekindled. There was something bracing about it, however futile, like desire for the dead.

I fingered the card, re-examining it for hidden messages. Of course there were none. It was entirely without context. A floating sign, like a stray line of a libretto from a lost opera, and I could not interpret it with any certainty. And yet the card itself gave me cause for hope. I chose to see it as a token of forgiveness. Surely, if Jack could forgive Edie sufficiently to post her a gaudy card of a Florida beach sprinkled with glitter, then perhaps, just perhaps, he might forgive me.

~

'A holiday?' said Clara. 'You want to take us all on holiday to Florida?'

'Yes. A week or so in the sun after Christmas. You certainly need a rest after all the nastiness with Ralph. I can play a little golf.'

'Have you ever played golf?'

'No. But Florida sounds like the sort of place one starts.'

She stared at me as though I'd finally cracked.

'Afterwards, I thought we'd take the children on to Disney World.'

'Aren't the girls a bit old?'

'You're never too old for Disney World. Isn't that their slogan? And besides, Robin will like it.'

'It's very generous of you, Papa, but wouldn't you prefer Vienna or Prague? Somewhere with music and culture rather than' – here she paused, as though about to say a particularly dirty word – 'golf.'

'Maybe I fancy a change.'

Clara did not look convinced. I did not tell her about Jack's Christmas card. I wasn't quite ready to confess to her the whole sorry business. Besides, I hadn't written to tell Jack that we were coming. He might have moved away. He might refuse to see us. He might be dead.

While Clara was bemused by the idea of the trip, the children were delighted. I'd not travelled for some time and had not been overseas since a year or so before Edie had died – she'd been too unwell to travel and I hadn't wanted to leave her. Now I found myself anxious about the journey and the prospect of being away from home. I woke in the early hours, fretting about details: suppose I mislaid my passport, or neglected to pack my good non-crease trousers, and what if my bags got lost? This new-found timidity irked and shamed me. I'd conducted concerts all around the world and had taken pride in my speedy, light-weight, last-minute packing – yet for this trip, I started to prepare my suitcase weeks in advance, fussing endlessly over what to take. At least, I consoled myself, Clara would be there to look after any last-minute fumbles.

Then, two weeks before the holiday, Ralph developed shingles and, as a consequence, both girls caught chickenpox two days before we were set to depart. Ralph, in my opinion, was a wretched father, but it turned out that he was a splendid virus spreader. Clara telephoned to cancel the holiday.

'I'm so sorry, Papa. You'll get it back through the insurance. We can go another time.'

I was horribly disappointed. I wanted to kick something gratifyingly hard. Of course it would be Ralph who loused it all up. Trust him to fall ill precisely when it was most inconvenient. He seemed intent on spoiling things for Clara. I was thoroughly put out. Then I had a thought.

'Wait a minute, what if I take Robin? I mean, he had the pox when the girls were away at tennis camp, didn't he?'

'Yes, he's already had it. But I'm not sure, Papa. Wouldn't it be a bit much for you?'

'I'll be all right. I used to travel the world, you know.'

'Of course you did, but you've not been anywhere for a while. And Robin's not the easiest.'

I was carried along now by the brilliance of my scheme.

'Yes, but it seems most unfair that he should lose his treat and be condemned to stay at home because his father and sisters are so inconsiderate as to fall ill.'

She laughed and then I detected a note of relief. 'Well, if you're quite sure you can manage. It might be easier to look after the girls without Robin trailing after me and complaining that he's bored.'

Almost as soon as she'd hung up, I did wonder whether I was being a trifle overambitious, but it was too late. Besides, any such admission of doubt would confirm to them all their concerns that I was losing my confidence and that soon I might not be able to cope alone. I was warding off that dreaded confrontation with the girls for as long as possible, steadily ignoring Clara's sighs and Lucy's prods of 'Isn't the house getting a little big for you, Papa?' as though it had spontaneously started to grow like rogue ear hairs. No, I would take Robin, and the trip would be a glorious success, and Lucy and Clara would leave me be for a year or two.

⁓

The night before we departed, it started to snow. I was too anxious to sleep and lay awake in the dark, watching the first flakes fall, silent and weightless. Then, after a while, seizing my dressing gown, I tottered downstairs and stepped outside onto the terrace. There was barely half an inch, just enough to glaze the hill and lawns. I stared out across the white expanse of garden. Edie would already have been out walking, hacking across the scrub and up to the huddled woods. I half expected to see her footprints.

The clouds parted to reveal a serving of moon, and its light reflected off the fallen snow, making it weirdly bright, as though the landscape were lit from within by a concealed lamp. The woods remained black. No matter what we did to the fields around them, the copse endured – with the knot of trees at its heart where no light or modernity seemed to penetrate. It had survived the slash and burn of two world wars. We told one another that it wasn't worthwhile felling it and putting the land to grass, as it was too poor even for cattle, but the truth was we loved those woods. The vast oaks and the alders, the tide of bluebells in spring followed by the stink of wild garlic and, most of all, the uncanny sense of eyes watching us. We dared one another to stay alone there after dark, and on one notable occasion my brothers lassoed me to a tree, leaving me screaming. I'd wrenched myself free and raced out onto the hillside, feral with terror. I'd had to wash the acid stench of fear from my skin before venturing downstairs for dinner.

Now, the white gleam of snow only made the woods blacker still. While the old songs receded from the world, dying as the last singers passed away, these woods remained, silent listeners to so many songs, as though they'd absorbed them through their roots and leaves. I imagined that when the wind blew, the music scattered into the air like pollen. In summer Edie had sung there as we walked with Clara and Lucy as children.

They'd been reluctant and had to be bribed along with treats. Jack told me once that our mother had often walked there too, and I liked to think that she did so singing.

In the cold I counted all the people I had lost like beads on a string. My mother. Only remembered as a warm shadow, a snatch of forgotten song heard sometimes when I started to drift off to sleep. George. Marcus. Edie. Jack. Here, I hesitated. His loss was different from the others. Jack I might find again.

I called out across the snow, 'Jack, does it make it better that I spent my life loving her? It was a terrible thing I did and I've lived with it for fifty years. Our happiness cost you yours. For that I'm sorry but I can't regret our life together. That would make the sin worse. You paid the price for our loving one another. I hope you went on to marry again and to have children and grandchildren of your own. I wish that you'd written to me to boast of your good life. Your deserved good life. But perhaps that's my punishment. Never to know what happened to you. If you are happy, then perhaps I don't deserve the relief of knowing it.'

No voice answered from the muffled dark. The snow continued to fall.

~

When I awoke in the morning every last flake had gone, as though it had never fallen at all.

I was grateful not to be travelling alone. I couldn't lose my nerve in front of the boy. The trip was remarkably straightforward. The airport staff appeared to find the prospect of an old man and his young grandson travelling together as endearing as a box of lop-eared bunny rabbits. As a result we were wafted through to the front of every queue and tended to with benevolent condescension. On the plane Robin watched cartoons and ate sweeties for ten hours – I saw no need to interfere – while I fidgeted beside him and counted which bits of me were aching with cramp.

I found Florida disconcerting. Every day brought the same unsullied sky, crocheted in baby-boy blue. The only rain that fell came from sprinkler hoses to keep the flowers pert and vivid. Wedding-cake tiers of apartments lined the beaches, each angled so as to allow the one behind a precise portion of sunset. Nature had been combed, shampooed and set. Spearmint-green grass grew everywhere, across the neat communal gardens and the ribbons of golf courses, as though it had been purchased on special offer from the same bolt of ghastly fabric. The moon-white sand was devoid of litter. Everyone spoke loudly and with excruciating politeness. I loathed it and found it despicably comfortable, all at once. This was a paradise for the elderly. A cornucopia of sunshine, handrails and extra-large parking spaces. I worried that, if I remained too long, I would never leave.

None of the restaurants offered early-bird specials as they were packed with white-haired diners yelling at one another across the plastic tables from a quarter to six, every restaurant empty by eight. I drove anxiously at twenty-five miles an hour, comfortably overtaking even more decrepit drivers who creaked along at under twenty. When the lights changed, there was always a pause before the first driver succeeded in telling his foot to press the accelerator, but no one ever honked their horn.

I'd rented an apartment on Long Boat Key, where I resented the usefulness of the handrail in the bathroom and the non-slip matting on the floor of the shower. The instructions for the air-conditioner were all in large print. The only convenience the apartment lacked was a piano, but Clara had warned Robin and, suitably prepared, he managed with great fortitude. We spent two days beside the pool, Robin swimming and me mostly napping, or at least pretending to.

I took him to a concert where, during the Moonlight Sonata, we counted fifty-three audience members asleep. I understood why the conductor pushed the brass section a little heavily.

I wanted to recover my equilibrium before we went knocking on Jack's door. I worried that my appearing with Robin out of the blue would be quite a shock, but on the other hand if I had warned Jack we were coming, he might have refused to see us. It was entirely possible that Robin was Jack's grandson. I doubted that Jack would say a word about that but I was unhappy at the prospect of hurting him again and reopening old wounds. Yet, the closer we came, the more important it seemed that he meet Robin and one day, I hoped, Clara. I'd brought with me the Christmas card, keeping it in my pocket whenever my resolve wavered.

∼

One morning, as drearily blue and perfect as all the others, I told Robin over breakfast that we were off to visit his great-uncle Jack.

'I didn't know I had an uncle.'

'A *great*-uncle. But I'm afraid that means he's old rather than that he's super-duper,' I explained, clearing that up before he was disappointed.

'I didn't know I had an old uncle, then.'

'No, you wouldn't. We fell out.'

'Why?'

'Well, I took something of his and didn't give it back.'

'What?'

'Grandma.'

'Oh.'

He studied me carefully, clearly interested. I knew that Clara would certainly not approve of my telling him – believing that

345

children ought to be sheltered from 'the truth'. Only she wasn't here, and it seemed rather pointless to conceal a fifty-year feud from an eight-year-old.

'Are you going to say sorry? That's what you're supposed to do when you take something that isn't yours.'

'I tried that already. Although it was quite some time ago. And the thing is, Robin, I'm not completely sorry. I'm sorry that I upset him but I'm glad that I got to keep Grandma.' I paused. 'I probably oughtn't to say that when I see him. I want him to forgive me. I want it very much indeed.'

Robin stared at me with great blue eyes so like his great-uncle Jack's and made no remark.

As I sipped my strangely moreish muddy coffee, I smiled at my grandson. He was smeared with sunshine and chocolate spread and appeared perfectly untroubled by my confession.

'Are you missing your mother and sisters? Would you like to telephone them?' I asked, thinking of the complicated phone beside the fridge. The instructions might have been in large print but they were still indecipherable.

Robin shrugged. 'Not really.'

'And what about your father? Your mother asked me to try to talk to you. I know it's all been a bit wretched at home.'

Robin shrugged and fidgeted. 'I'm all right. I don't like his girlfriend, Angela. Her voice is a semitone flat. She sounds like a wonky clarinet. I could never like a lady like that,' he added with uncharacteristic vehemence.

'I quite agree. Your mother has a nice voice. Melodic. Are you sure you don't want to call her?'

Robin shook his head.

'Good.'

I had promised to telephone Clara every other day, but after an initial phone call to tell her we'd landed, neither Robin nor I had fussed. I supposed I'd be for it once we returned, but here, amongst the red watercolour sunsets and

346

tangles of tropical flowers, home seemed sufficiently far off to risk her wrath.

My nervousness about our expedition showed: it took me four attempts to manoeuvre out of the parking garage. Robin tactfully said nothing, merely held the map open on his knee. I'd circled the address gleaned from the Christmas card in pink highlighter pen. In my anxiety, I drove more slowly than usual and a trail of bicycles zipped past, overtaking with a ting-a-ling of bells. We drove up a wide, sunlit road lined with palm trees and doctors' offices, proclaiming the diseases of the aged: 'Diabetes!' 'Cancer!' 'Baldness!' in a macabre echo of the billboards in other cities, advertising 'Coke' and 'Pepsi'.

I steered the car through a pair of vast gilded gates incorporating a pair of giant lotus flowers, their painted petals unfurling in the hot sun. The sign read: 'The Lotus Club Condos and Golf Course'. The lurid green lawns seemed to be stretched taut either side of the driveway. Vines of crimson bougainvillea were draped along a white picket fence, and I noticed uniformed gardeners scooping the blossoms into wheelbarrows as soon as they fell. Clearly nothing could be allowed to brown or to blemish those unnaturally green lawns.

White-haired ladies and gentlemen puttered by in golf carts, narrowly missing the car. They made me think of children escaped from a fairground dodgem ride, ageing improbably during the adventure. I parked the car at the front of a large building with columns, part Grecian temple, part suburban shopping mall. I did not immediately open the door. It occurred to me that I'd told Robin we would be seeing Jack, but all I really had was his address and the assumption that five years on he would still be here. He might be out or on holiday or even dead.

'We might not find Uncle Jack,' I said. 'I should really have said that before.'

'OK,' said Robin.

'He's not exactly expecting us.'

'OK.'

We sat for another few minutes, neither of us making any move to get out of the car, the air-conditioning whining in desperation. This was absurd. We'd come this far. I eased myself out of the car and into the heat. I was used to the tender warmth of an English summer; here in Florida, stepping outside always felt like opening the oven door and then irrationally climbing in. With Robin beside me, I was forced to keep my apprehension to myself. We padded up the steps into the thankfully cool marble lobby of the clubhouse. A pleasant-looking African-American woman smiled at us with great pleasure as though the simple act of our walking through the door was the highlight of her entire morning.

'Hello, how can I help you today? Are you here for lunch or a round of golf?'

'I was wondering if you could tell me the number of Mr Jack Fox-Talbot's condominium?'

Her smile drooped at the corners. 'Is he expecting you, sir? We have to be mindful of our residents' privacy.'

'It's a surprise. For great old uncle Jack,' chirped Robin. 'We've come all the way from England.'

She looked at Robin and then the smile grew perkier once again. 'Of course.'

'It's his birthday, you see,' I said, shamelessly building on Robin's line.

'Is it now? Goodness. Mr F-T is a dark horse. Shame on him.'

'So you know him?'

'Of course! Everyone loves Mr F-T. A genuine English gentleman,' she said, rhyming 'genuine' with 'wine'. She said it in the faintly patronising way that the young adopt when referring to the charms of the old – but I knew that if she'd known him forty years ago, she would have swooned with the rest of them.

'I can call up to his apartment for you. What's your name, sir?'

'Oh, but that would spoil the surprise.'

I hadn't come all this way to speak to Jack for the first time over a blasted intercom, with this woman eavesdropping on the whole thing.

'You sound just like him,' she said with a giggle. 'I love the English accent. Adorable.'

I winced.

'I'm his brother. I expect we must sound alike.'

'Well, in that case. If you're his brother, I suppose it wouldn't be bending the rules too much to say that Mr F-T is often on the putting green before his lunch. I always book him a table in the terrace restaurant for twelve-thirty.' Her face brightened. 'Would you like me to change the booking to three people?'

'Why not,' I said, supposing that if Jack sent us packing, a larger luncheon table than necessary was unlikely to be his greatest concern.

Robin and I left the refrigerated cool of reception, and descended into the midday heat. The air was full of the hum of bees and golf carts. I wondered why on earth Jack had chosen such a place. Its hygienic soul unnerved me. It struck me as an unlikely spot to visit in order to seek forgiveness.

I was sweating beneath my light-weight, non-iron travel shirt and, as I stroked my chin, I noticed I'd missed a patch shaving. I glanced down at Robin, relieved once again at his presence. My legs trembled and I suspected that, without him, I might have slunk off, still ashamed after all these years. Instead, I nodded, took a breath and said, 'Righto, can you spy the putting green, old sport? Ah, yes, there it is.'

We ambled over. Two men in improbably coloured socks hit balls, while a bosomy woman with a whiskery chin called encouragement. The group resonated with placid contentment.

'Hello,' I said. 'We're looking for Mr Fox-Talbot.'

'Oh, Mr F-T?' said the woman with an alert enthusiasm – his appeal apparently had not diminished for the older gal. 'He's popped inside to the little boys' room.'

I shuddered at the description while I thanked her.

'Are you here to visit with F-T?' asked the woman, removing her sunglasses.

'Something like that.'

'Because old F-T doesn't get many visitors now. Not since, you know, Pam passed.'

'Of course,' I agreed, not knowing at all.

'And who's this little man?' she asked, peering at Robin, a blob of coral lipstick on her teeth.

'My name is Robin Bennet.'

The men in the candy-coloured socks putted happily, ignoring us. Jack would appear any moment. He probably wouldn't hit me – he was over eighty – but beyond that I really had no idea what to expect. My heart began to do its awful thumpity-crash thing, and I tried to take slow breaths. It wouldn't be the thing at all to die right here on the lurid grass and abandon Robin in this strange, sanitised place. My eyelids started to sweat. I blinked, and then, through a gauze of heat and apprehension, I saw him. Jack Fox-Talbot emerging from the gents, buttoning up his fly.

We sat in the air-conditioned café, drinking lemonade and not talking, Robin poised between us like a very short vicar whose presence ensured an outward display of civility. Every thirty seconds, or so it seemed, another pal stopped by to shake

Jack's hand and wish him a good morning. His blond hair was now a perfect snowy-white and, to my envy, he appeared not to have lost any of it. His carriage was as upright as ever. He was as handsome at eighty-plus as he'd been at twenty-five and he had a light, pleasant tan, not the walnut furniture-polish sheen that I observed on others our age. He sported a dubious jazzy pink shirt but on him it succeeded in looking daring and dapper. The heat apparently did not faze him.

He did not look at me, and I sensed that he kept the well-wishers chatting for longer than necessary. Another lavender couple tottered off, chuckling improbably. Everyone here seemed to have been marinated in happiness. It was most disconcerting.

'You were just passing Long Beach, then?' he said.

'Not exactly.'

'You might have called to let me know you were coming.'

'I didn't have your number.'

'You could have written.'

'I could have but I didn't.'

Letters might be ignored.

'How did you find me?'

'A Christmas card you sent to Edie. I found it only a few months ago.'

He glanced at me and then looked away, visibly discomfited for the first time. 'I was sorry to hear—'

'You could have written.'

'I could have but I didn't.'

I studied him, this dashing stranger, and wondered whether I was really here to ask his absolution. I wanted the forgiveness of the man I'd wronged, not this handsome car salesman with gleaming teeth. I searched him for some sign of the man he used to be; the quick laugh, the playful charm. He stared back, unsmiling.

'Another lemonade?' we both asked Robin, who shook his head.

'I've had four.'

'Oh. Yes, best to stop then.' Clearly I'd not been paying proper attention.

We retreated once more into silence.

'You were married?' I asked after a while.

'To Pam. She passed around the same time as Edie.'

'I'm sorry.'

He opened his wallet and showed me a snapshot with some pride. 'She was a real doll. A super girl.'

The photograph showed a stout blonde woman in a sunhat on the golf course. She grinned at the camera, revealing a pleasant, warm smile and a splendid set of choppers. These Americans certainly knew how to do teeth. She looked frumpy and kind. Not the type to break his heart and run off with another man.

'She was a ladies' captain here. Magnificent golfer. Well, she was magnificent at most things she tried her hand at. A real good sort.'

The elegant shoulders sagged, just for a second, and I caught a glimpse of tenderness beneath the poise.

'She left me a list of her friends that I should marry, if I got too lonely.' He glanced uneasily over his shoulder. 'It's the only drawback about this place. Lots of widows on the prowl. You have to watch it. Better look out for yourself. If one of them sets her baseball cap at you, you'll find yourself beside the pool, a pina colada in one hand while she rubs sunscreen onto your moles. You won't ever leave.'

I laughed for the first time, glad that he hadn't entirely lost his sense of humour.

Robin, however, looked concerned. 'I don't want to live here, Grandpa.'

'It's all right, darling. Uncle Jack is only being silly.'

Jack wiggled his ears and Robin relaxed. Jack glanced at his watch.

'It's nearly twelve-thirty. I'm going to have some lunch. Thanks for stopping by.'

He stood without inviting us to join him and I thought, well, that's it then. I've seen him and that's all there is to it. There was neither forgiveness nor reconciliation. But how could one reconcile with a stranger? I would have preferred anger to this bland indifference.

'I'm hungry,' announced Robin suddenly.

Jack hesitated. His eagerness to be rid of us warred with his inbred politeness.

'Would you both like to join me?'

We traipsed back to the clubhouse, where the smiling receptionist greeted us with hearty enthusiasm.

'You found your brother! Happy birthday, Mr F-T.'

He stared at her for a moment, bewildered. I recognised his look – the sudden fear that one has lost one's marbles – and I took pity.

'Sorry, old chap,' I said quietly. 'We had to tell her that. Only way she'd tell us where you were.'

He smiled at the woman. 'Ah, yes. Thank you, Tabitha. Most kind. Twenty-one again.' He raised his linen sunhat.

She snorted with laughter as though it was the first time she'd heard the joke. 'You have a nice time, now, Mr F-T.'

We walked into the dining room, a fern-infested marble palace, with white driftwood walls and photographs everywhere of sunsets and the Y-tails of breaching whales. Framed signs, declaring banalities such as 'Don't worry, be happy!' and 'Tomorrow's another day!', shouted their drivel from the walls. The doors were thrown open to the outside and bright rays shone inside without being permitted to warm the room

353

above pleasantly temperate. A single sunflower had been placed on every table, like a child's drawing of the sun. The place reeked of cheerfulness.

A further parade of perky pensioners trundled past our table to talk to Jack, until I could bear it no longer.

'For God's sake. What's wrong with everyone? Are they cracked or simple? Why are they all so bloody happy? It's perfectly awful.'

Jack looked at me in surprise. 'They're content. How could anyone not be, here? We're all retired. We have enough money. No responsibility. It's a life of sunshine and ease. Golf and chicken dinners and blackcurrant martinis. What more could anyone want?'

A good deal, I wanted to say, but then I thought of the large empty house in Dorset that, no matter how much money I spent on heating, was never quite warm enough. Unless Robin came to visit, there were days when I spoke to no one. The winter lasted longer each year. Outside in the blue Florida afternoon the breeze made the fronds of a palm rustle like wrapping paper. It was seductive, I'd give him that.

We sipped our colourful drinks through straws, and ate fish, french fries and ice cream. The food on offer was like a children's menu with a better wine list.

We chatted uneasily. No, Jack had never had children. They'd not been lucky in that regard. Pam had had a series of small dogs; the last one died only last year. The Lotus Club had been very generous in bending the no-pet rule for them but after General was put to sleep, Jack had decided against another.

'You called your dog "General"?' I asked.

'Yes,' said Jack. 'It had a horrible temper. Barked orders at everyone.'

He caught my eye, and I saw the twitch of a smile. Perhaps there was a little of the old Jack in there after all, a hint of wickedness concealed beneath that sleek white hair.

Robin pointed to a piano in the corner of the room, half hidden by yet more ferns.

'Look, Grandpa! Can I play?'

'It's not an ordinary piano, Robin. It's a pianola. It plays itself,' said Jack. 'We can ask the waitress to turn it on, if you like.'

Robin stared at him blankly as Jack called to the waitress.

'Penny, my darling, would you mind awfully turning on the pianola for my young friend? He's never seen one before.' He smiled at Robin. 'Who would you most like to hear play?'

'Rachmaninov.'

Jack chuckled and shook his head. 'Don't think they'll have him. Put it on Scott Joplin, would you, Penny?'

A second later, the pianola started to churn out ragtime tunes, the keys rippling beneath ghostly hands.

Robin gazed at it in a mixture of wonderment and horror.

'Famous pianists record themselves playing onto discs, and then the pianola plays them,' I said. 'It's like a record player but with a piano instead of speakers.'

'It's creepy,' said Robin.

'It is a bit,' I agreed.

'I like it,' said Jack with a touch of defiance. 'I can sit here with my cold glass of something-something and listen to a great musician on a Friday lunchtime.'

'It's not a musician,' said Robin. 'It's a ghost.'

'Or an echo,' I agreed. 'A great musician plays the same piece differently every time. He can't play it in the identical way ever again, even if he wished to. Here, the music is trapped, forced to come out precisely the same. The exact nuance and expression.'

'Good God, you're just as much of a musical snob as you always were,' said Jack, snappish.

'And you're just as much of a philistine,' I said with a smile.

As he chuckled good-humouredly at the insult, I was relieved to have another glimpse, however watery, of the old Jack.

'Look here, why don't you record something, Robin?' he asked. 'Then I can listen to you when you've gone back home.'

'He's a splendid pianist,' I said.

Robin frowned. 'I don't want to be a ghost.'

'Every recording is a ghost in a way, Robin,' I said. 'You like it when we record you at home so you can listen to your practice. This isn't very different.'

'I suppose so. All right.'

In ten minutes the instruction book had been found, and Robin was seated at the pianola, an impromptu crowd of eager retirees huddled around him.

'Does he want some sheet music?' asked an elderly lady in shorts that revealed a tube map of varicose veins. 'I'm sure my granddaughter left some behind in my condo. I can run and get it.'

'That's very kind, but he doesn't need any. He keeps it all in his head,' I said.

Usually I was circumspect about Robin's remarkable gifts, until I came face to face with other grandparents, when to my chagrin I found it almost impossible not to brag just a bit.

He sat at the keyboard and played a few scales and then without a pause began to play a Mozart sonata in D major. The retired stockbrokers and real-estate agents, the housewives and lawyers, all listened, glancing around at one another, their mouths a series of surprised Os. This was a place of routine, where nothing out of the ordinary happened, where the menu always had the chicken and the sky was always the perfect colour-match shade of blue, and although every now and again a resident was carried out, never to return, even that was only to be expected. Genuine, goodness-gracious surprises were a precious rarity and here was four feet and two and a half inches of utter surprise and brilliance, sitting in the club-house restaurant in his sandals, a dab of tomato ketchup on his chin.

I felt a hand on my arm, and realised that Jack was squeezing me.

'Good God, Fox. Good God. He's a marvel.'

A second later, it occurred to me that this was the first time Jack had uttered my name.

Afterwards we strolled through the perfect gardens, which stretched down towards the golf course. Jack grilled Robin about his piano practice and he chattered back eagerly – there was nothing he liked better, if he wasn't actually playing.

'Five hours every day! I'm surprised you have time to sleep and eat.'

'Sometimes I don't shower.'

'Washing is extremely overrated.'

Robin studied Jack with clear approval.

A pelican soared above the palms, its vast wingspan an echo of something prehistoric. Even the long grass was all precisely the same length, as though it had been strimmed with a ruler. An enormous butterfly landed on a brightly coloured bush and posed there, preening at its own beauty.

'Look!' shouted Robin in some excitement, pointing towards a blue pool near a manicured green. 'A crocodile.'

A long brownish shape rested on the edge, a monster lurking in paradise, still as death and just as sinister. The butterfly fluttered beside its eye but it remained motionless, unblinking.

'Ah, an alligator,' said Jack. 'A rather large one. Perhaps we should take the long way round.'

'Are there many of them?' I asked.

'Oh yes. The club allows them to stay here until they're about five feet or so. Then they're carted off on a tour bus to the Everglades. It seems a bit unfair. Our little slice of Eden is built over their swamp.'

I glanced back at the alligator hunkered beside the pool, and the landscaped gardens seemed to shimmer as though they were a mirage. Beneath the layer of watered lawns peppered with sprinkler spouts, I sensed the ripple and ooze of the swamp. This manufactured paradise was only a thin layer; underneath the taut grass and the plastic pools, the wild and ancient shuddered and groaned. If there was old music here, it had been driven to the edges. Songs would seep out of the swamp in the dark.

We walked back to the car park, Robin running ahead, neither Jack nor I saying much. I paused beneath a cupola of sky-blue jacquemontia.

'Jack, why don't you come home for a visit? Come and see the old place once more?'

He frowned and looked away. For a second he looked old.

'No. I won't ever go back. I left and that was it.'

'But it would do you good. This place . . .'

I shrugged, somehow unable to explain how uneasy its perfection made me. I was relieved that Robin was here with me, to remind me of home and other things, otherwise I could see how tempting it would be to slide into a routine of early chicken dinners and rounds of sun-drenched bridge, surrendering all thought and desire. The magic kingdom wasn't in Disney World; it was right here amongst the retirement villages and flawless golf greens of southern Florida.

'I would very much like you to visit. Come for as long or as short a trip as you like. I want you to meet my girls. You really ought to meet Clara.'

I was conscious that it must seem tactless to press the point, considering his lack of children or grandchildren, but it felt terribly important to me that he come. Perhaps he no longer wondered whether Clara might be his daughter.

'It's very kind of you, but no thank you. With all this, why would I go anywhere else?'

Fronds of lurid flowers trembled in the breeze. The sprinklers clicked on with a whirr.

'Don't you want to see home again?' I asked, knowing I was stepping onto dangerous ground with both feet.

'Home?' he said. 'Home?'

And his voice was so ugly and bitter that I knew he had not forgiven me for taking it from him.

'I live here now,' he said at last, with an easy smile. 'I'll never leave. Why would I? This is paradise.'

He walked me to the car and shook hands with Robin. He did not invite us to come and see him again before we left. Two days later Robin and I flew to Disney World.

June 2007

I decided to sell the house. I'd had a bad fall before Christmas. My own fault; I was carrying far too much down the stairs and tripped on a step I ought to have had mended. I knew from the horrible crack when I landed that I'd broken something. Turned out I'd fractured my pelvis. It's another unfortunate thing about getting older – one takes for ever to heal. I creaked along on two sticks for most of the spring and into early summer, nervous about venturing outside in the wet, always fretting about slipping and having another fall, but irritated by the weeds in the herbaceous border. Apparently sensing weakness, they seized the opportunity to create an empire amongst the petunias and drifts of snow-in-summer.

When Clara and Lucy initiated The Conversation, it came as rather a relief. We sat on the terrace, surrounded by pink marguerites that gasped, unwatered, in their pots. Lucy poured me a very stiff gin.

'Papa, do you think that perhaps the house is a bit too much for you?'

To my shame, I wept. It was quite true. I couldn't bear the thought of anyone living in with me, but even I had to concede that a house with nine bedrooms, five reception rooms, a suite of attics and half a dozen ramshackle barns was a little large for one man approaching eighty.

'You were born here. You grew up here. So did your children,' I said to Clara, once I'd regained my composure.

'Oh Papa,' she said, and slid off her cushion, coming to sit beside my feet and resting her head on my lap as she did when she was a little girl.

'Perhaps you could take it on?' I asked her, knowing it was the worst of white elephants.

I spent nearly seven thousand pounds each year on oil for the boiler in a futile attempt to keep the place warm. I'd negotiated a special rate with the electricity company. There was always something to be done: trouble with the roof, damp in the attics, a barn threatening collapse. Even though most of the land was now rented out to other farmers, it was still my responsibility to maintain the hedges and footpaths, and to supply water to the cattle troughs. That cost alone ran into the thousands. The water pipe through the meadows needed replacing and I was facing a bill of another twenty thousand.

'I'm so sorry, Papa,' said Clara, trying very hard not to cry. 'A house like this needs so much money and so much time. I don't have enough of either. After everything, I rather like my flat. It's so easy and cosy. Even if I did have the money, I couldn't cope with a house like this and with Robin.'

I nodded and swallowed, not trusting myself to speak. What she said was perfectly true. Robin, now approaching puberty, remained consumed by music and uninterested in manners, showering or baths of any kind. In the hope of encouraging him to make friends, we'd allowed him to join the National Youth Orchestra, where to our dismay he'd entered the Young British Musician of the Year competition after forging Clara's signature on the entry forms. We'd raged at him, pointing out that he'd committed fraud, to which he replied, 'Either call the police and have them arrest me, or let me play the goddamn piano in the competition.'

We decided to let him play the goddamn piano. And docked two pounds fifty from his weekly pocket money. I'm not sure he noticed but this pretence at discipline made the rest of us feel better.

I turned to Lucy. 'How about you, darling? You've always loved this place.'

She drew her knees up to her chin, hugging them close. 'Of course I do, Papa. We all do. But I can't live here by myself. And I work in London.'

'Perhaps as a weekend cottage then? We could get you some help.'

'Papa, this would be a weekend cottage for a family of seventeen.'

I nodded again and took a large gulp of gin. They were being horribly sensible. I studied my daughters. Even though around fifty, they remained extremely pretty. Clara so fair and Lucy still so dark – a major and a minor key. I remembered that, once, fifty had seemed alarmingly close to being old – perfectly ridiculous. They seemed so young to me and yet both girls – women, I supposed I must call them – had a resolve and stillness that comes only with age.

'Would you like to live with us?' asked Clara.

Despite the tenderness of her tone, I sensed her reluctance.

'No thank you,' I said quickly. 'I want to be by myself. I like my own company. I don't want to be fumbling about in someone else's kitchen. And I play my music horribly loud.'

'You do,' she agreed, clearly relieved I'd declined but glad she'd done her duty.

'In that case,' said Lucy, 'how about moving into the little bungalow at the edge of the estate? It's all on one floor. It needs a new bathroom and the kitchen's a bit old-fashioned, but it's got a pretty garden and lovely views of Hartgrove Hill.'

'Yes, I must be able to see the hill,' I agreed.

I no longer slept well beyond the shadow of the ridge. I suppose some would have simply said that I didn't travel well any more, but I was certain that it was the hill itself that mattered.

'What do you think, Papa?' asked Clara.

They were poised, waiting. They'd clearly been discussing this for some time.

'My father stayed there from time to time during the war. Later so did your uncle George.'

'Of course we remember Uncle George living there,' said Clara. 'He grew the best strawberries. Scarlet as lipstick.'

'I suppose we could replant the strawberry beds,' I said.

'Of course we can,' said Clara.

'Is there room for the piano? I can't go anywhere without the Steinway,' I said, suddenly panicked.

If there wasn't the lure of the piano, Robin might not come to visit.

'I've measured the sitting room,' said Lucy. 'It fits beautifully.'

'All right then,' I said. 'I agree.'

~

A couple from London wanted to buy Hartgrove Hall. He'd been someone in the popular music business and she'd been a muse or a model or something or other. Although they'd been considering larger, grander houses elsewhere they liked what they insisted on referring to as the musical 'pedigree' of Hartgrove Hall, as though it had descended through a line of particularly splendid golden retrievers. Clara warned me not to be rude, as there hadn't been any other offers. After a flurry of initial ecstasy from the estate agent, he then had the colly-wobbles, declaring that viewers had been put off by the amount of repair work needed.

Nonetheless, Mr Too-White-Teeth and Mrs Shiny-Locks seemed very taken with the place when they came for tea. I'd taken one look at them, dispensed with the scones and jam, and brought out a large bottle of gin.

'My dad used to bring me to the festivals here when I was a kid,' explained Mr Too-White-Teeth. 'It had a real fusty charm. It wasn't smart or cool and it all smelled a bit of damp but I loved it.'

'Good,' I said, a little tightly. 'Fuddy-duddy charm was our aim.'

'Felix doesn't mean no offence,' said Mrs Shiny-Locks.

'Fuck, no,' said Mr Too-White-Teeth. 'It was fucking awesome. Like Glastonbury in dinner suits but without the slime.'

'Slime-free music, another of our goals,' I said pointedly, at which Clara walloped me under the table.

'We're going to turn it into a dead nice boutique hotel, comfy and chi-chi, and then throw a festival in the gardens each summer. Probably not classical, though, yeah?' said Mr Too-White-Teeth. 'It's hard to get bums on seats for that nowadays.'

'Not young bums anyway,' I agreed. 'Old bums here in the country are usually quite happy to listen to a spot of Ravel or Vaughan Williams. Even Shostakovich as long as there's some booze.'

The thirty-something couple in their expensively ripped jeans and studded T-shirts stared at me, then grinned good-humouredly. I understood that they simply weren't interested in tempting OAPs along to their concerts. They wanted their youthful audience to come all the way from London in their tiny shorts and fancy wellington boots. Clara berated me for being curmudgeonly, but the estate agent telephoned full of happiness, declaring that Mr Too-White-Teeth had found me so charming, he'd upped his offer.

'See,' I said to Clara in triumph. 'I'm remarkably engaging. Even when I'm trying to be rude, people are enchanted.'

After Clara left, I called Mr Too-White-Teeth and asked him to pop over the following day so that we could hash out the details. He arrived promptly after lunch and shook my hand warmly, while declaring, 'If this is to squeeze any more out of me, I can't do it, man. The wife's already giving me grief.'

'No, no, it isn't that at all,' I said. 'You're already being most generous. The place is falling to bits. You'll be cursing me for months after you move in.'

He laughed. 'Yeah, the wife reckons we should get a survey done.'

'Don't bother. Everything needs to be fixed. I can tell you that.'

'Well, no one can accuse you of mis-selling.'

'I should think not,' I retorted.

He stared at me, puzzled. 'What is it that you want to talk about then?'

'Come for a walk with me,' I said, dubiously regarding his much-too-clean trainers.

Suitably attired in a pair of borrowed wellingtons, Mr Too-White-Teeth accompanied me up the hill. It took me far longer than I liked, and he stopped tactfully to admire the view on several occasions in order to allow me to catch my breath.

'Constable once painted this view,' I said. 'The family had to flog the picture to pay for something or other before the war. It was a lovely painting, though.'

'I know,' he said. 'I bought it.'

'Really?'

'Yeah. Came up again at Sotheby's a few years back. Thought I'd hang it in the great hall.'

'What a good thought.'

We reached the woods. Spring was unfurling amongst the trees, while here and there appeared the feathered white of the hawthorn, like scattered brides. Catkins wobbled on the hazels and concealed in the branches I saw the smudge of last year's birds' nests, forlorn as abandoned cottages. The sun cast flickering spotlights across our faces and illuminated the scuttle of the woodland floor, the rush hour of earwigs and beetles. I led Felix further into the trees, and he fell silent, listening to the rustle of our footsteps and the mercenary squabble of the rooks. We paused at the pile of stones marking George's grave.

'This is my brother George,' I said. 'He's buried here. Illegally, I'm afraid.'

'Did you murder him?'

'Certainly not.'

'Then I can't see that it's a problem.'

'Thing is, one day, I want to be buried here too. Next to George. These woods are part of the estate, but you can't ever fell them. You must leave them as they are.'

'Wouldn't want to do anything to 'em. They're grand. Creepy. In a good way.'

'Good,' I said, relieved. 'But I also want your word that when my time comes, you'll let my daughters bury me here.'

'All right. I don't mind having a couple of old geezers buried in my woods. Could have worse neighbours.'

He shook my hand.

∼

The soon-to-be new owners of Hartgrove also agreed to let me remain in the house for one last summer. A date for moving was set for the end of October. Then in July, Mr Too-White-Teeth – who, it appeared, was still somebody in the music business – persuaded some bright young thing to include a sample passage from one of my CDs on a new recording of her own and, for the first time in some years, I received a very pleasant cheque from my agent. I decided to blow the lot on champagne and a party.

I invited the family, Albert and John, as well as, it seemed, most of the surviving members of the Bournemouth Symphony

Orchestra. I spent days fretting over the weather, but after a spell of drizzle the morning shrugged off the grey clouds like an old coat to reveal a freshly pressed blue sky beneath. I'd borrowed the marquee from the village hall and had it erected on one of the lawns, with trestle tables laid out in the shade of the lime trees. For once the lawns had been properly cut and rolled into stripes. I'd not been able to weed the borders, where wild poppies had seeded themselves but, with a sense of occasion, they all decided to pop at once and the garden was filled with scores of pink flowers, waving in the heat like dozens of chorus girls' frilly bloomers.

I left the catering firmly to my daughters, writing them a cheque and asking them to get on with it. Clara, Lucy and the granddaughters spent hours dismembering roast chickens, making cucumber sandwiches, spearing cocktail sausages, slicing up vast pork pies, buttering scones and cutting slabs of fruit cake. Albert, John and I poured gin and tonic into vats of ice and sliced lemon. The only trouble was that somebody put the empties into the recycling halfway through and so we had no idea how much gin we'd put in. Thinking of the orchestra members – retired or not – we added another litre or so, just to be on the safe side.

The musicians had offered to provide music in rotation. As I was determined that this should be a celebration, not a funeral, my only proviso was that they must not play anything in D minor – the saddest of all keys.

As the guests chattered on the lawns, half a dozen string players and a pair of flutes played a medley of my early folk-song collections. The English country garden of Hartgrove Hall was the most idyllic of settings for such music and I felt a pang at the thought of all the ghastly pop music that would make the windows rattle in years to come. I told myself sternly to stop, as this was sounding too close to regret. Annabel and Katy were dancing, teenage self-consciousness cast off in the wildness of the music as they whirled around and around with a couple of young musicians, yelping with joy. Home wasn't a place. Home was music. As long as I had that, the bungalow beneath the hill would be pleasant enough.

As I listened to the shouts and the furious pace of the dance – the fiddlers bowing faster and faster, scaling the old modal tunes as though they could play us backwards in time – I saw the concert-goers from the first festival, sipping champagne beneath the trees. They'd come here for years and years in their dinner suits, the women in cocktail dresses, wearing their grandmothers' pearls, to listen to our music. *The Song of Hartgrove Hall* was always the final piece of the festival. We'd performed it at the end by chance the second year, and the reception was such that we continued the tradition for years. I didn't hear it the last time it was played. Edie wasn't well during that summer. She'd been keeping her illness to herself, making light of her headaches, but that night she'd fainted. As Clara and I pleaded with her to let us call a doctor, she'd confessed. After that, there were no more concerts.

'You look dangerously close to misery,' said Albert, appearing by my side. 'I told you that gin was a mistake. Always makes one melancholy.'

I smiled. 'I'm feeling old, Albert. It's one thing to be old, it's quite another to feel it.'

He shrugged. 'It will pass. Like wind. Only comes in bouts.'

We meandered over to the potting shed. Several panes of glass were broken. I supposed I didn't need to worry any more about having them mended. We sat down on a couple of overturned pots in the middle of the flower garden, where no one had planted out any seedlings since Edie had died. In years gone by, at this time of year it had been a riot of pastel-coloured sweet peas, sprouting in tangles along wigwams of willow, alongside vast floppy-headed dahlias, sprays of stocks, lupins and sweet williams. Yet, as I looked closely, amongst the weeds I noticed that nasturtiums still clambered across the ground, while foaming white daisies and scarlet hollyhocks had all continued to bloom. It heartened me somehow.

'Come,' I said to Albert, 'enough maudlinness and nostalgia. Let's eat some pork pie.'

We helped ourselves to plates of food and retreated to the shade of a venerable oak. John joined us and we ate in silence, listening to the music.

'I hope Robin's going to play,' said John when they stopped for a rest.

'Oh yes,' I said. 'He's going to play the piece he's chosen for the final of Young British Musician of the Year. He still gets dreadfully self-conscious in front of audiences. He's all right with an impromptu crowd. He prefers it when people stumble across him playing, then shower him with compliments when he's finished.'

Albert laughed. 'Yes, I can appreciate the appeal of that, but it's not really a career plan, though, is it? To play the piano here and there, hoping one's audience pops by.'

'No,' I agreed. 'But he's still terribly young. I do worry about the competition being on television.'

We were all silent and I recalled the only and somewhat disastrous occasion Robin had played before the cameras.

Lucy hurried across the garden, stopping beside us and frowning. 'Papa, will you come? Robin's got into rather a pickle, I'm afraid. He's very upset.'

My heart sank. 'Oh dear. Is it nerves? It'll do him good to get them out of his system.'

Lucy shifted awkwardly, running her hands down her jeans. 'No. It's not nerves, it's gin.'

We found him alternating between apologising and vomiting in the downstairs loo. Clara crouched beside him, stroking his back.

'I'd be furious but I think this is punishment enough,' she said.

'Why on earth did you do it, Robin?'

'I'm so sorry, Grandpa—' he mumbled, breaking off to be sick again. 'I got scared. So many amazing musicians here. I didn't want to mess it up.'

I lowered myself awkwardly onto the side of the bath.

'Don't be silly. They're the most understanding audience you'll ever have.'

'I know. I know.'

'He said that he had a glass of gin and tonic to steady his nerves,' said Clara with a glare. 'It's bloody strong.'

'You said bloody,' said Robin from halfway down the toilet bowl. 'You never swear.'

'Oh bloody well shut up,' said Clara.

'It did have a good snifter in it, but you weren't supposed to be drinking it, young man,' I said.

'Sorry,' he said, and beached himself on the bathmat, his skin the same ghastly avocado green as the bathroom suite.

'Well, I don't think you'll be playing this afternoon,' I said. 'And if this is how the prospect of public performance makes you behave, then perhaps it's for the best if you don't play in the Young Musician competition. You can enter next year or the year after that. There's no hurry.'

'I want to do it this year,' he said, anger turning him a marginally healthier shade.

'Well, what do you think?' I said, turning to Clara.

She stared down at him, hands on her hips, her expression a blend of bewilderment and love.

'I want perfect behaviour up to the competition. One answer back or one stray sock out of the laundry basket and I'm withdrawing your name.'

He nodded. 'OK. Deal.'

'And no gin or any other tipple to steel yourself,' I said. 'It's a sign of the amateur and the hack. Are you an amateur?'

'No.'

'Jolly good. Then upstairs with you to sleep it off.'

Lucy helped him up and, leaning on his aunt, he swayed up the stairs.

'His grandmother suffered from just the same stage fright. It's why she gave up singing in public in the end. She managed the spectacular pre-performance vomiting without the aid of gin.'

'I hope he gets over it,' said Clara. 'If he doesn't, he won't get terribly far.'

'Oh he might, but it simply won't be as much fun.'

I put my arm around her shoulders and planted a light kiss on her cheek. She'd got rather thin after the divorce, but to my relief this last year she'd started to put on a little weight again and seemed happier. I wondered whether she'd taken a lover. I hoped so.

We returned to the garden where, to my surprise, an entire symphony orchestra had set up on the lawns. Nearly seventy musicians were perched on chairs, the brass section peering out from behind the hydrangea bushes, making their large clusters of blooms look like party hats. The percussion had chosen a spot on the loggia amongst the pots of marigolds and marguerites.

Clara squeezed my arm. 'They're going to play *The Song of Hartgrove Hall*. It had to be the last piece.'

I nodded and swallowed.

John and Albert joined us. 'Would you like to conduct?' asked John. 'I'm ready to step in, if you'd prefer to sit it out.'

I felt a wave of dizziness and glanced about for a seat. There was none. My heart began its horrible machine-gun pit-pit. I remembered the dreadful reviews last time John had performed my work. I'd never liked the way he made me sound. If this was to be the last time this symphony was going to be played here, I'd better jolly well do it myself.

371

'No thank you,' I said.

'Told you,' said Albert with a smirk at John, who to my satisfaction looked rather put out.

'I don't mind,' said John with a shrug. 'I'll play it after you're dead. I'm younger than you, remember.'

I patted him fondly on the arm and helped myself to the baton in his breast pocket.

As a young man I'd written this piece as my farewell to Hartgrove Hall. And yet the symphony itself, in the form of royalties and income from the festival, had helped to keep the house in the family for another fifty years. Up till now it hadn't been a farewell.

I climbed the rostrum.

≈

Afterwards, I drifted through the gardens quite spent, and yet thrumming with so much adrenalin that I couldn't rest. Paper napkins fluttered in the grass like tropical flowers. I heard the sound of a car coming along the driveway. Shading my eyes against the sun's glare reflected off the windscreen, I saw a taxi. I walked over as it pulled up outside the front door. The driver hopped out and jogged round to help the passenger. He eased himself out and with some effort stood, leaning against the car, slowly taking in the streamers festooning the trees and the scattered glassware.

'Hello, Fox,' said Jack. 'I seem to have missed a party.'

≈

We sat in Jack's old bedroom with the television, perched on the chest of drawers, displaying nothing but static.

'Whack it again, Fox,' he said.

'I'm trying,' I grumbled, repositioning the aerial for the umpteenth time.

The picture swam back into clarity. I settled back onto the chair. Jack lay in his bed, an oxygen cylinder beside him. Every now and again he took a puff.

'You sound as if you're smoking a Gauloise,' I said.

'Goodness, I do fancy a cigarette. You couldn't get me one, could you? It's not as if it could do me any harm.'

'It would blow us up. You're sitting beside an oxygen cylinder.'

'You always were a swot.'

'I'm not. That's simple common sense.'

We paused, Jack to catch his breath, and me to savour the pleasure of bickering with him.

'How long have I got?' he asked.

'Surely the doctors told you—?'

He smiled. 'No. How long do I have in which to shuffle off, before the movers get here?'

I looked at him in surprise. I'd not confessed that I'd sold the house.

'A good few weeks. No hurry.'

'Excellent. I never like to be rushed. Not over dinner. Not over dying.'

'Stop it.'

'Don't be such a drip, Fox.'

I glanced at my watch and turned up the volume on the television. It was the finals of the Young British Musician of the Year competition. The cameras panned across the families.

'Clara looks lovely,' he said. 'She's a pretty girl. I can't fathom why that idiot husband left her.'

'No. But I think finally she's rather happier without him.'

We watched as Clara fidgeted and reached for Lucy's hand.

Annabel and Katy sat beside them. The girls had come to watch Robin – I wondered whether they thought the disruption to their own childhoods had been worth it. The cameras held on them, slicing Ralph in half at the edge of the shot. I knew Clara would have preferred him not to come. As Katy leaned in to whisper something to her sister, the camera cut back to the presenter.

'Turn it down until Robin's on,' said Jack. 'I can't bear all that waffle they spout.'

'We need to hear the other performers.'

'Do we? I don't see why. I'm only interested in Robin,' said Jack.

I started to grumble, but decided it was bad form to argue with a dying man. Instead I set out a picnic on the bedspread. Pâté de foie gras from Fortnum's. Smoked salmon and caviar. A bottle of Grand Cru Chablis '99. I poured Jack a glass and we watched in silence as a girl of seventeen or eighteen strode into shot, holding her violin and exuding confidence. As she began to play, she plied her bow with dazzling ease and smoothness. I tried to work out what piece she was playing from her movements but I couldn't.

'Can't I turn on the sound? She looks jolly good.'

'No you can't.'

'Why not? This is silly.'

'It isn't. I told you. I don't care about the others. Besides, irritating you is tremendous fun. Like foie gras, it's a pleasure I've not indulged in for a while.'

I sighed and topped up my wine glass.

'I listened to him every day, you know,' said Jack.

'Who?'

'Robin. On the pianola. I had them put it on every lunchtime. The others all got heartily sick of it. I didn't. I ate my chopped salad and listened to him play. It was extremely pleasant. Then the pianola stopped working. Or so they said. One of those chirpy buggers probably complained to management. In any case they got shot of it.'

He closed his eyes briefly and took a few gasping breaths, then opened them and smiled.

'I wanted to hear him again. He's better than you ever were.'

'Infinitely better. I wasn't much good at all.'

We squabbled amiably through the programme. Robin was the last to perform.

'Look. Here he comes. Turn it up,' demanded Jack, struggling to sit up against his pillows.

I turned up the volume on the television set and sat back in my chair. I felt horribly sick. I had rarely suffered from nerves like this before any of my own performances. Robin was head and shoulders smaller than the other performers; he looked very young and an unhealthy shade of green. He was going to play Chopin's Piano Concerto No. 2. At first he'd wanted Rachmaninov or Beethoven but I'd pushed for the Chopin. This was a young man's piece written before the composer himself was twenty. Robin had a lifetime for the magnitude of Beethoven, and I knew that the poetry and fluidity of the Chopin would suit him. What it lacked in formal sophistication, it made up for in emotion and charm. Robin had eventually acquiesced. Like a Savile Row tailor who has an eye for the best cut and fabric to flatter a man, I possessed a knowing ear. I understood which piece was the best for a performer – especially one I knew as well as Robin.

'You could have gone to London to watch,' said Jack, quietly. 'You didn't have to stay with me.'

'If he doesn't win, I'll go next year.'

Jack waved at me to be quiet. The conductor signalled to the orchestra, and then, after a minute, Robin began to play. The dark bedroom filled with colour that poured from the television set in waves, the music painting the walls with russets and golds and circles of light.

It wasn't Chopin.

It was me.

And yet it was also Robin. He played my piano symphony *Robin and Edie* and shaped it with his own voice. I heard him talking to me through the music, laughing with me at its little musical jokes. I'd created a musical world and he was revelling in it, delighting in the shades, rushing here and there and calling me to follow, saying, 'Listen, listen to what we can do.' All his awkwardness had gone. He was unconcerned by the audience. I heard my world through his ears and it was marvellous.

In the second movement he played the uncanny Yiddish melody, his fingers tapping its swaying cadence, until I heard women humming in the Eastern ghettos, carrying their pots of *cholent*, steam hissing in the cold. Robin called to me but also to his grandmother. I heard Edie not only in the folk tune but also in his distinctive phrasing. He didn't have her eye colour or her laugh or her dark hair but he sounded like her. In the music, the three of us were united. My God, I thought, through this music he knows her.

The piano carried us across Hartgrove Hill, pushing further east until the bluebell woods were draped with snow and the trees with hoarfrost. In the darkness of the undergrowth a white wolf watched us with yellow eyes. As Robin played, the song made a forest grow that was both Dorset and Russia, the air resonating with old English and Yiddish tunes.

Afterwards, as he bowed, small and sweating from his exertions, the camera scanned across Clara, Lucy, Annabel, Katy and Ralph, all clapping and shouting. Jack and I shouted too, whooping our approval at the television set.

'What's next?' said Jack, applauding.

'The judges debate and then announce the winner.'

'Of course Robin's won. He's the best I've heard all night.'

I did not remind him that Robin was the only musician he'd heard all night. There was some dreary chit-chat with the presenters while the judges retired to discuss their verdict. We polished off the rest of the Chablis.

'They're back,' said Jack. 'Turn it up.'

The blonde presenter preened. She'd reapplied her lipstick, I noted. A paper was passed to her. She beamed at the cameras.

'And this year's Young British Musician of the Year, 2007 is awarded to David Julyan, Bassoon.'

'Bollocks,' said Jack. 'I can't believe it.'

I felt a wave of dizziness. I couldn't understand it. The camera lingered briefly on the winner before panning across the losing musicians. I saw Clara and Annabel trying to console Robin, who, noticing the camera upon him, showed it his middle finger and mouthed a very rude word.

'I think we may need to work on his gracious-in-defeat face somewhat,' I said, rubbing my forehead.

'Don't you dare,' said Jack. 'I think it's jolly refreshing.' He smiled. 'I'm sorry he didn't win. At least this way you can go to London and see him win next year.'

I turned off the television set and closed my eyes, grateful for the silence and relieved for once that I was not there to face Robin's fury and anguish.

'He's not quite twelve. The winner's nearly eighteen. He won't see that, though.'

I wanted to telephone Clara. I wanted to tell her that the competition didn't matter a jot. That it would be all right. That it was all worth it. The unpleasantness and the drives to London at four in the morning, the missed netball matches and the intermittent fury of her daughters, the spoiled marriage and the lack of family holidays. The boy was a revelation but, more importantly, he'd found how to open up his music, just a chink, but wide enough to allow us to slide inside. It was the closest I'd ever come to believing that he would succeed in making music not only his life but his living.

I glanced over at Jack. His eyes were closed, and if it wasn't for the faint movement of his eyelids I would have thought him asleep. I placed the oxygen mask over his mouth, and for once he did not object. He must be exhausted. I stood up to leave, but he reached out and caught my arm, shaking his head.

'It's all right. I'll stay,' I said.

Outside the window an owl hooted at the moon.

'Open the curtains,' said Jack. 'I want to see the woods.'

I did as he asked, turning off the light so he could see them better. The sky was a soft grey and the willows rustled in the dark, leaves fluttering like thousands of tiny wings. The woods crouched black against the hill, coiled into the curve of the slope. Above them the jagged line of Hartgrove Ridge divided the earth from the sky.

'Mummy used to walk in those woods,' he said. 'She was a lovely singer. Not a professional like Edie but charming. I loved it when she sang to us. You don't remember, do you?'

'No. What did she sing us, Jack?'

'Oh, this and that. Lots of folk tunes. She was like you in that regard. Loved old songs. But she sang a bit of everything. There was one she particularly liked. I taught it to Edie and she used to sing it to me sometimes.'

I stared at him through the gloom, his skin waxy and pale against the pillow case, the bones of his skull visible just beneath the surface, but when I closed my eyes, his voice was still the same.

'I would have loved to hear Edie sing that,' I said.

'Didn't she ever? It was such a silly song. About a blackbird. Or was it a nightingale? Do you know, I can't even remember the words properly.'

'No. She never did.'

Jack made no reply, but I saw him smile in the darkness and I realised that he was pleased she hadn't sung it to me.

'I probably asked her not to. You were always on one of your song-collecting jaunts and everything you found you remade into something new, shoved it into some symphony or whatnot. I didn't like the idea of you doing that to this. It was private.'

I swallowed, hurt. 'I don't think my music is like that. I'm sorry that you do. And I wouldn't have used it. Not if you had asked me not to.'

He said nothing for a moment, conscious he'd offended me. 'I could sing it to you now, if you like,' he said softly. 'I'm not much of a singer but I could give it a go.'

I smiled and shook my head. 'No. Keep it. It's yours,' I said.

I wanted to hear the song very much. I had the uneasy feeling that I'd spent most of my career searching for it, whether sung by shepherds beside hedgerows or in pubs, transcribed in songbooks, or hidden amongst the fragments in my imagination. And yet now I chose not to hear it, but I would continue to imagine it. I'd taken so much from Jack, I was relieved that he could keep this.

He appeared to fall asleep for a few minutes and then woke again, coughing. I helped him to some water.

'Did you videotape Robin's bit?' he asked after a minute.

'Of course.'

'Play it again.'

I rewound the cassette, then we sat and listened again as Robin created a world out of the void. From silence, followed by the static of the television set, came his glorious piano playing, conjuring order and magnificence. I saw the woods outside, both real and imagined through my music, one imposed upon the other, and I felt time stretch like a rubber band. I heard the layers in the music and, within Robin's playing, I listened to other melodies as well as the memories held within them. I heard the ghosts in the music of our other, younger selves.

'You'll bury me in the wood next to George, won't you?' he asked.

'Yes.'

He closed his eyes. 'I can't understand why Edie didn't want to be there too. It's where she ought to be. We all loved her, in our way. Even George.'

'I know. I was cross about it for a long time. But the thing is, Edie wasn't quite one of us. She felt the call of home, but hers wasn't here. Or not entirely. I like to think that she's in the woods anyway in the voice of the birds.'

I adjusted Jack's pillow, trying to prop him up to make his breathing easier.

'The soul is said to fly north, after death,' I said. 'That's without doubt the direction Edie's would have taken, flying into colder and colder realms, towards the creak of ice and the quiet snow.'

Jack coughed. 'Bloody hell. Mine's not. I'm going south. Back to Florida.'

The music stopped and I looked across at Jack, still and white.

'Do you need more morphine?'

'I can manage. I am cold, though. All that talk of ruddy ice.'

I pulled back the covers and slid into bed beside him, reaching for his hand, feeling its thinness. We lay there side by side in the dark, our ears ringing with music. Tomorrow I would be alone but that was tomorrow and not tonight.

July 1959

A row of dancers sleep under the beech trees. I'm not entirely sure whether their exhaustion is due to the sunshine, last night's performance or the party afterwards, strains of which floated up to our bedroom until after four. The General was aghast to discover several empty vodka bottles amongst the marigold pots on the loggia this morning. It's taken all of Edie's gentle diplomacy to soothe him and settle him back in the library with yesterday's newspaper.

The General can no longer cope with surprises. He reads yesterday's copy of *The Times*, reassured that it contains nothing so terrible that civilisation will not continue tomorrow. He misses Chivers and, since his old friend's death, he appears to have shrunk, bemused at the passing of his world. The modern one – filled with musicians and dancers who carouse and fill his flowerpots with empty bottles and who fail to understand the proper deference due to a man such as he – puzzles and frightens him. We keep him away from the concert-goers and the performers as much as we can. He enjoys visits from his granddaughter but can't fathom how Edie manages without a nanny, nor can he condone the fact that Clara is permitted to live downstairs when there is a perfectly decent nursery in the attic – which there is, although it is currently filled with most of the Bolshoi corps de ballet.

It's nearly five o'clock and the sun has dried the ground so that the edges of the lawns are cracked and hard, as threadbare and brown as worn carpet. The purple buddleias fill the afternoon with the scent of honey so that the garden smells like a Parisian patisserie. A smooth grass snake lies coiled on the path, its skin liquid and gleaming like molten metal. I step around him, unwilling to disturb his snooze.

I like this moment, this lull before the flurry of the evening's preparations. Soon someone will be unable to find her costume for Act Three, and Edie will search for half an hour until we discover it was sent to Wardrobe to be mended, and then one of the violins on the third desk will be found sobbing in the potting shed, lovelorn for a cellist.

'Here you are,' says Edie. 'I've been looking for you.'

'Oh dear. What now?'

'Oh nothing really. George says the strawberries are nearly over. He's brought some from the patch at the bungalow but we'll need to buy them in for next week.'

'Shall we have a drink? I think there's time before the chaos is scheduled.'

Edie smiles, creases appearing by her eyes, and she sits heavily in a chair. Her feet are noticeably swollen. She's almost seven months' pregnant. I kiss her on the forehead, which is slightly damp.

'Wait here, darling, you look absolutely fagged.'

I reappear a minute later with two glasses. Gratefully she takes a sip and glances at me suspiciously.

'There's the merest dash of gin. Medicinal.'

She laughs and closes her eyes. 'I ought to bathe Clara and find her some supper.'

'I'll do it. You have a rest. Go and lie under the trees with the dancers.'

She frowns. 'I feel like the matron of a boarding school. They're constantly switching bedrooms. I've absolutely no idea what's going on up there.'

There's a shriek and then Clara appears on the terrace, hands on her hips. She's a sturdy girl of nearly four, bossy and buzzing with opinions.

'I was looking for you and you weren't there,' she says to Edie, full of accusation.

'Here I am, darling. Did you want something?'

'Yes. You need to watch me. I'm a sylph.'

Edie and I do not meet one another's eye in order not to laugh. Anything less sylphlike than our podgy-legged, round-cheeked daughter is hard to imagine. A kindly member of the corps de ballet has neatly braided her yellow hair into two fat plaits. From the house, we hear the orchestra rehearsing snatches of the overture from *Giselle*. We sit back on the terrace and watch as Clara bounds across the lawn, twisting and flopping utterly out of time with the music.

'It's remarkable. She has no sense of rhythm at all,' says Edie, quietly, smiling.

'Absolutely none. It's a wonder to behold.'

Clara thuds to a stop and squats in a curtsey.

'Well done, darling,' says Edie.

Clara beams at us, her eyes the same summer blue as her uncle Jack's. I gaze at her and I can't help but wonder for a moment. I shake away the thought.

'Look, a dragonfly!'

She points with a short finger at the hovering insect, its wings beating. In the sunlight it glints green and blue like a ribbon of spilled petrol. She pursues it through the rose beds, trampling fallen petals into mush.

'Come on, darling, suppertime,' I call.

The orchestra strikes up again and Clara is whirling round and round on the lawn, a blonde blur amongst the white daisies.

'One more song, Daddy,' she shouts as she spins. 'There's time for one more song.'

A Note on Song Collecting

The history of Britain isn't just written in books or notched upon the landscape in holloways and long barrows, it's also contained in song. Parents and grandparents passed their songs down the generations, the words, melodies and rhythms shifting with each performance. They were sung on windswept hillsides and in muddy fields, around the fire and in the pubs, along the ice droves and the cattle droves; they were sung by carters and milkmaids, shepherds and shopkeepers, grandmothers and gypsies. Some were published as song sheets and sold at fairs by pedlars, while others survive only in memory. Some are centuries old with strange modal melodies, their origins unknown and mysterious, while others are more recent, recounting events such as the Napoleonic wars, which in time have become absorbed into the broad repertory of songs, their sources mostly forgotten too.

The subjects of folk songs are as varied as life itself: they are about love and death and murder, the passing of the seasons and of youth, of men lost in battle and at sea. Some are downright silly, and others tragic. Often the same tunes are sung to different words and vice versa. These variations are sometimes geographical – the version of 'The Foggy Dew' sung in the west of Scotland is quite different from that sung down in Somerset. The songs live with each singer and, as they make their journeys across Britain, they grow and change along the way.

By the nineteenth century, folk songs were already fading out of common life. Thomas Hardy complained that within a week of the railway arriving in Dorset, the hillsides and pastures no longer reverberated with traditional West Country songs but with the hits of the music hall. Soon 'The Lambeth Walk' was hummed in Langton Matravers and Batcombe, while the older songs started to be forgotten. The era where the singing of folk songs was an everyday pastime was vanishing, and with it many of the songs themselves.

Cecil Sharp was at the forefront of the first folk revival at the beginning of the twentieth century. The legend goes that while he was staying in Headington, a mile or so east of Oxford, a troop of Morris dancers appeared at the cottage on Boxing Day. They were a peculiar snow-covered procession, all the men dressed in white and carrying coloured sticks, with one dressed up as the fool. They danced and leaped to an odd-sounding tune that Sharp had never heard before. He was captivated. He wrote down the melody and declared that he must venture out across England to hunt out more. While staying with friends in Somerset, he overheard the gardener singing 'The Seeds of Love' as he mowed the lawn.

Sharp's song hunt led him across England and, later, America, accompanied by his devoted assistant, the evocatively named Maud Karpeles. Sharp and his contemporaries, along with almost every song collector since, gathered up folk songs as a way of preserving them from extinction. Yet folk songs have proved to be remarkably resilient. Even in the digital age, where it seems logical to assume that all songs must have been gathered and recorded, or long since lost, more are still coming to light.

Contemporary Song Collectors

The musician and folk singer Sam Lee is at the forefront of song collecting in Britain today. I met Sam one winter's night in a pub in Fitzrovia. He blew in and we huddled by the electric fire as he told me about song collecting – how he's light-footed as he walks through the woods, trying to leave no trace even as he searches for hidden things. Even though, like me, he's Jewish and was born in London, there was something Puckish about him; he was full of melody and charm. I was sure that, despite being in W1, I caught the scent of the woods.

Until I met Sam, I'd thought that song collectors were a vanished breed, but I was quite mistaken. He mostly gathers songs from the traveller community, the last custodians of ancient songs in the modern world. And he's always searching for one more song.

Benjamin's Book

When I moved house, I learned that our cottage had been occupied during the eighteenth century by a singer, song collector, alehouse keeper and mischief-maker called Benjamin Rose. In 1820, Benjamin sat down to write out all his tunes in a manuscript book. It contains a wonderful repository of tunes from the period – some are traditional West Country songs and dances; others chronicle great events like the Battle of Waterloo – all transcribed in Rose's beautiful, cursive script. Many years later the book found its way into the hands of the folk musicians Tim Laycock and Colin Thompson, who understood the significance of the find.

I'd heard that Tim was performing Rose's music, and so I pursued him, hoping to invite him to come to our cottage to sing it here once again. I finally tracked him down, aptly enough, at Max Gate, Thomas Hardy's Dorchester house, on a soggy autumn day. After issuing my invitation, I ventured into Hardy's rain-soaked orchard and scrumped a few apples, deciding that this must be good fuel for the imagination before embarking upon my new novel, *The Song Collector*.

A few weeks later, Tim came round to our house, bringing Benjamin Rose's book with him. We ate supper and then gathered by the fire to listen as Tim sang. The Rose family had lived in our cottage for several generations. Two of Benjamin's great-grandsons had drowned when their ship HMS *Good Hope* was sunk in 1914, and there is a small memorial to them in the village church. Tim selected a sailor's lament, 'The Blackbird', in memory of the two lost boys, and we sat and listened as he sang Ben's songs beside the hearth where they had been transcribed nearly two hundred years before. The boys had been lost, but the songs had been found again and returned home.

If you want to try your hand, or ear, at song collecting, Sam Lee runs the Song Collectors' Collective, which also contains a repository of folklore and recordings of folk singers: http://songcollectorscollective.co.uk/

The Great British Song Map

I'm still not finished with song collecting and I now want to create a portrait of contemporary Britain in song. Together with some friends in the folk community I have started a communal project to map as many songs as possible, put them up online freely available so that people can both listen to the music of their town, and if they like, learn their own local songs.

If you want to post or listen to a song please go to:
www.songmap.co.uk

Acknowledgements

I've been overwhelmed by the kindness and enthusiasm of the folk music community while writing and researching this novel. My profound thanks to Tim Laycock for singing lessons, impromptu concerts, friendship and apple cake. I'm indebted to Sam Lee, artist and song collector extraordinaire – this book was written to his music. My friends Hélène Frisby and Lea Simpson have been endlessly supportive, providing patient advice and support, and when all else failed: gin. Huge thanks to my parents, aka Mushki and Bup-Bup, and their unwavering confidence and childcare provision. I'm not sure how I would have managed without you. I realise that it's a gift to be able to sit down and write content in the knowledge that one's small son is happily dangling for tadpoles and hunting for trolls in his grandmother's garden.

Thanks to David Julyan, composer and friend, for checking the manuscript so carefully. I'm glad that in fiction I was able to help you fulfil your true ambitions on the bassoon. I'm extremely grateful to Kearn for sharing his extensive knowledge of vintage explosive techniques. Thank you to Stan for being the best of agents and of friends.

Huge thanks to my fabulous editors, Carole Welch and Tara Singh-Carlson, and the respective teams at Sceptre and Plum. Lastly, my gratitude and love to David and Luke for understanding that stories are sometimes more important than unburned suppers or tidy houses.

NATASHA SOLOMONS

Mr Rosenblum's List

List item 2: Never speak German on the upper decks of London buses.

Jack Rosenblum is five foot three and a half inches of sheer tenacity. He's writing a list so he can become a Very English Gentleman.

List item 41: An Englishman buys his marmalade from Fortnum and Mason.

It's 1952, and despite his best efforts, his bid to blend in is fraught with unexpected hurdles – including his wife. Sadie doesn't want to forget where they came from or the family they've lost. And she shows no interest in getting a purple rinse.

List item 112: An Englishman keeps his head in a crisis, even when he's risking everything.

Jack leads a reluctant Sadie deep into the English countryside in pursuit of a dream. Here, in a land of woolly pigs, bluebells and jitterbug cider, they embark on an impossible task . . .

'Subtle and moving' *Observer*

'An unusual, comedy-rich novel . . . a treat of a book' *Guardian*

'Prepare to be seriously charmed.'
The Times

SCEPTRE

NATASHA SOLOMONS

The Novel in the Viola

In the spring of 1938 Elise Landau arrives at Tyneford, the great house on the bay. A bright young thing from Vienna forced to become a parlour-maid, she knows nothing about England, except that she won't like it. As servants polish silver and serve drinks on the lawn, Elise wears her mother's pearls beneath her uniform, and causes outrage by dancing with a boy called Kit. But war is coming and the world is changing. And Elise must change with it.

At Tyneford she learns that you can be more than one person – and that you can love more than once.

'A deeply touching and blissfully romantic elegy for a lost world.'
The Times

'A vivid and poignant story about hope, loss and reinvention'
Psychologies

'Solomons's confident timing means that we sense what is about to happen only moments before it occurs, and are compelled to read on, not as one might expect for the frisson of a new event, but for the thrill of having our intuition confirmed'
TLS

SCEPTRE

NATASHA SOLOMONS

The Gallery of Vanished Husbands

At thirty a woman has a directness in her eye. Juliet Montague did anyhow. She knew exactly what she wanted. She wanted to buy a refrigerator.

But in a rash moment, Juliet commissions a portrait of herself instead. She has been closeted by her conservative Jewish community for too long, ever since her husband disappeared. Now she is ready to be seen.

So begins the journey of a suburban wife and mother into the heart of '60s London and its thriving art world, where she proves an astute spotter of talent. Yet she remains an outsider: drawn to a reclusive artist who never leaves Dorset and unable to feel free until she has tracked down her husband – a quest that leads to California and a startling discovery.

'Charming, mesmerising . . . brims with passion and skilfully evokes a bygone era . . . a beautifully written tale about a woman who was left socially dead but rose again by seizing life.'
The Times

'Captivates you with its charm, quirkiness and old-fashioned storytelling.'
Daily Mirror

'This brilliant novel is infused with empathy and humour. I adored it.'
Irish Examiner

SCEPTRE